Return to Berlin

E.V. McDermitt

VANTAGE PRESS
New York

This is a work of fiction. Any similarity between the names and characters in this book and any real persons, living or dead, is purely coincidental.

FIRST EDITION

All rights reserved, including the right of reproduction in whole or in part in any form.

Copyright © 2006 by E.V. McDermitt

Published by Vantage Press, Inc.
419 Park Ave. South, New York, NY 10016

Manufactured in the United States of America
ISBN: 0-533-14991-6

Library of Congress Catalog Card No.: 2004094937

0 9 8 7 6 5 4 3 2 1

To Genevieve and Jane, without whom this would not have been possible.

To Maureen & Edward, Edward & Maureen, mirror images of unique souls.

To Samantha and Mildred, wherever they are or might be.

I

The empty envelope lay on the dormitory desktop. Two handwritten pages lay beside it. The letter had served up only distant clues, what the reader called her "memory stews." That meant only impressionistic recall, at best. Seated on a straight-back, wooden chair embossed with Georgetown University's seal, the reader had not cried—not much, anyway.

There never would be sobs. Those would not have been dignified or practical. And Samantha Mildred Pemberton was both. She always had to be, when The Professor was not, especially after her mother's death.

She stood and looked at herself in a mirror on the closet door: 5´10˝, svelte, in a blue-skirt-and-white-blouse combination. The skirt had been a gift from her father. Her auburn hair, slightly beyond shoulder-length, was set in a French braid, pinned up in back. *Miss-Mid-Heel-Pump-Sensible-Shoes, Dutiful Daughter*, she reflected.

She was "Sam" or "Sammie" to her friends and family, except her father, The Professor. He called her "Milli," her mother's nickname as well.

The past months had given no warning of a sudden departure or disappearance: only nuance, subtle changes after each trip and its meetings. She had known there would be another scheduled series, but that was not until late in the Fall. Her father's phraseology lightly rubbed, rather than fully scratched open, her memory of: The Professor's non-academic consulting work for the State and Defense Departments? The family's travels? Whatever he expected her to surmise did not break from the darkness.

With a deep breath and sigh, Samantha reread the letter.

Dear Mil,
    Please DO NOT read this out loud, as you sometimes do.
    I didn't want to alarm Robert, since you know how he is. As for

the Twins, tell them nothing. You might be under surveillance. Trust me, Pumpkin, you may be watched or followed—or bugged, in weeks and months ahead. 'They' could be friendlies or hostiles, but you're not in immediate danger. Keep to school. Destroy these pages. Retain only the name and phone number I'll give you. And don't forget wiretaps. Probably brings back memories of our European nomad days. Don't expect to hear from me.

Second, got to leave NOW!! Bob's on his way to Hawaii. Still write me letters. All I can say is it'll soon be over, finally. Pity me—Berlin in Autumn.

Third, Daisy's been given a power-of-attorney. If you need anything, call her and use the words, 'How's the friggin' weather back home?' She'll know you're fine and will send whatever you need. She knows nothing else. If she leaves messages for you, do exactly as she asks.

Fourth, any problem with an unfriendly or want to know I'm all right, here's someone who can help: James McConneld, State Dept. You won't find his number in a gov't directory. So, don't lose it!! His private line's (555) 351-1789. He'll work the phrase 'a precocious person' into the first conversation. Answer, 'I'm not so sure anymore,' if he may speak freely. Any other response'll put him on guard.

Milli, I love you, Robert, Edward, and Maureen very much. You've been more than a daughter to me, since your mother was killed. Try not to worry. I'll be all right and back ASAP! I've got to do this—now that the chance's finally come. Especially after all I've seen and know. Till later then. Love, Pa.

P.S. Now you see why I had you promise not to open this until the morning after we left. I expect the amount of the check actually was a nice surprise, even if this letter couldn't be. Good luck finding the bugs. I love you.

Thanks, Pop, she thought. *I love you, too, you jerk.* She laughed. But then she felt her "stews," stirred up again. She had lidded them years before.

HER MOTHER. The minimal salt on her handkerchief came from a deeper mine. They had lost her mother more than a decade ago. Now her father, too?

What to do? Call Mr. McConneld? From a safe phone, of course!? Search her room? Like that time in Munich, when the Professor was attending those Cartel conferences. The family home had been under electronic surveillance before. "Industrial espionage," he had explained.

She never discussed Cartel business with her father. To discuss something one had to know about it.

THE CARTEL. Its formal name was "The Association of International Industrialists, Executives, and Entrepreneurs." The Professor had been involved in it for many years, as an analyst, consultant, investor. Wherever the family was, moving from city-to-city in Europe, every year or less, The Cartel was the reason.

"International business." "The Biz." Those were his descriptions, no others. He never allowed a conversation to enter its world. There were the consistently scheduled processions of perfectly dressed and groomed European, U.S., and Asian businessmen, old-line European aristocracy like The Baron, landed South Americans. Perhaps they were Fascists or Communists or terrorists with great tailors.Or worse! Republicans!

She laughed. Her father was a liberal-lefty Democrat, with more than a touch of *noblesse oblige*. But *business* had always been *business*.

"The Biz" had not seemed to affect his demeanor before. Not till the months preceding Sam's enrollment at her new school, Georgetown University. In those months he was more tense upon each return to Carbondale. Daisy, their housekeeper and his confidant, noticed, too. Before this letter, Samantha had not been interested, in "Pa's Cartel." But now . . .

She felt indignation, anger, defiance, hurt, at his keeping her in an unlighted academic closet. Abandoned. Not his right. Not right. She would not sit in Washington, waiting for his obit from a State Department spokesman, old friend or not. She would discover what this was about. If she decided he needed help, she would find and give it to him: in Europe, the Middle East, Asia, wherever he was.

On to immediate matters. The Professor had taught her about room searches from his days in "Army Intelligence" —no oxymoron in his case. His time in the Army pre-dated his Ph.D., academic career, and her life.

She felt a momentary, fleeting security, as she gazed at the baggage she had brought with her from Carbondale: boxes, a large steamship trunk that had belonged to her paternal grandparents, safe private places she could trust. But there were so many possible hiding places elsewhere, and so little time.

Sam knew the transmitters could be computer chip-sized, but also their ranges were very short. On the bottom of the closet door and under the sink she found what she only quasi-believed would be there, microphones the size of a quarter. The back of the bed's headboard disclosed another, the size of a dime. *It must have been like Grand Central Station*, she thought, grimacing. Geometric paranoia took over.

Later, she called home on an impulse, after flushing her father's note away. She used a pay phone in the Student Center, hoping against reality that her father would answer. But Daisy's voice greeted her, the same as always: maternal, controlled, emotional. Fantasies fled as she hung up. This was reality.

Her second call was to her father's State Department friend.

"Three-three-seven, may I help you?" a female voice spoke. Sam asked for the friend.

"Let me see, if Mr. McConneld's in," the professional-sounding voice continued. "Who may I say's calling?"

Samantha identified herself. The phone line felt numb. She fantasized about the friend. Paternalistic "stonewalling"? If, if, if. Her least favorite game.

A deep male voice gave the phone line feeling again. "Sure you'd be stomping around. But not this soon. Told you're quite a precocious person."

"I'm not so sure any more," Sam replied. "I need to see you. Today?"

"Meet you inside the lower level of Reiss Science Building in forty minutes," McConneld said, quickly.

Sam felt her first relief since reading the note: like after a migraine headache ends.

*   *   *

James "Buck" McConneld sat back in his brown leather office chair. "Betty," he spoke to his secretary on the desk-com. "Ms. Pemberton needs reassuring. Remind Washbourne his preliminary's due this afternoon. If anyone Up-Top calls, buzz me on the cell. Otherwise, out to a leisurely lunch."

She brought him a FAX from Office 4011, which also reported to the National Security Adviser's Office. The message read, "Neo-N. Act'y behind rash thefts AFCENT. Pemberton not arrived this A.M., as expected. Will investigate. Report follows. C."

Buck McConneld was a longtime veteran of clandestine and covert operations since the early-1970s, but had been on secret and longterm "loan" to the State Department from the early 1980s. Even within The Agency only his Deputy Director and the Director knew McConneld's double-agent status. Of course, CIA had many "moles," in the State, Defense, and military apparatus.

Now he was a "senior policy-maker," a cross between a "mole" and a legitimate source of policy recommendations for the Secretary, who was unaware of his continuing bloodline. Nevertheless, McConneld had always considered himself a field man.

It was in his field operations days, in Europe during the Cold War, that he served extensively with Professor Thomas M. Pemberton. "Old Doc," McConneld called him. College friends, they worked well together till "Old Doc" retired from "active service." McConneld's own assignments had included station posts and section chiefs' positions in every important NATO city.

But McConneld still doubted the Cold War was truly over: indefinitely suspended, but not over. Once the Russians sorted themselves out, and remained peacefully inclined, then... He had lost too many friends and colleagues to KGB, for him to be naïve about the Russians, though something inside him wanted them to be non-belligerent bystanders, at least.

Now there were this Pemberton matter and the investigation of the weapons thefts from NATO depots in the Federal Republic and elsewhere to run. His associated networks and allied governments reported "significant" rises in Nazi and Neo-Nazi covert activities, both in Europe and South America. Far more than reported in the U.S. media, even after Oklahoma City.

The survivors and descendants of ODESSA, et al. Were they only symptoms? Brown-shirted, seeping from sixty-year-old ashes, reinforcing the Russian right-wing in its own xenophobia. The Nazi phoenix... He was sure of something else: the Pemberton matter was like a main electrical cable, charging these elements.

McConneld put on workman's overalls. As he was leaving, his phone rang. "Deputy Director Simmons on the line for you, sir. Shall I tell him you've already left?"

"Put him on," McConneld replied. "Yes, sir. Nothing on Pemberton yet. Word from 4011 is he didn't arrive as expected. He didn't give me more than, 'Something big, within the next few months.' There're confirmed links between his group and Neo-Nazis."

"The Director's considering pulling you out of that State Department crypt and bringing you back over here," Simmons said.

"That might be premature," McConneld said, "if there's no connection between the Neon's and the 'big deal.' By the way, anything new on Israeli snatch operations in Southern Command's area?"

"Not since they grabbed a few ex-camp guards last month. *Mossad* missed the big fish they expected. Keep me up on Pemberton, Buck," Simmons said.

* * *

Samantha waited near the entrance of the Reiss Science Building. She alternated between calm and nervous. She had been there forty minutes and still no McConneld. *Diplomats were supposed to be punctual*, she thought. *Perhaps everyone in the State Department was not a diplomat.*

As she folded her long, thin arms in front of her, she shivered. The temperature outside the building was "hot-summer," too hot to wear hose or tights. Inside, it was autumnal.

A deep voice suddenly called her. She looked back at the oversized, wooden doors to a large lecture hall and saw a tall man in work clothes.

"You don't seem particularly precocious," he said. "Your father assured me you were quite that way." Sam joined him.

McConneld reached for the door handle, but Sam lightly swatted his hand away. She led him into the lecture hall.

"We'll be all right in here," she said. They sat at the back of the large, terraced classroom. She told him about her search. The cold and tension lingered. "Insights on this age-old problem, Mr. McConneld?"

"Ms. Pemberton—May I call you Samantha?"

"Call me Sam," she replied. "Almost everyone does."

"Sam," McConneld said. "It's not our people. There're plenty of unfriendlies it could be. Your father's doing very important... research."

"Spying," she said, agitated. "You people and your euphemisms. My favorites are 'Special Operations' and 'Executive Action.' Presumably enemy, but you're never sure."

"I can see you're angry..." McConneld said.

"Scared for him," she said, walking away. "And pissed at him, too. BS excuses. Damn it, he's not the spy type! A college professor." She hesitated. "Cordial. Addle-brained..."

She turned to him. "And my father! I don't want him killed." Sam felt tiny threads of tears on her cheeks. "First, Mother. Now him, too?... I think it's his way of punishing himself for losing her."

"I understand your anger."

"Do you? Well, I'm pissed at you, too. All you clinicians."

McConneld offered her his handkerchief. She refused it. "Is this your private hell? Or is it open for time-sharing?" he asked.

"I guess I deserved that," Sam said, sniffling. She took the handkerchief and blew her nose. "I hate losing control, especially in front of a stranger."

"Think of me as a long-lost family friend you hid from as a child. You're saying to me what you'd like to say to him." He put his index finger to his lips, stepped to the oak doors, and listened. He kicked one door open.

Across the high-ceilinged hall a tall, shaggy-haired man, in camouflage jacket and jeans, exited the building. He sat on the grass, across from the building and never looked back.

McConneld closed the door, softly. "You've been followed here." McConneld explained his plan. "Don't underestimate Doc.

Best shovel artist I've ever known."

"Will whoever 'they' are try something heavier?"

"Nothing's certain in a mess like this. You know things," McConneld said. "That could be indirectly of use. But my guess is you're too visible. It'd be reported to the police."

Sam rolled her eyes. "No one swift enough to snatch me would be deterred by the D.C. cops."

McConneld smiled for the first time. "Incompetent cops notwithstanding, disappearances draw attention. Pros don't want that."

"A tad reassuring," Sam smiled a sad smile. "But I've got to tell you: I've felt safer in my life. What about my room?"

"You'll have to live with it. If we debug, your listeners'll conclude you do know something important."

Sam sighed, "No kidding, Sherlock. I've seen all the flicks. With my father's business, I've picked up a few things."

"Sorry," he said. "I didn't mean to talk down to you. How about if we put you under surveillance?"

"Paternalistic," she said, resting her head on his shoulder. "But effective."

He gave her a fatherly hug. "You remind me of my own children," he said.

Sam looked up at him. "You have a family?"

"Doc didn't tell you about me at all, did he? Two sons and a daughter. The boys've finished college. My daughter's a senior at Harvard and deceptively strong. Like you. My kids used to snuggle up to me, too, in younger times. Doc told me not to underestimate you."

"Can you let me know he's all right?" She pulled gently away from him.

"I'll send word over, periodically. Now," he said, reaching into his hip pocket, "Here's a present for you. Keep it with you all the time." He handed her a compact.

"Looks ordinary enough."

"It's an electronic homing device. Here's what you do."

Later McConneld followed "The Shag," as he dubbed Sam's "tail," to a basement apartment off Reservoir Road. From his cell phone McConneld ran a check on its row house. His second call was to the agents for Sam's surveillance. He had arranged that before meeting her, for her own good, whether or not she agreed.

* * *

The mail still had not been delivered, and it was 11:30 A.M. Sam hoped for something from home, but suspected this day would, again, be routine: pre-approved credit card applications, magazine subscription come-on's, and consumption junk-mail. Two days had passed since her meeting with Mr. McConneld. Another student peered into her own mailbox, among the hundreds of 3″ by 4″ glass doors, lining one wall of the lobby. The young woman had flushed-red cheeks, natural, not the result of a hyper-active blush brush, and long, heavily streaked and frosted-blonde hair.

Sam had always wanted to have her own hair done that way, but had never gotten the nerve for such a radical change.

"You're Samantha Pemberton, Room 241, aren't you?" the other young woman asked, smiling and offering her hand. "Been meaning to introduce myself. I'm your neighbor in 247. The R.A. told me your name. Also told me you're a little older than the rest of us. You're the big sister on the hall, I guess."

Despite her heightened paranoia, Sam remembered her new acquaintance from silent hall encounters. "And you are?"

"Liz McGonnville. Transfer from Boston College."

"I'm a transfer, too," Sam said. "From Southern Illinois at Carbondale."

"That's where you're originally from?"

"No, my father's a professor there now. We've lived in a lot of places. Europe. The States."

"A real cosmopolitan sort, eh?" Liz said. "I'm just a kid from North Jersey. You know, that part of New Jersey The City should've annexed a long time ago?"

"I haven't had anything more than a stopover in Kennedy in the last so many years," Sam said.

"Had lunch?" Liz asked. "I'm famished! I missed breakfast!" She spoke with a special vivacity and panache. Sam could feel it, as though it were her own energy: very New Yorkish.

Sam put her arm around Liz, and in her best Humphrey Bogart imitation, said, "You know, Lizzie. I think this is the beginning of a beautiful friendship."

* * *

It was early evening. Sam had spent the day with Liz. After lunch, they registered for classes and shopped. They were walking on the campus road near the statue of John Carroll, the Founder of Georgetown.

"They dumped me here with most of my worldly possessions," Sam said.

"Bob, my brother, had to report to 'good, ole Pearl Harbor,' as he calls it. He's a Navy lieutenant commander."

"After living so much life, you wanted to live in a dorm?" Liz asked. "I'd have thought you'd want to be on your own."

"Something new for me, really. I don't mind it, though," Sam replied. "Very secure, easy. My father even encouraged me to." She trailed off.

"Don't take this the wrong way, but how come it's taken you so long to finish college?"

"We've got a housekeeper, who's doubled as a nanny to my younger brother and sister. But I guess I've been the real nanny to them, since Mother's death. The little ones've never had a female anchor, except me.

"I studied at different universities, including the Sorbonne and SIU. But it seemed we'd get settled and then we'd have to move again. Madrid, Munich, Paris, London, Vienna, Salzburg, Rome, Geneva. Berlin, too. That doesn't include the places we only visited or stayed less than six months. Semester here, semester there."

"How old're your brother and sister?"

"Half my age."

Liz stopped. "Twins?"

"Two loaded pistols."

"If you don't mind my asking, how did your mother die? Cancer? An accident?"

"I don't mind," Sam said. "There was a time, when I might've said, 'Pass.' But it's different now. She was killed in a terrorist attack in Europe in the early 90s."

"That's terrible! How you must've suffered!"

"We all did. Pa took it the hardest. He took the longest to come to terms with it. My middle name's Mildred, after my mother. Only Pa calls me that. Or 'Milli.'"

"May I call you that?" Liz asked, quietly. "We've known each other such a short time, but we're both sort of voyagers, alone here."

"Let me think about it," Sam said. "So tell me about yourself."

"Just been your basic student. Internships on The Hill. I transferred, 'cause I needed a better name on my resumé. The teachers here in Modern European History have great reps."

"Too bad we didn't meet when I first got here," Sam said. She was relieved the subject had changed. "I could've introduced you to my father. He's an authority, especially U.S. Foreign Policy, the Weimar and Nazi periods."

"What's his name? Besides the Pemberton part."

"Thomas Farnsworth!" Sam announced, with the verve of a leading actress singing the opening number in a musical.

"Christ!" Liz said. "I've read his books! Your . . . ?! No way!"

"Glad someone's read them, besides his students. Professors and their captive royalties. I've chided him about that."

"I like his politics," Liz said, blushing.

"You don't have to be politic," Sam said.

"No, really," Liz persisted. "I dug his approach to foreign policy. Sounds like ass-kissing, but it's not."

"Say all the nice things about him you want," Sam said. "If he makes it back, I'll introduce you."

"If he makes it back . . . ?"

"I mean, if he comes to visit me, that's all. I'm heading to my room. Are you coming?"

"No," Liz answered. "More picky errands. See you."

As she walked, Sam wondered if she could confide in Liz. At this time of vulnerability, she needed—and wanted—a friend.

II

In a rather undistinctive rowhouse in the Glover Park section of Washington, D.C., six blocks north of Georgetown University Hospital, a man was listening through headphones. His tie was pulled down, his pants shiny with days of overwear. He was auditing a conversation from St. Mary's Hall, Room 241.

He had planted microphones in the subject's room shortly before her arrival. He considered what he had heard "20s bullshit."

The buzz of a telephone came over the headset. He had not had time to tap her phone yet. He slipped the headphones onto his neck.

Two long raps and two short raps came on the door. His partner entered, carrying a brown paper bag and two large styrofoam cups.

"Anything new?" the partner asked. His clothes were as worn as the listener's. He tossed the bag to the listener.

"Same *ca-ca*, David!" the listener replied. "We told Control-West we should be tracking her father. I had enough university bullshit on our last assignment in St. Petersburg."

David laughed at his partner's bluntness. The red phone beside the bed released its bird-like ring.

"You'd better ask him," David said into the receiver, then handing it to his partner. "Control-West for you, George."

"Nothing so far, sir." George widened his eyes and shook his head. "If she knows anything. Right away. But . . . Yes, sir." He held the receiver away from his ear for a few seconds. "That's all very interesting. Yes, thank you, sir. Goodbye." He tried to drop the receiver onto its cradle on the floor, but missed.

"You make more noise, and the subject'll hear you," David scolded. "Eat your sandwich and shut up."

George, feeling tired and older than his thirty-ish age, fell back onto the bed. Ah, American chicken salad! Better than the sawdust deli-drek he ate at home, he reflected.

*   *   *

General Alexei Andreivitch Balkovsky, Head of the Fourth Department of the Russian Secret Service's First Chief Directorate and the boss of Russian Intelligence for Germany, took a long draw on his hand-rolled cigarette. The combination of the American and Turkish tobaccos tasted very good to him. *Someday he would quit, though*, he thought.

He was reading agent reports, and glanced at the portraits of Lenin, Gorbachev, and Yeltsin. They seemed to be reading over his shoulder. The Lenin portrait was probably the last one in the Kremlin.

As he stretched, a black telephone on his desk rang. He was angry at the interruption. *"Send him in."*

A young man General Balkovsky recognized as a cipher clerk from the cryptographic section came in. His civilian clothes bagged his thin body frame. *"From our embassy in Washington and from Germany, sir."*

Balkovsky looked at the clerk with compassion. He was sympathetic to the cipher staff. Lots of drudgery, no glory, nor medals for bravery.

"Leave me now, but check back in an hour for any responses. It's all right, Corporal. Dismissed."

There were three transmissions. The top message, from the Russian Embassy in Washington read: *"Senior State Department officials concerned, rising Neo-Nazi and Fascist activity Western Europe (Germany), South America, and Far East. Read Japan. Investigations ongoing. Possibly suppress identified rightist organizations. Our agents investigating. Further reports to follow."*

The second, from Washington, read: *"Professor T. Pemberton unaccounted for four days following trip to Washington Friday-Saturday. Daughter Samantha now residing Georgetown D.C. Grade 2 surveillance. Will report developments."*

General Balkovsky remembered, "T. Pemberton" well. Thomas Pemberton, CIA and State Department operative. Espionage, counter-intelligence against "Soviet" networks in the late-1960s and '70s. Balkovsky had been associated with those networks. Pemberton had avoided arrest many times.

Balkovsky respected the American, though he had discussed with his superiors "removing" the American. But he had never ordered Pemberton's disappearance.

Not only Balkovsky had been interested in Pemberton. Other branches within the First and Second Chief Directorates had been keeping him under semi-detached watch for years, after his apparent "retirement." Whenever they received information on Pemberton, they copied it to Balkovsky.

From Germany, the third dispatch read: *"Colonel-unit active. Europe. Training. Cover intact. Operation planned soon. Specific date not yet known. After-action report when feasible."*

This one, much more than the others, disturbed Balkovsky. It came from a source he had not used for years. A "mole."

"The Colonel." In covert operations. Someone Balkovsky had sought—and fought—before.

It was midnight, when Balkovsky stopped reading reports. He was frightened, unusual for him in his years of "espionage management," as he called his Moscow position.

"Lieutenant," he called into his desk intercom. *"Call Minister Torychenko's office. I must speak with him. Urgently."*

His secretary acknowledged. The intercom was silent for several minutes. Her voice returned. *"The Minister's office informed me he left hours ago, General."*

"Call his apartment," Balkovsky replied. *"I must see him. Tonight."*

*   *   *

Buck McConneld hung up the phone in his State Department office. His assistant, William Washbourne II, was with him.

"That was Analysis, Langley," McConneld said. "Message from Pemberton, dropped in the Main Post Office in Munich. They're e-mailing us a copy."

Bill Washbourne had been McConneld's assistant, since McConneld's "reassignment" to the State Department, and his ostensible Agency liaison. Unlike his boss, Washbourne had not been "detached."

Washbourne could have been a lawyer for a big, in-town law firm: striped, long-sleeved, button-down shirt, grey suit pants and matching vest. McConneld often wondered why Washbourne had not gone that route.

After their first days together, McConneld had called Washbourne by his initials. He once commented he was glad the younger man had not been the third person with that name. "Whatever you do," McConneld had said back then,"don't name any of your kids after yourself." Washbourne was not married.

"Did it come through a regular drop on time?" he asked.

"Scheduled time," McConneld said. "Last-resort drop."

McConneld's secretary brought him the e-mail message.

He read aloud, "Cartel's business with former and neo-nazis confirmed. Security tight. Expect rural locations. Alternate contacts. Deal to terminate two to three months. No firm date. Shall advise.' Well, WW2, what've you got?"

"Surveillance of Ms. Pemberton's s.o.p., so far, with the homer and directional mike. A bit shady, Boss. Not telling her it's there." Washbourne smiled a wry smile. "Our resident agent's on reassign-call, if necessary."

"What about the guy I tailed?"

Washbourne skimmed another file. "Ready for this? His name's Marshall, John D.," Washbourne said, laughing. "Goes by 'J.D. Marshall.'"

"His parents had big plans for him all right," McConneld said. "That's ironic praise coming from you, Dear Assistant."

Washbourne frowned at McConneld and continued. "Used his own name to rent that place. He's in his fifties."

"A little old for Ms. Pemberton," McConneld interrupted.

Washbourne continued, "Was a Major in the Army, when he got out. Excellent record. Could've been career. Vietnam, 1971–73. USAREUR, 1974–77. Embassy liaison, Tel Aviv, 1978. In Nam, an intelligence officer. Former Agency work, too. Recruited for Special Ops. File's murky on exact dates."

"There was a lot of that going 'round in Vietnam," McConneld said. "Funny I never met him before, though."

15

"Resigned from The Agency and the Service, at the same time. Reasons given: 'Irreconcilable differences' between himself and 'national policy.' His specialty was nuclear ordnance. Obviously no call for that in Nam."

"What the hell'd he mean by that? We've all had those. Where were his Spec Ops?"

"Europe, mostly," Washbourne replied. "Went back to school. Got a master's and a Ph.D. in physics." Washbourne whistled. "In three years, from Harvard and MIT. Bright boy. That was 1980."

"Any indication if he were infiltrating on assignment? Our friends in DIA or NSA ever had him? Or do?" McConneld asked.

"The file doesn't say. Anything's possible, but I doubt it."

"What's he been doing since '80? What brought him to D.C.? Samantha?"

"No family here. He's taught at private or state colleges and universities around the country, especially the Midwest. Checked with a guy I know at G.U. Marshall's a 'Special Student.' That apartment's been rented since mid-July. He's under regular surveillance. I took the liberty."

"With his background and experience," McConneld sighed. "He made our guys five minutes into their first shift and is playing with us. Initiative's why you're my protégé, though. If I ever leave, you'll be here to plague the higher-ups. Could Marshall be working for a former or future superpower?"

"Nothing from the file would indicate that," Washbourne replied. "My hunch is, no. He's a results-over-turf protection or CYA kind of guy. Maybe he's just a college groupie."

"Any emotional instability in his records?"

Washbourne shook his head. "And no apparent connection to Samantha Pemberton."

McConneld said, "So much for Mr. John Marshall—for now. Let's review the weapons thefts and related stuff."

Thus far, the investigations had been deadends. Stolen trucks and tags, no fingerprints, and no signs of the weapons surfacing had all led the U.S., German, and NATO investigators to what Washbourne termed at one point, "An endless country road." DIA investigations had also reached a deadend, according to reports from that agency.

The weapons had not been limited to the targets of usual thieves; i.e., small arms and ammunition. Grenade launchers, TOWs, LAWs, and Stingers had disappeared into the European netherworld. McConneld and Washbourne concluded the thieves were "pros, who wanted the arms for themselves, probably Europe."

Washbourne suggested a *coup d'état*. The weapons stolen could fit that purpose very well.

McConneld disagreed. The primary or secondary probabilities presented locations in the so-called Third World, not Europe.

As for the missing fissionable materials, there had been no reports of persons or groups, trying to sell "hot" plutonium, other than usual scares from the former Soviet Union or terrorist spooks. Enough was unaccounted-for to construct a very dirty tactical nuke of a kiloton or so.

"What about additional stuff one would need to build the bomb?" McConneld asked, finally.

"No way to trace those things," Washbourne said. "They could be bought anywhere, especially Europe. Marshall, you think?"

"Upgrade surveillance," McConneld said. "If he makes any sudden move to leave the States, have his passport pulled. But leave it to the Bureau. Pemberton's 'big business deal' could be some kind of terrorism. What terror groups head the most feared list this month?"

"Our NATO partners consider their own home-pollinated, leftist groups as the likelies. The Brits think fringes within IRA. Germans think descendants of Baader-Meinhof, or the Red Army Faction. Or they believe one group's responsible for the weapons, others for the plutonium. And there's always our *al Quaeda* whipping boys."

"The thieves can't approach the Russians," McConneld concluded. "Only we can be the victims. A *coup* doesn't seem plausible. Too hard, at least anywhere worthwhile in Europe."

"With all that ordnance loose," Washbourne said, "there could be multiple targets!"

* * *

It was the last week in September, when Sam received a full letter from her brother, Robert. He had been back at Pearl Harbor for some time, but had only sent her a postcard with a photo of the U.S.S. *Arizona* Memorial. *Toes-on-tongue*, she had thought.

His duty schedule was heavy, with the annual SEATO and ANZUS maneuvres. Central Pacific units had also been on Special Alert, Class 3.

> Pa hasn't answered my letters or my calls. Whenever I've called, Daisy tells me he's at school or is away. Have you heard from him yourself? The Twins think it's a big game. I try to recall I was an early-adolescent once. He's never been too busy to let us know he's alive.

If not for Mr. McConneld, she reflected, she could have been writing this. She, too, was between knowledge and ignorance: watching Bob, like a researcher observing a lab rat bounce through a maze.

But she was also on the "outside," another white rat, maybe even a "quisling rat," no closer than any other of the laboratory subjects she had to "stonewall" for The Professor and McConneld.

> Please call Collect, so we can talk. I think I'll start sending you audio-taped letters. Then, you can hear how I feel. Love, Bob.

Sam found the "McC" number in her address book and walked briskly to the Student Center in the Leavey Building and its public phones.

As she waited for the call to McConneld's office to be answered, she thought she heard more than the typical two or three call-routing clicks. Her paranoia was in geometric growth mode.

McConneld came on the line quickly. Sam told him about the letter.

"Don't tell him about Doc's trip," McConneld said.

She empathized with Bob, feeling like a hollow shield. "He's obviously worried."

"Share the worry," he said, finally. "Don't go into particulars."

"And if that's not enough?" Sam asked. "Even though he's hot-headed, Bob's never been stupid."

"Your father trusts you more than he does Bob, doesn't he?"

"That's an odd question," Sam replied. She felt her shoulders tighten, her emotions tense. "Logical, perhaps, but still off-putting."

"Off-whatting?" McConneld asked.

"Never mind," Sam replied, with a skyscraping voice that, she thought, could decalcify a spinal column, if used too much.

"Bob's a bureaucratic crazy at times," Sam continued, in her normal voice. "I suppose that's why Pa trusts me. My brother knows how to push things to the limits, but never beyond them. Which isn't to say he never goes off 'half-cocked.'"

McConneld said, "That's a good reason to keep him in the dark. Your father must've told you about 'grey truths.'"

Sam flashed back to childhood. "When you tell someone an untruth, but you do it, so as not to hurt that person."

"I've remembered it over thirty-five years. You've got to lie a little sometimes, Samantha," McConneld said, sounding pseudo-preachy to her. "If he doesn't buy it, there's always a transfer to the Aleutians or Antarctica, I suppose...Just kidding."

Maybe, he was, or... Sam reflected, as she hung up.

* * *

"Collect call from Samantha," the automated operator asked. A barely alive voice responded with a sound, closer to "yes," than "no."

"So what's bothering you, Big Bro?" Sam asked.

"Give me a minute," her brother said. "Middle-of-the-night for me."

"Who's in bed with you, Bob?"

"No one, for once," he answered. "But you know us sailors. I'm worried about Pa."

Sam replied, quickly, "If that's all you wanted to tell me, I could've saved you this charge." She wanted to coax him, even to coach him, to ask the most specific questions, so she could not avoid answering truthfully.

Sam told him what Mr. McConneld had suggested. It hurt to tell those half-facts. Even if she considered them "grey truths." She felt like a con-person, and a bad one at that.

"Why didn't Daisy tell me that?" Bob asked, speaking breathlessly. That was a sign of his skepticism.

"How the hell do I know?" she said. "Mother-hen and house orchestrator."

"I smell a hold-back here," Bob said.

"Not," she said, coolly. "Don't you think I'd tell you if anything were wrong? He didn't tell me anything. You were there."

"Before I got home? Any hint?"

"Nothing," Sam said. "I know you wanted to be a lawyer, Bob, but please don't cross-examine me." She tried to sound indignant. Now she felt the full hurt of the lie.

"Something about protesting ladies."

"Right, Bob," she replied. This time the indignance was genuine. "I'm lying. Never've told the truth. I'm always lying."

"OK, OK," he whined. "I'll take you at face. I didn't mean to call you a liar."

"Of course you did!" Sam said. "I'm still your little sister. Your personal, manipulatable doormat. Well, let me tell you something! I'm a woman who can take care of herself, Wise-ass!"

"You've got the mother-hen role down pretty well yourself. All those years of looking after the Twins."

"You're right, I do. Somebody had to, after Mother's death. I wasn't that old then myself, but I grew into it. And you weren't around, what with your Service duty."

"Always with the guilt," Bob said.

"I'm not trying to lay a guilt trip on you. I didn't mean it that way."

"Whatever. I'm getting to the bottom of it, and, if there's something going on—" He was not whining any more. "And don't get any ideas about getting involved in it."

Sam recalled how close Bob and their mother had been before her death. She felt his strength again.

"Your place's at Georgetown now. If I find you involved, I'll hire someone to escort you ungently back to school. Take care of yourself."

"Don't think you can order me around, Bob!" Sam said. "He's *our* father, not only yours." She no longer felt *angst* about "the tale." "I'll do whatever I think is best! Bye!" She slammed the phone receiver into its cradle.

Sam recalled Mr. McConneld's words: having to "lie a little." *Did ends justify means?* Perhaps. Sometimes. Was this one of those? But that was relativistic—too easy.

She considered telling Liz, if only to unload. As she leaned against the plexiglass of the booth, she thought how nice a trip to Europe in the Fall would be, could be. Time to order a long-term EurailPass?

"I'll show these bastards," she whispered, as she left.

At dinner that evening, Liz brought another resident of their corridor. Sam had only an occasional-smile-acquaintance with the new person.

Liz introduced each by her full name. "I'd like to introduce Regina Armstrong Foxwirth."

Regina offered Sam her hand, nearly motionless, at the end of a stiff, straight arm. Her verbal greeting reminded Sam of the late Audrey Hepburn at the Ascot Races.

"You've been too close to the 'brary," Liz said to Sam. "Not getting out enough. I've taken on the job of introducing you around."

"So nice to have one's own social director," Sam said, cocking her left eyebrow up and staring at Liz.

"I figured you and Regina have a lot in common," Liz said, undeterred. "Regina's lived in Europe, gone to school there. Isn't that right, Regina?"

REGINA. The name was right. Imperial presence and bearing. A smooth stride in her walk, very controlled gestures, starched uprightness: an expensive, private European boarding-school product. Sam mused whether Regina kept her school uniforms for use at University.

Regina's was a VERY moneyed appearance. Her dress was from Chanel. Black timelessness, padded shoulders, and its lines, sharply outlining her perfect, "super-modelesque" figure.

Her makeup was well-done, but not, what Sam called, "warpaint overkill." Her effect was completed with frosted and heavily highlighted blonde hair, swept back away from her face, with no part, and resting below her shoulders.

Except for a shade or two, a few glimmers, it was similar to Liz's. Sam had the same feeling as she had had when she first met Liz: almost envious, wishing she had the *chutzpah* to do her "do" so radically differently. A "do" change might be overdue, Sam reflected then.

But there was something else about Regina, submerged beneath the *haute couture* and the makeup, the well-exercised carriage. Regina seemed more the young matron, than the eighteen-year-old: more a late transfer, or a "very early second-childhood." There was also what Sam's father called *hauteur*, restrained and polite, or proper and correct, with the airs of self-absorbed and projected superiority.

"When I said I was having dinner with you, Regina asked, if she could join us. Anxious, weren't you, Regina? Well, as anxious as Regina gets."

"I tend to be more, how shall I say, restrained in my feelings," Regina said, "than Elizabeth. Or most girls."

Sam watched her place a forkful of food in her mouth, seemingly measured to proper amount. She fantasized Regina traveled with her own food-taster and chef, but she tried to put her own presuppositions aside and allow Regina space through the defenses.

"My family's permanent homes are in New York. Park Avenue. California. Near San Francisco. Also, Bel Air," she said, showing Sam clear blue eyes. "We sold our place in Manila, after the poor Marcoses were driven from power, and bought in Jakarta."

At that Liz's eyes bulged, and she was biting the insides of her mouth.

"Poor Marcoses?" Sam lipped the words. There were things she would discuss with Regina. Others she would not!

"My parents wintered there, occasionally," Regina was saying. "My father is in business. They spend time on the yacht in the Mediterranean—off Minorca, Capri, Nice. My father also owns places in Europe. I spend rather a lot of time over there, too."

"Whereabouts?" Liz asked, as though she knew the answers but wanted Sam to hear them.

"Switzerland. South of France. Germany and Austria. Italy," Regina said. *Like one speaking about the day's weather report,* Sam reflected.

"One thing I've wanted to ask," Sam said, "since I first saw you. How do you manage to look so good this late in the day? Especially in this heat?"

"I work at it constantly, my dear," Regina replied, breathlessly. "The only way to find the kind of man I want."

Liz sat up abruptly. "And what kind is that?"

"A perfect one," Regina said. "Brains, charm, style, resources to keep me well-heeled, well-tanned, well-oiled, and on the Continent."

"I don't look that far ahead," Sam said. She was still laughing inside about the "poor Marcoses." "Does age matter?"

"Young or old," Regina said. "It doesn't. So long as the other qualifications're met. One should always look to one's own class for companionship."

"Will you have to be in love?" Sam asked.

"My dear, love can be so transitory," Regina sighed. "So fleeting. Vast security is a much better basis. How about you? Elizabeth tells me you've lived in Europe quite a bit."

Sam was surprised when Regina departed from her personal script.

"We've spent most of the past fifteen years, maybe more, outside the States," Sam said. "In Europe mostly. I'm fluent in German, French, and Italian. Away from cities it helps. But I'm not telling you anything you don't already know. My father's an academic and consultant. He's taught politics and history at most of the universities in Europe. Follows his investments, too. They're not that much."

"Your father sounds," Regina said, hesitating, apparently for effect, "*very* interesting!"

"He's not your type," Sam replied, quickly.

"A great pity," Regina said. "I could be your stepmother—if

he's widowed or divorced. On a related note, I must say I've found the boys here a great disappointment. Too many junior executives and not enough senior material. Not like the men in Europe. This one in Nice. " She sighed, almost wistfully. "He was special. These want to fall into bed after the first coffee and give nothing in return. I put them in their places . . ."

I'll bet you do, Sam thought. Then aloud, "I haven't met that many." She wondered what Regina meant by "in return."

"Sam and I're both in the College," Liz broke in. "You're a freshman in Languages. Right, Regina?"

Sam softly kicked Liz under the table.

"D'you have a nickname, Regina?" Liz asked.

"I prefer 'Regina,'" she answered. "Samantha, I'm fluent in your languages. As well as Spanish. And I speak Russian."

"I'm getting something else," Sam said. She gave a short, sudden jerk of the head to Liz.

Regina was pulling a Dunhill cigarette from a box in her Chanel bag, and regally waved them off. She went outside to smoke.

At the salad bar, Sam said, "Were you serious? She wanted to meet me?"

Liz nodded, while laughing. "She's a real trip!" she replied. "I didn't mean to blind-side you, but you've got to meet Regina to appreciate her!"

"Did she say why?"

Liz stopped laughing. "Not really. She seems to need formal introductions. You should see her room! No roommate and all the closets are full. Shoes, boots, bags. Everything the best. Off Fifth Avenue, Paris, and the Chanel runways. I hope she loosens up."

"She's got more in common with Imelda than we suspected," Sam said, laughing again. "How old d'you think she is?"

"I've never been good at guessing. Eighteen or nineteen? Going on upper-class thirty-five or forty?"

"Older, I think," Sam said. "The clothes, the hair, the makeup. They're more than just safe. They're esteem-defining armour. Against people. Reality. Maybe even feelings."

"They ARE her reality," Liz said. "No vulnerabilities she lets us see."

Sam continued, "That perfect porcelain face from San Francisco. Something about Ms. Foxwirth isn't what it seems. And she's too perfect!" Sam said.

"Yeah," Liz said. "I guess I'm a little envious of that, too."

Back in her room that night, Sam tried to work. But she could not concentrate longer than a few paragraphs.

She fancied herself a female Walter Mitty. She wanted to be where she could help, leading the Marines, or a Navy SEALs team, like Robert had.

Even her fantasies were not havens of escape. She was tired, angry, afraid at friendlies and hostiles. She was unable even to feign a love life. Chaperoning-by-compact was as intrusive. Her "radio audiences" deserved tuning forks on every microphone, audio detonations, like nitroglycerine. Tonight, she wanted to send obscene "radiograms" to all. But she could not, would not, satisfy them. Not now. Not ever...

III

The sidewalk on Third Avenue arc'ed the corner at East 23rd Street in Manhattan. East 23rd Street in daylight was peopled by more than winos and homeless. Now it had only brown-baggers.

"There he goes!" yelled a man in a brown corduroy jacket and black turtleneck. He and three other men were chasing a middle-level specialist, named Erik Spurling, through the Lower East Side of Manhattan.

"Emilio!" the man in the turtleneck shouted. "Go left!"

"*Puta!*" Emilio said, as he turned the next corner.

"Jaime?" said another of the pursuers. "Jamael's car's up there, turning onto Park." He pointed to a light-green 1994 Ford station wagon. "He'll get Spurling."

They watched, as their quarry ran across the next intersection, a block short of the Ford, which turned south onto Park. He reached the median on Park Avenue, doubled over and collapsed. Jaime watched as Emilio and the others stuffed him into the back seat. "Still alive?" Jaime asked.

The driver showed him a tranquilizer pistol.

"Straight to the farm, Jamael," Jaime said to the driver.

* * *

The Ford pulled up before a large farmhouse. The trip to this New Jersey farm had taken several hours. Emilio and two other men carried Spurling in, with Jaime behind them.

"The drug should be wearing off," Emilio said. With Spurling tied to a chair, Emilio slapped him. "Wake up, *Puta*," Jaime shouted.

Spurling blinked hard. "Who're you?! . . . What d'you want?"

"You have my money," Jaime said. "As for what we want, Spurling, who's been buying your information?"

"You?! But I never..."

Jaime laughed loudly. "Me and fifty-seven flavors of couriers. When you didn't come through on 'Case Blue,' it was time for us to meet." He smashed Spurling's head against the cross-bar.

"I don't know anything about Case Blue!..." Spurling said, nearly crying. "D'you think I'd blow a good cash flow?"

"You're a whore, that's true," Jaime said. "But even whores won't do some things. Take his shoes off, and hold him."

Spurling struggled but his captors held him tightly.

"Look," Spurling blurted. "My bosses're having a big meeting in Berlin... November. I'm too far down the ladder."

Jaime put on black leather gloves and picked up a short piece of rubber hose.

"The Association," Spurling said, breath-heavy.

"The Cartel!" Jaime shouted. "Don't dignify it with the name 'association.' You're a two-sided whore, working for whores!"

"Please!" Spurling shouted back. "Please! No! I've told you!"

"I don't think so." Jaime slapped the hose against his left glove.

* * *

The four men stood around Spurling. His feet were bare, his clothes soaked. He was not moving, except for dog-like breathing.

"He was right," Jaime said. "He didn't know much. Directly."

"Want me to wake him again?" Emilio asked.

"Get rid of him," Jaime said. "His information's not been that good. We've got other contacts."

"He was babbling," Emilio said. He turned the pages of a notebook.

"Mongrel's breath tells what he's eating," Jamael said.

"Lots more comm-traffic between North America and Europe, especially Berlin and Munich. New York and Buenos Aires. Like acquisition activity. No acquisition's in the works. Key transfers to Europe. Lots of crisis analyses coming through New York. Oil, food, ferrous metals, plutonium, gold, silver, currencies. Lots of trading. Business with the Russians is shit. Next big meeting's in November in Berlin. And something we picked up ourselves. Their paramilitary affiliates will be there. Arms sales're way up. But nothing about Case Blue."

"The brush strokes screen too much. You're lost in the paint dots."

"We know one thing," Jamael said. "A one-handed thief can beg and scream."

"You'll have something useful to report to your agency," Jaime said to him. "It's September 15th. We'll be on Case Blue by October at the outside."

*   *   *

"*Good evening, General*," the butler said, as he admitted General Balkovsky to the foyer of Yuri Torychenko's Moscow apartment. He helped Balkovsky with his overcoat. "*The Deputy Minister'll be down in a few minutes. You may wait in the study . . .*"

In Torychenko's study Balkovsky poured a cognac, Courvoisier VSOP.

Among the paintings on the walls was a portrait of Lenin, rendered in less than the old revolutionary, "socialist-realism" style that one might have found, pre-coup. The other canvases were very traditional renditions of Eighteenth and Nineteenth century subjects by Western artists. The Deputy Minister had never been an ideological, threadbare Communist, even in the Brezhnev Era.

Torychenko's title was Deputy Foreign Minister for Foreign Political Education and Extension Service, his cover as Head of the First Chief Directorate, the primary foreign intelligence and operations branch of the Russian Secret Service.

Still, no ideology, except national interest, could have ensured Torychenko's survival. He was a pragmatist, a true survivor with an urbane manner, a "Dior-Marxist," as Balkovsky had called him. Now, only the "Dior" remained.

Torychenko came in. "*Alexei Andreivitch,*" he said, shaking Balkovsky's hand tightly. He poured himself a *Johnnie Walker, Black Label*, adding half-again as much water. He was dressed in a well-fitting, French-cut, three-piece suit in pinstripes. Torychenko always had looked more like a Western diplomat than a Soviet one in the "old days." Although Torychenko was gaunt and tall, and Balkovsky short and husky, they did have physical similarities. Both had fair, wind-burned-red complexions, brown eyes, and full heads of white hair.

"*Why the urgent call? I'm glad your secretary called me here. I've felt more secure here lately.*"

"*Trouble with GRU again?*"

"*Our military friends're playing the usual games,*" Torychenko replied. "*We caught one of their men tapping our communiques two days ago. We sent him back, after irate shouting with the uniforms. At least their hostility to the President's not under their greatcoats, not after Parliament and Chechnya. They've gotten over that business with the biological warfare materials, for example.*"

"*Coup?*"

"*Not from them,*" Torychenko said. "*And Mr. Z.'s not in a position for that ploy—yet. The uniforms're getting more aggressive about the things we're not telling them, with an eye to embarrassing us. Like the American CIA and DIA.*"

"*We still have to repay them, though, for those assassinations two years ago,*" Balkovsky said. "*The bastards.*"

"*Don't worry,*" Torychenko said. "*We shall. Those, who haven't paid already, soon will.*" He finished his drink, and reloaded each of their glasses. "*But you've not come to discuss our typical trifles, Alex.*"

"*Here's a report for you,*" Balkovsky said. "*It reads quickly. Then, a special communication.*"

Torychenko lit a French *Gauloises*, and read. Its smoke formed a cylindrical lattice-work on the way to the ornate ceiling, with breaks in the ladder, when Torychenko took puffs. He asked, "*Have you considered disclosing this to the Americans? Or a joint investigation?*"

Balkovsky replied, "*I don't trust them. No matter what.*"

Torychenko smiled. "*You rediscovered your old friend, Pemberton. Is your Department involved in his being unaccounted for?*"

Balkovsky said, *"I'd pre-clear anything like that with you."* He crossed his arms. *"Compliments on your memory."*

"I've been an anxious reader of all your exploits," Torychenko said, *"since I got you your first promotion."*

"How flattering," Balkovsky said. *"I've had no recent need to speak with the esteemed Professor Pemberton... Until now."*

"Why now?" Torychenko asked, taking a long draw on the cigarette and exhaling. The smoke speared toward Balkovsky along with the question.

"He's still a high-ranking member of the Association of International Industrialists, Executives, and Entrepreneurs," Balkovsky said. *"It should be named the Brotherhood of Corporate Capitalists. They call themselves..."*

"The Cartel," Torychenko said, quickly. *"Be careful, Alex. We're still doing business with those people, though on a much smaller scale than before. You're too pure. You must guard against that. These aren't ideological times."*

"Nevertheless," Balkovsky said, *"his Cartel has long ties to Nazi, Neo-Nazi, and extreme rightist groups. 'Subsidies.'"*

"Where're you going with this?"

"His disappearance and those activities're related. I've concluded his Cartel's behind these thefts. I'm certain it'll culminate in Germany."

"You think Pemberton's a Nazi... a closet one?"

"I don't know," Balkovsky answered. *"I don't think so, but that's irrelevant. I've checked with the heads of Eighth and Eleventh Departments, as well as with Department A and Executive Action."*

"You've been very busy, Alex."

"Mogorovski and Soeyetov agree with me. Not the Cubans, the Iranians, Arabs, disaffected Palestinians. Not even our former African clients or those of the Americans could've organized so well and kept it so quiet. I've been working with Second Department, on Latin American connections with Pemberton's Cartel."

"Oh, Alexei," Torychenko said, mock-scoldingly. *"Are you looking for a German Nazi under every Russian bed again?"*

"Being Cassandra's not an easy job," Balkovsky said. *"I expected this. So, I brought this other message. Every time I've*

received information from this source, it's meant something bad was about to happen in Germany."

"Alexei Andreivitch, stop wearing this anti-German badge," Torychenko scolded. *"Your father only died once. At Stalingrad. You expect the Germans to pay for that forever. Let the dead rest, Alex. We've survived the Cold War, and have more in common with the Americans and the industrialized world than you admit."*

"For now," Balkovsky said. *"But if we're at each other's throats again? Suppose the President doesn't last and hardliners return?"*

"I'm a surviving optimist," Torychenko said. *"Or an optimistic survivor. Things won't go that way again."*

"How can you be so sure? It seems we're on the brink of economic breakdown weekly, if not daily."

"The Western Germans've had over forty years of bourgeois democracy and peace. Why use force, when you can buy people off? They absorbed our former stooges without too many groans. It's cost them a fortune, but they've got it."

"That could be changing," Balkovsky said. "Now they know the price of neglect, plus Neo-Nazism's rising there."

"They're peacefully developing the former East Bloc. What more d'you need before you forgive the dead?"

"The only good German," Balkovsky said, *"is one under Russian control."*

"Very stale Cold War rhetoric," Torychenko said. *"Neither of us'll live to see that again."*

"Please keep my background out of this, Minister," Balkovsky said. *"I'm not the only person seeing more than coincidence. The other department bosses agree. If you think my prejudices interfere with my work, relieve me. Otherwise, please read."*

"Colonel-unit'... Is that...?" Torychenko asked, his skin paler.

Balkovsky was calm. *"Third-World Rightist. Mercenary. European origins. Apparently back after a multi-year hiatus. You're more attentive to my bothers now, Yuri. Why is that?"*

"Don't be impertinent, Alex. Any reference to The Colonel sets my alarms off, since Italy and Lockerbee. You set me up."

Balkovsky smiled. *"I had to show you I'm not paranoiac."*

"You think Pemberton can help us find him?"

"My agent might," Balkovsky replied. *"But I'm not sacrificing my mole. We take The Colonel, they'd only replace him. Pemberton's probably's been privy to it. My agent isn't, and won't be till target date."*

"How do we find him? I expect The Cartel's leaders've insulated themselves. Plausible deniability."

"His daughter," Balkovsky said, *"she knows where he is, even if she doesn't realize it. I recommend a wet operation for a few days. Then our people release her."*

"That'll alert American Intelligence and FBI. We shall have as much as told them we're interested in the girl and her father."

"Not," Balkovsky said, quickly, *"if we use local criminals, 'hired muscle,' the Americans call it. Americans'll do anything for money."*

"What makes you think she knows? If I were he, I'd have told her nothing. And what about the 'hired muscle'?"

"She's got access to his papers. As for the thugs, more dead criminals won't be missed in Washington. Especially now."

Torychenko said, *"I'll take it up with Department A, First Department, and Service One in the morning."*

IV

Velpke, Germany. A small town, northeast of Braunschweig. It wasn't exactly a name U.S. households would recognize: a place without a lot of excitement. When excitement did come, nary a Velpke resident ever knew it.

Outside Velpke were hills and woods, typical of Central Germany. Burrowed among them was the newly completed U.S. Army Strategic Arms Stockpile Command (SASCOM) Depot #E-917.

The depot was nine miles from the old Demarcation Line which had divided Germany into split national-personalities and schizophrenia. The Line was gone from the maps, but the social and cultural schism, between East and West, lived on in the "new" Germany.

Depot #E-917 had been built as part of "Operation Move-up." "Move-up" was intended to place the new, "clean" NATO, especially U.S., tactical nuclear weapons closer to the most-recently fancified frontlines of another unlikely war, as NATO tried to redefine its mission—and its rationale for existence.

This night was moonless, like so many other Autumn nights in Germany. Darkness, an onyx-colored bowl, had engulfed the depot and its surrounding hills and woods.

The guard and defense force, with equal detachments of the German *Bundeswehr* and the U.S. Army, was in place—or so it seemed. All appeared as it should have, but for the disguised and hidden presence beneath the uniforms and in the evergreens.

Huddling against the Fall winds were more than fifty men. They awaited delivery of the first redeployment convoy, bearing Medium Atomic Demolition Munitions (MADMs), one kiloton of TNT to Hiroshima-sized explosivity (and sometimes referred to as "madames" by Service personnel) and Special Atomic Demolition Munitions (SADMs), decimalized nukes.

The SADMs (sometimes called "mademoiselles," or "Mlles" by their handlers) were the so-called "backpack nukes," small-yield weapons, developed for two- or three-person Special Forces teams. These bombs' fusing/detonation materials came in the same convoy as the packs. The MADMs and their triggers were miles apart.

Around the outer perimeter ran two concentric, chain-link and barbed-wire fences. The Entry Compound was separated from the depot's interior by another gate. The bunkers, awaiting new tenants, smelled of young concrete.

There were three different uniforms here: *Bundeswehr* field-dress and G-3 automatic rifles, U.S. Army green-brown-and-black camouflage dress with M-16A-2s and Baretta 9mm pistols, including the "commander" and his aide.

The remainder of the "force," seven black-suited and charcoal-faced men, crouched in the overhead trees as snipers, armed with either Russian SKVD-7 or U.S. .50-caliber, single-shot sniper rifles, and "Starlight" gun scopes.

The "commander" of the unit wore a full colonel's insignia, a flat, black eagle: no random choice. He was known by friends and enemies as "The Colonel." With him were his aide, an ostensible U.S. captain, and a second man, a *Bundeswehr* major.

The leader seemed like other combat-experienced U.S. officers, with very young career-start in Vietnam, "can-do" tattooed in his brain. But English had not been his first language. Now he spoke it like a native of Texas.

His watch, a heavy, old-style timepiece from the Interwar period, had been his grandfather's, a privilege of young wealth in the 1920s. He recalled his grandfather calling the 1920s and '30s the "truce time."

The incoming convoy was scheduled to arrive at 2330 hours. The time was 2315.

Another U.S. uniform joined them. "*Das amerikanische Geleit hat.*" His voice was a Wagnerian baritone.

"English only!" The Colonel barked. "You know better, Sergeant Smith!"

"Sergeant Smith" stiffened to an unanticipated attention. "It won't happen again, sir!" he said. "Ten minutes ahead. ETA now 2320."

"About eight kilometers out," The Colonel said. "Problems?"

Smith said, "Recognition codes're holding up."

"Our guests?" The Colonel asked.

"Sleeping like babes," his aide replied. "It's sad to terminate."

"Why, Captain Frazier," The Colonel said. "Squeamish? You've never cried for our people we had to finish off."

"We weren't fighting Americans there," Captain Frazier said.

"The Americans've only been convenient allies over the years," The Colonel replied. "That back bunker's a good, air-tight chamber. Are the canisters ready?"

"For 0115 hours," Sergeant Smith said.

"Rendezvous with Force H's set for 0135," The Colonel said. "Des Site X. We no-show, they're gone. And, Smith, see NO ONE from the convoy gets near that bunker. Our guys in the trees?"

"Fire-defense, I mean, brigade," Frazier said. "Smith and Frazier. One d-merit each," Frazier said. "Our people in the trees're on opportunity fire."

The Colonel patted his right boot. He felt the luck. His companions nodded and smiled, as their leader had.

"Our American Santa," The Colonel said. He took out his Baretta 9mm pistol and pulled back the slide.

Truck engines were getting closer. Two minutes later the convoy was outside the gates.

Two men debarked from the lead HMMWV. One headed to the guards' kiosk.

"Captain Pierre Monroe, reporting, sir," the convoy man said. "Here's my DEPSEC i.d." He saluted and handed The Colonel a red plastic card.

The Colonel returned the amenity. "Colonel Allen. Here's mine." He introduced the others.

The convoy First Sergeant, Bill Bates, joined Monroe. The latter read from the Authentication binder, sealed since the convoy left *Syke* earlier that day.

"Request Authentication, Colonel," Monroe said. "Authenticate Bravo Six. Small Boys—Middle Son Delta."

"Authenticate Alpha Eight Continuous," The Colonel replied,

reading from a clipboard. "Package Delivery Tango. Zero. Zero."

"Three-Five. King-Zulu-King," Monroe concluded. "Authentication Correct."

"Back, sir, after I call TACOM, Corps Area Forward."

At his HMMWV, Monroe radioed to Fifth Corps' mobile field headquarters. "Convoy time is Zulu. GMT. Mission completed." He received an acknowledgment and returned to The Colonel.

The Colonel gave him directions for unloading. "How many troops in your party?"

"Twenty-eight, including Sergeant Bates and myself," Monroe said, holding his binder open and extended to The Colonel, along with a pen. "As soon as you sign off."

"What?" The Colonel asked. Then, after a moment, "Oh! Yes, of course. Stupid of me!" He signed the release, after a scan of the pages. "Times I'd like to forget this red-tape and red-card bullshit, and get on with being a soldier. You only brought five 'madames' with you? The rest're backpacks?"

Monroe nodded. "The W-45-3 'madames,' the W-54 SADMs. Twenty in all."

"Your last transmission indicated you were eight kilometers out. Sergeant Smith brought the message," The Colonel said.

"Smith" replied, "Eight kliks distant."

Captain Monroe returned to his HMMWV. "Do you remember giving a distance on our last check-in?" he whispered to Sergeant Bates. Monroe repeated the exchange.

Bates shrugged, "No, but maybe age's taking its toll, sir."

Monroe radioed The Colonel's instructions to the convoy, and unloading progressed. A forklift drove to the first truck, one of The Colonel's men at the wheel.

"Come on, people!" First Sergeant Bates shouted, as he supervised. "We're not paying you by the hour! Get your rears in gear and your minds out of park!"

Convoy men transferred backpack-sized crates into three Army-green pickup trucks. The Colonel's men were assisting, while their fellows were beyond the periphery, each with his M-16A-2 in his hands.

The first forklift rode to a storage bunker and its earthen mound fifty yards away. Two more forklifts, also driven by The

Colonel's men, followed. The first returned for the final MADMs, ferrying them to the same bunker entrance. The SADM unloading had also been finished.

Bates rejoined Monroe at the command vehicle. "Sir, I've been thinking," he said. "You're not slipping, Chip. They're lying."

"But why?" Monroe said. "Everything's been go. Strange the CO met us, though. When I offered him the release, he hesitated, like he didn't have a clue. Get through to TACOM, Corps Area Forward. Pass the word. Be ready for trouble."

The Colonel, with his aide, called Monroe. "Your boys finished, aren't they?" he asked, as he walked up.

"I noticed your men haven't put the hardware away yet, sir," Monroe said. "Mine could help put the 'madames' to bed for the night, sir."

"No need, Captain," The Colonel said. "My boys're up to it."

"In that case, sir," Monroe said. "It's been a pleasure doing business with you. Sorry we haven't crossed paths before. New assignment, sir?"

The Colonel said, "Your fulsome praise forces me to invite you in for a farewell drink. Your Top Kick, too."

"Despite military protocol, sir," Monroe said, "we'll take a raincheck. Besides, we've got to . . ."

"You've got to what, Captain?" The Colonel asked.

Sergeant Bates interrupted, "What the Captain means is."

"Does he need you to translate for him, Sergeant?"

"No, sir," Bates replied. "Just got an asshaul ahead."

The Colonel said, "Very good, Sergeant. How 'bout a little caffeine, maybe?"

"Appreciate the hospitality, sir," Monroe said. "But . . ."

"I insist!" The Colonel's voice was low, but tense and firm. He patted his holster. "Isn't that right, Captain Frazier?"

The aide stepped from behind his boss. Monroe and Bates saw Frazier's pistol. "No sharp moves," Frazier said. "Hand your weapons to Colonel Allen."

Monroe and Bates did not move at all.

"Do it!" the aide said in a loud whisper.

The U.S. soldiers glanced at the HMMWV, then quickly back

at The Colonel and his aide.

"You don't want to take us out, Captain," Monroe said. "If we're not back with Corps, MPs'll be choppering in before you get twenty feet."

Sergeant Bates said, "Got you covered. Right, Robinson?"

"Right, Sarge." A new voice spoke. Its owner stood from behind the command vehicle, holding an M-16A-2.

"Our hole card, doubles as our driver," Monroe said. "Now, please follow your own advice. You, first, Captain."

"Are you crazy, Captain?" The Colonel asked, angrily. "Tell your man to sling his rifle. This is a drill. I'm in from Washington."

"Sorry, sir," Monroe said to The Colonel. He took the pistol from Frazier. "But to do this officially, I challenge Authentication. We'll call Corps Area Forward and straighten this thing out. Your permission?"

"Preposterous!" The Colonel said. "I'll have you busted out of the Service!"

Bates and Monroe smiled at each other. "Maybe some Service, but probably not the U.S. Army, sir," Monroe said.

Monroe and Bates heard the blast of a high-powered rifle. Robinson fell to the ground. "That's no 16!" Bates shouted.

"Snipers!" Monroe yelled. "Robinson!?" More high-powered rifle blasts cracked the night silence open.

Frazier blew a whistle. The Colonel's men spread bursts of M-16 fire.

The Colonel fired at Sergeant Bates, wounding him. Monroe fired the aide's pistol, but missed.

Monroe dove onto Bates, log-rolling the two of them behind the HMMWV. He leaned Bates against its right side, beside Robinson's body.

The initial M-16 bursts found U.S. targets. More snipers' shots echoed. More U.S. soldiers went down. The men from Truck Six got their weapons to use. But one-by-one, they were hit by sniper fire.

"Play dead," Monroe said to Bates, "if you hear anybody."

"Shoulder's burning real bad," Bates gasped.

"We're getting outta this shithole!" Monroe whispered. Then, he shouted, "Fucking bastards! Killed my sergeant!" He fired Frazier's pistol, emptying it. Picking up Robinson's M-16, Monroe squeezed off short bursts, and reloaded.

He spread a longer burst that caught two of The Colonel's men and smashed them against a truck. Still crouching, he heard another sniper shot.

The M-16, loosed from his hands, discharged. Monroe reached reflexively for his back, then slumped to the dirt. Feeling cold earth and pine needles on his cheek, he smelled a foul aroma, as he lost consciousness.

* * *

After Captain Monroe fired at him, The Colonel jumped under a nearby tree, Captain Frazier with him. They stayed there through the firefight.

The automatic weapons fire became more intermittent. Single shots and short bursts replaced the longer staccatos. The Colonel's men scurried, firing between and into the convoy trucks.

Frazier checked his watch. "Not quite how we planned it," he said.

"Find Smith and Muller!" The Colonel replied. Smith joined him.

"Working parties!" The Colonel said. "At 0035 Hours they roll."

"We're already working, sir," Smith replied.

"Our people're setting charges in the CP," Frazier said.

"I'll do the final detonation myself and disable communications."

The Colonel jogged to the first storage bunker. He watched work parties load MADMs and SADMs into the cargo sections of civilian-style, enclosed Mercedes trucks. These, with two Rovers, had been parked near the fifth bunker, out of sight of the convoy. The loaders placed prefabricated walls into prepared grooves inside each cargo bed.

The Colonel's men changed clothes, uncovering civilian laborers' garb beneath their uniforms. The loading had been finished in only nine minutes.

"Colonel?" Frazier called to him from the command center. "Ten men killed. Six wounded. Two very badly."

"Load the wounded into our sixth Mercedes," The Colonel said. "Strip and dump the dead into the HQ. Leave some petrol. I'll handle the rest. Disperse as planned. No detonators for the MADMs, but that's being arranged."

"What about you, sir?" the aide asked. "We'll wait."

"Negative," The Colonel replied. "Someone's got to close this down. No telling how long."

"I could stay," Frazier said. "I'm expendable."

Sergeant Smith came up. "Everything's go, sir," he said. "Snipers're mounted. I'll ride with them." Sergeant Smith climbed into an army-green panel-truck.

The Colonel said, "Frazier and Muller'll lead. Get to rendezvous! I'll head in the opposite direction, and contact you. Now get the hell out of here!"

Frazier sighed. He formed the final detail. *What a miserable burial for good soldiers*, he thought, *to leave them, like charred bread in a toaster. He had known these men through combat, blood sausage, and death in the Third World.* The wounded were lucky. Perhaps the dead were, too.

In Africa and South America The Colonel had ordered other wounded comrades shot when they slowed down the unit. He knew that, *without* The Colonel, their next mission, whatever it was, *would* fail.

* * *

The last vehicle, except his Rover, had left into the forest nightshadows. He shone his light over U.S. soldiers killed in the firefight. Eyes were open, glistening with youth's last moment of disbelief when its mortality has been reluctantly accepted. The Colonel returned to the HQ.

Inside, gasoline fumes were ubiquitous. Around the command, control, and communications room were packets of C-4 plastique with radio-controlled detonators. He pushed a switch on each. Twin green lights flashed harmonically.

The bodies were on their backs, like in a morgue's anteroom. The Colonel picked up a gasoline can and poured its contents over the corpses, being careful not to spill any near the plastique charges.

As he back-pedaled to the front door, he noticed one of the detonators flashed irregularly, then went off completely.

Discovering a wire had become disconnected, he reached to his boot for his knife, his version of good-luck beads and the jack-of-all-tools, in one. It was not there. He searched the floor, and the Rover. Still, no dagger. He returned to the broken detonator.

Hell of a time to lose it, he thought, as he reattached the wire. His hands shaking a little, he turned on its receiver. The lights were operating again.

In the Rover, the radio transmitter for the detonators was on the passenger's seat. *Only two more loose shoestrings to tie up*, he thought.

As he drove through the outer gate, he looked at his watch. Sloppy, he reflected, but done in an hour-and-a-half. Next time, better. Below the detached analysis, he felt the loss of the dagger, almost like that of a trusted comrade. His watch had read 0050 hours.

*   *   *

"Major Williams?" the communications sergeant called to the Staff Officer G-4 for Nuclear Weapons and Ordnance, Corps Area Forward, Fifth Corps, temporarily northeast of Giessen.

"Sir, we've been unable to reach Convoy 442N," the sergeant continued. "Due, SASCOM Depot #E-917, Velpke, from Depot 112 near *Syke*. CPT. Monroe, P., OIC. Checked in on arrival. Expected five hours ago. Depot 235, where it was 'sposed to get a crew change and pick up cargo, is screaming."

The G-4 Staff Officer said, "I know Chip. Captain Monroe. By-the-book. Tried to reach them?"

"I supervised, sir, in case these cherries were fucking it up. Not a word. Depot 917 hasn't answered, either."

"What?! Why the hell?! Call HQ, Commandant's Office. He'll have both our asses if he reads it in the papers!!!"

V

Buck McConneld was at home that Sunday afternoon in September when the call came. It was the weekend after his phone conversation with Samantha Pemberton. Surprised, and angry, McConneld heard the preliminary report from Bill Washbourne. Experience reminded him nothing should shock him, but disbelief lingered.

"MPs discovered the theft," Washbourne said. He described the casualty situation.

"I'd hate to have to write those letters," McConneld said.

"Twenty weapons," Washbourne observed. He described types. "No stones completely out-of-place, but a few turned 'round. The unit skeletoning the place was neutralized: fifteen guys, in all, were in a bunker, asleep."

"Frigging James Bond didn't chase so many bombs! The Army's story?" McConneld interrupted. "Who's in the express-five-items-or-less-no-wait-line? Ransom notes?"

The frustration McConneld detected in his assistant changed to relief. "First answer: take a number and stand in line."

"Silly question," McConneld admitted. "What's the Army's line?"

"It hasn't started notifying next-of-kin yet. Two DIA teams and an ordnance/E.O.D. unit are on site. The post CPs a wreck. The walls were a ready-made oven."

"The Army's waiting to debrief their beauty-sleepers. DIA's doing background checks on the crews."

"How're the Germans taking this?" McConneld was imagining U.S. authorities informing them "a few of our BOMBS're *missing.*"

Only humor helped him control his anger: at the Army for its can-do, life's-a-football-game attitude, at the thieves, for "upping the ante" on the international "political Richter Scale." At least they weren't perfect. McConneld had never been a "budget bureaucrat," working for ever larger appropriations and justifying his employment by bending or manipulating intelligence estimates, an old trick of the Reagan/Bush/Bush people. "Has the Army broken the news to the FRG yet?" he asked.

"We did," Washbourne said, "but at the top. Too many leaks inside the Defense and Foreign Ministries to take a chance. If the Russian right-wing..."

"Hold the Russians. How are our German buddies taking it?"

"Typical Germanic stoicism, I suppose," Washbourne replied.

"I've got to get over there right away, WW2. You know Simmons."

"And, if he didn't order it, you'd go anyhow," Washbourne said. "A plane's at Andrews for us. I'll meet you at the helipad in an hour."

"I'm going solo," McConneld said. He knew he was stepping on Washbourne's feelings. "But I need you here. If anyone's after Tom, they could go after Sam, too."

"And is she a 'Sam'?"

"Dump all your presuppositions," McConneld replied. "She's her own, unique person. And she won't take crap from anybody."

McConneld packed, and kissed his spouse good-bye. Minutes later he was on his way to the helipad in a Lincoln limousine, where, as promised, Bill Washbourne awaited him.

"Tom Pemberton's due to contact us. The schedule's in the file. His option. This is no R 'n' R. See you soon—I hope."

"Bummer not being on the first string," Washbourne said, as McConneld boarded the helicopter. Within an hour McConneld was bound for Wiesbaden, Germany.

* * *

The sound of the U.S. Army Bell "Huey" transport helicopter engulfed the ravine, with its hyper-rhythmic thunderclap and artificial winds. Its sound was like the flogging of a Persian carpet, on a clothesline, with a baseball bat.

McConneld looked for the men, who were to meet him. One was a young Agency station officer, Charles Channing, his soon-to-be assistant. Reports he received in Washington on conventional weapons thefts had come from Channing. The other was the chief of the DIA investigation teams, Colonel Harvey Barsohn, U.S.A.

Three men walked from an Army limousine, parked nearby. Charles Channing, his short, brown hair blown back by the "Huey's" wind-storm, introduced McConneld to Colonel Barsohn and his deputy, Major Henry Martin.

The ride to the site took ten minutes. The car turned onto a dirt and graveled road lined with thick underbrush and tall evergreens.

"I heard about the CP," McConneld said.

"It was an ambush in the jungle," Colonel Barsohn said. "Two survivors, convoy CO and his Top Kick. One's in a coma; the other seems catatonic. Medics haven't reached him." He shook his head slowly.

"The skeleton crew was asleep in a bunker?" McConneld asked.

"Damnedest thing!" Barsohn said. "MPs thought they'd found more KIAs. Then realized they were breathing."

"Debriefed?" McConneld continued.

"Interrogated most of them by now," Barsohn replied. "My deputy can fill you in. Hank?"

"Post was awaiting its *Bundeswehr* contingent," Martin said. "A unit of twenty or so men, in the right uniforms, along with a 'Major Muller,' showed up and checked out OK. The *Bundeswehr* men took over the depot. They must have hit our people with tranqus. The real *Bundeswehr* crew, it turned out, was delayed."

"Insider trading," McConneld said.

"Tell them about the gas canisters," Barsohn said.

"Pressure tanks, labeled 'lethal nerve agents,'" Martin said, "contained non-lethal sleep gas. One tank failed to release. Here're the reports."

"They meant to kill everyone," Barsohn said. "They just screwed up."

"Any composites on the thieves?" McConneld asked.

Martin answered, "Contradictory. Example: 'Major Muller.' Medium and a heavy build. Light complexion, medium one. All agree he had a German accent."

McConneld said, "He'll be a snap!"

The major smiled. " 'Muller.' It might as well've been Smith or Jones."

"Or Schmidt," Channing quipped.

At the depot, two sentries, after seeing Colonel Barsohn, waved them inside. A sharp, bitter stench of acrid char swept into the limousine.

Troops were searching, dissecting, and collecting the scene for reassembly of the jigsaw evidence they discovered. Outside the shell of the command post five soldiers, two men and three women, stood talking.

Colonel Barsohn called one of the women over, identifying her to the CIA men as the OIC of the E.O.D. team.

"They used delayed or radio-operated detonation devices, with C-4 Plastique or something like it," she told McConneld. "And gasoline, like Hollywood special effects." She described the debris and the human remains.

"John Does," she concluded, "probably thieves, bought it in the firefight. No dog-tags." She returned to her work.

"So much for the accident theory," Channing said.

"Did any locals hear anything?" McConneld asked, rubbing his eyes.

Barsohn replied, "The nearest house is miles from here. Whoever planned this chose well. They knew routines VERY well. Are you all right?" he asked McConneld.

"My eyes've only had a blinking acquaintance with sleep for thirty-six hours," McConneld said. "Meetings all yesterday. The Germans've begun their search within a fifty-mile radius of here. Total blackout on the affair."

Barsohn was shaking his head again. "If the Germans think they'll find them that close, they're crazier than in their last war."

"Colonel, I want to see the survivors," McConneld said.

Barsohn nodded. "They're in the Post hospital. The fifteen from the post, too?"

"When and where?" McConneld said.

Another DIA soldier, an Army lieutenant, hurried to Colonel Barsohn. "Sir," he said, "casts of the tire marks're ready. Something else you should see, too, sir."

McConneld, Barsohn, and the others followed the soldier to a large evergreen, with blackened singes, a short distance from the command center.

The handle of a knife showed, after the soldier pushed branches apart.

"Found it minutes ago, sir," the soldier said. "Almost missed it."

"I haven't seen one of those in a while," Barsohn said, whistling. "Not nice."

McConneld said, "Every *SS* boy got one from Himmler after initiation into the death's-head club. Doubts about former or Neo-Nazis are now in the trash can."

Channing agreed. "Whoever owned this was into serious homicide," he said.

His hands gloved, Channing carefully picked up the *SS* dagger. He held it, as one would hold a dead rat. The dagger's glossy blade showed no corrosion or rust, only mud. He placed it in the lieutenant's evidence box.

"Museum quality," Barsohn said. "The owner's a camp follower or groupie."

"It could've been a souvenir," Channing suggested. "Or an unaffiliated nutcase. Or planted by the thieves to throw us off. Left-wing whackos—or worse."

"It would've been more conspicuous," Barsohn said, "a right-wing flake, my guess."

"A fresh generation of Nazis," McConneld said, quietly, "as worse as it gets."

McConneld and Channing shuttled back to Frankfurt late that afternoon. On the way Major Martin accompanied them on two stops, where vehicles believed by DIA teams as having been used in the theft had been discovered.

At one stop, west of *Hanover*, they examined a large commercial Mercedes truck, abandoned on a secondary road near an *Autobahn* exit. The truck's serial number matched a vehicle stolen six months before in *Oldenburg*. Its tags were also stolen, from *Aachen* the preceding year. The cargo bed had been fitted with a false divider and separate compartment.

On the second stop, near *Kassel*, was an Army-green van, accidentally found by MPs from an armored cavalry unit. The van had come from E-917's own motor pool, but produced no new clues. Major Martin stayed at the second stop.

When they reached *Rhein-Main* Airbase, a car was waiting for them. It drove them to McConneld's impromptu command center at a nearby U.S. Consulate. Channing's secretary handed him a fax.

"From Colonel Barsohn," Channing said. "German authorities discovered two more trucks they think were involved. One's west of *Braunschweig,* another near *Luneburg.*"

"Both north and south of 917, hmm?" McConneld said, as he made notations on a large wall map of Germany. A red "x" indicated the depot's location, while McConneld added new ones. "Does he say why the Germans think so?"

"Both abandoned, stolen. Tags, too. Outfitted like the one we saw. Tire slashes match impressions at the depot," Channing said. "One had large amounts of blood in the hideaway section."

"Get me Colonel Barsohn," McConneld said. "If the 917 thieves stole those for this job, they'd been planning it at least a year. That requires long-term storage capabilities and networks in place."

Minutes later, McConneld was on the telephone with his DIA counterpart.

"The knife's on the way to you," Barsohn said. "Analysis found fingerprints on the handle. We're running them now."

"I'm sure this ties with that chain of jobs over the past year," McConneld said. "You're not the OIC on those, are you?"

Barsohn replied, "One of my former subordinates at the Pentagon is."

"Can you get me his files, Harvey?" McConneld asked. "On the QT?"

"I'll see what I can do," Barsohn said. "It might be quicker if you did it yourself."

"I don't want anyone else to know I'm poking around," McConneld said. "There was too much they knew about our procedures."

Barsohn said, "When d'you want to see those convoy guys?"
"Is this evening too soon?"
"Major Martin'll meet you there at 2000 hours."

* * *

The black limousine turned onto Yeltsinsky Prospekt near the Kremlin and pulled to the curb. General Balkovsky got in beside Yuri Torychenko.

"What's this about, Alex?" Torychenko asked, after the glass partition closed between them and the driver. "Our lunch date's not till next Friday."

"It couldn't wait, Yuri!" Balkovsky replied. He read a report aloud.

"The Colonel and his men?" Torychenko asked. Balkovsky nodded. "We won't read that in Der Spiegel tomorrow," Torychenko said. "How'd you? . . ."

"I received an emergency contact through Bonn," Balkovsky said. "My mole hasn't found why, or where they're hidden."

"Will you disclose this to the Americans?" Torychenko asked. "If we help them get the bombs back, without GRU or STAVKA being involved, we would be the heroes."

"GRU already knows, Yuri," Balkovsky said. "They have their own networks in the German Ministries, and in ours."

"What about the Americans?"

"No matter how friendly we're supposed to be," Balkovsky said. "I don't trust them. They're too arrogant. Also, the Colonel's organization must have infiltrated NATO or the American Nuclear Command. I'll lose my agent."

"I'm not suggesting you compromise the agent," Torychenko said. "Only disclose what bear's on the theft. Don't source it."

"My agent's still endangered. The Colonel'll know the information could only have come from inside."

"I could make that an order, General," Torychenko said.

There was an unpropitious quietude between the two men, as the car traveled through a workers' neighborhood.

"Your mole can't do the job?" Torychenko asked, after he told the driver to return to his office.

"As I've suggested before," Balkovsky said, *"not in time to be useable."*

"What if your agent DOES get us the material in time?"

"Americans give me sudden attacks of amnesia," Balkovsky said. *"Besides, we were hating them for fifty years, give or take. A break in tension doesn't make the flu go away."*

"That leaves the Pemberton Connection, doesn't it?" Torychenko asked.

"Did you discuss my plan with First Department and the others?"

Torychenko replied, *"The operation's already in motion."*

"You old bastard!" Balkovsky said. *"You didn't tell me?"*

"I don't have to explain things to subordinates," Torychenko said, *"even favorite ones."*

VI

Purplish streaks spread across the dusk clouds and turned black. Wearing his brown leather jacket, Jaime huddled with Emilio and Jamael under a grey stone foot-bridge in Central Park. The shadows under the bridge melted into darkness.

Jaime's GRU contact was half-an-hour late, unusual for her. On past occasions she had been the one waiting for Jaime and Emilio. Jamael had never met her before this night.

"She's not coming, Jaime!" Jamael said, angrily. "That's what you get for trusting a woman. And a Russian."

"She'll be here," Jaime replied. He was calm. "She's not a courier. She's a colonel in Russian Military Intelligence."

"My neighbors," Jamael said, quickly, "would call that more of a contradiction in terms than 'American Intelligence.'"

"I trust her," Jaime replied, "more than I do you sometimes. She's a good friend and doesn't like their politicians."

"She's using you," Jamael hissed, "like the Russians always used your people."

From behind them, reverberating into the far end of the small tunnel, came the sounds of running footsteps, rhythmic getting closer with each thump.

In the farther semi-circular opening, the noise stopped suddenly. A tall, thin figure stood, fuzzily outlined by the light of an argon lamp.

It was the woman, wearing a black, epidermal running suit. As she lodged herself against the interior wall, she motioned to Jaime and the others.

They crouched beside a large trash can. Jamael pulled his pistol from a shoulder holster and released the safety. There was a sound suppressor on the end of the barrel.

More running noises, only doubled this time, echoed through the tunnel. Two more figures stopped further from the tunnel than the woman had.

Two *CLICKS*! Jaime saw switchblades, as the pursuers headed toward the tunnel, one ahead of the other.

As the first one passed the woman, Jaime heard the dull thud of a sound-suppressed gunshot. The lead pursuer crumpled.

The woman struck the second pursuer with a kick in the back. An elbow blow to the head and a finalizing kick in the face finished him.

"You idiot!" she yelled, with an accent that could have come from London's fashionable West End. "You incompetent! You could've killed me!"

"This is Jamael," Jaime said, abruptly. "The one I told you about."

Jamael noted the woman was taller than his own 5´6˝. "That would've been a pity. But so goes the war."

"Jaime!" she replied. "Why'd you bring this moron?!"

"Who're these two?" Jaime asked.

"Hoods," she replied. "They followed me since I left my flat. Looked hungrier than ordinary rapists or muggers. At first I thought they were FBI. Put the pistol away," she hissed at Jamael, "or I'll make you eat it!"

"That's enough!" Jaime said. "You and he've got lots in common."

"What could that be?" Jamael asked. He exhaled displeasure.

"Remember who needs whom, you superstitious herder!" the woman said, spitting the words toward Jamael. "Cutting you off was the best thing my government did!"

They concealed the bodies in the bushes. Then, Jamie and the woman walked up a hill, to the sidewalk on top of the tunnel.

"I've got important information. What you do with it is your business, Comrade," she said. "I'll not give your compatriot shit. If *you* do, I'll find out."

"As though that would stop me," Jaime replied. "Emilio's your spy."

"Don't be a fool," she answered. "Emilio's yours. If you did spill, and I didn't want you to, you'd never see another scrap. I'm the best contact you've got."

Jaime was impatient, though he agreed with her about Jamael.

"If you trust your rugman there," she continued, "there'll be a time when you'll have to choose between your two interests. They're not the same. One of our nets in Germany reported party or parties unknown relieved the Americans of an undisclosed number of tactical devices," she continued. "A tight-lidded search's on. We're not involved. Did your people...?"

"If only," he replied. "Does your Secret Service have this, too? What're they calling themselves this week?"

"Does it matter?" she snickered. "Those buffoons know. Perhaps before us."

"Will they help the Americans get them back?"

She replied, "Anything to keep the President on Washington's good side."

"Why're you telling me this? You've never given me such hot stuff before?"

"Let's say, the world's too rigid," she answered. "My government abandoned the revolution business in the name of chauvinism."

"Can you help us get to the bombs first?"

"Not overtly," she said, somberly. "You...perhaps. Not your carpet salesman. The thieves'll probably sell to the highest bidder. Your carpet man could beat you."

As they parted, Jaime reflected on how he would not allow that.

* * *

"I told Control we'd get nothing from her room," George said. "Three weeks and nothing, but numb eardrums and cow *ca-ca*."

"Stop complaining," David replied. "Team Zed's on this now. Our briefing with Control's in twenty, at the Hoya Café."

"I've got one regret," George said. "I wanted to see this kid before we left."

"Amorous, are you?" David asked.

"Curious," George rejoined.

Twenty minutes later, George and David were at the Hoya Café, two adjoining rowhouses, that had been converted into a two-story restaurant/bar on 36th Street in Georgetown. On the second floor they settled into a booth, which looked like a sawed-off church pew. The man they knew as "Control-West" arrived five minutes after them.

"Here's background," Control-West said, "before I give you your new assignment." He spoke in a soft, though firm American-English voice.

"Our contacts inside the PLO informed us," Control-West continued, "that radical Palestinian factions were approached by shadowy groups during the mid-summer, trying to enlist disaffected's in a terror and assassination campaign in Western Europe. Maybe one country. Maybe more."

"A nightmare, but been there," George said, "seen that."

"The leadership's not condoning this," Control-West said.

"What would the rebels gain?" David asked.

Control-West said, "No immediate gratifs. That's why they rejected the overtures. For now, anyway. The Palestinians would've been the grunts, not the generals."

"What country's support?" David asked. "The EU? Only three count there: Germany, France, and Britain."

"They're all having their own troubles right now," George said.

"Interesting choice of words," Control-West said. "This one's coming from the right, no question. Your assignment."

"Should we accept it," George interrupted, "is to save Western Civilization from barbarism. Again."

"No choice but to accept it," Control-West said, drily. "You're the best team I've got, but I'll send you home if you crack too wise with me. "

"No, thanks," George replied. "I'm used to American food."

"You'll begin," Control-West continued, "with a new contact, code-named 'Marbison.'"

"Marbison?" George asked. "Sounds like a refugee from a sci-fi flick."

"He's your contact," Control-West said. "Meet him this time tomorrow. He'll notice you on place and recognition code."

"What's the arrangement with...with 'Marbison'?" David asked. "Do we pay him? Work with him?"

"He's a source and a guide, you might say," Control-West

answered. "He's been a field man, a good one. But not for us. Trust him. One other thing. If he chooses, he can tag along with you."

"Does he expect anything in return?" David asked.

"Nothing tangible."

"A true believer, eh?" George asked. "A patriot?"

"A professional. He's done us plenty of favors. We've reciprocated. You go where he guides you. Probably New York, Europe, or both."

"With him?" George asked.

"I told you," Control-West said. "It's his option."

"Do we check in with you before we leave?" David asked.

"No more F2F," Control-West replied. "Drops only, until further notice. Good luck, gentlemen." He put a $5 bill on the table and left.

The unstamped postcard from "Marbison" the next morning directed David and George to a small wooded, sand-peninsula near Thompson's Boathouse on the Potomac River. It was within easy glance of the Kennedy Center and the Watergate Complex. The code phrase, "Who're you?" was to be followed by the response, "Uncle Fester," and completed with "He's shorted out." The code prompted George to quip to his partner,

"Now, who's been watching too much TV?"

The peninsula was a fossil, from the days of an operating C&O Canal, surrounded by the River, the Rock Creek, and the Canal orifice. Its foliage had been overgrown for years, providing solitude and privacy to the occasional fisherman or lovers.

David and George checked the underbrush. No one else was there. They sat on the dirt, back-to-back, far enough from the shoreline that they were concealed from river-bound passersby and rowing teams.

"4:20," George said at one point. "This clown's not showing. So much for unpaid professionals."

"Control wouldn't rely on somebody who'd miss," David said. "Besides, without him, no new assignment. You want back on dormitory surveillance?"

"You got me there," George replied. He noticed an aluminum canoe with one rower, heading closer to their beach. "Company."

George took a .32 caliber pistol from under his warm-up pants and palmed it.

The boater beached the canoe. He secured the boat's line to a spike in the rotted timbers of the canal lock.

George saw in black letters, "R.M.S. *Titanic*," stenciled on the canoe. The boater, wearing a trunk-only wetsuit and a scuba cap, walked slowly toward the grove where George and David were.

"Who're you?" George asked, standing.

"Uncle Fester," the boater replied, sweeping his hand over the cap.

"He's shorted out," George said. "You're 'Marbison?' Where'd you get that code-name?"

The boater smiled. "You don't need to know that yet. Maybe on the second date."

"We flushed this place before you got here," George said. "You're late."

"*I* flushed it, before *you* got here," Marbison replied. "I saw you arrive. If we weren't alone, you would've got a note in a bottle."

"Is your boat's name a dream or a wish?" George asked.

"You've got to be George. Control warned me you have a big mouth," Marbison said. "He didn't tell me if it was because you're hungry, young, or stupid. Are you David?" he asked, offering his hand.

David chuckled. "Control said our next assignment depended on you."

"I do this my way," Marbison said. "A piece at a time."

"What kind of chicken *ca-ca* is that?" George asked.

"Forgive my partner," David said. "He's a country boy. Sand beating his butt has made him a hardass. But he knows the aroma of a privy when he smells it."

"No privy here," Marbison replied, "only good stuff. We think the principals are members of several private concerns."

"What's with 'we'?" George asked. "I thought you worked alone."

"It's the imperial or regal 'we,' Junior," Marbison said. "A primary group's an organization called The Association of International Industrialists, Executives, and Entrepreneurs. 'The

Cartel,' to the initiated."

"They're rumored behind recent military coup activity in Latin America, the Caribbean, and Western Africa," David said. "Nothing provable, though."

"Good homework," Marbison said. "I didn't think those parts interested you guys much, except for specialized purposes."

"Shelters and havens always interest us," David said.

"A second group is the World Anti-Comintern Coalition Order," Marbison said. "It's a secret satellite of The Cartel and headed by a former U.S. Air Force general from Mississippi named Tripleleaf. He's so hardcore, he resigned when Reagan signed the INF Treaty. He accused Ronnie of selling out to the Russians."

"Ironic, in light of recent developments," David commented.

"Tripleleaf's operation brought almost every right-wing nut group under his umbrella, from Latin America to the industrial Pacific Basin. They joined with Neo-Fascist and Neo-Nazi organizations. European and American factions dominate."

"On the surface, The Cartel and The Coalition Order aren't associated?" George asked. "But in reality they're incestuous?"

Marbison replied, "Parasitic, symbiotic concurrently. The Cartel uses Tripleleaf as a procurement and Ops officer. His people approached the Palestinians."

"No daylight connections?" David asked.

"They're submerged in red herrings, dummy corporations, holding companies, legit businesses," Marbison answered. "The Cartel fronted him the capital to start his operations and business covers. He's been working with them at least thirty years, especially while he was on Active Duty, on his own agenda. Unless you're inside, it'd take you years to find any connections."

"Its own cadre army, hmmm?" George asked. "How d'we get in?"

"Its own arm*ies*," Marbison replied. "Tripleleaf's a general contractor. Subs out the work to freelancers. His people supervise from a distance. Like Top Cover. Any trouble and they make sure the freelancers don't talk, one way or another. Permanent termination's the method of choice."

"History lessons're fine," George said. "But do they get us in?"

"And what do we get from it, if we do?" David asked.

"Patience, fellas," Marbison responded. "The Cartel'll support practically any right-wing or far-right regime it decides is in its business interests. It controls manufacturing, finance, shipping, chemicals, communications, and oil and other resource rights, to name a few. Billions. It hovers in the resource-rich Third World. South America and Africa for resources. Asia for labor. Ring a bell now? Havens and cubby holes, maybe?"

"Specifics?" David asked.

"How about a little less general?" Marbison said. "Western Europe's too democratic and visible for it to gain the political clout it wants by ballot, even Italy. A coup, in a key nation, changes the whole calculus, especially with East European investments. Think of what crawls from the woodwork, if there's a neo-Fascist takeover in a European country with big economics in the East. The power to throw those economies into chaos, or pull them from the brink, is heavy politics. The way in's through Tripleleaf."

"D'you believe the Americans'll sit back and let a dictatorship take over a core NATO country?" David asked. "I mean, Greece and Turkey were one thing, but Germany, France, or Britain?"

"They probably won't mind, given current conditions," Marbison replied. "The political winds here aren't conducive to democracy. There's another way: through a small, direct-action unit The Cartel's got on permanent retainer. It works for others, but its first loyalty's to The Cartel. It uses them only when the job's vital. The unit's independent of Tripleleaf. Rivalry between the two's exploitable."

"*You* can get us in there, right?" George said.

"Sarcastic and stupid," Marbison replied, "hardly a propitious combination. Step one: Cartel information from a New York contact. Next stop: Manhattan. And bring lots o' dollars. Unlike me, this guy's cash-corruptible."

"And what're you corruptible with?" George asked.

"I collect markers," Marbison replied. "Consider me your banker. Real solvent. Payback comes later."

He unzipped his wetsuit to mid-chest, took out a plastic

ziplock, and handed it to David. "The name and address in New York."

"Control said you 'guide.' This is ongoing?" David said.

Marbison answered, "After New York, get back here. Put an American flag in the window of that townhouse you're using to keep track of the woman."

"How d'you know about that?" George asked.

"I'll be in touch," Marbison said, "with more for you."

"D'you know what this New York guy'll say?" David said.

"I wouldn't be sending you up there, if I did. By the way, I suggest you send your Control any Latin American leads you uncover. You focus here and Europe. The shortlist's France, Britain, and Germany. Maybe, Italy, Spain. All have right-wing maladies." George and David watched, as the canoe slipped down river.

* * *

The hospital waiting room on the fourth floor was a bland affair: pale, "government-green" walls and a yellowed, white ceiling. Yellowish-brown and black stains pocked the tile and linoleum floor. Magazines and newspapers in English and German lay scattered on tables. The black and white vinyl couches showed varying levels of use and abuse.

As good as an Army hospital could be, McConneld thought, as he waited with Chuck Channing and Major Martin. A figure in a white lab coat with red-thread cursive writing appeared. "Mr. James McConneld?" she asked.

McConneld shook hands with the questioner. "This is Major Martin, our Army liaison, and my assistant, Charles Channing."

"Of course. Colonel Barsohn phoned and said you'd be along," she said.

"My parents were funny folks," Channing said. "I'm the Number One Son."

The doctor looked confused, then nodded. "I love *kitschy* flicks," she said. "Major Rosa Gallo, physician on the Monroe and Bates cases. How may I help you?"

"When may we see them?" McConneld asked.

"Doctor," Martin said. "You'll render these gentlemen whatever assistance they request. Within feasibility, naturally."

"It's urgent," Channing said, "national security, literally."

"Colonel Barsohn used those words, too," Major Gallo said. "I'll tell you what I told him." She described the men's conditions.

"I must insist on seeing him, Doctor," McConneld said.

"If he's awake, I'll let you in for a few minutes. If it overtaxes him, I'll ask you to leave. Both were lucky. Hypothermia saved them."

Channing said, "He's our only lead to stop a nightmare."

"Persuasive Number One Son," Major Gallo said. She left, returning a few moments later. Her face was care-loaded.

"His eyes're open. But he doesn't speak, or acknowledge being called. Come along, gentlemen."

McConneld, Channing, and Martin followed the doctor to a small, white and tiled room, with one bed, a sink, a sick-table, and two chrome chairs. On the bed lay Captain Pierre Monroe.

His white hospital gown was padded under the right shoulder with bandages. The doctor and the others entered, past the MPs standing security in the hall. Monroe's eyes gave no recognition to the arrivals.

"Pierre," Major Gallo spoke softly and gently. "These gentlemen want to ask you a few questions."

Monroe did not respond. His eyes locked on the ceiling, not releasing their grasp of its sound-absorbing tiles.

"They need to know about Friday night and Saturday morning," Major Gallo continued. No reply. "Pierre, can you hear me?"

Monroe did not react to the doctor.

"Well, gentlemen," the doctor sounded regretful. "I didn't understate it. Best to leave him now. Perhaps in a day or two he'll be more receptive."

"I can't do that," McConneld said, firmly. "I'm getting SOMETHING, and I'm afraid I'll have to ask you to leave, Doctor." He looked at Channing. "Chuck, if the doctor disagrees, see she gets wherever she should be going."

Major Gallo harumphed at McConneld's remarks. "It's your responsibility, if you harm this patient. I'll file a complaint against you with the Post Commandant."

"Doctor," Major Martin broke in. "Post Commandant's Office will merely repeat what I said. Do yourself a career favor and forget it. And tell the guards to stand down for ten minutes."

"Career be damned, Major," the doctor replied, as she left. McConneld heard her murmuring, "We never get respect."

Martin followed the doctor out, instructed the MPs, and returned.

"Shall I try what we discussed?" Channing asked. McConneld nodded.

"What've you got in mind?" Martin asked.

"One of my specialties as a trained psychologist," Channing said, "is non-electro-shock therapy. Sometimes with hypnosis or drugs, but not always. Using noises and dialogue close to the original, you recreate what caused the patient's condition. Try to find a trigger or door into the patient's mind. It's chancy and could cause the patient to go deeper into the psychosis. But if it works, the patient spills."

"We're trying it," McConneld added, "without drugs or hypnosis, first. They're Plan B, if this doesn't work."

"Need my help?" Martin asked.

"You're another voice," Channing replied, "one of his men calling. Seeing them get waxed caused this, despite his combat experience."

Chuck Channing walked to the doorway, McConneld with him, and took off his shoes. He directed Martin to a corner away from them and Monroe. Channing slammed his shoe against the wooden doorframe, causing a loud *THWACK*. The sound bounced around the room like a rifle shot.

"Captain! Can you hear me?!" he yelled, as he continued to bang the wood with the shoe. "It's Sergeant Bates! Where're you, sir?"

The first hit on the doorframe caught the soldier completely unprepared. He jerked violently, rolling and tossing. He fell off the bed, away from Channing and the others, cringing on the floor. Channing continued his banging.

Channing signaled Martin. "Captain!" Martin cried out. "Orders, sir? They're all around us!"

"That you, Robinson?" Monroe yelled. "Thought they got you!"

"It's me, sir!" Martin said. "What d'we do?"

"Sergeant Bates!" Monroe yelled. "That you?"

Channing replied, "Gotta get outta here, Captain! Captain?! Can you hear me?"

"Sergeant!" Monroe yelled, as he leaned on his elbows. "Go for Captain Frazier. I'll get Colonel Allen!"

"Colonel?" Martin asked. "Who, sir?"

A nurse's face appeared in the window of the door. Her expression showed annoyance, but also wonder. McConneld slipped out between Channing's blows.

"What the hell're you doing, sir?" Her eyes widened with polite anger, as she spoke softly. "This is a hospital! I'm calling the MPs, if I can find them."

McConneld reached into his jacket pocket and pulled out his identification. Major Martin joined them, as Channing's wall-banging continued.

"Sorry for the trouble, Lieutenant," McConneld said. "We're questioning this patient in a VERY important investigation. Your lack of security clearance prevents me from explaining. Confirm what I've said with Post HQ, if you'd like."

"Lieutenant," Martin said. "Call Post Commandant's Office and mention my name, Major Henry Martin. They'll explain."

"This is very weird," she relented. "I'll call Post Commandant, sir, like you said. Your name's Major Martin?... And yours is Mc."

She read the identification. Handing the i.d. back to McConneld, the nurse-lieutenant headed to the nursing station.

McConneld and Martin re-entered the room. The loud banging had stopped. Channing was near the door, speaking loudly. Monroe was back in bed and sitting up, as though at attention.

"They got Sergeant Bates and Robinson," Channing said in a deeper, rougher voice. "Report, Captain! I'm Colonel Emery, DIA."

"In the trees, sir," Monroe yelled, holding the sheets as though, in a tugging match with an imperceptible opponent.

"Snipers!... Arrived OK... Authentication Correct... no Recognition problems... Unloaded cargo. Little things... Strange. Then, Colonel Allen. Captain Frazier. Gunpoint. Call

Corps...Bates and me...Robinson stopped 'em. Call Corps...But then." Hysterical, tears and sweat dripping from his face, Monroe hesitated. "But then..." Monroe repeated, and fell onto his back, covering his head with the sheet.

"But then what, son?" Channing asked, at the bedside. Channing uncovered Monroe's face. The soldier quickly covered it with his arms.

"Then, what?" Channing repeated. "Tell me, Captain!"

"Robinson dead! Snipers! God! Bates down!...Bastards! Killing my men...Killing us!"

Channing held Monroe's arms and forced them to either side of his face. Monroe's eyes were irises drowned in white, not seeing anything in the room.

"Muller's guys. Colonel's...Shooting! Get the bastards! My men! Down!.Hit...All hit!...God!...Let me die, too!...Gotta get outta here!...Bates!...Bill, we'll make it!" His expression loosened, as his body did, and his eyes closed. He had passed out.

"Authentication Correct. No Recognition Code problems," McConneld repeated. "SASCOM's penetrated. Maybe Frankfurt HQ, too. Somebody's in business for himself."

"Bought or compromised," Martin said. "And what about this 'Colonel Allen?' A pseudonym or alias."

"When we get back," McConneld said, "Chuck, contact HQ Langley for personnel checks on anyone, who might've had access to the convoys' and the depots' info. We don't know whom we can trust over here."

"Understood," Martin said. "Colonel Barsohn should be informed."

"Whoever it is will go to ground," McConneld said, "if we start checking through channels here. From now, we don't rely on USAREUR/NATO channels."

The door opened suddenly. Major Gallo came in with the nurse-lieutenant. "I checked with Post Commandant's Office, Doctor," the nurse said. "They confirmed the Major's story. I still thought I should tell you."

"You did the right thing, Lieutenant," Major Gallo said.

She scowled, though her tone was not loud or disrespectful. "Where d'you, gentlemen, get off, coming into a hospital, disturbing and abusing my patient? I don't care who you are. Please leave, before you injure Captain Monroe further."

"I suggested you forget it before." Major Martin started, but McConneld interrupted him.

"Believe me, Doctor," McConneld replied, firmly. "I'm sorry for what we had to do. But I didn't have time for your care to bring him around. We got what we came for. Only answering any charges you *try* to bring will force me to act. And for your information, I think you're one hell of a doctor, officer—and woman. Later," McConneld said, putting his coat on.

"Thanks," Major Gallo said. "You available yourself?" she asked, as they walked away.

* * *

Back at their offices, McConneld and Channing examined more reports. Checks of the name, "Colonel Allen," with spelling variations, had been sent to OPO, Pentagon, via CIA-Langley.

The replies revealed apparently loyal officers, most not on tour with USAREUR. McConneld ordered background checks on those, attached to European Theatre Commands.

"I thought that name'd get us nothing," McConneld said, after they read the responses. "But there was something slightly familiar about it."

Other reports showed inconclusive results. The Army was still inventorying its nuclear detonator materials and could not confirm that the "madames" would remain "virgins." Analysis of the blood from the abandoned truck had been unhelpful. The fingerprint analysis and checks of the *SS* dagger were incomplete. The dagger itself sat on McConneld's desk.

As the two men finished their review, the buzzer on the direct-line to Washington/Headquarters-Langley went on. Channing handed the receiver to McConneld. "Mr. Washbourne."

"Any progress?" Washbourne asked. "Heard from the thieves?"

"Not even a thank you," McConneld said. "We won't hear anything from them, unless you count an explosion as e-mail."

"You don't think extortion?"

McConneld said, "A hunch tells me this is for personal use. So far no direct link between Pemberton's Cartel and the theft. Neo-Nazis aren't the only coveters of nukes."

"Need anything at this end?" Washbourne asked.

McConneld told him about the requests to Langley. "Contact DHS, FBI, INS, and Treasury," McConneld continued. "My DIA colleague's already passed the word to the Pentagon about overseas security. Any contact from Tom Pemberton?"

"Not since the first," Washbourne replied. "He missed a drop-time, but it was his play. I got a report, though, from an agent near *Stuttgart*. She saw what looked like a mini-U.N. tour, with plenty of security bruisers. Our agent followed to an estate near Ulm. We identified the address through the German Federal Police. It belongs to a big international industrialist/financier named Otto von Markenheim."

McConneld said, "'The Baron,' with holdings in Europe and the States."

"Africa, South America. You name it," Washbourne added. "High-ranking member of Pemberton's Cartel. Maybe the leader, but that's unconfirmed. Do you want the lowdown?"

"Give me the five-minute sound-byte," McConneld said. "Encrypt the rest."

"He's in his eighties now, but still active in businesses," Washbourne said. "Father and family supported the Nazis financially in the '20s and '30s. Pleaded ignorance after the war. He ran one of the family's war production plants during the late stages of the war. Our side confiscated most of their holdings, but they were never tried for anything. Von Markenheim made a big recovery through shrewd post-war deals. Unclear where he got his working capital. It's rumored he hasn't voted in an election since 1933."

"Obviously more conservative than the Christian Democrats," McConneld said. "What about family?"

"He married late, with a younger wife. One daughter. A stepdaughter, actually."

McConneld thought. "They must not suspect Tom after all," he concluded. "It's a mandatory drop next time, isn't it?"

Washbourne replied, "His choice of drop-site."

"They're moving around, so the first message's on point. If he misses the next, we'll know something's wrong. How's Ms. Pemberton?"

"Well," Washbourne's voice went high and squeaky. "You know, Chief, Pemberton's Cartel might have its suspicions."

"I asked about Samantha, not Doc," McConneld said.

"Well." There it was again. McConneld recognized the symptoms.

"What aren't you telling me, WW2?" McConneld said.

"You sitting down, Chief?" Washbourne said. "I've got quite a story for you."

VII

In her evening *Advanced German* course a week after her phone conversations with Bob and Mr. McConneld, Sam was paying little attention to her old professor. He was babbling about the reading assignment from Hegel's writings. She had read Hegel before, in German, and thought of his work as literary "jello": enveloping and drowning the reader with long, congealed, and rubbery sentences. Her notebook was open, with doodles around the name, "Hegel."

Besides, she thought to herself, *Hegel was not the only dense idiot in her life right then. There were two more, but she had no choice being related to them.*

"*Fräulein* Pemberton," the teacher said abruptly.

Sam did not hear him at first, as she drew daydreams in her notebook. He called her name again, louder this time. Her family-induced stupor passed.

In his inimitably stiff manner he asked her to translate and explain a passage.

Sam apologized quickly. She tried to find the paragraph he mentioned, before she felt completely routed and foolish. The pages seemed to conspire against her.

"*Fräulein* Pemberton," the teacher repeated, sternly. "*Bitte, be better prepared next time. Which for your sake will not be this session. If you need to prepare, go home.*"

"Herr Professor," Sam said. "*I apologize again. I did read this material yesterday evening . . .*"

"*Bitte, read it better tomorrow.*" He turned brusquely, calling on another student.

Sam crumpled into the chair, hoping it could and would swallow and devour her. The old bastard humiliated people for fun, she concluded, with his "old school" bullshit. She was angry: at teacher, father, self.

"Let me out of here," she murmured, as the class ended. She

was the first person from the room.

The night air shocked her face, as she exited the Walsh Building on 36th Street, two blocks from the Main Campus Gate. An old, black Chevy Nova pulled from the curb and sped past her, toward N and 35th Streets.

The occasional streetlamps, with their 19th-century-style opaque covers, yellowed the brick sidewalks. Shadows. Darkness. The faint, but bouncing, echoes of traffic in the Wisconsin Avenue Corridor reached up O Street from five blocks away. Townhouses along 36th Street, tenanted mostly by students, were atypically unlighted and quiet. She saw no other pedestrians up the street.

That was the problem with a 7 P.M. to 10:30 P.M., four-credit class, Sam thought.

Wanting to get home faster than her usual route, she took a short-cut near Georgetown Visitation Convent School and the wall that ran along its property-line on P Street.

Sam rounded the corner at P Street. A car passed her, driving slowly. It looked like the same Chevy as before. Its driver's side windows were down.

The Nova pulled to the curb of the hardly lit street. Shadowy and shoddily dressed men emerged from it and headed toward her.

Frightened, and preferring to run than confront, Sam dropped her purse and books. She took one stride backward without turning.

A hand clamped over her mouth. Its arm slammed her against a body that felt more like a concrete pillar.

"That's a blade against your ribs, lady," the sandpaper voice whispered. "Scream and I'll tear your mother-fuckin' head off!" He lowered his hand slowly.

"You bastard! Let me go!" Sam shouted, struggling.

"Shut up!" the sandpaper voice whispered, as he locked his hand over her mouth and slammed her against himself again.

Pain leaped through Sam's back. The assailant dragged her toward the two men from the car. One was holding something clear and tubular.

Sam kicked, while Sandpaper held her. She pushed him off-balance, though these victories were rewarded with body-slams. Still, she fought, extending her breathing more deeply.

"Hurry up with that needle!" Sandpaper said. He kept his hand over her mouth. One of the others grabbed her arm.

Sam pulled in her deepest breath and held it. In the next instant, she bit hard into Sandpaper's hand. He shrieked, and uncovered her mouth.

She exhaled a loud shout, planted her right foot, using Sandpaper as a push-off board. She landed a kick in the belly of the thug holding her arm.

He stumbled backward. The third man, with the syringe, did not join in.

She delivered a strong left elbow, where she expected Sandpaper's *solar plexus* to be. Sam felt the soft, fatty tissue give way, as he screamed. She turned in time to follow the first blow with a second, point-blank.

Sandpaper straightened, as the switchblade fell to the broken sidewalk. He fell forward, unconscious.

Sam broke free and spun around. The two muggers were spread apart, facing a shaggy-haired man in an Army fatigue jacket. Sam's kick victim had recovered and was holding a stiletto, which he jabbed at the long-hair.

"Stay back, Sam!" the shaggy-hair shouted, sweeping his arm backward, like a policeperson pushing back a crowd.

"Drop the needle!" he yelled, "or you're dead meat!"

"Come and get it, sucker!" the mugger replied. His partner jabbed at Sam's new ally. Another jab backed the shaggy-hair once more. The syringe-man watched, urging his partner on.

On the third jab, the shaggy-hair was ready. He seized the extended arm by the wrist and cracked it over his own leg. The stiletto fell to the ground.

As the former mugger slouched, the shaggy-hair struck him two more blows, one to the face, the other to the throat. His nose bled, as he tumbled against the brick facade of a stanchion.

"Your turn!" the shaggy-hair glared at the last mugger.

The third man dropped the syringe and sprinted away, but the shaggy-hair caught him after several all-out strides. A cross-body-block crashed the last mugger into a parked car. The shaggy-hair turned him over and was sitting on his chest.

Sam had followed her rescuer and could hear him talking to his prisoner.

"You're crazy, mister!" the mugger whined.

"Who hired you, maggot?!"

Before the mugger answered, screeching tires sounded from down the block. Two pairs of headlights turned the corner at 36th and P Streets. One pair stopped where the first two assailants lay, while the second sped toward the long-hair and his prisoner.

The second car's doors bounced open. Two men in suits crouched behind the doors and held the long-hair and the third mugger at gunpoint.

"Please stay back, Miss!" one of them shouted to Sam.

"Both of you," the other yelled. "Up slowly! Hands in the air! No fast moves!"

"I've got the situation in hand," the shaggy-hair yelled back, "with her help. Who the hell're you guys?!"

"Up!" the second man repeated, gesturing with his automatic.

The other man hustled from the car. He pushed both men into "the position" against the hood.

"I'm J.D. Marshall," the shaggy-hair said. "I broke up this attempted robbery and rape. Check with Sam Pemberton."

The two finished their pat-downs of Marshall and the mugger. They found no weapons on either man, and marched both to the other car.

Three of their fellows had Sandpaper and the other mugger handcuffed and restrained. A fourth agent was speaking to Sam.

"Who're you guys?" Marshall repeated his question. "Cops?"

"None of your concern, sir," one man said. He had been speaking with Sam.

"I'd call that a big 'No.'" Marshall said. "FBI? How 'bout some i.d.s from you guys? Your man there's seen mine."

"She's confirmed what you said," Sam's questioner continued. "She's a little shaky and banged up, but tough."

"Here's Marshall's wallet," the man guarding Marshall said, handing it to Sam's questioner, who strip-searched it.

"I see a military i.d. in here, Marshall. Are you on Active Duty? DIA, maybe? Or NSA?"

"I don't have to tell you, till I know who you are," Marshall replied. "If you're cops or FBI, let's hear some *Miranda*. Otherwise, get out of my face and identify yourselves."

"We know who you are, Marshall," the man with his wallet said. "Those men were assigned to you. We're on Top Cover for the girl." He took out his own wallet and handed it to Marshall.

"William Kearney, Central Intel." Marshall stopped abruptly. "Operating domestically these days, boys? Thought that was against the rules. Reagan and the Bushes let you off your leashes, but I figured after a few recent *faux pas* you'd be lying low, not to mention Ames. In answer to your questions, no."

"Never mind us," Kearney replied. "What the hell're you doing here?"

"Your job, obviously," Marshall answered.

"We had the situation under control," Kearney said.

"More control like that and Sam'll be dead," Marshall said.

"Listen, Smartass," Kearney shot back. "We could turn you over to MPD and let them roust you. Maybe you need a night in Central Cellblock."

"Go ahead. And I'll sue you for wrongful prosecution," Marshall said. "I'm a fucking hero. I've got friends at *The Post* I could give the story. But you don't want publicity. And the locals don't like you playing in their yard."

Marshall looked at Sam, as she leaned on a parked car. "Sam, are you all right?"

"Fine," she answered, out of breath. "Thanks. But, who...? How'd you know my name?"

"Ex-student friend of your father's. He asked me to look after you," Marshall said. "I thought The Professor was laying proud parent stuff on me, about taking care of yourself, but you were doing great."

"Did the one you pummelled tell you why? Or who?" Sam asked.

"No chance," Marshall said, "before Agent Kearney and his boys swooped in like Batman and Robin."

"I hate to break up tea-time," Kearney interrupted. "You can finish this indoors. The first order of business is to get Ms. Pemberton checked at a hospital. Our superior'll want to speak with you, Mr. Marshall, at HQ-Langley. Art," he turned to Marshall's cover team. "You and Mel turn these maggots over to MPD, but be sure the Mets know we'll question them, before they're cut loose."

"I'll talk with your man, Kearney," Marshall said, "but when I choose. Give me a number to call."

"Black belts in judo and jiu-jitsu, you bastards," Sam hissed at the prisoners, as they were ungently stuffed into the CIA cars.

Sam's check-up at the Georgetown University Hospital showed no broken bones or internal injuries, only brush-burns, bruises, and scrapes. Marshall, Kearney, and two of Kearney's men had taken her there. Emotionally she was also bruised, according to the attending resident, who had her admitted inpatient "for observation" and prescribed a mild sedative and tranquilizer.

After she was registered into a private room, with Kearney's men alternating eight-hour surveillance shifts, Kearney and an off-duty agent left. Marshall stayed.

"How much d'you know about your father's business?" he asked her, after she was in bed.

"Not much about The Cartel," she replied. "He always said he didn't want it to be the 'family business.' I knew he had a trip coming, but not this soon."

"He said you don't miss much," Marshall said. "Something unexpected moved everything up."

"How much do you know?" Sam asked.

"Some." One side of his mouth curled into a smile.

"Can't you tell me?" she said, her eyes praying to him, as she spoke.

"You're in deep enough. Too deep really. If those slugs hadn't shown, you wouldn't know I was here."

"I'm glad you were," she said. "Let me show you how much." She motioned with an index finger for him to come closer and kissed him softly on the lips. "Now will you tell me?"

He kissed her back. "That's attempted bribery."

"It is not!" she responded.

"Not bribery?"

"Not attempted," she laughed.

"Your father wasn't kidding. You CAN take care of yourself."

"Perhaps," she said, embracing him. She grimaced once, when she moved a certain way. "But I meant the thanks."

"What I can tell you is he's doing a special investigation," Marshall said. "Once and future Nazis and his Cartel. He's documented everything. Europe, the U.S., the Pacific Basin. He got vibrations of something BIG."

"Our family's been living in that thing's shadow," Sam said, "since way before Mother was killed. But I always thought it was legitimate."

"It is," Marshall said. "That's what's frightening. 'Legitimate' is whatever the people with the most guns say it is."

"That sounds more than a bit cynical."

"Let's say I've seen too much ever to be starry-eyed again."

"So, where's my father?"

"In Europe, somewhere," Marshall replied.

"You won't tell me, will you?" Sam asked more sternly, though she held his shoulders. "I've got a right to know! He's my father."

"You've got no rights in this at all. Besides, I couldn't tell you where he is, even if I wanted to. He's moving around a lot. The next meeting's supposed to be very important, but he didn't know why—not yet, anyway. He calls The Cartel 'The Orphan Merchants' and 'Death's Land Office.'"

"Has he contacted you?"

"Indirectly," he answered, "through an old friend."

"You're not telling me where he's been?" she persisted.

Marshall said, "He knew you'd try to follow him, if you got a clue. So, he wanted you kept *sans* clue."

"Goddamn him!" Sam said. "And what the hell d'you mean I've got no rights? Like I'm not in it now? I get roughed up, nearly kidnapped, drugged, and God-knows-what-else. And I've got no rights?!"

"I was there, remember?"

"It WASN'T a chance mugging or rape attempt, right?!"

"No question in my mind," Marshall admitted. "They knew

who you were, had a plan, and scoped you out ahead of time."

"Right again, Sherlock!" She let go of Marshall and crossed her arms.

"His damn crap's intruded into my life, and you've got the balls to tell me I've got no rights?! You won't even tell me where he's been!"

She rolled away from him. The pain in her back made her grimace.

Marshall walked around the bed. "I empathize. But, you're smart enough to know, if you go blundering in, you'll put both your necks in danger. Maybe even get you killed. I don't have to remind you."

"Cute trick," she said.

"I thought so," Marshall said, smiling. "OK, I'll tell you more. He got word to me through an old contact in *Heidelberg*. He's not there now. There'll be scheduled contacts in lots of possible drop-points all over Europe. Satisfied now?"

"Yes," she said. Her anger had sunk back inside her. Her stews were cooling.

She put her arms around his neck again and kissed him, harder than before. "Quite satisfied—for now," she whispered.

* * *

CLICK. The lights went on, as the sound pinballed between the thick, concrete walls and the twenty-foot ceiling in the large, underground warehouse room. There were five large, wooden crates along the far wall, with fifteen much smaller containers piled around and on top of the crates. Fifteen other packages were stacked nearby.

Two men walked through the cone-shaped light. The first was an old man, in his eighties, dressed in a well-cut tuxedo. The other was in his fifties, with a green, Bavarian jacket and brown, suede knickers.

"*Good work, Colonel,*" the older man said in German. "*Your father would've been pleased, too.*"

"*Thanks, Baron,*" The Colonel replied. "*We had a spot of trouble. Firefight. Lost a few men, but they've already been replaced. I* made sure their bodies wouldn't be identified. We killed all the Americans."

"This part of Case Blue went better than expected," the Baron said. "Our partners'll be placated. It has been tough keeping them under control. They're so impetuous."

"How's General Tripleleaf taking my score?"

"He's still stung we didn't let his organization do the job," the Baron said. "Storing the devices here on his turf's a bone I threw him."

"You're accommodating, after his people barely pulled off some of the depot jobs?"

"He's sulking, but he'll get over it. We'll control his ilk this time, if Case Blue succeeds. If it doesn't, we're safe. He'll twist slowly in the wind very nicely."

The Colonel nodded. "We're recruiting people to make the bigger devices operational, based on your recommendations. Your Eastern contacts were real helpful. They're in, no reserve. The Western ones've been slower. They want assurances."

"Always hand-holding with them," the Baron said, contemptuously. "If our Western friends aren't committed in three weeks, our ship sails without them. I want you to maintain security. Don't tell them anything more."

"I haven't," The Colonel replied, patiently. "My Number Two doesn't even know where these are. I'll brief the team leaders, late. In November. There're still a few loose ends to snip off, but all's fine. Are your people ready?"

"The Board'll be in place," the Baron said. "The network's already testing. Contact throughout Blue won't be any difficulty. The political economy's worked out. Professor Pemberton's seen to it. Thomas's been a Godsend. I've taken a few personal measures, in the interest of loyalty."

"Anything I should know?"

"No, Colonel," the Baron said. "Our insulation's intact. If the worst happens, we can always sell these to deserving, underdeveloped countries with the right political views and resources. What about the smaller ones?"

"That stack over there," The Colonel said, pointing to the smallest packages. "They contain all the detonation materials we'll need for the SADMs."

"*Splendid!*" the Baron said. "*Most obliging of the Americans. Still, we don't want anything to go wrong this time. Not like ODESSA. Well, I must get back to Ulm, to our dinner party.*"

The Colonel said, "*Call if you need anything, sir.*" He was confident. At least he wanted the Baron to think so. If only he had not lost his good-luck "charm" . . .

* * *

"Take a look at this report, Fearless Leader," Chuck Channing said to McConneld, handing him a fax. "Fingerprints from the SS dagger. Langley came up with a match through INTERPOL and the Anti-Terror Network."

McConneld read the report aloud. "'Krattmay, Johannes Eugen. Alias Shorall Allen. Alias Audran Arnold. Alias Johannes Johnston. Alias Vernon Stelek. Alias Ellis Eriks. Alias John Conrad. Alias Shorall Win-Smith. Alias Barry Kelly. Alias Rexald May. Alias The Colonel.' Christ! Sounds like we're dealing with 'Sybil.' Now I remember why that name, 'Colonel Allen,' bothered me! He used it in Angola. I know this guy. Or, I know who he is. Angola. Mercenary. He had his own troops, recruited and trained. I saw him during meetings my Agency superiors and I had with FNLA and UNITA."

McConneld read on. "'Positioned Far Right, Anti-Communist.' That's a mild understatement. 'Suspected terrorist. Believed behind acts of terrorism in Europe late-'70s, '80s and '90s. Last known whereabouts 1983–93.'"

"What else d'you know about this nut?"

"First served in the Argentine Army," McConneld said. "His father was a wealthy German supporter of the Nazis, who went into the SS himself. The father escaped to South America and disappeared. He probably changed his name and identity. I don't know, if Krattmay's The Colonel's real family name. That past history never bothered The Agency."

"Fun family," Channing said. "One's a full-fledged Nazi. The other's your garden variety killer."

"Our man cut his teeth on rounding up and executing opponents of the *juntas*. Also fought for the old South African Government. Say 'white' and 'Anti-Communist,' and he'd be yours. I can't imagine it paid well enough to allow him such an expensive hobby. Probably like Mengele."

"And he was there, fighting with black Africans?"

"It's the 'Anti-Communist' part that counted most," McConneld said. "He had a reputation for shooting deserters, stragglers, and wounded soldiers, on both sides."

McConneld thought for a moment. "There's a rumor he was blown up in one of his last jobs. I never saw the dagger during those meetings years ago. I guess it's his father's. So, he's moved from our payroll to our most wanted. How delightful."

VIII

As J.D. Marshall took the exit on the George Washington Parkway for the CIA's Langley Headquarters, he was chuckling. Through the late-1960s the sign read only, "Federal Highway Administration." He never learned what "pathetic lemming" had arranged the "camouflaging" of CIA; it was probably a former head of Counter-Intelligence. He called officers like that "brass lemmings."

At the main gate a uniformed Federal Protective Service guard took his name and identification, sending him to the building's public entrance. Marshall knew the way well.

From the visitor's check-in he was led to William Washbourne II's suite, by a young, blond-haired woman, in long-sleeved silk blouse and grey skirt. He read her first name from her plastic i.d. card, "Denise."

During the interview's "first furlong" J.D. Marshall felt he must have been "beamed" to another planet. Washbourne was personable, had a sense of humor, apologized for inconveniencing him. He was more like a PR person, than an operations officer.

His office, particularly his desk, looked like the result of an explosion in two overstuffed filing cabinets. Marshall wondered in what piles the microphones were hidden.

Washbourne said, "Let me see if I got you straight. Your story is Tom Pemberton asked you to keep an eye on Samantha, right?"

Marshall nodded.

"You're an old friend of his, but he never told why, right?" Washbourne leaned back in his atypical, government-issue padded chair. "Didn't that seem odd to you?"

Marshall shook his head. "I owed him a few favors."

Looking up at the ceiling, Washbourne yawned.

"Am I keeping you up?" Marshall asked, his irritation awakened from the anesthesia of Washbourne's charm.

"No, John," Washbourne replied. "Not right now."

"I go by J.D.," Marshall shot back.

"As I was saying, John," Washbourne replied. "Tom Pemberton trusted you with Samantha's life. It sounds like she didn't need your help."

"Or yours."

"Whatever, but he didn't trust you with why, or what?"

"A need-to-know basis, I guess," Marshall replied. "They taught you that in spy school, didn't they? He didn't want her bothered by rowdy college guys. How do I know?"

"You were there to chaperon? For free? That's your statement?" Washbourne's eyes widened. "Guys like you keep me up nights. How do you support yourself? Free cases?"

"None of your business. I'm just a loyal friend."

"Well, you know what I think, Loyal Friend?"

Marshall shook his head, like an auction bidder refusing a bid.

"You're lying through your teeth," Washbourne said. "Funny that Samantha's never seen you before. Tom Pemberton can't confirm."

"He knew I'd do things you're not supposed to," Marshall said. "Which reminds me. Imagine my surprise discovering Kearney was yours. The Bureau wouldn't like that. You guys'll lose your magic attache cases for that."

"That's not your affair," Washbourne replied.

"It's every citizen's affair when you government guys go beyond your limits." Marshall returned the CIA man's glare.

"What if I told you the Bureau knows we're doing this?"

"I'd never believe it," Marshall replied. "The FBI's made a life's mission out of protecting its turf. Now who's doing it through his teeth?"

"Stop trying to change the scent. Know what I think?"

"No, Miss Marple," Marshall said. "I can't wait for your next revelation."

"You arranged it, anonymously, but they don't know you're coming. You invent this bullshit to cover yourself, particularly when it looked like she was doing the job herself."

"In with those morons?" Marshall asked. He laughed a loud, derisive cackle. "Thanks a lot, Washbourne. I owe you one."

"Watch my lips," Washbourne said. "*Mr.* Washbourne."

"Before this bullshit, this wasn't personal. I was pissed you Agency assholes'd put me through this. Or tail me. But that's your job. I could understand."

He stood suddenly and kicked his own chair backward. "But now it's personal. Suggesting I was in with those low-lives, those maggots."

"Not with them," Washbourne replied, "with the people who planned it and recruited them. They didn't expect those knobs to pull off that caper. Who are they?"

"Ask the low-lives," Marshall answered. "The only reason you're giving me this one man good-cop/bad-cop is you didn't get the answers from the slugs. I don't know any more than you do. But I'm right about the maggots, aren't I?"

Washbourne said, "*Didn't* know. Hired by phone. Cash from a locker in the Greyhound Terminal. No foreign accent. The drugs and paraphernalia with the cash."

"Trace it?"

Washbourne snapped back, "A booth in Union Station. Surveillance produced nothing." Washbourne was imperturbable again. "They *didn't* know anything. Cops found two with their brains splattered in an alley near 14th Street. MPD figures it's drug-related."

"They think everything's drug-related these days. Wait a minute. You mean, they were loose?"

"Somebody paid their bail," Washbourne said. "The locals had to cut them loose. We don't know who the benefactors were."

"The third?"

"Made bail, too, but hasn't been seen since. He probably won't be at trial in any way but spirit."

Marshall watched Washbourne, like a critic at a film premiere. The CIA man was like an android with a few emotions, dispensing and absorbing data.

"I swear to God!" Marshall said, finally. "I thought you were different from other Agency clowns I'd worked with. But you're all alike. You fooled me with that charm bullshit."

"Why, Mr. Marshall, whatever d'you mean?"

"I saw plenty of guys like you in Nam. They shoved captured VC from choppers at a thousand feet and called it 'mercy-killing.' Just another numeral on a piece of paper. 'Body counts.'"

Washbourne replied, "Whoever blew those two losers away weren't people I'd chum with, either."

"Don't give me your relative morality, Washbourne. You and your little plastic i.d. cards." Marshall headed for the door. "Same old, same old," he said. "If you get more than daydreams to back up those charges, you know where I am. Otherwise, tell your boys to get out of my face. Otherwise, you'll find yourself mentioned prominently in *The Post*, or a lawsuit."

"Marshall!" Washbourne yelled. "If you're clean, stay that way. Leave the Pemberton matter to us, or I'll come down on you like a *samurai*. Amazing what creative things can legally happen to you."

"Threats?" Marshall smirked. "So unattractive. Try some *Miranda* before bedtime. It does wonders for cop-wannabes. If you'll excuse me, Sam Pemberton's waiting for me." He left.

Bill Washbourne smiled a self-satisfied smile and shook his head. "Denise," he called his assistant on the intercom. "See that Mr. Marshall makes it to Reception. Then get me Mr. McConneld on a secure line." He felt more relaxed and hoped his performance was what McConneld had wanted.

* * *

"Sure it's the right house?" George asked David. They were dressed as delivery people. Their van, parked across the street, belonged to their New York contact, a garage owner.

They rang the doorbell of the townhouse again. It was a brownstone on New York's East 33rd Street.

"It's what the 'Marbison' Company gave us," David said.

Someone answered on the intercom.

"Mr. Agnello?" David said. "Marbison Company. Books."

George heard the locks being released. The door opened as far as a security chain allowed. A middle-aged face looked out at them.

"We phoned earlier about this delivery of first editions," David said, as though reading from his clipboard. "Early Dickens and Twain."

"My collection's got those, but books're heaven," Agnello replied. "Bring your truck in the alley to the garage."

Moments later George backed the van into the otherwise empty one-car garage, with its alley entrance, while David directed him.

Agnello closed the outer garage door. He was a short, heavyish man in his fifties, completely bald, by razor. "Got the money?" he asked.

"Fifty thousand dollars," David said, taking an envelope from his overalls. Agnello reached for it, but George pushed his arm away.

"First, the information. You sound a little less altruistic than our last contact," George said. The man was perspiring and nervous.

"You're lucky I'm talking to you at all," he said. "My partner was found in Central Park three weeks ago, murdered. Our recent customers likely took him out. The stuff's not here."

"So, where is it?" David asked. "And what is it?"

"In a locker in the Port Authority Terminal," Agnello replied. "The key's here. Let's have the money."

"Half now," George said. "Other half when we've got the package."

"That wasn't the arrangement," Agnello protested. "The stuff's worth ten times what I asked for."

"You didn't tell us we had to fetch it from the asshole of Manhattan," George answered. "Half something's better than a whole bunch of nothing. Why the discount? Going out of business sale?"

"Everything you've got left is in this locker?" David asked.

Agnello nodded. "I've got to disappear, with what my partner and I saved."

"You sound heartbroken," George said. "Who did it?"

"We were selling to Cubans through couriers," Agnello answered. "My partner didn't know who. We sold them Association stuff about Latin America and other deals. He wouldn't have gone along, if he'd known. It's my fault he bought it."

"And you're all eaten up with contrition?" George asked. "You owe it to him to take all the money?"

"I want the Cubans to get theirs," Agnello said. "I only know the head one by his first name, Jaime."

"What makes you think your employers didn't catch up with him?" David asked. "Maybe a warning? To you?"

"If they'd killed him," Agnello said. "He wouldn't have been found. I'd be gone, too. They don't waste time with warnings. It was Jaime. He wanted to know about something called Case Blue. I wouldn't help. Here's a picture of him. He hangs out at a Spanish club in Harlem."

David counted out $25,000, and was holding it.

"All right," Agnello said, resignedly. "Give me half. When you've got the suitcase, I expect the rest. One thing about the material. You need a laptop."

"We'll leave the rest in the locker," George said. "Unless there's more, I don't see you again."

"I'm more broken-hearted than you know," Agnello said. "I'd almost give you the money back, if you'd pop Jaime. But pick another place, 'cause I'm not going near that locker."

"We'll get it to you, if the material's good. I guarantee it," David said. "Sorry, but we don't do private vendettas."

"And who're you? Lloyd's of London?"

"The men from Marbison," George answered. "What was your friend's name?"

"Erik Spurling," Agnello replied. "When he wasn't at his own apartment on East 66th Street, he lived here."

George and David left. Later that evening, they drove to the Port Authority Terminal. George waited across the street in the van, while David picked up the brown, leather suitcase. At the parking garage, they examined disks. There were over a hundred floppies in all.

"Look at this," David said, after several hours of reading. "They've assembled special satellite and cable communications set-ups in the past six months, connecting New York, London, Paris, Berlin, Bonn, Frankfurt, Brussels, Tokyo, Rome, Madrid, and Buenos Aires. And paid for private satellites to be put into orbit."

George said, "Maybe they're starting their own TV network?"

"These are copies of the shakedowns. They're due to be a complete, scrambled and closed-circuit network by next week, with cable back-up."

"I show staff rosters from the Western Hemisphere," George said. "Most staff's been transferred over the last five months, especially upper, to the cities you reeled off. This side of the Atlantic must be a ghost town."

David scanned another disk while George read on.

"The Association's been doing heavy commodities trading for the last two years. Gold, silver, plutonium, wheat, euros, currencies," David continued. "Here're memos, noting increased sales by their subsidiaries of those same commodities."

George said, "Depress prices with oversupply. Drive other suppliers out of business. Sharp business. But nothing illegal."

"Here's another list," David said. "Bank accounts in Europe and the Bahamas. The cash from those transactions've been accessed through currency exchanges and funneled into what they're calling 'operations and services accounts,' separate from their visible accounts. Different banks. The Association's name isn't on them. MILLIONS in the laundry!"

"Whose name or names?"

"Ding-dong! 'Tripleleaf Enterprises,' 'Audran Arnold Associates,' 'Johannes Hoquette,' 'Shorall Win-Smith.' Many others."

"More interesting stuff," George said. "Let's play NATO Disintegration,' 'Soviet/Russian Collapse.'"

"That's a moot game," David said. "Although."

George read from the monitor, "It's a model simulation, marked 'Top Secret.' 'Case Red,' 'Case Blue,' 'Case Yellow,' 'Case Green,' 'Case Red-Blue.' Lots of mixed colors and scenarios: *Coup d'état,*' terrorist-siege,' 'financial collapse-depression,' 'Western Europe,' 'America,' 'Far East,' 'economic depression'."

"What's the difference between those 'depressions?'"

"Haven't got that far," George said. "Soviet invasion. Another dead issue. 'Eastern European takeover.' Too many right now. We can play when we get back to Washington. I'd say Agnello earned his other half."

"We'll Fed-Ex it in the morning," David said, "bearer bond.

Now what about the Cubans?"

"What about them?" George asked. "We don't have time for private contracts. Fuck them."

"Copying to Control and recommending surveillance. How's your Spanish?"

*   *   *

At the end of McConneld's first week Colonel Barsohn sent him copies of the DIA chief-investigator's personal files. Barsohn's team obtained copies, without involvement of European-based personnel. The probe had produced no arrests, identifications of suspects, or recoupment of weapons.

As McConneld and his analysts compared the copies with CIA's and DIA's Washington files, they discovered discrepancies. The investigator had omitted field reports and leads from his agents.

There were discrepancies between what he had disclosed to CIA in Europe, too. Parts of the investigator's files, referenced in other documents, were missing. Barsohn and McConneld decided to confront the investigator at home.

Barsohn arranged with Post Commandant for MPs to accompany them, but would not disclose their destination, until they were *en route*.

For McConneld Monday was a "routine," some would say "boring," day: receiving, reviewing, discussing reports and communiques with his analysts and with Channing.

Deputy Director Simmons was assigning more agents, bringing his complement to one hundred-plus operatives. Colonel Barsohn's DIA detachment also received reinforcements. His crew totaled more than two hundred personnel.

Around 7 P.M., Barsohn and Martin arrived at McConneld's offices. With them were specialists and MPs. A convoy of Barsohn's limousine, three vans, and several Humvees drove to the investigator's home.

The house was located in a section of Frankfurt that Barsohn's driver described as "upscale, full of German yuppies." McConneld noticed Mercedes, BMWs, and Jaguars along both sides of the street, with only a sporadic hint of cheaper cars. The house reminded McConneld of the Upper East Side of New York: rows of houses, varying in their peaked heights like members of a family portrait.

The investigator had been away from his office all day. A random phone check at 4 P.M. showed he was home. Barsohn had already ordered surveillance of the house.

Barsohn's on-site team reported no one else but one delivery person had come or gone. Nor had anyone left by the roof. The investigator lived solo.

MPs joined the surveillance team at the rear entrance, on a back alley, while the rest of the party remained with Barsohn and McConneld.

The entry hall and the first floor were dark. The MPs, with 9mm automatics ready, entered first. One tried the switches on the nearest wall, but no lights came on. They went off to search the house further.

"It smells like he forgot to let out the kennel," Channing said, as he passed through the foyer. McConneld, Barsohn, and Martin followed.

McConneld noticed the smell, too. It reminded him of European public toilets in the 1970s, when disinfectants had been used in prescription-like teaspoon doses. The stink emanated from the central staircase.

An MP came to Barsohn. "Sir?" she said. "The electricity's off in the whole house. The first floor's clear."

McConneld sniffed his way up the center-hall steps to the second floor, using a flashlight from another MP. The hallway was dense with the stench. In a bedroom at the end of the corridor, he discovered the cause.

There, lying back-spread over a reclining chair, was the body of a man. He was nude, but for a robe that covered his shoulders. His eyes and mouth were open, with the tongue bloated and perched over his lips. At the base of the chair was an electric foot-massage/water-bath. His feet were submerged.

"Chuck!" McConneld called. "I found the kennel." The others joined him.

"That's our man," Barsohn said, as McConneld shone the

light beam over the corpse. "How?"

"No bullet or knife wounds I can see," McConneld replied. "I didn't see any blood. Better get the forensics guys up here."

The overhead chandelier went on just then. There was a flash and loud *CRACK!* Sizzling sounds came from the foot-bath. The corpse was jolted and slammed back into the chair. The lights went off again.

"Your guys found the electric box," Channing said to Barsohn. "Hold them off till we get this thing disconnected."

The lights came on again. The corpse reacted, as though wired back to life momentarily. The lights were off once more.

Barsohn sent Martin to stop more attempts at closing the circuits, since the MPs did not respond to a headset call. Before the aide reached them, the dead man was re-energized by the current one more time.

"Talk about dark comedy," McConneld said, while he and Channing pulled the bath's cord from the wall. "I hoped he'd be giving us more than horrific sight-gags."

"Another dead fucking end. We'll find the bastards," Barsohn said, "even if he IS a traitor."

"We can safely assume he was," McConneld said.

"Somebody *really* fixed *his* feet," Channing said. "It's so awfully sad, but why is it I feel like laughing?" The lights were back and remained on.

"Call Post Commandant's Office and the German police," Barsohn said to Martin, who rejoined them, "after we search. I don't want anything disappearing before we get a shot at it. The major'll keep a while longer."

"Somebody cover him up, at least?" McConneld asked. Channing threw a bedspread over the corpse.

The chandelier's crystal light shone on a Persian carpet with little depreciation. The furniture included mahogany canopybed, matching armoire, chests and nighttables, which would have sold as scarce antiquities back in the States.

There were file cabinets in the cellar, a wall safe in the victim's bedroom, and, what particularly interested McConneld, specially tailored, inside pockets with black, plastic zippers in the dead man's dark-green, winter-uniform jackets. The contents were inspection slips, with the same inspector's number, "131425."

"What're the odds?" he asked Channing and Barsohn. "Non-regulation pockets with inspection tags and the same number?"

"The combination? From the looks of this house," Channing said, handing an inspection slip to the locks specialist, "this guy was compulsive. Everything's perfect. Why wouldn't he have a back-up?"

Within seconds "131425" had unlocked the safe. McConneld felt like he was salivating over the contents, Pavlov-style. There were papers, a binder, notebooks, and lots of cash.

"His Alpine retirement fund, no doubt," Channing said, as his boss dropped two-inch-thick stacks of 1,000DM notes, in wrappers, onto the bed. "That's a hell of a Christmas Club, or somebody owned him, lock, stock, and wrapper. But why involuntary retirement?"

"Just because you buy a guy," Barsohn said, "doesn't mean he stays bought. But we don't know his owners took him out. It might be payroll."

"After 917," McConneld said. "He was just another mouth that could roar against them, if he got pissed off. Better get through that stuff in the basement."

"The trucks're already on the way," Martin said. He also phoned the Provost-Marshal's Office and the Frankfurt police.

* * *

His brain still lightly singed by the interview with Washbourne, J.D. Marshall took Samantha Pemberton to lunch at a French-style café in Georgetown. *The* Agency would not chase him away from a special promise, he decided.

Over chef's salads, cheap for a Georgetown restaurant, Samantha and he found common memories—as though in the past they had been on the circumference of a circle, obscured from seeing each other by a large center crowd.

"I wish we'd met before," Samantha said.

"You were too young then," Marshall said. "And there was a time you mightn't've liked me."

"I find that hard to believe," Sam replied.

"I didn't like me back then, and your father always sheltered his 'little mademoiselle.' It's ironic he asked me to watch over you. I guess he figured he'd guilt me." He imitated a buzzer on a television game show. "Wrong answer."

"That's like him," Sam said, lifting her wine glass. "A toast. To John Marshall, my guardian angel. Late of the Supreme Court. Very late, but well-preserved. Long may he wave."

"Thanks, ma'am," he replied. "So my parents were lawyers and had a sense of humor." They sipped from their glasses.

"Here's one to you, Samantha," Marshall continued. "To Sam Pemberton, the toughest co-ed I ever met. Oh, sorry! They don't say that any more, do they? Co-ed? I just fossilized myself."

They drank again. "And the only Sam I ever kissed. Maybe I shouldn't have interfered. How'd you get so good?"

"Lessons and lots of practice. Didn't Pa tell you?"

"Only what I told you before."

"He became a fanatic about my self defense, after Mother was killed. Judo, jiu-jitsu, aikido. Wherever we were living, lessons and a place to practice. Checked me out on small arms and rifles, too."

"That's right," Marshall said. "It *has* been over ten years since then. I can't believe that much time's gone. A good lady, your mother. Good head, good heart. Didn't drink much, but could drink most men under the table when she had a mind to. By then she was out. Quit The Agency years before that. That's the real irony."

"Pa took Mother's death real hard," Sam said. "He blamed himself for it."

"I went through that with him, too. Your father lost a lot of self-esteem in that period."

"Tell me about it!" Sam said. "On an intellectual level he knew it wasn't his fault. But emotionally, the guilt. If he hadn't been in this business. If he hadn't brought her along on that trip. Etc."

"The longer I live, the more I'm convinced the root of all evil's lack-of-self-esteem. But guilty or not, he's still a good man. And he's been a friend to me, since before my 'Special Ops' days."

"You were in 'Special Operations'?" Sam asked.

"I went to Vietnam, a bright-eyed, naïve kid. Thought America was the land of the little guy, fought for the underdog. It didn't take me long to see that's all bullshit. I probably hung in too long."

"But 'Special Operations?' That's a euphemism for murder and assassination."

"I never murdered *anyone*," Marshall replied. "I killed the enemy. That was my rationalization. Not pretty, but it worked then. I'll not apologize, though. But Spec Ops days were just more bullshit and self-flagellation. Your father was the only person, who understood. He was real. Not like the rest of those brass lemmings. He helped me deal with the pain."

"Brass what?" Sam asked, smiling.

"Lemmings. You know the kind. Be a good soldier. Ask no questions. 'Only following orders!' My country right or wrong still pays my pension after twenty good ones."

Sam laughed. "I'm sorry. I had no right to judge you."

"Sure you did. And I learned something about myself in Nam. I'd never make it as CEO of 'U.S. Army, Inc.' No brass lemming, I. What about you? How'd you take her death?"

"I was angry," she answered. She felt her stews. "I guess I am at times."

"Guess?"

"OK, so I'm angry. I remember hating, but there was no one there to hate. Only faceless 'them.' Asking why it was *my* mother, but no one could answer me. Not Pa. Maybe that's why he felt so guilty. But I grew. Lots of others've died, innocently. I had to grow. For the Twins' sake, Edward and Maureen. I had to be strong for them."

"And not for you?"

"I like to think I found inner power and strength over the years. But it still hurts, knowing her then losing her. Bob took it the best of all of us. He didn't fall into the denial game, even subconsciously. He cries even now, when he thinks no one's looking. But never in public."

"It's tough when someone close dies, not to feel like it's your fault. It's also tough not to feel abandoned.

"I lost buddies in Nam. It took me a long time not to feel guilty, 'cause I survived. But I finally got tired of fighting that goddamn war. Tired of hearing Middle America moan, 'cause it got suckered into going. Sick of hearing about draft-dodgers! Goddamn war wouldn't have gone on, if Middle America'd had guts sooner! And on the subject of fermenting, you want to know more, right?" Marshall asked. "Take another sip. What a bedtime story I've got for you."

Two glasses of wine later Marshall had limned the frame, back- and foreground, of her father's mission.

"Why didn't he confide in me?" Sam asked. "His trust is reassuring."

"I guess he didn't want you to get involved, or hurt," Marshall said. "He told me he didn't want The Cartel to be the 'family business,' too."

"That's lame. Not telling me hasn't kept me out. Anybody interested in him doesn't know I know nothing." She stopped. "Does that make sense?"

Marshall nodded. "Best to avoid double negatives." He leaned closer to her. "I don't have to remind you to stay out of it. You're a bright lady."

"If you don't have to, why'd you bring it up again?"

Marshall shrugged.

"Let *me* guess now," she said. "You're trying reverse-guilt. Keep me barefoot, ignorant, and in the dormitory. Otherwise, I might get him killed. That's what you want me to think. Why must you men always do this to us? Try to control us? And you're no better, John Marshall, with your innocent, 'How-should-I-know?' face. My father might get himself killed without help from me, if what you've said is true."

"Your father wants you all to survive," Marshall said, patiently, "even if he doesn't. But he wants the word to get out. On the self-esteem thing, look at the Nazis. If you're abused as a kid, you start believing you deserve it; that's all you're worth. A bunch of scared, angry little self-hating men with no self-esteem and a hate on against the world. Not unlike some of our current politicians. Each generation fights this battle."

"Well, I can't argue with you. But I'll be the one to make *my* decisions. Not Pa, you, or anybody else, by guilt or manipulation."

"You're a good kid, Sam," Marshall said, taking her hand in his. "I've gotten accustomed to *your* silly face, and I don't want anything to happen to it."

"That's the wine talking," she said.

He shook his head. "Are you serious? This water?"

Samantha squeezed his hand. "Thanks," she said, softly.

Marshall dropped her off at the dormitory, after a farewell kiss-on-the-lips. A pink telephone message slip was waiting for her there. It read, "Edward's very ill. Please come home immediately. Don't call first. Just come. Daisy."

IX

The atmosphere was a thick, hovering, tobacco smog. Latin music, drum- and guitar-driven, varied between quiet mood and carnival. To George and David, this Harlem nightclub was a throwback to their Central American and Caribbean assignments. Here, too, Spanish was the first language, English merely a tolerated convenience, or inconvenience.

They sat to one side of the stage, watching the band and its lead singer, and their quarry, the man whom Agnello had identified as "Jaime."

Late the previous week their local contact had given them Control-West's approval of David's request to shadow "Jaime." They were to maintain stand-off distance and only stay on if he led them to more than rackets, drugs, and prostitution.

"Jaime's" surname was Rodriguez *y* Wessin. He appeared and claimed to be a modestly prosperous El Salvadoran refugee, popular among the Latino community and merchants. He ran a commercial janitorial business and had contracts for large, high-rise office buildings in midtown. Further inquiries proved Agnello's Association had its New York offices in one of those. His income was sufficient for him to keep a condominium on Central Park West, to which George and David tracked him, and a farm in North Jersey.

There were rumors of less-legitimate activities. It was said he ran prostitutes and drugs on the underbelly of his legal concerns. Some spoke of his being "borderland," his accent and lifestyle not Salvadoran. The term "Cuban Mafia" had come up.

This was the fifth night of their surveillance. The previous four he had been accompanied by the same three men, and a catalogue of lively, but different, women. After closing, Jaime returned to his apartment with one of the women. His was a top-floor unit with plexiglass-bubble skylights, George and David had learned the first night.

"We've lent new meaning to 'nurse a drink,'" David said, taking a sip from a Scotch-on-the-rocks that had lost its "rocks" hours before.

George slapped him on the chest. "Our man's on the move."

Jaime and his men were leaving. Jaime gave his woman of this evening, a tall blonde, a demeaning swat, to chase her away.

"I'll wait for you at the taxi," David said, leaving.

George dropped a tip on the table, but then sat while Jaime spent the next ten minutes saying good-bye to half the patronage. Finally, Jaime and his party left.

Outside, George joined David in a cab driven by a colleague of theirs. Jaime and his party, less women, drove away in a Ford station wagon that had been double-parked, but unticketed.

The Ford drove directly to Jaime's condominium. The four men, after parking the car illegally again, went upstairs.

George and David waited for someone to leave or enter. Several couples entered together. David and George slipped in behind them past the *concierge*.

On the roof, through the bubble skylight, they saw Jaime and his men, plus one new man, sitting around the table. With microphones on the plexiglass, they recorded the conversation. It was in English.

David nudged George. "We've seen that one before," he whispered. "Remember Madrid three years ago?"

"Yeah, yeah," George whispered. "He was a double, working for Iranian Intelligence, I think."

"Another good oxymoron," David said.

"Almost nailed the bastard, but he escaped."

Jaime was talking about a "Dr. Pola," who was due from Los Angeles the next afternoon. He ordered one man, called "Emilio," to meet "the doctor" at Newark Airport. Pola was a physicist, Jaime continued, who would become a full member of the team, but would be lodged at "the farm."

"Isn't this a little early for that?" the new man asked. "We might not get close to the bombs."

"Be optimistic, Jamael," Jaime said. "I have new info from my GRU colonel tonight. The bombs're still in Europe and haven't been moved yet."

"How the fuck does she know that?" Jamael asked.

"I never ask how," Jaime answered. "Only how much."

David tapped George. "Different name, same asshole. We did get off cheap with Agnello."

Jaime mentioned other information from a new informant, working inside Agnello's Association. "Subsidiaries of The Cartel've been general and sub-contractors for the new nuclear storage dumps for the American Army in Europe," Jaime continued. They're overcharging the stupid Americans, slipping cash through bank accounts and using it to buy far more construction materials than're needed, from U.S. suppliers, shipping from America and Mexico to Italy and Holland via Bremen, into Germany. Big contracts from the German government. Leipzig, Berlin, others."

"Normal stockpiling?" Jamael asked.

"Not with detours like these," Jaime answered. "As soon as my Russian lady gives me a trail, we'll be off. Said she'd have it late this week or early next."

Jaime's visitors were leaving. George and David returned to the cab. They followed the station wagon.

"Stay with them till they drop the one called Emilio," David told the driver. "He'll lead us to their physicist and the farm at the same time."

"One of us'll have to hook up with Marbison, while the other stays," George said. "Control will want to hear about this Iranian development. Iranians and nukes! No fucking way!! Cubans, too?!"

"Solidarity? Mercenary?" David said.

"A marriage of convenience. Go to D.C. I'll stay on Jaime."

"With luck these clowns'll lead to the bombs themselves," David said. "Jaime *et al.* could be out of here within the week."

"If they split while you're off?" George asked.

"Go to the regular destination drop. I'll scamper after you."

"How about the million-dollar question?" George asked. "Hunt for owners or keep the nukes ourselves?"

"We can guess who the owners are. But that's for the policy-hounds," David said. "Maybe we give back. Maybe we don't."

* * *

Lying back on her pillow, Samantha let her mind fill with swirling *non-sequiturs*. Her lunch with J.D. Marshall. The Professor. The Twins. Bob. Images of her mother.

Sam felt a slow emotional rain, but also ambivalence. She could not expect security in the memory of a mother dead for over a decade. A mother who had not lived to help her through adolescence.

Daisy's message. She wondered if it were genuine, or another attempt to get her to where she could be kidnapped. She trashed doubts that it was false. Going now would provide the chance to prowl through The Professor's papers and his "stash."

There was a knock on the door. "Who is it?" she asked, shuffling to the sink. She bent over the basin, and splashed her face with water.

"It's Liz," came the answer. "Ready for an early dinner?" Liz asked, as she came in.

"Not yet," Sam said, crossing her lips with her index finger. "I had a late lunch, but I could use a cup of coffee. Let's go down to the lounge."

Sam gestured Liz out and followed her to the corridor lounge. There were concession machines and a small kitchen. They were alone in the common area, with its permanent-press couches and chairs.

She decided to unload to Liz. Sam bought coffee from a machine and considered looking in the kitchen, but chose not to, since its lights were off.

"I just *had* to get out of that room!" Sam said.

Liz asked,"You can't talk in your room? Why?" Liz's hands were near-praying, around the styrofoam cup.

Sam replied, calmly, but out of breath, "You've won my lottery for unofficial couch. I've got to go home ASAP. But I don't expect to be there long. Something's wrong. Period."

"Can't your family handle it?" Liz's supplicating body language was pleading harder for information. "Your father?"

"He's nowhere in sight," Sam sighed. "I don't know where he is. Try this one. Remember that night I was away last week?"

Liz nodded. "You said you spent it with friends, off campus."

She told Liz the truth. Sam's discomfort had faded, replaced by a slight brush-stroke of anger. "I half-wasted two of them. A friend of my father's finished them off, before some authorities showed up."

"Police? FBI?" Liz sounded incredulous and restless.

"Would you believe CIA?" Sam whispered to her.

"Oh, really?" Liz replied. It was a more subdued and polite response. Almost like she knew!

"You half-wasted them? How? You don't have a gun, do you?!"

"Of course not," Sam replied. "*Jiu-jitsu*. I've studied it for years. Thank God, they were only armed with knives!"

"Remind me to have you along if I ever go down dark alleys," Liz said.

"And, of course, there's that friend of my father's," Sam said, as she lay back on the cushion. Her mental vision's big screen was broadcasting J.D. Marshall, with vast anatomical and poetic license.

"So, what happened?"

"Obviously, the rumors of my kidnapping were greatly exaggerated."

"Tell me more about that later," Liz said, slyly. "I'm talking about the guy. That look. A guy, right?"

"Yes," Sam sighed again. "But I can't tell you that much. I don't know much about him, myself—yet."

"You're planning more, right?"

Sam felt confident, happy, at least for this second. Her imaginary Marshall blurred and disintegrated into dots, like a photograph that had been enlarged too many times.

She told Liz about Daisy's message. "St. Louis's the closest major airport, without those commuter air-crates. Our phone's probably tapped. Even if it weren't, which I'm sure it is, I can't call from my room. It's bugged." Sam fingered her lips, like she was having a nervous breakdown.

"What's your father into?"

Sam shrugged. "What do I know? I'm just someone in a checkered jacket."

She told Liz some of what Marshall had told her.

"Thanks for trusting me," Liz said, when Sam finished.

"I've probably put you in danger, too. Not sure what I planned with you. Everything flowed, once I let out my cork. I know you keep your mouth shut."

"Anyone else involved, other than The Agency?" Liz asked, quickly.

Sam shrugged. "Well, I have errands, but I really appreciate your ear and your heart, Liz, my comrade." They hugged tightly, before Sam left. Liz remained to read for a short while alone.

* * *

Liz McGonnville sat in the old-style, brown-wood telephone booth in the hallway outside the lounge. The booth was fully indented into an alcove. Liz listened.

While she and Sam had been speaking, she thought she heard soft noises in the kitchen. She had not wanted to panic Sam or alert whoever might have been in there.

Now, she suddenly heard footsteps, soft, though high-heeled, getting louder. They stopped.

Liz peeked around the side of the booth, but the lounge door blocked her view. The footsteps resumed. She hunched against the rear wall. The sounds stopped nearby.

"Hello, Regina!" Liz heard a call from far up the hall. "Looking for something?" the new voice asked.

"No, no," Regina Foxwirth replied, in her ever-proper English. "I was sitting alone in the lounge for the past half-hour. Collecting my thoughts."

As Regina walked away, Liz heard her embellishing the lie. Hidden by the lounge door, Liz slithered from the booth.

The conversation broke up. Regina returned to her room.

Hurrying to Regina's door, Liz could hear movement inside. Alone in the hall, Liz took a seeming mini-Walkman, with a microphone and earplug attached, from her purse. She held the mike to the door and listened.

"I should like to send two telexes, please," she heard Regina saying. "One to France. The other to Germany. That'll be Cannes, France. Here's the reference point."

A door down the opposite hall creaked. Liz stuffed the device into her purse, trotting to Sam's door.

"Hello, Liz, how're you?" It was the same student, who had called to Regina.

Liz answered in the rote manner she had learned at the school. "I'm fine. How're you? Seeing if Sam's home. Have you seen her?"

Regina's door opened slightly, and she glanced out, with a cell phone to her ear. After supplementary innocuous-speak, the other student departed. Liz and Regina looked across the hall at each other.

"Hi, Regina," Liz said, after awkward seconds. "How's life?"

Regina nodded. It was her regal nod, as though she were dismissing Liz.

While she walked away, Liz felt Regina's laser-like suspicions burning into her back. When she was around the corner, Liz broke into a run to the lobby.

Rats! Liz thought. *Regina knew. So much for her cover!*

In another phone booth, in the Georgetown University Hospital foyer, Liz punched in a familiar number and awaited an answer.

"Three-four-two," the voice replied. "May I help you?"

"Put me through to Washbourne! Emergency!" she said, short of breath.

* * *

"Two down, one to go," Sam murmured, as she tapped the final number into a public phone in Lauinger, G.U.'s central library. This call was to Mr. Washbourne.

The preceding calls had been easy and painless. The first reserved a First-Class seat on the next open flight to St. Louis, the following morning's 8 A.M. Flight 442 from Dulles Airport, rather than from National. National would have been easier, but on such short notice, only Dulles flights were open.

Her second was a credit card call to Daisy. The housekeeper greeted her with, "Didn't I tell you not to call?" Sam gave her the flight information into St. Louis Airport and rang off.

The third call was answered after five rings. "Three-three-seven. May I help you?"

Sam asked for Mr. Washbourne. She was anxious to *inform* him of her plans, cutting off any discussion he might try.

"I'll transfer you. Hold, please," the female voice said. The subsequent ringing ended quickly with a CLICK and, "Three-four-two. May I help you?"

Sam repeated her request.

"He's on another line. Do you want his voice-mail, or would you care to hold?"

Sam identified herself and said she would hold. After a few moments, Washbourne was on the line.

"I'm letting you know, I'm flying home via St. Louis tomorrow morning," Sam said. "Our housekeeper said it's urgent."

"Is it really a good idea right now? Or necessary? It could stretch our ability to protect you."

"This isn't a request," Sam said, "but a courtesy call. I didn't want you guys to freak when I went off the radar screen, or whatever contraption you're using."

"I love *faits accompli*," Washbourne replied. He sounded in resignation- or surrender-mode. "Airline and flight number?"

She gave him the information. "I always fly United," she concluded.

"It'll be tough, but we'll handle it," he said. "How're you getting from St. Louis to Carbondale? Commuter flight? Limo?"

"Our housekeeper's picking me up."

"Remember to keep the compact with you at all times. And we'll see you in St. Louis. But, I trust, you won't see us."

* * *

"So what'd the New York boy tell you?" Marbison asked David, as they had drinks in a rear-alley pub with a titled English name, in Northwest D.C.

"Directly?" David asked. "Or indirectly?"

Marbison replied, "Bluntness first, then subtlety."

David gave him a summary of the meeting with Agnello and of the contents of the bag from the Port Authority locker. "Pieces fit together for a picturesque puzzle. But the indirect leads're even better."

"Where's the stuff now?"

"I brought it back with me, after making multiple copies of the disks for Control. I noticed him on it already."

"Tell me about the indirects," Marbison said.

"Agnello had a partner."

Marbison nodded. "Erik Spurling."

"He's dead," David said, quickly.

Marbison inhaled vodka up the back of his throat and coughed. David gave him time to clear his nostrils. "I'd only heard he dropped out of sight."

"Agnello figures Jaime Rodriguez or his men killed him. He offered us a contract on Rodriguez."

"You dusted him off, didn't you?"

"But we followed up on Rodriguez. Agnello said he was a Cuban agent, not that we're that interested in Cuba. Control cleared it."

David stopped, and took a deep breath. "And Rodriguez's led to a trail of 'stolen bombs.' They were talking about bringing in a physicist."

"Nukes?" Marbison said. "Who was stupid enough to be burgled?"

"We heard Rodriguez say he got the info from a Russian military intelligence 'lady.' I'd guess the Americans. We were watching him the whole night. He must've made the contact under our noses."

David recapped their inquiry into Rodriguez, including the farm, the physicist, and an expected expedition to Europe.

"What's the sidekick's name?"

"Emilio. I've got the conversation on tape," David said. Marbison seemed to recognize the name.

"If that weren't enough, at Rodriguez's apartment, they met an Iranian agent George and I tangled with in Madrid three years ago. Real chummy, they were."

"Iranian?" Marbison asked. "It's getting weirder all the time. Christ! As if the world weren't unstable enough! The Russians're helping them?"

"I don't know for sure. She could be a renegade agent," David continued. Rodriguez and Co. could be leaving any day. The Russian's giving them a start. I've got to get back tonight."

"I thought the Russians'd be low profile for a while. Their intelligence services're going in for industrial espionage now. More bad news for you. Radical Palestinian factions and the IRA signed on with Tripleleaf. PFLP and the Provisionals' grandsons. New players, too. One calling itself the United Front for the Liberation of Kurdistan."

"It was only a matter of time before Kurds got *very* internationally militant," David said. "People'll be doormats only so long."

"Jaime's taking the physicist with him to Europe?" Marbison asked. "He must be sure they'll get near those boomers."

"Rodriguez seemed *macho*-cocky. But you said players?"

"Nothing definite. I've heard east winds blowing west. No names out of the fog, though, besides the Kurds."

"How reliable's your info on the Palestinians *et al.?*"

Marbison smiled. "Arafat should have my sources. There's a good chance I'll be joining you in Europe."

"Control called you a 'guide,' but said you stayed here."

"Things're coming together sooner than expected. But I'll be along, only if I can escape quietly from my work here. If I *do*, I'll need you along."

"Along?" David asked. He felt irked. "It sounds like you think we're carry-on luggage, working for *you*."

"Check with Control, if you don't want me around over there. You'll find it's *my* option. I've got the contacts," Marbison said. "There's no reason to get on each other's nerves. As far as I'm concerned, we're allies, not cowboys or gunslingers."

David smiled. He trusted the contact, in spite of his pique. "How'll you catch up with us? We'll have to move fast."

"Clear Control by drop with your first, expected touch-down. I've got a good nose for trails," Marbison said.

X

The scrambler phone was purring in burp-sized rings, as Chuck Channing came into his office. He was returning from a conference with NATO and German Defence Ministry officials.

Channing answered the call. "E-mail me with it." He hung up.

By the time he sat at his computer, an e-mail awaited him with an attached copy of the report. He printed out the contents, perused them, and, with it and other files and printouts, went to McConneld's command center.

McConneld was examining his wall map of Germany. Map sections of Austria, Switzerland, Eastern France, and Western Poland had been added to it.

"Another unscheduled drop from Tom Pemberton," Channing said.

"Read it to me while I do this," McConneld said.

"You know we do that with computers," Channing said.

"I'm old-fashioned," McConneld said. "A computer screen's never replaced the feel of paper to me."

"Neon, N. & C. plan Case/Operation Blue due completion 30 Nov. Starting date likely post-30 Oct. West Euro believed where. How why unclear. Baron, Gen. involved. Contingency plans U.S.-Russian responses destabilization NATO/EU, esp. France, Italy, Britain, Germany. Further contact difficult. Expect Sequestration. P."

"Optional contact near Vienna," Channing added.

"'Sequestration.' *Incommunicado*, if he isn't already. How'd he make the drop?"

"In a café WC. Our man used the same booth as Pemberton," Channing said. "Pemberton left it in a recess of the bowl, in a plastic capsule."

"We'll call this drop Vienna," McConneld said, as he stuck a locational pin into the map. "The contact?"

"Resident operative," Channing replied, "a waiter. It's a regular drop."

"Sure it was Pemberton?"

Channing nodded. "That op's on the PemWatch. Pemberton was with a group of executive-types and security muscle. Private dining room. Private bus. Our station people're following that up."

"Pemberton's not made any scheduled drops lately, has he?"

"Not since the first one," Channing said. "What've you got there?"

"Printouts," McConneld said. "First, names, etc., of all USAREUR personnel, qualified to make a 'madame' operational. With or without regulation materials. Second, USAREUR-assigned personnel trained on SADMs. Third, a services-wide list of SADM personnel. Fourth, a services-wide version for 'madames.' I want everyone on those checked, and *our* people to do it, not Langley. We've got to have Pemberton's 'sequestration' site pinned, before hibernation."

Channing said, "These'll take time. So will locating Pemberton. Why not let HQ do the backgrounds?"

"The fewer hands, the better."

"Are you assuming the MADMs or the SADMs're the more likely usables?"

"Both," McConneld said. "I'm not discounting *anything*. Those last two lists were cross-referenced by OPO, Energy, HS and FBI. Washbourne's coordinating with us."

"We got the autopsy report on that DIA major. Cause of death, 'myocardial infarction, due to massive electric shock.' The foot massager had been rewired. It fried him the second he turned it on. Our official line's 'ventricular fibrillation,' the result of overexertion and a history of heart trouble."

"That saves Army cheeks and family embarrassment," McConneld said, "not to mention the cost of an espionage trial."

"We also got his Service record through Langley. Forty-four years old. Single, never married. One dependent, his mother in Idaho. Right-wing affiliations and organizations. Army ROTC in college. Commissioned second lieutenant, 1986. Active Duty since. Assignments around the States. Over here. Far East, too.

Multiple postings to Washington. Recruited DIA, 1990. Gulf War. Passed over for lieutenant-colonel twice. Retirement recommended."

"Someone else made that decision for him," McConneld said. "There was some anger in him all right. Any children?"

"None. And that theft investigation probably would've been his final assignment before the Army forced him to retire."

"Colonel Barsohn's and our people have been analyzing the stuff from the file cabinets and the safe. Swiss, Luxembourg, and Bahamian bank accounts've surfaced. The money in the safe was payroll or travel money. Lots of names, addresses, contacts, dates and places. Documents seem to be missing, though. Whoever murdered him, must not have had time to clear the files."

"And how was the briefing?"

"Well," Channing said, in his best Ronald Reagan imitation. "The Germans're divided. Some think the bombs, or part of them, were gotten out of Germany. Some think the MADMs're still here. Some don't know what to think. Their investigation's going on the 'still-here' assumption. No agreement on why, but consensus that only European thieves're to blame."

"And the other NATO officials?"

"They're berserk. The British, French, and Italians're on full alert," Channing answered, his Reagan-*persona* gone. "They're not discounting the weapons' being used in their own countries or in Germany, but prejudice in favor of known terror groups. And they rubbed in the fact they wanted the SADMs out."

"They discount their nationalist or right-wings? Neo-Nazis?"

"They claim there's no hard evidence to confirm 'non-Communist, non-terrorist involvement.' Especially since the FRG officials're talking about a new group, thought to be terrorist, calling itself the East German Black Army. Smoother and more elusive than Baader-Meinhof or their grandchildren. This group's thought to be former members of the National People's Army and *Stasi*."

"I wish Tom'd turned up something linking the bombs with this Case Blue stuff."

"Why don't we share the message with them? It might convince them."

"We can't. One leak and he's dead. Some of your fellow attendees might be a little too right-wing, too. The right-wingers have been in an identity crisis, since the USSR died. They've been looking for new spectres, all the better to scare their publics. That's why they bandy 'terrorist' around so easily."

"They're trying to do what the German Nationalists during Weimar thought they could do: pander to the Nazi-mentality, but control it," Channing said.

"Thank you, Professor Plato," McConneld quipped. "Now what've we got on this East German Black Army?"

"Not much more than our NATO friends," Channing said. "It's too recent. I should have the best profile to date by tomorrow."

"30 October to 30 November," McConneld reflected. "Less than four weeks to head it off. Let's chew over the possibilities of this Case/Operation Blue."

"Well," Channing was back in his Reagan-mode.

"Enough, Ronbo," McConneld said. "Major league assassination?"

"Too much ordinance for that," Channing said, "unless they plan to wipe out a whole city to swat flies. Early thefts could have been a way to get something to sell, to finance the nuke job. Or a diversion for the next one."

"Your last supposition doesn't add up," McConneld interrupted. "Why pull thefts that would put us on the alert? If you're using a diversion."

"It obviously didn't put us on enough alert," Channing said. "But if you've bought off the opposition's chief investigator..."

"On the other hand, these guys might be arming themselves to the teeth. Not traceable, even through the international blackmarket. Ordnance."

McConneld repeated the word. "Shit! I wonder!" He pushed the intercom switch. "Get me a secure line to File Section, Langley HQ right away!"

*   *   *

With her sable coat caped over her shoulders, Regina

Foxwirth walked from a telephone stand outside the Post Office on Thirty-first Street in Georgetown. The weather was not cold enough yet, she had decided, to wear her favored coat as more than a drape. Not as cold as the Alps would have been. She avoided using a cell phone, for fear of being traced too easily.

Her initial instructions had been ambiguous, vague. Watch Samantha Pemberton's day-to-night activities. Report "anything unusual." Only report. Their fathers were colleagues, she knew, perhaps even friends. Strange how they had never met, though related by fathers and business all those years.

Her father had asked her to do this chore. She hated chores, but she would do anything for him. "Industrial espionage." His name for this and the other cases on which she had worked for him. This would be easy, too.

A short time later, Regina was knocking on the door of a shop, a small rowhouse, nineteenth century slave quarters, compressed along the C&O Canal Towpath. Curtains covered its window and door, with a "We're Closed," sign displayed.

The door opened. Before her was a tall, slim, and tanned man, in tightly clinging, European-style jeans, shirt, and leather jacket. His blond hair covered his ears and collar.

"Ah!" he said, loudly, pulling her to himself snugly. Regina's body went board-like, as she feigned a reciprocal greeting. Passersby looked over.

He apparently enjoyed this ritual. She did not. Or she did not want him to know, even if she did tingle with the touch of his body. She pulled away quickly, going past him.

"*Enough!*" she said in French. "*When'll you learn you're NOT interesting to me?! At all?!*"

"*When'll you admit*," he replied, also in French, "*That I am?*" He closed the door and locked it.

Regina hated his arrogance. He had been her contact on other cases, though she had been meeting him only a few weeks for this one. He had made passes at her each time.

"I told my father I didn't want to work with you," she said, coldly. "*He didn't listen to me. Do you have my new instructions? Be quick. I've got an appointment for dinner.*"

He grabbed her arm, trying to embrace her. She broke loose

from the attempt and slapped his face. "*You're not meeting anyone. You forget I know you. No man's good enough for you.*"

"*Your French is good, for a lower-class Hun,*" she said. "*But your manners, or lack of them, give you away. My instructions! IMMEDIATEMENT!*"

"*Very well, Putana!*" he said. Regina felt his contempt. "*Your lieber Papa,*" he said, with sarcasm seeping from the remark, "*has the desire you follow the Pemberton girl. Wherever she goes. Especially if she travels.*"

"*A fine time to tell me!*" She returned his sarcasm. "*I overheard her planning a trip home. A few days, I think, but she's coming back. It'd be awkward for me to chase her there.*"

"*Do not concern yourself this time. But we also need to know, if she has information about her father's work,*" he continued. "*Here, take these. You know how to use them.*"

He handed her two, small, hand-sized, black leather cases, which she placed in her large Chanel purse.

"*I overheard her say she was nearly kidnapped. You?*"

"*Kidnapped? No, not us. Find more about that, if you can.*"

"*What about finances?*" Regina asked, "*to chase her? What if she takes a flight I can't get on?*"

"*Taken care of,*" he answered. "*We're hacked into any reservation system. All you do is check in. Has your Papa denied you anything? You'll only have to do this a few more weeks.*" His sarcasm was back.

"*He denied me a better partner.*"

"*I repeat.*"

"*Never when it suits his purposes,*" she answered. "*And mine. Jealousy becomes you well.*" Regina showed her own arrogance, which was not easily defeated. "*If it weren't for mein 'lieber Papa,' as you put it, you'd still be a street thug in Hamburg. Or worse, cherish the thought. You resent him . . .*"

"*On the contrary,*" the contact said. "*I'm not jealous of your Papa. I respect and owe him much. He pays me well, to tolerate you. It's you who're a contemptible witch!*" Still cool, he had spoken quietly.

Regina envied his control and calm, though she maintained her usual self-control. She found him attractive, physically, but below her class and, thus, only momentary fantasy-in-flesh.

"I've never had to do so much for his cases."

"New type," the contact replied. *"Be prepared to leave whenever necessary. Light traveler that you are."* He snickered.

"I've been ready," she answered. She reveled in her own coldness. "What am I to do with that busy-body McGonnville? I'm sure she knows I was spying."

The contact looked at her, his own expression impenetrable. "The Baron leaves that to your discretion. So long as you draw no attention to us. We can arrange something for you, if need be."

* * *

The uniformed Russian Secret Service sentry handed General Balkovsky and his driver their identifications and waved the limousine on. Two other guards had opened the gate to Yuri Torychenko's country retreat.

The car drove along a one-lane road, defined by snow-coated evergreen trees. As the driver turned the car on a wide curve, Balkovsky could see the *dacha* ahead. It was a white, three-story house, with columns at the front door. It reminded Balkovsky of a CIA safe-house in rural Virginia, USA.

Torychenko was waiting for Balkovsky, as the car stopped in the circular driveway. They walked off together, leaving the driver and more guards at the house.

"You know, Alex," Torychenko began, when they were beyond ear-range of the others. "Our attempt against Professor Pemberton's daughter failed."

"Our people should've done it themselves," Balkovsky said, "instead of relying on those stupid American thugs. I was wrong for recommending that."

"It wasn't the plan, but the execution. No matter," Torychenko said. "Our people took care of them. We still need the information, though. The daughter's out of-the-question."

"And my agent hasn't reported lately," Balkovsky conceded.

"Alex, approach the Americans. Offer to cooperate."

"We'll find Pemberton!" Balkovsky said, angrily.

"Not in time, my dear Alex," Torychenko replied. "Our chance is with the Americans."

"You know my feelings. No matter what the President finds expedient."

"And if I ordered you to, General?" Torychenko asked.

"If I refused?"

"Don't force me to relieve you. Recall you were a lucky survivor," Torychenko said. "Alex, I know it's hard for you, but let go of the past. Contact American Intelligence on your advance trip. There's a senior American CIA official in Frankfurt now."

"Yes, I know," Balkovsky replied. He was angry—but also grateful.

He was thankful to the Deputy Minister, but would never tell him, even if Torychenko ordered him to do what he should already have done: Begin to trust again.

"I'm a good soldier," Balkovsky continued. "I'll follow my orders. But you still can't order me to like them, Yuri."

"I knew when the borscht was at stake you would bring it home," Torychenko said, patting him on the back. "These matters are too important to leave to politicians. Anything else?"

"Yes," Balkovsky said. "I've been receiving information and reports, fragments really, about a group called the East German Black Army. It's made up of former members of the National People's Army and Stasi. Other terror cells, too. I've got some evidence GRU is supporting them. Without approval, of course."

Torychenko asked, "Can I take this higher?"

"Not yet," Balkovsky said. "But my informants tell me the group's planning major disruptions. They may have even infiltrated the Bundeswehr."

"Any timetable?"

"October, November, we think. We haven't had time to infiltrate it yet. But I'm working on it."

"And on the seventh day you should rest, Alex," Torychenko said.

* * *

The early morning light over St. Louis was streaked with shades of red and yellow against a pale aquamarine and blue sky. The sun cast long, westward shadows over the city from behind the airliner, on its final landing clearances to St. Louis Airport.

Sam watched from her window seat. A purple haze hovered over the city and the Mississippi River. Arriving in a haze. *How appropriate*, Sam thought. She laughed sadly.

The trip was simple so far. Packed the night before. Up at 5 A.M. Caught a cab to Dulles Airport. Paid for the ticket and waited for the flight.

She saw no cover team, but was too tired to see much. Sure they were there, or hoping they were, Sam kept the compact in a sidepocket of a new purse. She had left her old reliable handbag in her dorm room.

The toughest part had been dissuading the male passenger in the adjacent seat from making passes. Sam faked drowsiness. His spouse, named "Denise," a blond woman in a blue suit, silk blouse, and silk scarf, was away from her seat a lot.

As they landed, Sam said good-bye to them and was surprised when he responded, "See you again soon?"

Daisy was at the gate, the same skinny, middle-aged woman with silver-golden hair Sam had left in Carbondale. But now she looked tired, very tense.

Her body spoke a language of discomfort when they embraced. Small innocuous blabber was what they spoke in the airport. On the highway, Sam cracked through Daisy's body jargon. Sam said, "Why the hell d'you get me back here?"

"Lots of reasons," Daisy replied. "Edward's got a viral infection. They're both upset about your father being away. You're the one they look to for support."

"Well, that's got to change, doesn't it? St. Louis-to-Washington's a hellacious commute. You didn't get me back here 'cause Edward's got a fever."

"Bob was here two days before I called you," Daisy sighed, "madder than hell. He wanted to know where Professor Tom was and didn't believe me. He called me a liar and wanted into the Stash. I'd not let him. The combination's been changed. And he didn't have too many kind words for you, either."

Sam said, "I did what I had to. What else?"

"I think the house's been burglarized, but nothing was taken. Things were out of place. I want to know more than Tom told."

Sam signaled with a slashing gesture across her own throat. "I could use a Coke," she said. "Stop at the next fast-food joint. I've got to shake loose of these dustballs in my head."

Daisy nodded and the conversation went innocuous again.

*   *   *

"So now you know what I know," Sam said, as she and Daisy sat in a mom-and-pop diner off the Interstate, drinking coffee. "Pa certainly told you more than he told me. It pisses me off he didn't confide in me."

"He didn't want to worry you," Daisy answered. "Don't be too cross with him."

"I'll be as pissed off with him as I care to. I *do* have the solace of knowing he didn't tell Bob anything," Sam said. "Pa's got faults, but he's not a genderist. I want to look in the Stash."

"I'll not let you do that," Daisy said. "You'll go off crazy like Bob did."

"After what I found in my room at school," Sam said, "I wouldn't be surprised. But you won't let me look through Pa's papers out there?!"

"What good'll that do?" Daisy asked. "Ignorance isn't just bliss. At a time like this, it's heaven. Nothing but bad can come from that."

It was stupid to dodge truth that way, to avoid pain, Sam thought. *She must get into The Stash, with—or without—Daisy's help. She wanted the truth about her father—whatever it might include.*

XI

Bill Washbourne's assistant, Denise, came into the upstairs sitting room. "Anything going on?" she asked Washbourne.

He was looking through a large video camera on a tripod. Beside it was a 35mm digital camera mounted on a telescope.

"Nothing, fortunately, Dee," he said. "How are Chip and Jack?"

"Bored, cold, pissed you gave the duty-teams off," she said. "There are limited options in a van."

She picked up a headset. The headphones were plugged into a bank of amplifiers, and reel-to-reel tape recorders, like an electronic spider's web.

"Developed a protector-complex, haven't you, Boss-man?" she asked, laughing.

"No, just my job, ma'am," he replied. "I don't want to explain another screw-up to Mr. McConneld. Besides, I got the feeling she's up to something."

"Sounds like more," she said. "You've got a crush on her."

"You're way over the edge on this call," Washbourne said. "Anxious to return to the steno pool, are you?"

"Me thinks the gentleman doth protest too much. You were coming on to her pretty heavily."

"Only having fun. After your trashing, I need a shower," he rejoined. "Keep an eye on things, will you?"

"A serious question," she said. "Between you and me and whatever microphone's monitoring us, how long's the Agency had this set up? It looks like a while before the father disappeared."

"We're on a need-to-know regime," he said, shrugging. "Somebody upstairs decided we didn't." He left for the bathroom.

"What's this 'we' stuff?" Denise murmured, as she adjusted the console.

* * *

"Feeling better?" Sam asked her brother, Edward, as he ate in his sick-bed. His usually scarlet cheeks were pallid, his brown hair a stark frame around his face.

"Daisy told me you're back," he replied. "I'm lots better than yesterday. I'm not throwing up. Why'd you come?"

"I heard you're sick, so I came right away," she said, nodding to his twin sister, Maureen, at the other side of the bed.

"Sammie got here this morning," Maureen said.

"Pa's away, and I knew you guys needed hugging," Sam said.

"I miss him," Edward said, between mouthfuls.

"Me, too," Maureen said, quickly.

"When's he coming home?" Edward asked, in an uncharacteristic whine. "Daisy doesn't know."

"I'd be telling you a grey truth, if I said I did," Sam said.

"Maybe a grey truth's better," Maureen said, "than no truth."

"That's another reason I'm back," Sam continued. "I recall how it was as a baby-teenager, after Mother died. I wanted to talk to you about things. Grey truths. And Mother."

"I miss her, too," Maureen said.

"You didn't know her good," Edward snapped. "Neither did I."

"I miss her all the same," Maureen replied. "And Sammie's gone most time now, too. And Bobbie. Daisy tries, but she's not Mother."

"Do you feel like everybody's abandoned you?" Samantha asked.

"It would be a grey truth," Maureen answered, "if I said I didn't."

"Well," Sam said. "You know there're times we don't want to hurt people. So, we tell them a grey truth."

"Papa told us one this time, didn't he?" Edward asked.

"Perhaps," Sam said. "I don't know for sure. If he did, it's to keep us from worrying while he's gone."

She felt sorry about her own "grey truths," but telling them they might soon be orphans was not possible. Pulling Maureen over to her, Sam hugged them both. A good hug, but so inadequate as a parent substitute.

"At times we have to do things we don't like or want," Sam said.

"Pa likes to go away," Edward said. "He likes to."

"No, he doesn't," Sam replied. "He has to sometimes."

"Nobody has to do anything," Edward said. "He wants to."

"I used to be angry at Mother for dying," Sam said, parrying his obstinacy. "Till I realized it wasn't her idea."

"I'm angry she's not here sometimes. Other kids've got mothers. We've only got Daisy," Maureen said. "I ask myself why Mother had to die."

"And Papa never even gave us a step-mother," Edward said. "But it's silly to be angry at Mother. She didn't want to die."

"Maybe it sounds silly now," Sam said. "It's a whole lot easier to know it's silly, than to feel it is. You each have a special friend in the other. If you feel lonely sometimes, call me."

"We're a damn good family," Maureen said, firmly.

"And we're not going to let some nuts with a bomb a long time ago destroy us," Sam said, before returning to her own room.

Out in the hall she saw Daisy, who handed her an envelope and whispered, "Bob's note to you."

Back in her room Samantha considered her Carbondale agenda. The "bug-safari" was first, squeezed into chances when she and Daisy could work unwatched; then, a search of her father's study and desk. Finally, there was "The Stash," the most important search she would do.

She had to get into it, though she did not know how—yet. Her father, the perfect documenter, would have left the new combination in "triplicate parchment."

Sam read the letter from Bob. It began with, "Samantha," a clue that it was full of anger.

> By now Daisy's told you my story. And she's told you I'm pissed off at all of you. But especially at you! Daisy gave me the Big Stall. When she didn't let me into Pop's Stash I knew something was wrong. I found the combination changed, too. I don't understand why Pa didn't tell me about it. As for you, 'Dear Sis,' I thought we had a special bro-sis trust. Guess I was wrong. You've been lying to me from the start, so why stop now?

"Thanks a lot, you bastard," Sam whispered, but she was crying inside, beneath the whisper.

Sam recalled what Mr. McConneld had said. More "greys." Big-time. It was one thing to tell a "grey truth," but didn't it hurt more when that someone deserved the whole truth?

> Pa's probably in some shady deal with his Association.
> Doesn't he care about himself? Or us? More *Kamikaze* missions, like for The Company. I used to get more insight from our deep-cover field guys than I'm getting from you. Do you know what really does cut, Samantha? That he didn't trust me enough to tell me as much as he told you. And knowing him, I don't think that was much. Something's better than nothing. Well, I'm not so thick as you all think. I've got my own sources in the Community. IF I CATCH YOU IN THIS IN ANY WAY, I'LL THROW YOU ON THE NEXT BOAT, PLANE, OR SHIP—ROWBOAT, IF NECESSARY, TO D.C. OR CARBONDALE!!! Bob

"Do the words 'tough shit' mean anything to you, Bob?" Sam said, as she folded the pages. Bob was as care-worn, in his own way, as she was. But he could be such a jerk, the "soul of un-tact."

Over the next two days, Sam and Daisy had a mixed relationship: warm when others were around, cold when they were alone. The search for "bugs" did go easily. Daisy abated as a "quasi-maternal *kvetch*." It took hours and produced an average of three or four different microphones per room, like the ones at school. Sam left them in place, but noted each location. After that, it was time for a visit to his study.

* * *

An aging male rock-star's voice detonated from the stereo speakers in The Professor's study. The radio was set on an FM "Classic Rock" station, running a special on late-60s "legendary groups," Sam's favorites. The singer was bemoaning a lack of fulfillment.

"Tell me about it, chum," Sam said, as she sorted through her father's desk.

Lecture notes from courses, financial information in numerous folders, thicker files of research and personal notes, were stuffed into the desk. It was a replica of Roscoe Pound's desk at Harvard Law School and engulfed the occupant in rotund mahogany.

The research and personal notes were at the bottom of a drawer, otherwise full of dated financial records. In their unhewn shape the research notes were an outline for a book. She did not recognize it. The next one?

He usually discussed topics with her, even before he did any research. Then again, nothing of this showed his usual cadences.

Sam listened. More lack of fulfillment in 1965! No change, either then or now!

Been there. Done this. *Can definitely empathize*, Sam thought.

The Professor's research outline followed a clear theme: the resurgence of fascism and of Neo-Nazism from the 1950s through the 1990s into the New Millennium. The U.S., Europe, Japan, and select, resource-endowed Third World nations were covered.

The notes referred frequently to "business transactions." There were dates or footnote numbers, but no footnotes in the file or the desk. She hoped they had not been stolen by the mike installers, and concluded, "they" had not searched well.

She went on to the personal notes. They were written diary-like, memoir-style, with entries being mostly undated.

There were also short stories, doodles, caricatures, drawings, anecdotes. She did not know her father wrote prose fiction. And poems. These interested Sam the most, more than fifty of them in free verse, meter, and limerick. *So*, she thought, *writing poetry was in her genes, after all.*

Everything in the file, including the stories, was numbered with Roman or Arabic characters, but not sequentially or logically. Numerals had been changed from Roman to Arabic or *vice-versa*. The predecessor designations were lightly crossed out in pencil.

Sam was repacking the desk when she noticed one drawer shallower than it should have been. She turned it upside down and found wooden flaps on either side, held in place with tape.

Excited, she pulled the flaps. A wood slab slid out. Inside the hiding space, she found folded papers. The top sheet had her brother's handwriting on it, while the other, much smaller one, held The Professor's script.

"Too bad," the first paper began. "Beat you here. Now you know how it feels. Left Pa's limericks. They don't help. HA! HA! A few other goodies. Sorry I can't share! You might find the first limerick interesting. ENJOY! Bob."

The limerick read,

Milli

Milli was a young girl of U.S. Nativity,
Who had rare sensitivities.
She could sit on the map
Of Nazis and flap,
And detect their Fifth Column activities.

I. Roman Numerals are so much fun.
    You never need more than ONE.
    Whether the line goes up or down
        this way or that,
    It's always a straight old slat,
    And functions and additions like ours
    Are none.

She assembled the personal and outline folders, while still listening to the radio. The new song was reminiscent of the first half of the twentieth century, the carnage, the dark-spiritual inspiration for the worst butchery in human history. Echoes of the future? Sam wondered.

* * *

"Deputy Director Simmons on Line One," Chuck Channing said to McConneld.

"I read your reports, Buck," Simmons said. "So did some people higher up the ladder. There's good news and bad news."

"Save the best for last," McConneld replied.

"The president's National Security Adviser's on the way to see you. He arrives tomorrow morning," Simmons said. "He wants a briefing from you and DIA, too. The White House's real concerned this hasn't been wrapped up yet."

"Christ, Mac!" McConneld said. "All I need is an ex-brass hat expecting royal treatment. What do they think we've got? A TV script ending happily six minutes before the hour?"

"He wants on-site briefing. Some hand-holding to take back," Simmons said. "The White House's scared blankless."

"You used to say the word 'shit,' regularly, before you became a Deputy Director, Mac," McConneld said. "He'll compromise my operations. Public attention and press follow him."

"You know his penchant for secrecy," Simmons answered. "In and out."

"Fat-mouthed brass hats give me hives, and you know that! Is that the good news?" McConneld asked.

"I haven't got there yet. The adviser's bringing someone with him, on 'indefinite visit' and a direct liaison with the White House."

"In other words," McConneld said, "I'll still be wet-nursing some political yes-man and stooge."

"'Stooge' is such an ugly word."

"Who's running this operation? The White House staff or me?" McConneld asked.

"You are," Simmons replied. " 'Cause if you fail, then they can blame you."

"That sounds typical of this crowd."

"Nothing changes. The liaison's a leftover from the first administration. The adviser liked him and brought him back."

"Does that mean this interloper has to go through me?" McConneld asked. "Or can he go over my head at whim?"

"It's your case, Buck," Simmons replied. "Do what you think's best. I'll try to back you up."

"What's this 'try' stuff?" McConneld said. "I've saved your ass plenty of times. I can't *wait* for the good news."

"Your team's being souped up. You'll have over 300 to 500 additional personnel. The DIA teams're beefed up again, too."

"Thanks," McConneld replied. "But no thanks. Shifts like

that draw flies. Overkill in bureaucratic bullshit, underkill in results. I can imagine headlines, now. 'Fifteen McBombs Ready For Use On The Loose.' I'm being set up to fail."

"The offer's not refusable, Buck," Simmons said. "It comes from the very top."

* * *

With his oversized briefcase and a clothes carry-on, Alexei Balkovsky was chauffeured to Moscow Airport, for a chartered *Aeroflot* flight to Frankfurt, Germany. He was traveling with a large Commonwealth of Independent States trade delegation, scheduled for talks with EU "working groups."

As the jetliner took off, Balkovsky thought about his "German Agenda." He would contact his spy-masters, network bosses, for leads to Pemberton, as a substitute for Torychenko's order.

He still hoped to avoid it. Nevertheless, he knew he would, in penultimate finality, obey, and meet his CIA reflection.

Balkovsky wondered about that reflection. *"Apolitical," a bureaucrat dedicated to the bureaucracy rather than to the ideology? A professional? Someone he could learn to trust? Or an ideologue with a shallow world-view?*

Balkovsky would work with this counterpart, would force himself. He would grant his trust like installment loan payments.

* * *

Samantha rubbed her neck and stretched. The alarm clock read 8 A.M. She had spent the night reading her father's notes, for clues to the new combination. Her father must have had mnemonic triggers, but she missed them. Ten hours and no lodestar.

THE STASH. It was the remaining place her father would have left explanations. Since Daisy had not changed her bunker-like stance, Sam had no formal "Plan B"—yet. *Trust in a "tolerant Deity?"* she wondered. Only the notes she read held "manna potential."

Mnemonics were always his style, so much so that Sam thought it was written on his DNA structure. He left himself trip-wires: punch-in-the-face closeness, only for those with enough savvy *not* to duck.

Her night of reading provided memory triggers of her own. Cryptic and obvious allusions to the family's overseas, nomadic days snaked through the notes. The Professor had spoken during those times of "business deals" or "transactions," without added definition. They were like the book outline without footnotes.

The limericks and Bob's removed pages were probably the crib sheets to this quiz. But with only half of it, the useless half at that, Sam was discouraged.

She reread the limerick page. She felt ambivalently embarrassed and honored. She recognized nothing of the "return uppercut" she believed was there, especially as she fancied herself the least-likely math major in the Western world.

Bob was right: no help. *The "goodies" he took? The bastard*, she fumed. *Was this her punishment from a less-tolerant Deity for "grey truths?"* She dozed for a while.

When she awakened, she resumed. She suspected the short stories were fictionalized versions of her father's experiences with The Cartel, like pastel water colors brushed over old, slimy oil paintings.

The poems were a different challenge. She worked on the sequence numbers for each verse, looking for patterns. No consistencies showed, though she found repetitious progressions. When she took breaks, she reread the poems, heavily political tomes, or romantic references to her mother.

Frustrated after hours of unrewarded decoding, Sam read the limerick page for the *ad nauseumpteenth* time.

There was "Milli." He used it for her mother, too. Perhaps he had meant the elder, or for Sam. Did it matter? It seemed too obvious a clue.

There were enough numbers, with the poems, to make combinations for the Fort Knox vaults. Did he mean those? All of them? The ones lightly crossed out? The replacements? The unchanged ones? The numbers in the limericks?

Sam converted the numerals to Arabic form, made lists of permutations, and planned to try them after dinner. With Daisy doing laundry and the boarders in their rooms, Sam walked to the barn, fifty yards from the house.

She took a flashlight, the lists, and notes with her. She was worried that whoever bugged the house might be waiting for her to lead him/her/it/them to her father's papers.

Sam disregarded those concerns. She needed to know what her father was doing. If someone tried to kidnap her again, she would scream enough to arouse the entire vicinity.

In the deep charcoal shadows of the barn, Sam kicked through heaps of hay to an empty horse stall at the back. She felt for the metal handle she knew was there.

When she found it, she pulled the handle upward with both hands. The flashlight made a quick parabola across the rafters. The straw fell away, as a metal hatch rose from the floor.

Into the round hatch opening, with the light pointed downward, Sam climbed, locking the hatch behind her. She descended the cylindrical stairs and turned on the light switch at bottom.

Before her was a four-room fallout shelter, 1950-ish, which came with the property and which her father had refurbished. He had the original hatch behind the barn concreted closed and buried, replacing it with the one in the stall. He also had "The Stash" built. It was a walk-in vault with steel door, and combination dial/ locking wheel, which enclosed a once-fifth room.

Sam felt it was, in the years following her mother's death, a metaphor for her father's life. Keeping his feelings to himself, he often worked alone there. Until this episode began, Sam thought of it as his "refuge against invasion by the world."

She tried her combinations on the vault door. Her frustration crescendoed when none opened it.

At a desk in the adjoining room Sam sat. Her handwritten pages were before her, the limerick sheet on top. She stared at it, reading the verses over and over.

"M-i-l-l-i," she said aloud. Nothing. She read the second.

"Functions and additions," she repeated. "There aren't any with Roman numerals! You admit it yourself, Pa!" she shouted.

There was the numeral "I" on the page, but it was the sole Roman character. *Could he have meant the letters on the page? The "M" could have been one, but there were too many other possibilities.*

"I'll never get this goddamn thing!" she yelled. Even the letters in the title were lowercase. "But what if . . . ?"

She capitalized the remainder, and slumped back in the wooden chair: all Roman numerals, except "LL."

"Additions! Of course!" Sam shouted. Then she recalled her father's love of puns, and worked the "Fifth" from her namesake verse, as a function. "Two fives for a ten!" she said.

Excited, she finished the math, and variations. On the fourth possibility, the unlocking wheel turned, and the door clicked loose.

"Ta-da!" Sam cheered, pulling the door open.

Inside, there were five, four-drawer filing cabinets, all olive-drab, where Sam remembered two before she left for school. The first two were the same tenants, still full of similar dust-carriers, as she found in his desk, plus family valuables.

The other three were shoe-horned full of notebooks, binders, and files. There were handwritten, typed, and printed-out pages, dating from the 1950s.

The notebooks, etc. corresponded to the numbers and numerals of the short stories and poems. Where a number had been crossed-out and changed, its matching file, binder, or notebook had been likewise renumbered.

In the top drawer of the third cabinet, Sam found a thick, looseleaf binder with the missing footnotes from her father's outline-manuscript. She read some, lengthy and detailed.

They identified Cartel members, employees, business dealings, operations, "special operatives," "contractors," and "suppliers": names, dates, places, events. All were specific to various "Special Operations," to "contractor(s)" involved, to other notebooks, files, and binders.

Enough to fry lots of folks, corporations, and conglomerates, Sam thought, as she read the files and notebooks.

Sam wondered why her father had not reduced these to computer disks. He had been resistant to using personal computers and eventually overcame that inertia, but still valued handwritten or -generated materials over electronic results. "Loss of electricity won't turn my hands off," she remembered him saying many times.

She scanned pages, then refiled them. In one binder, captioned "Open Cases," Sam read about terrorist operations and bombings during the 1980s and 1990s, in newspaper clippings, her father's narratives, and xeroxed pages. Lockerbee, Brighton, Bologna were among the subjects. The corner-points of her eyes overflowed. Parallel tear-streams trickled south to her chin.

In an accompanying binder, Sam found photographs. They were dated from the 1920s and '30s through the 1990s.

From more recent periods she saw pictures of the same man, clad variously in dress military uniforms (different countries), civilian clothes, and camouflage fatigues. Another man was dressed in U.S. Air Force uniforms of escalating ranks. She removed photos, placed them in her own folder, and returned the binder to its drawer.

She also found captioned folders and binders, whose contents were missing. Their subjects were provocative, even scandalous. Many people would have liked to have destroyed these, but she decided her father had removed those, no one else.

As she read, Sam realized there was too much for her to ingest. Nor did she want to know much. Better to be a very poor witness against The Cartel, she had decided. She wanted The Professor back, although what she had seen verified her intuitions.

Concentrating on material with 1980s and '90s dates, she discovered files with the titles of colors and many permutations of them; e.g., "Case Green," "Case Blue-Red," etc. Each had outlines, like sketches for novels or simulation board- or computer-games.

Sam found a manila envelope in a folder with neither number nor numeral. The envelope itself was marked "Old Friends—Must Stops on Holiday." It contained names and addresses spread all over Western, Central, and Southern Europe, as well as Central, East, and South Asia, and Central and South America.

She knew some of the names: longtime family friends. She found key envelopes, with the top halves of broken keys in them, with names taped to them. Stuffing the pages and key envelopes into her own file, Sam returned the envelope to its cabinet.

When she finished, Sam gathered her own thickened folders in a tight hug. She relocked the vault, and munched and swallowed the paper strip on which she had written the possible "M-I-L-L-I" combinations.

In a bottom drawer she had found one item and its accessories, but she left it there. It was her father's .45 caliber service pistol, extra clips and shells. It was the one with which The Professor had first trained her.

Even with her recent experiences, she knew she could not carry it like a toy. She was certain that names on the "Holiday" list could get her something appropriate, when the need matured. She hoped that maturation would not come, but . . .

Sam unlocked the hatch cautiously and climbed into the darkness. Quickly relocking the hatch, she covered it with hay. She was already planning when and how she would get to Europe—and how she hoped to lose everyone on the "Sam-watch."

In the dark quietude, Sam felt the cold fingers of surveillance surrounding her like a cage. A flashlight search of the barn did not allay or dispel her fears.

Next stop, United, Sam thought, as she walked back to the house to pack, with the files under her coat.

* * *

"Bill!" Denise called. She stepped to the love-seat where he was napping. "Our Ms. just phoned United!"

"So? She's going back to D.C. some time."

"She was doing more than that," Denise answered, "asking about overseas flights. Latin America. Japan. For November. She's on the 7:30 A.M. flight from St. Louis to National Airport tomorrow."

"I knew it!" Washbourne said. "She's up to something, and she's doing it from D.C. She probably found her father's files. We want those. United? Well, she's consistent, I'll say that for her. Get packed. Tell Chip and Jack to be ready at five A.M." He was pacing. "We'll get them on her flight. Call HQ-Langley to alert Kearney. Resume top-cover at National."

"Is that all?"

"Yes. I mean, no," he added. "While you're doing all that, I'll talk to this detachment chief about a little job I need done."

* * *

Sam leaned back in her seat, after watching St. Louis in a final, rush-hour light. The drive from Carbondale seemed shorter than before. Daisy, her chauffeur again, was reticent, sullen.

She suspected something, Sam thought. Had Daisy discovered her "Stash cracking"?

When the subject of whatever-should-they-do-about-Bob intruded into the atmospheric quiet, Sam repeated: more grey truths. Stick to the script.

"Ask me no questions," she had murmured, as Daisy hugged her tighter and harder than usually.

With the flight attendant's muzak-voice as background, Sam worked on her plan. The queries to United, she was sure, were overheard. It was time to do what "they" expected, but not quite the way "they" expected it.

Did that include J.D. Marshall? Yes, he would try to stop her, if he knew. That was too bad, too: she liked him—and she could use him along. But now she hoped her ruse worked.

Sam was tired, dozy. The few hours sleep before leaving for St. Louis, were multi-dream burnout, what she had always imagined an LSD "trip" to be.

As she heard the plane's engines, Sam remembered her father's files and the photographs. Those photos. Those photos. Those photos.

When she arrived at Dulles Airport, Sam cleared the plane and baggage claim quickly. In an airport limousine finally, *en route* to Georgetown she dozed—again.

* * *

"*Herr Baron?*" the secretary's voice on the intercom asked.

"*Ja? What is it, Elke?*" Otto von Markenheim replied.

"*The General's on your private line. Calling from Vicksburg,*" she answered. "*Will you speak with him now?*" Von Markenheim nodded.

"*Otto?*" The General asked. "*Sorry I missed your calls. Just got back from Tokyo and Osaka, about the project. I missed you in Frisco. Things goin' good at your end?*"

"*Very well, Walter,*" von Markenheim replied. "*Completion date's . . .*"

"*Our date's a good touch,*" The General interrupted.

Von Markenheim agreed. "*The teams're in dress rehearsals.*"

"*No hitches with our little whorehouse?*"

"*The specialists're on top of things,*" von Markenheim said. "*And the little bastards're fine, too, Walter.*"

"*Those fucking assholes're getting what they should've a long time ago,*" The General said.

"*On a similar note, mein lieber Walter,*" von Markenheim said. "*I have heard rumors about friction between your people and ours, secret arms sales without permission. 'New player' in the market can ship ANY NATO weapon in quantity, except APCs. Everything's got to be cleared with us. You know that. Nearly bungled operations were bad enough, but, if these're true, too . . .*"

"*Nearly bungled?! That junior-grade boy of yours filling your ear full of shit again? I don't know what you're talking about. I'm tellin' you; I'll take care of it. Whatever it is!*"

"*You'd better,*" von Markenheim said. "*We'd hate to close you down after all these years, even if you're not personally involved.*"

"*No bullshit from my end, Otto!*" The General said. "*I'll see y'all as scheduled.*"

"*You'll see me before then, Walter,*" von Markenheim replied, coolly. "*I want this laid to rest before the operation. You'll be notified when.*"

Von Markenheim tapped the intercom switch. "*Elke? Bitte, get me Herrn Doktor Hauptmann, on my special line.*"

"*Colonel?*" von Markenheim spoke softly into the receiver. He recounted his conversation with The General. *"Proceed as we discussed yesterday. We want him and his people ... Chastened."*

* * *

When Sam opened her eyes, she was lying in a scantily lit place, with fog or mist, stenchy and stifling, lingering near the ground. A strange aroma, and something else. Dense, overwhelming, stagnant and rat-like, like carrion. It reminded her of an antebellum, Virginia coal tunnel. Or a cave. Shadowy shapes rippled over the walls from flickering torchlights. Dark walls on either side of her, with deep ridges.

Sam felt something sharp cut her cheek. PAIN! A sticky wetness. She dabbed it to her lips. It tasted good to her. Her forehead and neck were wet and cool.

She got up slowly. Off-balance, she fell against one wall, then straightened. She staggered toward the torchlight ahead.

Through the darkness she looked for traces of the driver or the car. Wonderment at how she got there, not fear or panic.

Behind her only blackness and lost shadows performed for other lost spirits. Up ahead she heard a low-pitched, continuous moaning sound. Occasionally, a higher-pitched noise broke the monotone. She called out. No answer.

The torches were wooden clubs, tightly wrapped at their fiery ends with rags and hanging from iron brackets on the walls. In the dirt below the first torch, Sam found an olive-drab, long-handled flashlight.

Sam could see her clothes, in flickering yellow and gray light. They were smudged with dark brown stains. Her jacket drooped from one pocket.

She reached inside it and came out with a small-caliber pistol. Its safety was on. Sam put the .22 back into her jacket.

Continuing down the tunnel, Sam heard the moaning. It was no louder than before. It reminded her of when she had visited open military hospital wards.

The smell was still there, pervading her nostrils and taste buds. She spat, trying to be rid of it, but it returned stronger. Ahead, Sam heard squealing and scurrying noises. Whenever she shone the flashlight's beam, she saw no rats, though the scurrying sounds preceded her in the darkness.

Sam stayed close to one wall. She scanned the ground, seeing crushed gravel, coal chips, and a broken pick handle.

Laying beside it was what appeared at first as a large greyish-white stone. But, as she passed the "stone," she saw the front of it.

A sinister, full-teeth smile looked up at her, beckoning her to pick it up. Her perspiration froze. Frigid fear seized her chest. Another white stone, in the dirt ahead, lying on its side. Another after that, and another.

Nauseous and near vomiting, Sam ran up the shaft. The light from the flashlight bounced wildly. The moaning sounds became louder. When she came to a Y-shaped split, Sam took the left side.

She fell, smashing her face. Her earlier wound throbbed more. The flashlight flew from her hand and crashed against the wall.

Stunned, writhing, she upchucked violently, uncontrollably. Exhausted by the involuntary convulsions, she passed out.

When she came to, Sam took deep breaths and looked for the flashlight. She found it nearby. The pains in her knees rivaled her facial wound, but she went on.

The stench was as thick as before. She tiptoed toward the light from the right side of the fork up ahead of her. The moaning sounds were louder again. Was she in some remote sewer system and meant to die there?

She heard a scream ahead. At least there seemed a live answer to the moaning riddle. Startled, she felt her heart go cold again. The screaming voice was very familiar. It cried out, "Never . . . again . . . bastard!"

Sam hurried through the tunnel toward the cries, ignoring her pain. A second voice, shouting profanity in German. She reached the end of the shaft and leaned against the jagged wall.

Loud slaps on human skin sounded close by. Groans followed.

The light came from her left. She saw a room, partly obscured by the tunnel wall. Bright, artificial light washed over a grey, linoleum floor. Sam caught a fast picture of the chamber. The moaning, louder than it had been, chorused on.

In the room were five men. Three wore Nazi uniforms. The

other two were her father and J.D. Marshall, both stripped to the waist. Both were tied to primitive wooden chairs, arms behind their backs.

Their faces and upper bodies had bloody wounds. The Professor's nose was broken, Marshall's chest swollen with welts. Their eyes were the donut holes of bruised cheekbones and brows.

One of the Nazis, the only officer, had his back to her, as he interrogated the prisoners. He was dressed in a black *SS* or *Gestapo* uniform with a red, white and black *swastika* armband.

His Nazi companions were two guards, with *feld-grau, Allgemeine-SS* uniforms and coal-scuttle helmets. They were at attention, with M-16s slung on their shoulders. Sam could not see much of their faces. No one had seen her.

The officer slapped The Professor across the face. Marshall spat at the officer. One of the guards broke attention-stance and hit Marshall on the back of the head with his rifle stock. Marshall's head slumped forward for a time, then back up it came.

The Nazi officer spoke in German-accented English. "Who're your contacts in Vienna, *Herr* Pemberton?"

He punched her father in the abdomen. The Professor leaned forward, only as far as the bindings allowed. "And what did you pass to them about Case Green and Case Red? Or Case Blue?"

"Don't... know..." her father gasped. "No contacts... Swear."

"Soon you'll tell me all I wish to know," the officer said. "After, you'll beg me to kill you swiftly. But I won't!"

"Never," The Professor said, in shallow breaths, "give you... satisfaction... Not let you... happen... again!"

"Oh, but you already have," the Nazi said. "You and the Baron. The old fool thinks he's doing it all for the *Vaterland*. Your Cartel's been most helpful. Keeping us alive, nurturing us. You wonderful corporatist fools! Tomorrow-the-world isn't just a slogan anymore. It's here!"

Sam still could not see his face. Her anger grew redder with each second. She leaned back into the tunnel.

Reaching into her jacket pocket, she took out the gun, but it felt different to her, heavier and more bulky. It was her father's .45 automatic.

She clicked off the safety and pulled the slide back. Holding it firmly with both hands, she swung around the corner toward the Nazis.

Her father saw her first. His eyes widened through the swelling. The officer did not notice. He screamed another question.

"Freeze, asshole!!" Sam shouted at the *SS* officer.

He turned, surprised, then smiled. In that moment Sam recognized him from the photographs, the one in the camouflage uniforms, among others.

The guards quickly tried to unshoulder their weapons. One was faster than the other, but, before he could fire, Sam coolly squeezed the trigger twice.

The slugs caught him in the chest and forehead. He was thrown back against the door-sill behind him. His body slumped, and he did not move again. The gun clattered to the floor.

The second guard, seeing the fate of the first, lowered his M-16 carefully to the ground and held his arms in the air. His face was also familiar to Sam, but she did not place it.

The officer had been struggling with his own holster, when Sam pointed her pistol at him.

"Don't even consider it, slime!!" she shouted, "unless you want to be ant food tomorrow. It's your decision."

"I was wondering when you would join us, *Fräulein* Pemberton," the officer said, as he raised his arms slowly. "Very good! I always knew there was some of us in you."

Sam was surprised he knew her name. "Expecting me?"

"We know a great deal about you, *Fräulein*," the Nazi smiled. "You handle yourself excellently. You'll make a good addition.For a woman."

"Untie them!" she shouted. She felt raw, naked hatred and wanted a pretext to shoot this composite of disgusting human nature. She controlled her feelings, but was ready, if he gave her a reason.

"I said untie them!!" Sam clenched her teeth, and raised the pistol. "Addition to what, you filthy bastard?!"

"Pay NO attention!" The Professor said. "He's trying to get you off-guard!"

"Or what?" the Nazi asked, smiling contemptuously. "You'll shoot? I think not. You Americans've got no stomach for it. You won last time because of your industries and because we ran out of..."

"Move anywhere but over to untie them," Sam interrupted him, "and you'll get a real surprise from Santa."

"As I was saying," the officer said. "We ran out of men. It won't happen this time. We own your industries and our manpower's unlimited. Hate's a marvelous motivator. Put that gun down!" His swaggering arrogance was apparent. He stood with hands on hips, impatient at her intrusion.

"Perhaps you're right," Sam said, pretending to lower the pistol.

As quickly, she raised it, and released three shots, striking the officer in the chest, neck, and head. His eyes opened, as though his eye sockets would empty. His jaw drooped, and blood dripped from his mouth.

He staggered backward, falling over The Professor's lap. His body tightened, as he tried to get up, but couldn't. He went limp sliding down The Professor's legs to the floor.

Sam remembered the skulls in the tunnel. She realized that the moaning sounds had stopped.

Pointing the pistol at the surviving Nazi, Sam motioned to him toward the prisoners. She spoke to him in German, to untie them, but he stared at her.

"Untie them!" she said in English, finally.

"Yes, ma'am!" he answered in a Mississippi accent. "Don't shoot! Anything you say!" At that, he hurriedly untied her father and Marshall. They massaged their wrists and were breathing heavily.

"Want to join your friends?" Sam asked the third Nazi.

"Don't, Milli," The Professor said, as he pulled the pistol from the officer's holster.

The guard looked pale. "Just followin' orders! Please don't! Listen to your old man. Like you always do! Please don't shoot!"

"What're you doing here?" her father asked Sam. "I told you to stay out of this. Where'd you come from?"

"I'm saving you, Pa!" Sam said. "Come back with me! But

please tell me where we are."

"Under the crematorium," The Professor answered.

"They call them 'disposal chambers' now," Marshall said. He picked up the M-16s and stripped the dead guard's and the survivor's belts of their clips.

She saw her father's and Marshall's lips move, but she could not hear them.

"What's the matter with you?" she heard Marshall ask, finally. "We'll take him with us for cover."

"Where are we?!" Sam yelled.

"Later," she heard her father say. "Your shots alerted the others!"

"Which way?" Marshall said.

"Milli's way," The Professor said, "through the mine."

"Where's it lead?" Marshall asked.

The Professor shrugged. "Away from here."

He pushed the Nazi toward the shaft opening. Marshall took the prisoner. They headed into the tunnel, with Sam following. She remembered the flashlight at the entrance, where she had left it, and gave it to her father.

Sam felt weak. She hurried on, trying to keep up with them, but could not. The flashlight's beam became smaller. Her father called to her to stay close.

She could not see him or the others. His voice was clear, as though beside her, but he did not come back for her. She heard only her name, as the light finally disappeared. Blackness once more. Even the lights from the room behind her were off. Torches burned down to glows. Sam heard scurrying sounds all around her.

She called to her father. He answered, urging her to hurry, but he did not return.

When she bumped into the wall, she followed it slowly. The jagged edge cut her hands. She felt a corner, and came around it. There was bright light ahead of her. Sam ran toward it, shading her eyes. She heard automatic rifle fire.

When she reached it, there was silence. Sam found no other people. She came into the light, but it blinded her. She covered her eyes, and felt herself floating. She called to her father again, heard his voice, urging her to hurry, over and over.

"Pa!" she answered, still unable to see. "Come back! Please come back!"

Finally, she felt someone shaking her shoulders. "Oh, Pa! You came back for me!" she said.

As she opened her eyes, she could see again. The flight attendant with the muzak-voice was leaning over her and holding her shoulders.

"Ms. Pemberton, are you all right?" she asked. Sam sat up. Other members of the crew stood at her seat.

"We've landed at National," one said. "You must've had quite a nightmare."

"It's only started," Sam whispered, as her head cleared.

XII

On a dingy, rainy morning after his telephone conversation with Deputy Director Simmons, McConneld waited in a small Mercedes limousine. It was parked on the rim of a runway at *Rhein-Main* Airbase. Chuck Channing was with him.

An Air Force jet landed. Aboard it was the President's National Security Adviser and his very-abbreviated staff.

"Still so glum, Boss?" Channing asked.

The plane stopped taxiing. Its front door scooped open, and an Air Force truck-mounted staircase docked with its entrance.

"I'm tired of brass-hats and political hacks," McConneld said. "Besides, he's a marine with a brain. That's a dangerous combination." Channing laughed.

A retired marine general, the Adviser was sixty-ish and bald, about 5´6″ tall with a tree-trunk torso. His chief-of-staff was over six feet, younger, with a full head of chestnut-brown hair.

The Adviser and his aide rode in McConneld's car. His remaining four staff members were in the security cars, as the short convoy drove to McConneld's offices. Colonel Barsohn and Major Martin awaited them there.

Once in McConneld's office the ex-marine was less cordial. "Colonel, Major, this is Mr. Jack Kinnean, my chief-of-staff. He's a retread from Reagan-Bush."

"I've known Mr. Kinnean by reputation for quite a while," McConneld replied, coolly.

"I'm leaving him over here," the Adviser said, brusquely. "He'll be my liaison with you and Colonel Barsohn and will report directly to me. See he gets an office, and whatever else he needs. Stat. Understood?"

"With all respect, sir," Barsohn said, "to what end?"

"Hold it, Harvey," McConneld broke in. "I saw this coming. General, I'm sure he's good at his job, but he can't help us do ours. By the way, he's cleared, isn't he?"

"Still the wise-cracker, eh, Mr. McConneld?" the Adviser said. "Mr. Kinnean has top clearance. You knew that. I don't like your impertinence, Mister."

"It's not impertinence," Barsohn interrupted. "It's practicality, sir. I agree with Mr. McConneld."

"Let me finish, Colonel," the Adviser said. "Mr. Kinnean's function'll be to keep me up to date. Which means the President's up to date. The President's very concerned about this situation and wants it resolved. Favorably—and quick."

"Concerned?" McConneld said. "He should be shitting in his pants!"

"If you gentlemen can't get the job done," the Adviser continued, "he'll find people, who can. My smart-assed CIA man."

"Sir," Barsohn broke in again. "You're here for a full handholding. Don't go for our throats yet, OK? As for your assistant, unless he's got a direct line to the thieves or is clairvoyant, he's of no use to us."

"I'm not getting through to you, Colonel," the Adviser replied. "The President's in a . . . a delicate position. Mr. Kinnean's presence isn't for you. It's for the President and me. He's worried, which means I'm worried. Mr. Kinnean stays, till completion of the mission. Understood?"

"I know we've had differences, General," McConneld said. "But those were in your active duty days. I'm not comfortable with an uninvolved civilian observer reporting out-of-channels over my head. That's how I get sleepless nights, sir."

"Your sleeping habits don't worry me," the Adviser said. "And the past's still very much alive. But in the interest of doing the job, I'll make a deal. Mr. Kinnean clears everything through your office. Does that keep you and Colonel Barsohn happy?"

"Modestly satisfied, sir," McConneld said.

"Any problems with that *m.o.*, Jack?" the Adviser asked.

"None," Kinnean replied. "If you can live with it, I can, sir. But I expect my needs to be met. And, no censorship of my reports."

"I've never been afraid of the truth, Mr. Kinnean," McConneld shot back. "Unlike your bosses." The assistant seemed to him not to have lost any of his "Beltway arrogance."

"Well, that's settled," the Adviser said. "I'll take my briefing. Now. And forget the hand-holding. Leave it to my wife."

* * *

His favorite nightclub was more crowded than on a typical weeknight. Jaime was at his table with Jamael and Emilio, listening to the band and flirting with its lead singer, a brunette woman, with a five-octave range. In the smoke and Latin music, which bothered Jamael, Jaime was energized.

"Your Russian's late again," Jamael said. "Let's get out of here."

"It's just getting hot," Jaime said. "How d'you know she's not here?"

Jamael shrugged. "I haven't seen her."

"Check out the redhead I danced with. She's got a fur coat on now. At the bar," Jaime said, "in the red-sequined miniskirt and red thigh boots."

"That's her?!" Jamael asked. "She looks great! Did she pass you anything?"

"Not yet," Jaime answered. "We're going upstairs."

"I liked her hair natural. Blonde," Jamael said. "But don't tell her I'm attracted to her. She lives on that."

"Don't worry," Emilio said. "You're the farthest thing from his mind."

"Emilio," Jaime said, "if I'm not back in ten, go to the apartment. I'll be back."

He and the Russian agent left through a back doorway, with hanging beads for a door, up two flights to a room at the end of its corridor. The hallway and room smelled of aged tobacco smoke, urine, and disinfectant.

Jaime locked the door and pushed a chair under the doorknob. The woman hung her fur coat on a hook on the door. She handed him a folded envelope from her purse.

"Here's a contact name and phone number in Paris. A new player in the European market," she said, "no previous visibility, and we haven't infiltrated them. They're able to provide first-line American weapons, except vehicles."

"Not a Western sting operation on terrorists, is it? CIA?"

"Not as far as we can tell. We suspect they're connected to the bombs. Too much good, new stuff. That leaves out Southeast Asia or Afghanistan. Memorize the number and eat the paper. There's also a contact point to a mercenary I've done business with before. But he doesn't know I'm GRU. Better bring your physicist, in case."

"Why're you helping us? And how d'you know about her?"

"Good sources. And I'm helping *you*, not your rug-man."

"OK, helping me. Why?"

"I told you. The world's too rigid. I'm nostalgic for clearer times."

"That's not it," Jaime responded, tearing the envelope open.

"That's part of it," she said. "Come with me right now. I keep a house not too far from here. I'll show you . . . everything."

"Show me what?" Jaime asked. He softly ran his fingers through her hair, after she took off the wig.

"This," she said. She put her arms around him and kissed him hard on the lips. "I've wanted you out of your pants for a long time. I want you, before you go to Paris." She kissed him again.

He kissed her back, long, hard, and swept his hands along the sides of her dress, then under it. The feel of her body soothed him.

"Don't trust that bastard," she said, out of breath. "He's like his government. Treacherous."

"No politics now," Jaime whispered, as he kissed her neck. He helped her on with her coat. She stuffed the wig in her large purse, and brushed her hair out. They left from the room's sole window, down the rust-bubbled fire escape.

In the alley he checked if they were followed. The couple walked past a lone derelict, sitting in a doorway.

They found a cab a block away. During the ride, between excited embraces, Jaime thought briefly about Jamael, considering his own trust of the Persian agent. The Russian believed it was wrong-headed. Had he begun to think so, too?

* * *

"He's got to come back some time tonight," George said, "unless he's staying all night in this flea-trap."

"Look!" David said, quickly. "They're leaving."

"Set-up!" George said. "Take the cab and stay with them. Call the garage, when you've pinned them down. I'll join you later."

David left. George found a rear exit onto an alley.

The rain had stopped. But the air was thick, with wet fog. He watched for would-be muggers, as well as the Cuban agent.

George saw a fire escape, extended to the ground, apparently stuck there. He also saw a street person, dozing on a doorstep across from it.

He smelled the penumbra of a woman's perfume, trailing down the alley, but not from a cheap street-walker. A more classic, uptown scent.

The street-person, through an alcoholic haze, told George he had seen a man and a blonde-haired woman leave, minutes before. George slipped him a ten-dollar bill.

George called the garage on his cell phone, but David had not checked in yet. George walked to a coffee shop in an apartment building. After coffee and more phone tries, there was a message.

At the condominium, he found David in another taxi. Parked across from the front entrance, he and the driver, another colleague, were listening to conversations in the apartment.

"I looked in," David told him. "Our man hasn't shown yet. The physicist is there, though."

"Something big's on the way, if she's there," George said. "That's the first time she's been here, since they picked her up."

"Give us a warning on the radio when Rodriguez gets here," George said to the driver.

Minutes later George and David were on the roof, listening to the apartment's small-talk. The physicist was pacing and talking nervously to Emilio.

She was a short, thin woman, possibly in her later thirties or forties, with olive-skin and straight, asphalt-black hair.

"Easy, Doctor," Emilio was saying to her. "Lighten up or you're going to pop a vein."

"I haven't ever been on an operation like this!" she said. She took two quick draws on her cigarette. "I'm no lab flower. Been around. Moscow, Beijing. But never like this." She smiled and shook her head. "Cloak-and-dagger stuff." She stubbed out the cigarette and lit another. "Thought you said we'd be leaving soon," she said, through clouds of smoke.

Before he heard Emilio's response, George saw a call blinking on his radio. The driver said only two words, "Rodriguez incoming." The Cuban arrived moments later.

"Emilio," Rodriguez said. "Get seven seats on flights to Paris. Tomorrow or the next day. Split them in two, if you can."

"What took so long?" Jamael asked. "I hope she was good."

"Better than you can imagine," Rodriguez answered.

"Don't give me any of your *macho* bullshit," Jamael replied. "I can imagine a lot. What'd you get from her, except fleeting gratification?"

Rodriguez told Jamael and the physicist about his meeting with the Russian agent.

"What d'you need me for?" the physicist asked. "If you can make a deal?"

"My dear, naïve Dr. Pola," Jaime replied. "No one's going to sell us a nuke, for what we'd offer. Even if a sale occurred, you have to verify the merchandise."

"You want me along on the theft?" she asked, puffing heavily on yet another cigarette. "When I was recruited, nobody told me I'd have to do anything like this. I can't. If something happens to me—?"

"Nothing's going to happen to you," Rodriguez replied. "I've never lost a man, even in this country, and no one's more triggerhappy than Americans. If it didn't happen here..."

Emilio came in. "Got reservations on two flights out of Kennedy, Friday, the 19th. British Airways Flight 311 at 8 P.M. and *Lufthansa* Flight 108, scheduled to leave two hours later. Jaime and the doctor'll travel as husband and wife. Jamael and Juan'll be on the British Air flight. Manuel, Nadim, and I'll be on Lufthansa."

"Get Manuel and Juan," Rodriguez said. "They stay here tonight. You'll take care of your man?" he said to Jamael. He put his coat back on and headed for the door. "I've got an appointment. I'll be back."

"With that Russian whore?" Jamael said. "You shouldn't go. We should stay together till flight time."

Rodriguez walked back to Jamael and put his hand on the Iranian's shoulder. "Look, motherfucker," he said, softly. "It's none of your goddamned business. If you call her anything like that again, fuck cooperation. I'll cut out your tongue and stuff it up your ass! Then I'll tell your government you swallowed it yourself!"

He turned to leave. Jamael swung a fist at the back of his head, but Rodriguez anticipated it and ducked. He grabbed Jamael's arm and twisted it, flipping the Iranian backwards onto the floor. Jamael smashed against a coffee table. Rodriguez put a foot on his chest. "Why'd you have to go and do something like that?" He pushed harder.

"Jaime! Jamael!" Emilio yelled. "Break it up! No reason to screw up the partnership over a woman! We need each other!"

Jaime stepped back. Jamael got up slowly, gasping and rubbing his shoulder.

"OK," Jamael wheezed. "I'll watch what I say about your woman. I still think you shouldn't go."

"I agree with him," Emilio said.

"I hate to outrank you, *amigo,*" Rodriguez said. He left.

David and George reached the street, ahead of the Cuban.

"After we pin this guy down," David said, "we get seats on one of those planes. Preferably the *Lufthansa* one. I'll catch the shuttle to D.C. and meet 'Marbison,' tonight," David said. "I can contact Control, too."

"We don't need 'Marby' along," George protested.

David said, "I've got an idea I want to chew over with Marbison. You don't like him, but he's a good man. Those creeps have a heist in mind. We could use him."

"What's this idea you want to talk about with him?"

* * *

In a park in Northwest D.C. named Fort Stevens, a one-time Union Army fortification where President Lincoln came under Confederate fire, David waited for Marbison. David's late shuttle had arrived two hours before.

After exchanged phone calls with Control-West, in lieu of a "drop," he drove to the fort, as instructed. He already had his return ticket to LaGuardia.

He stayed atop the fort's hill, behind one of its earthen mound/gun emplacements. The Fall winds were wet and piercing, as the first hour ended, but still no Marbison.

David was tense. What he heard in Rodriguez's apartment worried him. The sounds of passersby caused him to reach for the pistol he picked up at the Glover Park townhouse on the way. After another half-hour he heard a whisper call his name.

"I made sure you weren't covered," Marbison said. "Now, what's so important?"

David told him that evening's developments. "Let's firm up a sure drop point in Paris. We'll neutralize them."

"Terminate, you mean," Marbison said. "I didn't think your crowd was squeamish about that, when necessary. 'We?' Is George his thrilled self about having me around?"

"It's my call," David said.

"I hope they're not quick finding the boomers," Marbison said. "I'll try to get over there ASAP, but I've got loose ends here to knit together."

"Here's the name and address of the hotel we'll use. It's a passable fleabag on the Right Bank. *Rue St. Antoine*, near the *Rue de Rivoli*."

They shook hands. "Good luck," Marbison said. "See you on the Right Bank."

"I look forward to it," David said. "Oh, there's one other matter I'd like to talk with you about."

* * *

"A messenger delivered this for you," McConneld's secretary said, as she handed him an envelope. Inside it was a sheet of paper with handwriting in red ink.

The note read, "Important information re: your stolen devices. Hotel Continental 6PM tonight. Alone. Wait at desk. Mr. Alfred Smith."

"Mr. Alfred Smith?" McConneld read aloud. He laughed and called Channing to his office.

"Whoever it is saw *The Maltese Falcon* too many times," Channing said. "Seriously, folks. It could be a hoax, or genuine. You're not going alone, are you?"

"Into a hotel room, yes," McConneld said. "But not *into* the hotel. You'll be nearby."

He checked his Baretta 9mm pistol. "The note read 'come alone,' nothing about being unarmed," he said, as he waited for his call to the motor-pool to be answered. "Get our people over there. You and I'll follow."

"Going with a 'wire'?"

"I considered it," McConneld replied, "but decided against it. I'll take a homer, instead."

Channing arranged the dispatch of agents to the hotel. He himself changed clothes to work overalls and boots.

McConneld and Channing took one car, while additional agents followed.

The hotel was an older accommodation, rebuilt after World War II. Its brochures described it as, "Old World comfort and *Gemütlichkeit*."

McConneld entered the lobby ahead of the others. Channing, carrying a toolbox, came in from a rear service area. McConneld saw the early-arrival agents around the lobby and elevators.

At the check-in desk McConneld was handed an envelope by the desk clerk. The note inside directed him to a room on the third floor.

On the elevator ride with McConneld were two other men, a casual boarder, and an advance agent sent by Channing. The agent remained on, after McConneld exited.

McConneld looked down the hall, as the lift doors closed behind him. Two men in service uniforms were loading laundry into a large cart to his left. To the right the corridor was empty. The room, #308, was down the left hallway, past the laundry men.

McConneld knocked on the door. There was no answer at first. Impatient, he knocked again. Still no response.

After a third tap, the door opened suddenly. All the CIA man saw was a figure, wearing a gas mask, shoot something into his face.

His next breath was short, too short. In those seconds his body relaxed, beyond his reach. He was falling... He felt himself scratched or tickled. He blacked out.

* * *

McConneld opened his eyes. He was on a sofa, and shaded his eyes from a lamp, until someone turned it away from his face.

"No ill effects?" a man's Russian-accented voice asked.

There was only a thick, dark shape in the space between lights. McConneld's brain cleared. He was in an apparent warehouse.

"I apologize for this introduction. But I wanted this first meeting between us *not* to be on your home court, so to speak."

"Who the hell are you?!" McConneld asked, angrily. "Where are we?! Show yourself!"

"All in good time," the Russian accent replied. "Please, feel free to move around. This is not an interrogation. We did take the liberty of relieving you of your weapon and your fountain pen, among other things, at the hotel. As I was saying, this first meeting, I wanted it on neutral ground."

"Show yourself, goddamnit!" McConneld yelled.

"As you wish." The emotion behind the voice was cool, subtly hostile, distant. The thick shadow came around a light pole and stood before him.

"General Alexei Balkovsky?!" McConneld said, "of the former KGB or Russian Intelligence. Which d'you prefer?"

"It doesn't matter. You recognize me?" Balkovsky said. "I'm honoured. But you may call me 'Mr. Smith.'"

"I've seen your photograph," McConneld answered. "I didn't know you had a sense of humor."

"Care for my autograph?"

"You lured me with damned effective bullshit. Why am I here?" McConneld asked, still angry.

"Mr. McConneld," Balkovsky said. "*I'm* here, because I was ordered. My superior ordered me to collaborate... I mean, cooperate with you. I was against it."

"Freudian slip, General?" McConneld asked. "You're earning your merit badge. Deportment and playing well with others, hmmm?"

"You're making it easy to disobey my orders," Balkovsky replied. "Please don't, eh? We'll both lose. I could've had you killed or done it myself."

"You were just doing your job, is that it?"

Balkovsky nodded. "As a professional, I expect you to understand that. It's nothing personal. Other sections of our respective governments *have* been collaborating. *I* don't trust yours."

"So, I shouldn't be put out, being gassed, snatched, and brought to these upscale, pre-World War I surroundings? My only question is how did this place escape air raids?"

"I understand your anger," the Russian said. His tone seemed less distant, perhaps warmer, if only a few degrees. "Please consider my position. I didn't want your people to know I was here. I couldn't walk into your office and announce my arrival, now could I?"

"That'd depend on your motives," McConneld shot back. "By the way, what was in that pen? That *was* you in my face?"

"Our standard nerve neutralizer, with temporary effects only. And you suspected it was I?"

"A hunch," McConneld replied. "After I read your note, I remembered a friend's comment about you. This isn't the first time you've used 'Mr. Alfred Smith.'"

"A friend of yours?" Balkovsky asked.

"It doesn't concern you now."

"Thomas Pemberton, perhaps?"

"Gifted insight?" McConneld asked.

"Obviously. The rest doesn't concern you now."

"*Touché*," McConneld said. "One son-of-a-bitch to another." They shook hands.

"I'm afraid all the same you must earn my trust," Balkovsky said.

"What've you got?" McConneld asked, his anger thinned.

"Rules of engagement, first," Balkovsky said. "I'll deal only with you, though I shall come to your office after this. To everyone else but you, I'm 'Mr. Smith.'"

"There're two others I've got to have along now," McConneld said. "Or at least disclose what you tell me."

"I don't trust the upper echelons of your government."

"Is that the position of your intelligence community?" McConneld pursued. "Or personal caprice and convenience?"

"The enemy we're facing has spies everywhere," Balkovsky said. "We've got good reason to believe they're resident in your upper reaches: the career ones undisturbed by cosmetic changes."

"One of the men I'm talking about's from DIA in Washington."

"That doesn't matter," Balkovsky replied.

"*We* know there's been penetration." McConneld said.

"This goes far beyond your dead major or his network."

"Speaking of having spies everywhere," McConneld said. "You're well-informed."

"Not as well as I'd like. That's why I'm here. Neither of these is German, is he?"

"Both Americans," McConneld reassured him, "my local assistant from the Agency and the head of DIA's investigation. Why?"

"Personal caprice."

"You've been ordered to help *us*, right? Your superiors are just eaten up with guilt for the past fifty years and want to make up for it?"

"What're you saying, Mr. McConneld? You don't want my help?"

"I want to know what's in it for your side?"

"My superiors want to help you recover the bombs," Balkovsky replied, "keeping them away from terrorists. My president wants to run up points."

"The old KGB's become the new Russian Boy Scouts? Telling me I've got to earn your trust, you've given me no reasons to trust you. What's in it for you? Not just a few aid bucks."

Balkovsky sighed. "There's deeper self-interest involved. Forget your newspapers about reforms and markets, even your own agency's estimates. Russia's still Marxist-Leninist under the national skin. You don't undo seventy years of political culture in one or two, or even fifteen years.

"Our military's looking for pretexts to take matters into their own hands. Any Western-based rightist uprising'll be used as a threat, or blown into one by our generals. In other words, our internal and external survival is at stake."

"You and your people don't trust the 'new Germany'?"

"I didn't say that, though that term might conjure up other images for some of our people. I said 'personal caprice.' Call it as you like," Balkovsky said. "I don't trust them."

"So far you're not giving me a reason to trust you."

"My dear Mr. McConneld," Balkovsky said. "I've offered my, I mean, our help. If you don't want it, I'll go back to Moscow. There's no time for us to be vodka-partners."

"Your terms're unacceptable," McConneld replied. "If your info's as good as you say, I've got to disclose the source, discuss it with those two special exceptions."

The Russian was quiet. Finally, he said, "Sell them to me. Here. Now. Persuade me I can trust them—And you, ultimately."

McConneld spent the following hour representing his colleagues, like a defense attorney would to a jury. He argued, cajoled, used humor. When he felt his appeal was emotionally exhausted, he looked up into the skeleton of raftered darkness.

"Very well," Balkovsky said. "You're principled. I respect that. Bring them in. But give me your word they'll treat what I say in absolutely strictest confidence. Arrange for my clearance to your offices, as 'Mr. Alfred Smith.' Not a word to your superiors here or in Washington and no one from the German Government."

"I've got no superiors here," McConneld replied. "Only a pain-in-the-ass I avoid anyway. It'd help if you gave me something on account."

Balkovsky walked from lighted view, returning with documents he handed to McConneld.

"This is the man, who led the raid on your installation," Balkovsky said. "Johannes Krattmay, also known as 'The Colonel.'"

"Among other names. He's got more aliases than some Hollywood actresses have ex-husbands," McConneld interrupted. "He was i.d.'d from something on-site."

McConneld told Balkovsky about the dagger. "We don't know where to find him. He dropped out of sight, after The Wall came down."

"After he stopped working with your side in Africa," Balkovsky smiled, "he's been running a special operations unit for Pemberton's Cartel. He was on their payroll, while on yours. He answers to Baron Otto von Markenheim, but they don't claim his exclusive services."

"What's your evidence?"

"Good sources," Balkovsky replied, without looking up, "I can't disclose at this time."

"Someone inside?"

"Neither confirm nor deny that," Balkovsky said.

"Non-denial denial, Nixon-style," McConneld said, laughing.

"It's difficult to prove the connection to the Cartel. They are too well insulated from The Colonel and his unit."

"It doesn't matter—yet. Save anything else for my office. I'll expect you there tomorrow night. I've got meetings before that. About eleven P.M.?" Balkovsky agreed.

"I'd say we're finished for now," McConneld said. "Could your people drive me to my office?"

Balkovsky said, "I'm afraid you'll have to be blindfolded. I'll return your pen and weapon when I visit you tomorrow."

"In other words," McConneld said. "You trust me, but only to a certain point?"

XIII

"Jesus!!" Samantha cried, after pushing the door to her dorm room open. Her spirits dropped more quickly than the luggage.

Fear passed, giving way to anger at this latest affront, at her father, at "others." Her room had been searched, with a visible absence of civility, or finesse. Drawers were rummaged and dangled on the edge or were already on the floor.

Also from the floor, aging rock stars and their groups seemed to grimace up at her from CD covers amidst pleats, hems, and blouses. Books and papers topped the piles like icing or whipped cream.

"Lousy bastards!" she cried, slamming the door.

"They" must have known she was gone. How? Did it matter? The hall traffic during the day was often like an Interstate through Death Valley, so anyone could have got in. Someone from the dorm? More paranoia and anger.

She considered calling the police, but knew she could not be candid about the "why?" or the "who." They would never solve it, and probably not try very hard. They'd tell her she was lucky she wasn't there. Just the facts, ma'am. She laughed sadly at paranoia's narcosis: victimization.

The memory of the dream lingered between the front and the back of her mind. Her father. J.D. Marshall. The Nazi officer. The Nazi soldier with the Mississippi accent. *CLICK! CLICK! CLICK!* Like exposures through a camera lens. The Nazi officer and his man. Familiar. Frightening, that they were.

The officer's face flashed into her mind again. His words returned. Phrased fragments, like the leftover chalk marks on a blackboard cursorily erased.

Her father, The Cartel "nurturing them over the years." "Case Green," "Case Red," "Contacts in Vienna." "A bit of us in you," the most frightening.

Dreams were wishes, according to Freud. Was she wishing

The Cartel had helped the Nazis? Her saving her father. That was the wish. Saving Marshall? Was that it? Shooting Nazis?

Enough "investment opportunities" for it. "Investment opportunities." How typical that language was.

She recalled her memories of youth, of childhood. The Professor telling her of his father's "Anti-Fascist Work," his OSS days. The Nazis. *Willful, deliberate.* Murderers.

But the war had not ended it, her father had said many times. She had not understood then, not till she saw his files. Had he done business with escaped Nazis over the years. Then Neo-Nazis? She felt betrayed.

That passed, too. It was only a dream. But dreams were wishes, according to Freud. Oh, what did he know about anything?

Her family's history was anti-Fascist and anti-Nazi. Her father had spied on them, she decided. He was a "secret agent" all those nomadic years. Talk about an oxymoron: him as a "secret agent." She resented her father's compartmentalization of his life: the relationships he never disclosed.

Something else from the Nazi officer rebounded. "A little bit of us." Ends justified means? She had not thought so before, but now? Was it her cool, quick manner on the trigger, her willingness to shoot?

But that was in the dream. The bastards had deserved it! No, she rebuked herself. No one deserved to be killed.

In the dream it had been easy. The coldness of the pistol grip. Steady the weapon, like her father had taught her. But that was firing range or trap-shooting stuff. Could she shoot or kill another human being? Even a bastard?

GUNS. Filthy things. Hated them. Reluctant to learn. Last resort, her father reassured her during the hours of lessons and practice. Was she a killer? Willful, premeditated, deliberate, like a . . . a . . . a Nazi?

She hoped not. Hoped it would never be easy for real. Wished not. Dreams were wishes. Damn Freud!

"I wanted to see if you were back," Regina Foxwirth said, as the door opened. Her words trailed off. She seemed controllably surprised, artificially shocked. "My, my. What happened?"

Perfect Regina. Her streaked-blonde hairs locked in place, with dress and makeup to match.

"What's it look like?" Sam asked, perturbed at this *haute couture* Doll-in-Chanel-pumps, trying to be cooler, more sophisticated than everyone else.

"As though you've been burglarized," Regina said, dryly. "Have you called the police?" She came in, looking pained at stepping around the wreckage of Sam's belongings. "Any clues? Anything missing?"

"No, on all counts," Sam replied. "Did you notice anyone unusual around the hall while I was gone?"

"Not really," Regina shrugged, effortlessly. "Where were you, by the way?" Sam told her.

"Perhaps one of the maintenance people did this," Regina said, shivering a haughty shiver. "They're so untrustworthy. And dirty, too. I saw a telephone man repairing the pay phone down the hall a few days ago. Funny, I didn't know the phone was broken. But he didn't look like a burglar."

"And what does one look like?" Sam asked.

"You know," Regina said. "Not one of us."

"I don't have time for your personal prejudices!" Sam said. "More stupid, obnoxious comments, and I'll suspect you, Regina!"

"What did I say?" Regina asked.

"Look, Regina," Sam said. "I hate to be rude. But if you're here to help, fine. Otherwise, I don't have time to chit-chat."

"I should love to, darling," Regina sighed, exhaling the words in her inimitably breathless, I-can't-be-bothered-with-such-mundane-things-way. "But I can't stay. I'm happy you're back, Samantha. *Ciao.*"

Sam went to the door. She watched as Regina and her disgustingly perfect figure and hairstyle went back into their room.

At Regina's door, Sam heard her speaking French rapidly. When Regina's footsteps came closer, she ducked into her own room, and watched Regina leave.

Sam examined her door. There were scratches near the keyhole, perhaps fresh, perhaps vintage.

She continued her clean-up, and checked for anything missing. All her quasi-valuables were present, but the letter and postcard from her brother were missing. She needed a secure place for her father's papers, but not for long.

Sam planned to leave for Europe within the week. Her mind wandered back to "who." She recalled Regina's reactions.

No, Regina would not "dirty" her hands with something like this. She would be the only spy, with a servant to do the messy work. Besides, what possible reason or motive would she have had?

* * *

The door to the shop, along the C&O Canal, opened. Regina Foxwirth, her sable coat over her shoulders, passed her contact.

"*You took too much chance calling me on your own phone,*" he said to her in French. "*Such short-order cooking. The FBI's got many ears.*"

"*You're expendable,*" she replied in French. "*I wanted guidance—immediatement. I searched, as you suggested. All I found were these.*" She opened her *Chanel* bag and removed a picture postcard and a letter.

"*From the father?*"

"*Non,*" Regina said, exhaling a bored French sigh. "*But Professor Pemberton's mentioned.*"

"*You shouldn't have taken them. She knows now why the search.*"

"*After what I did,*" Regina smirked. "*She can have no doubt why . . . And what I overheard her telling that nosey so-and-so McGonnville.*"

"*In typical fashion,*" the contact said, sarcastically. "*You chose the wrong time. Papa won't be pleased. If I tell him.*"

"*I can't go back in there,*" Regina replied. "*I was following your suggestion, you arrogant bastard!*"

"*Temper,*" he chided. "*Where's that expensive toilet-training and breeding your lieber papa's lavished on you?*"

"*I don't duel with an unarmed man,*" Regina hissed.

"*You should find a new writer. Your lines need freshening.*"

Regina picked up the shop's telephone. "*Call mon pere. Right* now," she said, holding the receiver out toward him. "*I doubt he'll fault me for being overanxious, but he hates failure in hirelings.*"

The contact hung up the phone. "*Jousting gets us nowhere.*"

"*It's good you recognize that,*" Regina replied, triumphantly. "*If Miss P. sneaks off and I follow her, she'll know it. I had an uncontrollable urge and picked her plane? I can only disguise myself so far . . .* "

"Dressing down might help," he said. "*How about a new logistique? I'll take over outside surveillance. The same plane or train. Once I'm patterned, I call you.*"

"*How'll you know when she's moving? She'll hardly announce it in her room. Campus Security's been tighter since that rape attempt on campus. I don't suppose you . . . ?*"

The contact gave Regina a cold glare.

"*Well, someone like you might set off alarms,*" Regina retrenched.

"*We'll have to get a tracking device like this on her. You'll arrange it.*"

He showed Regina a small electronic homing device. "*Preferably in clothing she's likely to keep with her.*"

"*She wears this one blue skirt at least twice a week,*" Regina said. "*She's wearing it now, in fact. But I'm no seamstress.*"

"*Repetition of clothes isn't a problem for you. I do have a plan,*" he smiled. "*Now, if I have your attention, sans whip, I'll outline it for you.*"

* * *

After restoring ordered chaos to her room, Samantha made her list of things to do. Airline reservations, train passes, money, travelers' cheques, maps. A safe place for her father's papers. She had already been given Incomplete grades by her professors the previous week. And pack, if only a few things, besides the "road map," from her father's papers. In Europe she would buy whatever else she needed.

She walked the suitcase to Liz McGonnville's room. Liz was not there, but her roommate was. After a short gab session, Liz joined them.

Sam felt relieved the case would be secure and realized she had not eaten since a rubber-eggs breakfast on the plane. Sam and Liz left for lunch at *"Chez* Cafeteria."

While they were wandering through the serving area, Regina Foxwirth and her plate of saucy lasagna ran into Sam, making a tomato-cheese-and-pasta pancake down Sam's front. Regina's shoes only suffered a splatter or two.

"Oh, Samantha!" Regina cried. "I'm so sorry! Look what a mess I've made! I'm so sorry!"

"Regina!" Sam said, suppressing her anger, trying to substitute pity for it. "My good skirt!"

"I said I was sorry," Regina whined, with a blush, a full-facial, purple blast of embarrassment, even through the perfect makeup. *So nice to see Miss Perfect wasn't*, Sam salved herself.

Regina returned with moistened dish towels and a ream of paper napkins.

"I'll make this up to you, Samantha," Regina continued, as she and Samantha dabbed at the orange stains.

"You don't have to," Sam said, still hiding her feelings. "I can do my own laundry."

"No, no, I insist," Regina added. "I loathe being so vulnerable or indebted. I'd like to dispense this as quickly as I can."

Ah, Sam thought. *The "real" Regina reappearing.* Sam's anger nearly overwhelmed the sympathy, but she controlled it. She did not want to destroy what was probably Regina's only considerate impulse of the entire Fall.

Sam went to her room, showered and changed clothes. The dirty clothes left with Regina.

Back in the cafeteria, Sam could not find Liz. She settled for a hurried lunch by herself, feeling less angry than before. The accident, she had decided, would delay her escape, until she could take her "lucky" skirt with her, one her father had given her. Times like this required superstition.

However, she would not wait too long. It was now Monday. She hoped to have left by Wednesday. Now she pushed that to Friday, depending upon flight availability. Even "lucky" skirts were replaceable.

* * *

In a phone booth in the Student Activities Center, near the U. Medical Center, Sam listened to the travel agent on the other end confirming her reservations. "Ms. Pemberton, you and your sister-in-law're confirmed on Metroliner to New York, leaving Union Station this Friday at 8:45 A.M. October 19th. There will be a limo waiting for you there." And you two're booked on Flight 235 to London-Heathrow from Montreal at 7:45 P.M., same date," the smooth, automatic voice continued. "You'll have a plane change at Heathrow, and Flight 235 will end in Paris."

Sam would return to London that same day, Saturday, by Channel boat-train or hovercraft. She did not like the "Chunnel." She would push on to Oxford the next day, for the first stop on her father's list: "Must-do's on holiday."

"Shall I place both reservations under your name or hers?" the agent asked. "With such short notice I'm sorry you're not eligible for our discounts. Remember to bring your identification."

Sam replied, "It's a spur-of-the-moment visit to my brother. Put them under my name."

Sam still had to get to the bank. She would pay for the tickets in cash. Then to National Airport for a New York shuttle to purchase rail passes, at the midtown Manhattan office that sold them.

Thank goodness for AmEx, she thought, as she glanced at the credit cards in her wallet. But she would only use them for cash advances, before Europe.

All was in place for her escape and chase to Europe. She was worried about so much time in Montreal. Perhaps Mr. Washbourne would catch up with her.

Sam made other phone calls quickly, among them an "appointment with radical departure." She left the telephone booth, for the bank, other errands, and, eventually, National Airport.

* * *

In a small, side-street café off the *Champs Elysees* in Paris, Jaime, Emilio, and Jamael waited for their first in-person contact with the arms seller, whose number Jaime's Russian lover had provided.

It was late afternoon, nearly 5 P.M. Jaime and the others had been in Paris since that morning, when they had checked into a large *pension* on the Left Bank.

After Emilio's arrival, Jaime called the phone number. The French-accented, male voice directed him to the restaurant, with contact by 5 P.M. Jamael had reached his own resident agents, who provided them with pistols and ammunition.

When Jaime and the others reached the café, they found a table reserved for them. As usual, Jamael was antsy, anxious.

While the three talked, Jaime recalled his Russian lover's comments. Five o'clock passed, no contact. The early dinner crowd began to filter into the place.

"It looks like your woman's wrong," Jamael said. "I told you, you shouldn't trust Russians."

"We settled this back in New York," Jaime said.

"*Monsieur Rodriguez?*" a waiter asked. "There's a phone call for you. Take it at the bar over there, *S.V.P.*"

"Rodriguez?" said the same caller as before. "Go out front, and through the alley. Wait there."

Jaime and the others emerged in evening's darkness and the high-walled alley.

As they turned the corner, they were seized and held at pistol-point by three men. The men blindfolded and shoved them into a corrugated panel truck, pushing them to the truck bed.

"Search them and don't miss a spot!" a German accent shouted. "Make sure we're not tracked. Here, overalls and boots."

With their jackets, shirts, and shoulder-holsters stripped from their bodies, Jaime and the others were wrestled into coarse overalls and high, ankle boots.

"You'll get your things back," the German accent said, "when we're through with business. You amateurs."

Jaime felt the truck stop, a door open and close. Cold air blew into his face. Then the truck started up again.

"My apologies for the treatment, gentlemen," the same French accent from the telephone, said in English. "The *Sureté*,

British Intelligence, and the CIA have undercover operations everywhere. Our employers are nervous types."

"T'would be too bad," the German voice interrupted, "if you're trying to 'sting' us. We'd be obliged to kill you."

"But if you're genuine," the French voice continued, quickly, "we shall do business, as long as your cash is good. Which of you is Rodriguez?"

Jaime sat up. "These're my associates."

"You're the leader, *non?*" the French voice asked. Jaime nodded. "We deal only with you. My friends'll keep your colleagues entertained." He laughed. "We'll speak more, after we've reached our destination."

Jaime heard city sounds for a while. Sharp turns rolled him side-to-side, like a cigar, bouncing into Jamael and Emilio, or the truck side.

As they drove, Jaime counted seconds and minutes in rough time. He guessed they had been driving forty-five minutes, when the sounds outside reduced to what could have been countryside.

"For Christ's sake, aren't we there yet?" Jamael asked at one point.

"*Herr Rodriguez,*" the German voice said. "Please instruct your man we'll answer no questions."

Jaime heard Jamael grunt, but he did not speak for the rest of the ride.

After what seemed to Jaime another hour, he felt a hard turn. Distantly he heard a turbo-propeller airplane's engines getting closer. When the truck finally stopped, the airplane noise was very loud.

Hands grabbed Jaime and led him from the truck. The plane's noise deafened him, its winds blowing against his side.

"Step up," a new voice said in a cockney accent. Jaime walked up steps, as other hands pulled him into the plane. He was pushed into a seat.

"Can I take off this blindfold now?" Jaime asked, loudly. "Emilio? Jamael?"

"Don't worry about your friends, *monsieur*," the French accent said. "You're making this trip alone. We'll tell you when you may take off the scarf. Enjoy our friendly skies."

Jaime counted time again during the flight. There was turbulence as the plane rose and fell. When he sensed the landing cycle in progress, he thought they had been flying for more than an hour. Seemingly ten minutes later they were on the ground.

More hands got Jaime up, turned him around, and shuffled him down the aisle. Across a smooth runway he was led, and spun around, before being shoved into a car, between two other people.

The air was colder, thinner than Paris. The pavement was slippery. Ice crunched under his boots. He was still dizzy as the car drove off.

"Not much longer?" Jaime said, trying to chuckle.

"No comment, *monsieur*," the French voice replied from his right. Its tone was colder than the air outside the car.

Jaime resumed counting. He listened for noises, any hints. The car's interior shielded riders well from the outside. Then, as though cued to happen as Jaime felt most frustrated, chimes sounded, far off at first, gradually getting louder.

They repeated a tune, a Christmas song, whose title Jaime could not remember. The bells stopped, then began anew.

This he recognized as *Silent Night*. *A little early for a Christmas medley*, Jaime thought. As the bells faded, Jaime heard a third familiar song.

* * *

It was after midnight when Samantha arrived back at St. Mary's Hall by taxi. The two shuttle flights had not taken as long as her rides to midtown Manhattan and back to LaGuardia.

She traveled light, not dressed up: jeans and a blue blazer, coat over the shoulders, with a small purse and one slight appearance alteration, a red-haired wig she bought earlier in the day before leaving for New York. She loved New York, to visit, but knew she could never live there: too frenetic, even if chaotic order.

Back in her room, Sam checked her voice mail. There was a message from Mr. Washbourne. He wanted her to call him as soon as possible.

She wondered if he could know the compact was in Liz's room, if she ignored the call. If she returned it, she would have to lie, beyond "grey truths." Yet, she was curious.

A quick trip to Liz's room retrieved the suitcase. Liz was not there, but her roommate, studying for a midterm, once more was. Back in her own room with the case, Sam checked it. Nothing from Illinois was missing.

She must find a safe place for the papers, until her return. Before she left for Montreal, she would send the stuff to a Jesuit priest at the University, a friend of her father's, with directions to turn it over to "the proper authorities in the event of my death." It sounded goofy, clichéd, she knew, but clichés could still be good ideas.

*　*　*

The alarm went off in Liz McGonnville's room at 8:25 A.M. that Tuesday morning. Her roommate got up and saw Liz's undisturbed bed. Liz apparently had not been home at all, even after Samantha Pemberton's visit. Studying late, she wondered? That guy she had been seeing socially? Both?

When she was ready for her 9:15 A.M. class, she was fingering through her purse, and came across a compact she found in their room the previous evening. It was a nice one. Maybe she would not bother Liz about it after all.

*　*　*

"Samantha?" Regina was calling to her from the hall that Tuesday afternoon.

"I tried last night," Regina said, after closing the door behind her, "to return these to you."

In one hand, she held Sam's skirt and blouse, on hangers and covered in dry-cleaner's thin, clear plastic. The other held a large Saks Fifth Avenue shopping bag.

"Where'd you get it done so fast?"

"My secret," Regina said. She hung Sam's clothes on a closet doorknob. "Missing you allowed me to finish a little shopping."

She opened the bag. "For you," she said, handing Sam two gift-wrapped boxes.

"Oh!" Sam said, feeling quite shocked. "What's in them?"

"Stop asking questions," Regina said. "Open them. I hope they fit."

Sam found a new *Chanel* white blouse and navy-blue skirt in one box and a large *Chanel* purse/tote in the other. "Tasteful, but not gaudy," she said. "But you really shouldn't have, Regina! This has got to be the biggest *Chanel* bag I've ever seen! I can't. What you did wasn't THAT bad. These must have cost a fortune!."

"I insist!" Regina said.

Sam saw Regina's anxiety was genuine. *She was caring, after all*, Sam thought. *It took spilled lasagna to bring it out.*

Regina looked down at the floor for a second. "I wouldn't think of letting you say no," Regina replied, slowly looking at Sam. "I don't like being vulnerable. Besides, now you have two good skirts. In case I get clumsy with food again."

"I really can use these, especially the bag. Now," Sam caught herself. "I mean, since I've got so much to lug around. For classes. This'll be great!"

"You're babbling, Samantha," Regina said, returning to her typical manner. "All I want is a promise you'll use them."

* * *

The truck's taillights were visible through the darkness about a hundred yards ahead of them. Through downtown Paris in late afternoon traffic, they had driven, after watching Jaime Rodriguez and colleagues thrown into a truck.

The truck stopped once along another Right Bank sidestreet. The driver threw something into a parked Citroen. Then the truck hurried off.

Once into the countryside the truck turned onto smaller roads, leading them southeast along the Seine. They followed the truck for two hours, when it turned and disappeared.

The taillights reappeared, between high hedges on what appeared to be a private road. As they passed the entrance,

David read a sign in French, *"Private Property—No Public Egress."*

George parked the car in a grove of trees beyond the entrance. They could still hear the truck, and a new sound, too. "They're flying out of here," George said. "Shit! And I thought this was going to be easy."

"Watch for guards. I'll call our transport. Come in, Ari. Over," David said, waiting through the static for a reply. He repeated the call.

"This is Ari. Over," a voice crackled from the microphone.

David answered, "Do you have them? Over."

"Roger. Small airfield. Couple kilometers, your position. Down in five minutes. Over."

Winds swept the trees as a jet-equipped, civilian helicopter, with inside cabin behind the cockpit, landed in the middle of the road and hesitated long enough for George and David to board it.

It gained altitude, but waited carefully for the other plane to take off. It was a short while before the propeller-driven plane started away. David and George changed their street clothes for black overalls and boots.

David squeezed between the pilot's and co-pilot's seats. "You still have them?" he asked the pilot.

The pilot nodded. "They're faster than us without the turbo. I've got them on radar. These American night-vision goggles're handy."

"Heading?"

"Southeast to east-southeast at one-four-five," the co-pilot answered.

David slid back into the passenger compartment and sat down with George, who was working on two unloaded Uzis without rear stocks. Magazines for them were on a seat beside him.

"Uh-oh, sheriff," David said, in his best Walter Brennan imitation. "Looks like there's gonna be a shootout. You got enough artillery for it, son?"

George smirked, but became somber again quickly. "Wherever these bastards're going, we'll need more people."

"Eventually, but not tonight," David said. "They're feeling Rodriguez out. The trick will be fouling him up, without letting the sellers know. If that happened, they'd move the bombs."

George shook his head and kept working on the Uzis.

David removed a small, compact Geiger counter from a box. He tested it with the phosphorescent elements on his wristwatch.

Sitting back, he remembered what they heard in the Cuban's apartment. He hoped that Marbison would be joining them soon, along with whatever personnel he could manage, if any.

He also scratch-planned the next step, including whatever personnel he would request from his European Control or his service's headquarters.

The co-pilot called David back to the cockpit. "They've changed course," he said. "Due east and seem to be descending. I make it central Switzerland."

"We'll have them by their ground lights," the pilot said. "We have to be quick, though. If they're not too paranoid, they could miss us."

"Not too paranoid?" David laughed.

"Got them!!" the co-pilot shouted. "See flashing lights? I make it sixteen kliks."

"On approach, all right," the pilot said. "Now it's your call."

"We'll play shadow," David said. "Note the location."

* * *

"Take off the blindfold," Jaime heard an American voice say. The accent was southern U.S. He uncovered his eyes. They were overwhelmed as suddenly by flood lamps.

"Am I here to buy weapons? Or be interrogated?" Jaime asked. "I've been real patient so far. Now I'm pissed. My money can go someplace else."

"So it can," said the American voice from behind the front floodlamp. Jaime could see the outlines of a large desk, as he hooded his eyes. "But if you didn't need us, you wouldn't be here. The arms market's good enough that we don't need you."

"We heard you could supply almost anything from the American inventory, mostly," Jaime answered. "Straight cash. No questions asked."

"Amend that to 'a few select questions asked,'" the American said. "Such as 'who's we?' How'd you hear about our little shop?"

"I'm here to buy arms. I've got cash," Jaime said, standing up. "Talk to me face-to-face." As quickly, two sets of hands pushed him back to the chair.

"No more precipitous moves," the American said. "Back to 'who's we?' And how'd you hear about us?"

"My people and I're planning a takeover in the Caribbean."

"Communist?"

"Since when does ideology matter to a high-class gunrunner?" Jaime asked. "As it happens, we're non-ideological. Unless opportunism's an ideology."

"That's our kind of ideology. Target?"

"*Habana*," Jaime answered.

"Cuba?!!" the American blurted, excitedly. "You're shittin' me!" the American said, still excitedly.

Jaime said, "I was seeing if you were listening."

"You've got my attention," the American said.

"An island off the Haitian coast," Jaime said. "We found oil deposits on it. Future developments're possible from there, too. East and West."

"Back to 'we' again," the American repeated. "You still haven't told us about 'we.'"

"What's it to you?" Jaime said. "We're businessmen mostly. Now do we do business or not?"

"Not," the American said, "unless you give me more. You need us more than we need you."

"We're a consortium of Latin businessmen, some Cubans," Jaime said. "We've got bigger plans than sucking oil and lying on the beach. At least that beach."

"Now you really *are* talkin' about Cuba," the American said, quietly. "But my men tell me there's an Iranian in your party. Hardly a Latin, is he?"

"Who better to know about oil?" Jaime shot back, quickly. Silence from the American confirmed his momentary triumph.

"We like doin' business with funny men," the American continued. "How'd you hear of us? This time don't be a comic."

"A contact in Russian military intelligence gave me your number."

"A triple oxymoron, eh? What's his name?"

"*She's* a colonel," Jaime corrected, and told him one of the Russian's aliases.

"I don't recall us doin' business with or through Russian GRU lately," the American said. "One shaky reference. Any others?"

"The Russians were your middlemen, between factions in the Horn three months ago," Jaime said, repeating something the Russian had suggested to him, before a love-making session. He smiled at that last thought. "You recently supplied a *compadre* of ours in Guatemala. Name of Ortiz."

"Score one for you," the American said. "Ortiz's a good customer. He'll confirm this?"

"Our money paid you."

"Let's find out," the American said. "I can reach him. Direct. If your story checks out, we do business. If not, yours is a dead language."

Jaime heard a door open and close. The room was quiet again. He also heard only infrequent footsteps or breathing.

Did Ortiz still believe he was an Anti-Castro operative and would he confirm his story? He heard a door open and close again.

"Just got off with Ortiz," the American said, angrily. "He doesn't know your 'consortium,' or whatever you call yourselves, for shit. Looks like we got a hangin' to do."

Jaime felt frozen, desperate. The overalls were wet and cold on his back, as he thought quickly—to what his Russian lover had told him.

"You couldn't've found him that fast!" he said, finally. "You bastard! He told me he'd be *incommunicado* at least a month. You're full of bullshit!!"

"Why you sweatin', boy?" the American asked, smirking. "If your story's true, there's nothin' to sweat about, right?"

"You bring me in here, like some kind of asshole!" Jaime shouted.

"You are some kind of asshole," the American laughed.

"You feed me bullshit and threaten to kill me! Fuck it! Take me back to Paris! Now!"

"Relax," the American said. "In fact, I got him. He confirmed what you said. He wants in on anything in Cuba. I had to see how you'd react, if you thought you were cornered."

Jaime slumped back in the chair, sighing. "Did I pass?"

The American said, "But God-help-you-bastards if *you're* bullshittin' us. There's not a jungle dark enough to hide you."

"Let's get down to negotiations," Jaime said.

"What kinds of stuff you want?"

"The typical. Small arms and ammo. LAWs. Some TOWs we could mount on jeeps. .50 caliber machine guns. We're told you've got Stingers. Lots of them."

"Everybody's had Stingers since the Russians were in Afghanistan."

"Yours work like they're supposed to," Jaime said.

"Everything you've mentioned is possible. How many men?"

"About a brigade-size, without the rear tail."

"Mercenaries?"

"Some," Jaime replied. "But dedicated ones, too."

"They're in trainin' now?"

"I want weapons, not help," Jaime said.

"You're goin' to need instructors."

"Is that included in the price? We only need it for the anti-air. LAWs are easy."

"It's a surcharge, percentage per units bought," the American said, "for the expertise factor." He sounded typically American to Jaime: proud and arrogant.

"The thing we're worried about is U.S. intervention, even though we're not Communist."

"Now that's the trick, isn't it? Not getting squashed by Uncle Sam, before you're ready to give the Marines or the 82nd Airborne a bloody nose."

"We're looking for insurance," Jaime said.

"We might be able to help you there, too," the American said. "We've got connections in Washington. But it'll cost more than cash."

"What? And how much?"

"A percentage of your oil revenue. Gross. Rights to future interests in Cuba."

"You've got more faith in us, than even we do," Jaime said.

"We can afford to," the American said. "We've got nothin' to lose."

"We were thinking more in weapon-style insurance," Jaime said.

"The conventional stuff you're after won't give you that."

"A more political variety. Use-it-or-lose-it kind. You've got connections that way, haven't you?"

"That's a different ballgame," the American replied. His tone was more tentative, less sure. "Maybe we do, and maybe we don't. Can't say right now."

"If you don't have the authority, I want to talk to the man who does."

"You're talkin' the antepenultimate. I don't think we can help you there. Not without more."

"But you do have access to the material?"

"I didn't say that," the American said, hurriedly. "That's for later. We're finished for now. Take him back to Paris."

"But what about our negotiations?" Jaime asked. "We haven't agreed on anything."

"Details," the American said. "We'll contact you in Paris to firm that up. You won't be seein' me again. We'll be in touch."

"But..." Jaime said, as a blindfold swept over his eyes and the floodlights went off.

* * *

"Take a look," the co-pilot said, handing David a night-vision scope. "The car's moving away from the house."

In spite of the altitude, the scope gave him a full scan of the limousine, as it drove down the long, private driveway.

The house that stood at the top of the horseshoe drive was a mansion, by anyone's measure. Its windows supplied enough light for the scope's mechanisms to reveal the full outline of the stone edifice.

The estate itself was secluded, distant from the closest village, in the finest custom of the super-rich. *A fine location*, David thought, *for covert operations and arms deals.*

In the cockpit again, David tapped the pilot's shoulder. "They making any evasive moves?"

The pilot shook his head. "They haven't made us. But it's going to be a tight return, fuel-wise. I hope they don't dawdle."

* * *

The wood paneling in Baron von Markenheim's *Ulm* library conference room had been polished. So had the leather couches and chairs, which bordered both sides of the long, mahogany table. The chandelier, hanging from the high marble ceiling, had been cleaned an extra time. Other preparations around the estate had been hurriedly completed, before the limousines arrived for this emergency meeting of The Cartel's Board of Directors.

Around the table were Baron von Markenheim, "Dr. Schmidt," a/k/a Colonel Krattmay, and twenty other corporate executives and clones. The executives' names, though less known to any public, could have introduced a list of the world's wealthiest business leaders.

There were also The Baron's two personal assistants on either side of him. He sat at one end of the table, with seniority determining the others' seats.

"*Have General Tripleleaf join us*," The Baron said to an assistant in German.

General Tripleleaf was 6´2˝ tall, in better physical condition than most men over fifty-nine years old, and dressed in his "retirement civies": dark grey, two-piece suit, long-sleeved, white shirt and navy-blue striped tie. His close-cropped hair, white all-round, seemed at attention as he sat at the opposite end of the table from von Markenheim.

"I'll come straight to the point," The Baron said in English. "It couldn't wait until our next scheduled meeting. General, someone in your organization's been selling weapons from our caches. We're here to give you the chance to confront this evidence and refute it, if you can."

"Cut the bullshit, Otto," Tripleleaf said, angrily, leaning onto the table. "Are you accusing me, personally, of profiteering?"

"Are you confessing to it, General?" asked a dark-haired man, with grey at his temples. "Posturing and overreacting?"

"Is this the procedure, Otto?" Tripleleaf asked. "You sit back, while Boy Professor carries out this inquisition? I don't have to stand for this!"

"You're not George Patton," the dark-haired man said, angrily. "And I'm not the slap-victim in Sicily."

"Patience, Professor," von Markenheim said. "You'll see the evidence, General. Then you decide if we're accusing you of treason."

He nodded to his assistants. One turned a switch. A section of wall paneling lowered and a projection screen filled the opening. He turned down the lights. The other hooked up a laptop.

"These first tallies're rough for now," the second assistant said in English. "Our people did random audits, based on leads from reliable sources."

"What goddamn 'reliable sources'?" Tripleleaf interrupted. The assistant looked at von Markenheim, without responding.

"I'm persuaded of their reliability," von Markenheim replied. "If I told you, you'd only retaliate against them."

"You're accusin' me, and I don't even know who?" Tripleleaf roared.

"You're the one who keeps saying we're accusing you," von Markenheim replied. "I said nothing of the sort. But a commander's always responsible for his men. Right, Colonel?"

Colonel Krattmay nodded. "You, above all, should know that, General," Krattmay said.

"*Bitte*," von Markenheim said. "No more interruptions, Walter, until we've finished the presentation."

The General sat back in his chair, still diffident.

The assistant resumed. "Our tallies show American small-arms, anti-tank missiles and Stingers, unaccounted for and missing." He went on for another half-hour. "At each site, we're conducting full audits. The pattern is slow-siphoning. These final sheets show bank accounts where we believe some of the monies have surfaced. The names on the statements are false.

They're all in Luxembourg and Switzerland. We're checking the Bahamas."

"Now," von Markenheim said, after his assistants were reseated beside him. "What have you to say, Walter?"

"Let me ask you a question first, Otto," Tripleleaf replied. "You're not accusing me of this shit then?"

Von Markenheim nodded to his assistant, who did the presentation and answered. "We've no proof of direct involvement by you, General."

"You're goddamn right you don't, Boy!! Ain't none!" Tripleleaf shouted. "Do you have leads on the real traitors?"

"We have some suspects," the assistant continued.

"Good, Junior!" Tripleleaf said, quickly. "'Cause I want their asses fried for Sunday... for puttin' me through this."

"Until the matter's settled," von Markenheim said. "Colonel Krattmay'll oversee security. You can manage that, and still keep our principal project on schedule, can't you, Colonel?"

"No problem, Baron," Krattmay said. "What's the protocol between General Tripleleaf and me? Do I report to him or to you?"

"General Tripleleaf will report *to you*," von Markenheim said, "for the remaining time before Case Blue."

"Wait one fuckin' minute!" Tripleleaf yelled. "I 'report' to your candy-assed yes-boy, Otto? What do I report to him? When I go to the latrine? 'Cause that's the only end he'll hear from. I guarantee."

"And I guarantee, my dear Walter," von Markenheim interrupted, more shrilly, "that he'll hear from your front orifice, or else we'll close you down. What a pity. Your Coalition's been a good cover for us."

"I've done too much for you guys," Tripleleaf said, pleading, while trying not to look like he was, "to be treated like shit-in-the-can and flushed away. Bad enough you put him in charge of Blue. That should've been my baby. I earned it!"

Von Markenheim said, more calmly, "Someone working for you doesn't share your dedication or loyalty. I suggest you find out *who*. It would be better if you work *with* Colonel Krattmay, especially since *I* want it that way."

General Tripleleaf nodded, stiffly, the gestures of a temporarily defeated, but still-unconquered foe. "You boys haven't heard the last of this," he said, softly, but loudly enough for all in the room to hear.

"I'd hope not," von Markenheim said. "Unless you've anything else to add, General, you're dismissed." Grumbling, General Tripleleaf left.

"*Also, meine Herren,*" von Markenheim said. "*Let's discuss the situation,*" he continued in German. "*The floor's open . . . Professor Pemberton?*"

The dark-haired man with grey temples, who had earlier argued with Tripleleaf responded. "*Even if we don't have proof—YET—that's the word Kurt omitted in his answer to The General—YET. It's clear, General Tripleleaf knows more than he's told us. I'm inclined to the view he's directly involved, even the architect. He's at least guilty of gross negligence.*"

"*How can you be sure?*" another executive asked. "*The General's been loyal. Even when he was still in the American Air Force.*"

"*He's been on the edge, sehr viel,*" another executive added.

"*We all know that,*" Pemberton said. "*Tripleleaf's not averse to making a profit, probably at even his mother's expense. He's not some icon.*"

"*There was that business in Latin America,*" the second executive to speak added. "*He nearly brought our operations into the press and into the American Congress' investigation. I agree with Herrn Professor-Doktor Pemberton.*"

"*And that theatrical resignation over the INF Treaty,*" Pemberton said. "*Attention-junkie that he is.*"

"*But his companies have all our important contracts for Blue,*" the first executive said. "*We can't afford to shut him down yet. And he knows that. He's having the last laugh.*"

"*I repeat, he's an attention-addict,*" Pemberton said. "*A primadonna. He's got to posture for the public or he'll die.*"

"*An apt choice,*" von Markenheim said. "*But change the conjunction, Thomas . . .*"

* * *

Late Tuesday night, Sam finished her packing and other preparations. She stayed light. Only a few skirt- and-blouse combinations, including her favorite and the one Regina had given her as a peace dividend, other special and personal necessities, a few things from her father's papers, her "itinerary" and photos. Anything else she would buy, as needed.

Sam had reservations at a small, northwest Washington inn on Florida Avenue and 19th Street, near Dupont Circle, for the few nights before her train. This was a break, to see if she had eluded all of her escorts. That included J.D. Marshall, she had already decided, him and his "cutesy guilt." She still liked him, though, but that would have to wait.

Awakened by her alarm the next morning at 5:30 A.M., she dressed, and finished packing her father's papers for mailing to the Jesuit priest. She bade her room farewell around 6:30 A.M., almost ritualistically, and waited in the lobby for her taxi. She would rely on cabs, rather than rent a car.

There was no one else around, not even a concierge, when the cab picked her up. Her suitcase and new *Chanel* bag were beside her, with the box of her father's papers.

On the ride downtown she wrote a note to the priest. Although she had one final appointment to meet, a pampering one, before she departed, she was leaving with a whisper, Sam thought, as she taped the box.

*   *   *

"Ms. Pemberton! You look beautiful!" the hairdresser exclaimed, as she handed Sam a styling mirror. "No one'll ever know you were anything but a blonde! You're a natural!"

Sam looked in the frontal, and then into the hand-held mirrors, as the stylist slowly turned the chair around. Her new hair color scheme could have been Regina's or Liz's. She had finally found the *chutzpah* for that "rendezvous with radical departure," deciding on a full day at the Elizabeth Arden Salon in Chevy Chase. She was now redone from scalp to soles.

"They did a fabulous job with your face, and the makeup's very flattering to you," the hairdresser bubbled on. "I'm sure your boyfriend'll love your new look. Your new clothes're awaiting you at Reception. You can pay there, and they'll be happy to get you a cab to your hotel."

After she changed to a leather skirt, matching jacket, with long-sleeved, silk blouse and thigh boots, Sam gave her servers good tips, took her new wardrobe purchases, and left by cab for the inn.

XIV

The day after his "formal introduction" to General Balkovsky, McConneld had conferences with investigators and high-ranking officials from the Foreign, Defense, and Interior Ministries. The Germans had had little progress.

McConneld dissuaded them from literal, village-to-village, house-to-house searches. He reminded them "tightened security" was a spasmodic thing: too long and everyone slackened again. The press would break the story, especially the foreign press, lacking German legal constraints.

Fortunately, they postponed that option for ten days, until 1 November. However, their restraint, they warned, depended on American progress in the case.

When McConneld returned to his office after 5 P.M. Chuck Channing had news from the dead major's files. There was also a telephone message from "Mr. Smith." He wanted to see McConneld that evening at 7:30 P.M.

"Did you call Colonel Barsohn about this?" McConneld asked.

"He had to rearrange, but said he'd be here," Channing said. "We've identified what we think're payoffs, courier exchanges. D.C. Other places. Between the major, or his agents, and some big fish. His calendars map out travel records, flight numbers, airlines, and destinations, dates and pretty big dollar amounts."

"How big?" McConneld asked.

"Six figures, at least. Plus there's the notation 'WH' on them. The trips he didn't take himself have other initials. Entries go back over 20+ years."

"Did you inform Langley?"

"No, I thought you should be the one," Channing replied.

"I want Deputy Director Simmons on a secure line," McConneld said. "That 'WH' could mean many things. How about those checks on USAREUR personnel?"

Channing told him that most had been cleared. There was a

small number remaining. One State-side inactive, whose file had recent entries from Langley and elsewhere, had come up.

"He's still on USAREUR's rosters?" McConneld asked. "I'd have thought he was off long ago."

"Once Reserve, always Reserve," Channing said. "Our friends at DIA and Fort Meade are also interested."

"Ask Harvey Barsohn to check," McConneld said. "Is there an overseas address?"

"General Delivery, Paris."

"When I talk to Langley, I'll have them double-check him at his local address. Get me Simmons now. If he's not at HQ, get him at home."

Minutes later, McConneld's call to the Deputy Director was through to his home in Virginia.

"Real trouble," McConneld said. "But I think we can make it stick. We believe there was a spy in the Administration, working for the bomb thieves."

"What d'you mean, 'think'?" Simmons asked. "You better make it stick, WITH dry powder."

"I need more info to do that, Mac," McConneld said. "Whoever it is might still be inside. Here's what I want you to arrange." He described his plan to Simmons.

"Are you crazy, Buck?" Simmons replied. "I can't authorize that. I'd at least have to go through the Director."

"Do that, and you tip off whoever it is," McConneld said. "If the shit-hits-the-fan, I'll be there to take my share. But I need that stuff."

"Damned right you'll be eating it," Simmons said. "We both might be filing unemployment. We're too old for second childhoods." After the call, McConneld and Channing continued through the major's travel records for hours.

"What I don't understand," Channing said, "is how his bosses let him go all over God's creation, without calling him on it. We're talking hundreds of trips."

"He obviously didn't have to explain," McConneld said. "Till we have this D.C. connection nailed down, we tell that Inane Kinnean nothing. Got that?"

The intercom went off. "Security calling, sir. There's a 'Mister

Smith,' at the Personnel entrance," his secretary said.

"Tell them to escort him to my office," McConneld said.

"Colonel Barsohn's also here," she added.

McConneld met General Balkovsky at the door. Barsohn and Channing gave promises of confidentiality.

"What's the big emergency, General?"

"I'll get to that," Balkovsky said, quickly. "Professor Pemberton's Cartel recruited radical Palestinian factions, IRA, other terror cells... New ones, too. They've got a continent-wide terror campaign in mind. Your bombs could be at the core, as a *coup-de-grace* or a threat-in-being." He handed McConneld files.

"The ultimate objective?" Channing asked. "Terrorists can't afford those risks, unless the return's huge."

"I believe it's directed at our president. He's due to visit the West in less than a month," Balkovsky said. "That mightn't explain the whole, but it's a large segment. The Cartel cut business with us when he refused resource concessions."

"He's offered resource concessions for foreign debt before," Channing said. "He's the golden goose."

"He's also holding the whole thing together. Without him, complete chaos. The Balkans were mild in comparison to us."

McConneld said, "But everybody loses in the break-up scenario."

"For a short time," Balkovsky said. "In the long run, The Cartel strikes deals with the bits and pieces—on its own terms. Our military can't hold things together, without the President. It may be backing its own candidate for his job."

"There's got to be more to it than that, General," Barsohn said. "Those terror organizations will be wiped out in an operation like that. Like the VC in Tet."

"The beauty is the surrogates won't be around afterwards to talk."

"The road to hell's paved with promises," Barsohn shot back. "Try collecting on that contract."

"Don't mix metaphors, Harvey," McConneld said. "But I agree. What's your evidence?"

"Not at liberty to say at this time," Balkovsky said. "Don't ask me again."

"The Cartel and its Ignoble Lie?"

"It'd be manufactured in time," Balkovsky said. "If I were The Cartel, I'd not let the terror troops near the bombs. Which brings me to the urgent matter. We've found a storage site for some of your stolen weapons. Before you get your hopes up, non-nuclear ones."

"You know about those, too?" McConneld asked. "The German Government is a damned sieve."

"The Cartel people are moving them," Balkovsky said.

"Why didn't you say so in the first place?" Colonel Barsohn asked.

"You'd have been too preoccupied to listen to my other information," Balkovsky said. "They're relocating, tonight or tomorrow. They're shaking up their command structure. It's in Luxembourg, opposite Trier."

"Chuck," McConneld said. "Get onto the Luxembourg government. Call the French Brigade commander near Trier. General Guy DeChampbonneau. He's a friend of mine."

"General, do you know where they're moving the stuff?" Barsohn asked. "How about other relocations?"

"Colonel," Balkovsky said, sighing. "They're spooks. We're lucky to have this."

McConneld interrupted, "Harvey, get us escort and transport to The Big Lux. Do you know their current storage arrangements?" he asked Balkovsky.

"A farm," the Russian said, "with specially built, underground storage."

McConneld himself called the Consulate motor-pool and ordered a car. "There'll be three of us," he was saying, when Balkovsky motioned.

"I'm coming," the Russian said. "I was there, earlier this morning. And, remember, no Germans along."

"How'd you get there so quick?" McConneld asked, then caught himself. "Correction. Four. No need for a driver."

Balkovsky took maps from his briefcase. "I can give the vicinity and heading from this. Once on the ground, I'll use this."

Barsohn came back. "Got us choppers and a fifty-MP detachment."

"The general's coming with us," McConneld replied.

"Ridden in a Huey lately, General?" Barsohn asked.

"The first time was after Saigon fell," Balkovsky said.

McConneld called to the other office. Channing replied, "They're trying to locate that friend of yours. He's not at his HQ or home."

Finally, the French located their general. McConneld spoke with him. The French officer agreed to cooperate and to lead the convoy himself.

"We'll put down near *Temmels*," McConneld concluded. "We'll radio the exact LZ, when we're airborne." McConneld handed Balkovsky a set of credentials, in the name of "Mr. Alfred Smith."

Channing drove them to the *Rhein-Main* Airbase. Their assigned helicopters were warmed up. The MPs, dressed in light combat gear, were already boarded. McConneld and the other three changed clothes, to U.S. camouflage fatigues and were issued sidearms.

McConneld and Barsohn briefed the O.I.C., introducing Balkovsky by his pseudonym. The General put on a very convincing New York accent for him. The O.I.C. confirmed the unit was equipped with night-fighting equipment.

"We need an LZ, sir," the unit commander said.

"Mr. Smith can help us," McConneld said. It was decided "Mr. Smith" would fly in the point chopper to pinpoint the meadow he had discovered. McConneld decided to ride with Balkovsky in the lead.

"You never told me you're from New York, 'Mr. Smith'," McConneld said, after they were in the air. "Been away, huh?"

"Yeah," Balkovsky agreed. "I haven't seen the Big Apple for a while. I miss hot pretzels at Fifth Avenue and East 59th Street, hot chestnuts and *shish kabob*. There was this family place in 'Little Italy.' The best veal in town. The Village. Those were the days."

The flight took less than an hour. En route, the flight leader contacted the French general and his convoy, with "Mr. Smith's" landing zone on the German side of the border. The French knew the spot. They used it for their own maneuvres. It was five kilometers from *Temmels*.

On the ground, McConneld was greeted by General DeChampbonneau. The general had brought a detachment of paratroopers. They and some MPs would go ahead of the convoy, with "Mr. Smith," McConneld, and Channing, as scouts.

The remaining MPs would accompany Barsohn, with "homing" equipment. The helicopter flight would follow at "stand-off" distance and remain in contact with Barsohn and the MPs.

General DeChampbonneau, Balkovsky, McConneld, and Channing crammed into the French command vehicle. The scouts' truck was close behind them. Before rendezvous, the French had arranged with the repopulated border station for quick passage. The security measures the German authorities were otherwise taking, were rigorous, a departure from, post-European Union non-measures.

The area was heavily wooded, with voids, where farms had been cut into the forest. The closest town or village was *Herborn*. A short while later, Balkovsky announced they were within a kilometre-and-a-half of the site.

General DeChampbonneau ordered his driver off the road. The spot had good cover. From it, a trail led into the forest. Balkovsky took "the point," with McConneld, Channing, and the French officer in tandem. The French paratroopers and U.S. soldiers fanned out on either flank. Guards were left with the vehicles, to meet Barsohn and his convoy.

The trail wound through thick brush and conifers. Balkovsky seemed to know, almost without looking, his way along it.

Thirty minutes into the trek the Russian stopped abruptly. The bare sounds of natural night had been complemented with distant human ones.

Balkovsky waved a change in direction. DeChampbonneau sent orders to the flankers. The sounds became steadily louder, though still soft. At the top of a ravine, edged with thick foliage, dead tree trunks, and a sheer-drop, the four men squatted behind cover.

McConneld used his night-vision binoculars. Two hundred yards down the ravine, in a clearing, were typical-looking European farm buildings, complete with house.

With trucks parked near the buildings, loading operations

were underway. Balkovsky had brought them to a close, side boundary of the property.

McConneld swept the area with his binoculars. The closest guards were a hundred fifty yards away: thirty or so men, armed with various assault rifles and small arms. Another thirty or forty were loading the trucks, from a silo and a barn. A road ran parallel to the ravine, seemingly the only paved way in. While he watched, trucks arrived and departed.

"I wish Barsohn'd get here," McConneld whispered to Balkovsky, who was using his own night-scope to observe. "It would be nice to have those trucks shadowed." He crawled to DeChampbonneau.

"*Guy? Try to raise Barsohn. Do you have a link with our car?*" he whispered.

Shortly, he had an answer: Barsohn and Co. had not arrived. McConneld was concerned. The convoy was not that far behind them.

"We've got to get a closer look," McConneld whispered to Channing. "But we should wait for Barsohn." More minutes passed. Still no convoy.

"*I'm getting a look-see,*" McConneld said, finally. "*Have everybody sit tight, Guy,*" he said to DeChampbonneau. "*When Harvey Barsohn makes it, tell him to have the choppers shadow those trucks.*"

Balkovsky took "the point" once more. They stayed well inside the woods-line, along the edge of the ravine. Over the first fifty yards of the semi-circle, McConneld saw flankers.

Well beyond where their flankers should have been, McConneld stopped suddenly. An armed man, probably a guard, was twenty yards ahead.

The guard was wandering slowly, his rifle slung. He lingered in one place, then continued. They waited for him to move on, but he was in no hurry.

Balkovsky accidentally tripped over a small log and fell into bushes. McConneld ducked down, to help him, and looked for the guard. He was gone.

"So much for your night-vision," McConneld whispered.

They reached the spot where the guard had been. He was

lying in a leaf pile, apparently drugged. Was McConneld's "guardian angel," watching over him?

About a hundred yards further on they found another man, drugged and unconscious, just inside the tree line. McConneld's musing became more serious.

Barsohn and his men? New players? A less malevolent presence, perhaps? McConneld screwed a sound suppressor onto his Baretta. Balkovsky did the same.

The sounds of the loading had not abated. McConneld heard more truck noises.

Nearly to their preferred observation point, they stopped. Another guard paced through the foliage ahead of them. He turned unexpectedly toward them.

Balkovsky and McConneld went prone. The guard continued toward them, weapon unslung. Within feet of McConneld, he pointed his rifle at the CIA man. McConneld did not move.

He saw the guard jolted, as though shot. Three human figures were quickly around him and got him to the ground. His rifle did not hit the ground.

The figures were dressed in U.S. camouflage fatigues. A fourth man crawled over to McConneld and Balkovsky.

"Colonel Barsohn's compliments, sir," he whispered to McConneld. "Sorry we're late. Unavoidable." He led them to Barsohn and the unit commander.

"Where the hell?!" McConneld said to Barsohn, who quickly waved him off.

"The damn directional finder went dead. We were winding around on these roads, till a chopper reported this activity from way off," he whispered.

"I thought I heard a Huey, but it sounded miles away," McConneld said. "We're lucky it didn't spook these clowns."

"Our guys and the French are two's and three's around the perimeter," Barsohn said. "We've been shadowing you two for an hour or so."

"We have you to thank for letting sleeping guards lie?" McConneld asked.

Barsohn nodded. "More than you saw. A couple were about to nail you. There's a perimeter inside the tree line."

"How long've we got before the sleeping beauties wake up?"

"Till way after noon. It's a real potent tranquilizer," the MP commander said.

"We were praying for you to get here," McConneld said. "We need a tailjob."

"That action's going already," Barsohn replied. "But the flight commander had to call *Rhein-Main* and *Bitburg* for backup and followup birds. He didn't know how long their fuel would hold up."

"Are we stranded?" McConneld asked.

"We can get back. What's wrong?" Barsohn asked.

"If they had a line behind us, they probably had one—" McConneld said, excitedly. "Shit!"

They heard a high-powered rifle shot, from their left. Then, more shots. McConneld and the others ran the fifty yards to the edge of the woods. Guards on foot and a jeep with other guards in it were racing toward the far side of the ravine, where General DeChampbonneau and his men were.

"So much for a quiet look!" McConneld said, when they reached the tree line.

Colonel Barsohn gave orders to the MP commander. "Fire at will! But take prisoners where possible!"

Single shots and bursts rang out from the woods to their right. The troops with them also opened up.

Shots hit the jeep, as it drove across the open ground. It turned over. The guards were taking cover and firing back, toward DeChampbonneau's position. Rifle-fire came from McConneld's left. Trucks were speeding down the road, with their rear doors or tailgates still swinging open. Men were scurrying wildly.

"I sent guys to cover that road," Barsohn said. "Have we heard from them?" he asked the MP officer.

"I've got to have a look," McConneld said. He broke from the tree line into open ground and wove toward the barn, with Balkovsky close behind.

"Wait!" Barsohn yelled.

McConneld sensed someone else had joined him and Balkovsky. He turned to see two MPs, one on either side, with their M-16s cradled to their chests.

Rifle shots whizzed by as he covered the sixty yards to the barn. He was winded when he finally bounced onto the wood exterior. Balkovsky was behind him. It seemed to McConneld the MPs were humoring him, without breaking a sweat.

A guard, with rifle ready, came around the side of the barn. McConneld aimed his pistol hastily and fired. The man crumpled against the wooden wall.

Along the back of the barn, McConneld raced with one MP. Both men swung around the right side, firing their weapons. The second MP joined them. Two guards fell to the ground. The second MP was wounded. The first MP leaned him against the barn wall, and continued with McConneld and Balkovsky.

McConneld saw the rear of a truck's cargo bay, yawning open. The truck was pulling away. McConneld sprinted, garnering whatever breath remained.

With a final leap, he was inside. A pair of hands helped him in. He saw, by an inside light, one other man, apparently one of the loaders.

McConneld pointed his weapon at the other man, who lunged at him, and belly-flopped on the floor. McConneld shoved him, and he tumbled from the truck.

As he sat up, McConneld noticed Balkovsky also chasing the truck. The Russian jumped over the man McConneld had ejected.

McConneld found a long, steel bar on the floor, and held it out to the Russian. Balkovsky dangled from it, as McConneld drew him onto the truck bed.

Balkovsky lay, exhausted, dribbled like a basketball, by the truck's bouncing. McConneld, too, was panting. The rear doors swung uncontrollably.

"I'm too old for this stuff," Balkovsky wheezed.

"You shouldn't have tagged along with me," McConneld muttered.

"No way I was letting you go off on your own," Balkovsky replied.

"Half of me wants this truck stopped," McConneld said. "The other half...."

As he was speaking, they heard rifle shots. The truck swerved, going off the road and side-swiping trees. They were thrown back and forth against the walls. Crates fell around them.

They were prone on the bed-floor, as bypassed MPs fired through the open doors. The truck did not slow.

"Those idiots'll kill us!" Balkovsky said.

"Who're the real idiots?" McConneld said.

"Not to worry," Balkovsky said, reaching into his jacket pocket. "I picked up a homer, before we left *Rhein-Main*." Balkovsky showed it to him.

McConneld moved a thin flashbeam over their surroundings. The crates had assorted markings from the U.S., British, and German Armies. There were also pry- and crow-bars, and other tools, spread on the floor.

There was no window from the cab into the cargo section, only large plywood sections across the front wall. He noticed a hatch in the ceiling, large enough for a person to climb onto the truck's roof.

"There's enough ordnance to hold off a battalion," McConneld observed. "It reminds me of the Gulf and this one Special Forces team. I wonder if your purloined DF's attracted attention." He motioned upwards with his thumb. "I feel a heavy attack of *déja vu*."

"It's a hangover from the gas I used on you," Balkovsky said.

"That reminds me. Your New Yorker's very good," McConneld said. "Is that from spy school? Or on-the-job training?"

"A little of both, actually," Balkovsky smiled. "There really was this family place in 'Little Italy.'"

The truck sped up. Its driving had become more controlled, less erratic. But the driver had not stopped to close the rear doors yet.

A half-hour passed. Still, McConneld could not resolve his *déja vu*. He wondered how Barsohn and DeChampbonneau had fared. There was something about that plywood facia. McConneld took a closer look. He found an involved latch on the left side. Then, he remembered. The truck was slowing. Outside, the country night was still and dark.

* * *

A truck was still burning nearby, as Colonel Barsohn, Chuck Channing, and General DeChampbonneau surveyed the farm. The commander of the MPs was with them.

The firefight had ended only ten minutes before. Rubble and debris were all around the ravine. U.S. and French troopers were searching the farm, leading prisoners to quickly improvised holding areas, and guarding the perimeter.

"They're nowhere around, Colonel," DeChampbonneau said to Barsohn, in English. "They've got to be here, General," Barsohn replied. "Where the hell're those two MPs I sent with them? Are you sure they weren't among the KIAs or WIAs? How many people'd we lose?" he asked the MP captain.

"Pretty sure, sir. Our casualties were light. Only seven wounded, no KIAs," the U.S. officer answered.

"Be absolutely sure, goddammit!" Barsohn said.

"Easy, *mon ami*," DeChampbonneau said. "We'll find them."

"How many did you lose, General?" Barsohn asked the Frenchman.

"Two killed, three wounded," the general replied.

"How many trucks got away?" Channing asked the U.S. captain.

The captain replied, patiently. "A couple got through, even after our men fired on them. No report from the choppers yet, but they had surveillance progressing."

"What *do* you know, Captain?! Find those damned MPs," Barsohn said.

Meanwhile, Barsohn and the others examined the contents of the barn. While the barn's exterior had a semi-dilapidated look, the interior was refurbished and modern. The lighting was good, with storage closets, lock-ups, and shelving. There was an attic, semi-finished, with cots, and a multi-level basement. There was a wide range of Western weaponry, from small arms to anti-tank and anti-aircraft missiles.

The MP captain returned. "One MP with Mr. McConneld was wounded in a firefight, sir," he said to Barsohn. "He's unconscious. I passed the word for the other to report. I'm roll-calling as soon as the situation's fully stabilized, sir."

"Sorry I shot out of-turn at you, Captain," Barsohn said.

"You're just worried about your friends, sir," the MP officer said.

"Copy a preliminary report of this to EVESTOFF, DIA, Frankfurt. I want my interrogation teams to be ready. Now let's find McConneld and Smith!"

An hour later they had not found the missing men. The MP commander spoke with his troops, but none had seen McConneld or his companion, after the firefight started.

"Sir?" the MP officer came to him a while later. "We got a weird report from one of the choppers. It picked up a homer transmission from someplace that has no business sending."

"What double-talk's that?" Barsohn asked.

"The source's moving, sir," the officer replied. "The chopper's been following, using passive radar. Southeast of here."

"One of the getaways, I'll bet!" Barsohn said. "Captain, inform the choppers. We're going after that bogey."

"But, sir," the MP officer replied. "It's a million-to-one shot."

"When those're the best odds, son, you roll," Barsohn said. "Are you coming, General?" he asked DeChampbonneau.

"I wouldn't miss it," the Frenchman replied.

* * *

McConneld felt in his pocket for the pen-light. The blackness of the truck's secret compartment promised no opening or window into the truck cab.

The compartment was narrow and high, four feet wide, with extra depth, and floor, lower than the regular truck bed. The walls were covered in a material, resembling sound-proofing tile.

"Do you think we'd better get out of here?" Balkovsky said.

"And blow the best lead we've had?" McConneld asked.

"He's bound to come back here," Balkovsky countered. "What then?"

"Surprise him. Force him to take us to the source."

"What if he's not alone?"

"They've got us," McConneld said. The bouncing continued. *The driver must have taken every back road in this part of*

Europe, McConneld thought.

"I didn't know Luxembourg was so big," he said to Balkovsky. The truck slowed.

McConneld and Balkovsky took out their pistols and reentered the truck's open bed. Seconds dragged, like hours. The truck jerked abruptly, then stopped. They heard footsteps.

McConneld tapped the Russian. Balkovsky turned on the flashlight, finding the man's face. The man squinted.

He struggled with something in his belt, but stopped, when Balkovsky dropped the light down to his waist. There was a pistol under the belt.

"*Ich schiesse!*" McConneld said. The man stood still.

McConneld told him to drop his gun. The man slowly removed it from his pants with one hand. Balkovsky picked it up.

The man was heavy-set, not as tall as McConneld, with old workclothes on.

"*Sprechen Sie Englisch?*" McConneld asked. "*Sind Sie allein?*"

"*Ja, allein. Ein bißchen Englisch.* A little bit," the man replied, his arms in the air. "*Wer*... Who are you, please?"

"Your friends... *Ihre Freunde*..." McConneld said, touching the muzzle of his gun to the prisoner's neck. "*Fahren Sie uns, wo Sie diesen Lattenkisten austragen müssen.* Take us to where you must deliver this cargo."

"*Der Mann würde mich töten!* He would kill me!"

"And I'll shoot you now," McConneld said. "*Wenn Sie sich mich weigern.* If you refuse! *Verstanden?*"

"My friend *will*," Balkovsky added. "*Zuweilen ist er verrückt!* Crazy! Better do as he wants!"

They shuffled him from the truck. It was parked on grass, between a two-lane road and woods. There were no lights nearby, or buildings.

"*Haben Sie Landkarte?*" McConneld asked. The man nodded, reached onto the seat, and took out a folded roadmap. He pointed to a section of it.

"We're just this side of the French border," Balkovsky said.

"Quite the way," McConneld observed. "We could've been here a couple hours ago. *Wohin fahren wir?* Where're we going?" McConneld asked.

The driver hesitated. *"Nein, ich kann nicht..."*

"And I'll shoot you, if you don't," McConneld said, placing the muzzle to the driver's temple.

"Mein Freund ist vernünftig. Reasonable, *verstanden?"* Balkovsky said to the driver. "But you must do what he says, right? If you do that, I convince him to protect you. *Nichts schadet Ihnen.* Nothing will hurt you. Understand?"

The driver looked, alternately at Balkovsky and McConneld.

"Aber, wenn Sie es nicht tun, kann ich Ihnen nicht helfen," Balkovsky said. "No help. And *mein Freund* will feel compelled to shoot you. *Schiessen."*

The driver opened the map and pointed to a spot, south of Stuttgart. "I... stop here *und* here. Before." He showed them other places, along the French border.

"Die Wahrheit?" Balkovsky asked. The man nodded, nervously.

"Smell any wild geese?" McConneld asked Balkovsky. "Or a trip down Viet Cong or Afghan lane?"

"Methinks our man here," Balkovsky said, in vintage New York brogue, "has already lost it in his pants. If you get my drift... and his."

"Wann sollten Sie am ersten Punkt kommen sein?" McConneld asked the driver.

"Um drei Uhr morgens," the driver answered.

"We'll be a tad late. *Wir denken an eine besondere Geschichte, nicht wahr?"* McConneld said. *"Weil wir spät sind..."*

"Better get out of these uniforms," Balkovsky said. "And find work clothes."

Hustling the driver into the truck bed, they had him push the crates into the concealed compartment, and close it.

Balkovsky drove, with the prisoner between them, McConneld keeping him at gun point. The man gave them a route number and directions. McConneld instructed the prisoner to explain their lateness, with the raid, engine and tire trouble. He told the prisoner to identify him and Balkovsky as comrades from the evacuated depot.

They spent an hour, looking for farmhouses, with laundry on outside clotheslines. In a small border village, McConneld left

Balkovsky with the prisoner.

He took clothes from different houses, returning to the truck, in a side alley. McConneld musedly worried about encountering the "local constabulary." He found the prisoner asleep. Balkovsky looked bored, as he kept guard.

"Is this what you Americans call, 'borrowing from the rich and giving to the poor'?" he asked McConneld, who was sorting the clothes by size.

"I'll see they're dry-cleaned, before we return them," McConneld replied. "When did our friend conk out?"

"Right after you left. I think he's faking."

"We'll take turns watching Bozo," McConneld said. "You go first. I hope they fit."

"Damn skinny Westerners! They're too tight," Balkovsky complained, after returning. McConneld changed clothes quickly, and relocked the cargo doors. "You've got to lose a few pounds," McConneld joked, as they started off. "What reeks? Don't take this the wrong way, but did you...uh...?"

"Did I what?" Balkovsky asked.

"You know...while I was gone?"

"No," the Russian replied. "Maybe he did."

"Hey, *Struntzie*," McConneld said to the prisoner. "Wake up."

McConneld shook him, but his body was limp. The Russian shoved him toward McConneld, but he fell back against Balkovsky.

"Pull over," McConneld said, feeling the man's wrist. "I can't get a pulse. I think he's dead."

"How?! I was with him the whole time," Balkovsky said.

McConneld opened the man's mouth. "Didn't you guys learn from Himmler?" he asked. McConneld put his ear to the man's chest. "I think I hear a faint heartbeat. Find a police station or hospital!"

The truck sped back toward the center of the village. Near the village square, there was a small police station, with police cars parked in front. Inside, McConneld found a dispatcher and three or four uniformed officers. In French, he concocted a story.

He told the official they were movers and their colleague had suddenly collapsed. The official sent two of his men to help. The dispatcher contacted the village clinic nearby. Balkovsky and the two officers took the unconscious man there.

Meanwhile, McConneld called Frankfurt, on an outside pay phone. He gave his location and the clinic's phone number to the Duty Officer.

When McConneld arrived at the clinic, Balkovsky was in the lobby. One police officer had returned to the station. The other was speaking with two white-dressed nurse-practitioners.

"No one's asked me his name yet," Balkovsky said to McConneld. "Here's his wallet."

A white-lab-coated man, who had joined the nurses, walked over to McConneld and Balkovsky. The police officer was with him.

"*I'm Dr. Vaucher. You're the gentlemen who brought this man?*" he asked McConneld and Balkovsky in French.

Just then came the sound of an approaching siren. It stopped abruptly.

Suddenly, the police commander came through the front entrance, followed by Colonel Barsohn, General DeChampbonneau, and Channing.

"*Monsieur Le Docteur,*" the police commander said, quickly. "*These men must speak with you immediately!...*"

General DeChampbonneau did not wait for the policeman to finish. He identified himself. "*The man you have is an important prisoner. You must do what you can.*"

"Guy," McConneld said. "I think he poisoned himself, under our noses."

"*Sorry, but you'll all have to be kept in our custody,*" DeChampbonneau said to the hospital staffers and the policeman, "*while he's your patient.*"

A nurse from the clinic's interior spoke to the doctor. "*He's not my patient any longer, I'm afraid,*" Dr. Vaucher said.

"You got our messages!" Balkovsky said to Barsohn.

"Is the convoy out there, Harvey?" McConneld asked.

"Only a little insurance. A few MPs and paras," Barsohn replied.

"Glad to see you, Boss-man," Channing said. "I thought I had to break in a new one."

"For a while, I wasn't sure you wouldn't," McConneld said. "We'd better powwow." He and the others congregated in a corner of the room.

"Square one?" Barsohn started the impromptu conference.

"Not this time, Harvey," McConneld said. "A way in's mapped out for us."

"Do you have anyone in mind, Boss?" Channing asked. McConneld smiled.

"Aren't you a little senior," Barsohn asked, "to be following truck trails?"

"I'm not that much older than this guy," McConneld said. "I'm a field man. I've always been a field man. I'm sick of a desk."

"But, Boss," Channing said. "I'm more expendable. Let me."

"What about a more immediate problem?" Balkovsky interrupted. "Can we keep this quiet?"

"We can't hold these people for long, before the word might get out," DeChampbonneau said. "But I'm sure the police chief can be reasoned with."

"Don't tell them much," McConneld said. "Someone here could work for the badboys."

"He was a terrorist escapee," the French general said. "You were transporting him, *incognito*," DeChampbonneau answered. "You had to maintain your cover story."

"Now for the question of the hour," Barsohn said. "Whatever shall we do with Buck?"

"Why, Harvey, you actually have a sense of humor," McConneld said.

"Channing's right," Barsohn replied. "He's more nimble."

"I've been working on this case for months," McConneld said. "The bastards have been ahead of us every time it looked like we've gotten somewhere. I'm going in there myself."

Barsohn said, "We'll run this guy's identity and particulars." Balkovsky handed him the wallet.

"You still need an accomplice," Balkovsky said. "Somebody with connections."

"Are you volunteering, Mr. Smith?" McConneld asked.

"You bet your ass," Balkovsky said. "I've got more depending on this."

"This time I'm insisting you go wired," Channing said. "And with a homer."

DeChampbonneau rejoined them. "As you Americans say, 'the fix is in.'"

"Get him to release the body in your custody, Guy," McConneld said. "I don't want him having any time to think. Harvey, you have techs with you?"

"No, but we've got field sets and communications," Barsohn said.

The Frenchman returned to the police officers, while Barsohn got what they needed from his truck. After a barrage of official French, the police chief and his men left. Barsohn had a portable evidence kit.

The clinic physician led them to the enclosure where the body lay. Barsohn fingerprinted the corpse.

DeChampbonneau told the doctor to store the body, until his men claimed it. Barsohn and McConneld searched the deceased's effects. Inside one shoe they found half of a blue poker chip. In the other was a scrap of paper with an address on it.

Outside, Barsohn used a mobile phone set-up to fax a printcard to Frankfurt. They waited another half-hour before an answer arrived. From the portable fax pages of print and dot-like photos poured.

The deceased was a former *Stasi* agent. His whereabouts until then had been unknown. He was wanted by the German Federal Police for questioning in connection with terror bombings in eastern Germany. They were offering a 5,000DM reward for information leading to his arrest.

"Maybe Mr. Smith and I should split the bounty," McConneld laughed, as he skimmed the streamlined dossier.

"You don't look that much alike," Barsohn said. "Can your German hold up? If you run into anyone from that farm?"

"Been there. Considered that," McConneld replied. "I also thought where we are without this lead."

"Let me tag along," Channing said. "I could be another loader."

"Too many people," McConneld said, "will make his buddies more suspicious than if I showed a week late. Mr. Smith and I're going. But, Chuck, I expect you guys to be within earshot. We'll take mikes, but uninstalled."

Channing sighed. "Let's get you set up."

*　*　*

"Herrn Doktor Hauptmann, to see you, Herr Baron," the secretary said, after opening The Baron's office door.

The familiar visitor sat in a leather chair. He waited, though impatiently, for his host to finish some work.

The Baron said, with finality. *"What's this 'super-urgent' matter?"*

Colonel Krattmay spoke quickly, telling The Baron about the raid the previous night.

"Will anyone talk?" The Baron asked. *"We need to move up Fall Blau, even after the move-up from the 30th?"*

Krattmay shook his head. *"Those were cheap Eastern fanatics. They think they're doing it for the 'New Dawn.' Everything's still on schedule. The problem's how the Americans found it."*

"Do you have *suspects?*" von Markenheim asked.

"Not many had that specific information. Too specific . . ."

"Specific? . . . or general?" von Markenheim said.

XV

Jaime lowered the binoculars. The European countryside seemed like an enormous and bottomless hole to him. Wherever he was taken, could have been in any small nook along the shaft. "It smelled like an estate," he had told Emilio.

They had overflown numerous villages, towns and farms, for three days, with little result. He looked at his map, tracing the helicopter's course.

The pilot was a resident operative from Jaime's agency. The aircraft was part of his cover business.

"*How far're we out?*" Jaime asked the pilot.

"*Central Switzerland,*" the pilot replied. "*At the speed you were probably going... Time in the air... Probably about five hundred kilometers. We're going to have to refuel soon.*"

"*We've still got daylight left,*" Jaime protested. "*If we turn back now, we'll lose too much time.*"

"*We can reload at Zürich,*" the pilot said. Fifteen minutes later they were on the ground at *Zürich-Kloten* Airport.

The thinner and colder air frosted Jaime's face. He tried to remember smaller details, and later conferred with Jamael and Emilio.

"The pilot thinks we're at the outside," Jaime said. Emilio and Jamael looked at their own maps.

"There's still lots to cover," Emilio said.

"According to the weather reports," Jaime said, "this area had rain or sleet within the past week. How many airstrips can there be?"

The pilot rejoined them. "A controller told me there aren't many small airfields. Enough to take time, though." He showed them the locations.

"We need a car," Jaime said. He told the pilot to scout churches and chimes.

"Are you kidding? Every village's got its own music bells.

There're hundreds!" the pilot replied, before he left them again.

He returned half-an-hour later. "Lots of small churches start playing their Christmas chimes about this time," he said. "Maybe later in November."

"We'll check all of 'em, if we have to," Jaime said. "I want to win this pot." Soon they were in the air, heading south-southeast.

When they reached the vicinity of Lucern, they turned southwest, toward the *Thunersee* and *Interlaken*. They saw a few airfields, each secluded and removed from the accidental or curious. Most were small public fields. They continued west, then northwest, in the direction of Berne, and saw more snow-covered strips.

Jaime was frustrated, like before. This time there would be no "miraculous wake-up call," not at this altitude. Nevertheless, the prize was too close, to quit.

After more hours, and darkness coming swiftly on, they turned back for Paris. Jaime and the pilot planned a schedule, to investigate each airstrip.

Jaime had expected this to be a long, typically tedious job, like too many jobs he had recently. Knowing the Russian in New York had made it tolerable. He was looking for rapid action—real action—and not surveillance or "babysitting."

In Paris at their pension, Jaime decided on an early night, foregoing the Parisian nightlife—for now. There would be time for that, after they found the bombs. That would be *his* time to celebrate.

The next morning before dawn they were back in the air, en route to northeastern Switzerland. When they reached Lake Constance, they turned west.

They saw more small airfields, though some looked like wide roads shut at one end. One, near *Winterthur*, interested Jaime and he noted it.

After more hours they refueled in Zürich. While they were waiting, Jaime had Emilio and Jamael inquire about the real estate market and private estates nearby. Again, there was a list of sites.

They continued their sweeps, along the Franco-Swiss and

Swiss-German borders, before turning back for Paris.

That night they reviewed the locations they had. They cross-referenced the airfields and estates, along with churches. There were still days, perhaps weeks, of work and travel ahead of them.

* * *

The pilot called back to David and George from the cockpit. "We'll be passing that estate in a few moments."

David squeezed up into the cockpit. "Do wide swings to give us a look. Then stand off. We don't want too much attention."

As the helicopter did broad oval passes, David shot with a 35mm camera and long telephoto lens. George used video and digital cameras.

Limousines were parked to the side of the grey-stone mansion, near closed garages. Guards, armed with automatic rifles, were patrolling the immediate vicinity of the house, and the rear grounds. There was a large storage shed and stables, set back from the house by several hundred yards.

Further from the house and the stables, was another storage barn. A dirt and gravel road led to it, with overhanging trees and foliage.

"Impressive," George said to David. "It will take a while to go over it. I wonder, if Rodriguez and his crowd're anywhere close yet."

"We'll have to deal with them sooner or later," David said.

"Then, why not sooner?" George interrupted. "Why not take them out now? We know where we can find them."

"Does that include the physicist?"

"Why not?" George asked. "She's helping them."

"Marbison is right," David replied. "You're impetuous."

"That guy!" George scoffed. "Do you really think we'll see him?"

"I'd bet our Swiss bank accounts on that," David said. "To terminate we need orders."

"Unless, 'in our judgement, they pose threats to our lives or our mission.'"

"I know what the book says," David snapped. "Confucius says, 'Never kill man, when you can leave him in the dust some other way.'"

"Our ace-in-the-hole will help us there," George said.

"We'll need a full recon team," David said. "Head for the nearest airport," he told the pilot. "We need background on the house."

"Zürich is a short hop," the pilot replied, as he turned the aircraft south.

David and George left the pilot and the helicopter at the airport. They phoned Paris, for reports on the Cuban.

According to their contact, most, including the physicist, were still there. Rodriguez and two men were on another day of helicopter rides, and had not returned.

George and David visited real estate firms downtown. The well-renowned Swiss respect for privacy was an obstacle, until they found a small firm, owned by a self-described iconoclast, named Fischer. He helped them run the local village and land records on databanks for a cheap fee.

The estate was titled in the name of a U.S. corporation, "TeaLeaf, Inc.," with a European subsidiary, "T.E.I., S.A.," listed as well. The real estate man made inquiries, receiving names and addresses of agents for the two businesses. One name was no surprise to them.

They helicoptered back to Paris and drove to their contact's offices near the Opera. His cover was an import-export and merchandising business in farm machinery and equipment, to and from the EU. He was short, balding, fifty-ish, and favored European-cut business suits.

"Anything on Rodriguez?" David asked him, after his secretary showed them into his private suite.

"He and his friends're back at the hotel," the contact replied. "Our people are there. They reported heavy, cryptic phone traffic from Rodriguez' rooms."

"How fast can you get us a recon team?" David asked. "We've located the estate where Rodriguez was taken. He's getting close."

"I say we take him and his people out," George said. "Now.

Before they cause us more trouble."

"We settled that for the moment," David said, irked.

"That's between you and your Control," the contact said. "I'm not getting into the middle of that. I'll get the extra team, but any hits have to be ordered from the executive suite. I'll have the men here by morning."

"Do it," David said, still angry that his partner argued with him "in public," even if in front of a fellow agent. "Meanwhile, we'll have a look at Rodriguez."

"You two leave your car here." The contact called another agent to drive them to the Rodriguez stakeout.

The surveillance was in a hotel across the street from Rodriguez'. Three men were on duty.

David nudged a man with headphones. "On the speaker," David said to him.

"Start at this place near." Rodriguez was saying..., "*Schaffhausen*. Then, *Baden*, *Winterthur*. After that, we'll head down the *Aare* Valley."

"Those bastards're closer than we thought," David said. "That only gives us a day or two. Maybe, three."

"Hit them," George said. "I'm telling you right now. We'll be sorry we didn't, if that Iranian bastard gets near a bomb."

"Rodriguez must know that," David interrupted. "At least give the bastard that much credit. Our main concern is our own touch-raid."

They listened to the Cuban's planning. Afterward, they returned to their own hotel on the Rue St. Antoine for the night.

The next morning they were back in the contact's offices. The contact had assembled a six-man team. Each was a resident agent from Paris, drawn from other assignments.

David briefed them, working from a hand-drawn map he made during the over-flights and from the photographs and videotapes. They would fly to Switzerland that evening and would be met by other contacts.

The group was divided into two four-man teams, George and David each leading one. As David had earlier requested, the Paris contact provided them Geiger counters and similar detection devices.

The surveillance teams covering Rodriguez had already reported. He and his men left by helicopter again, with a flight plan for Switzerland and return to Paris. His colleagues stayed at the hotel.

David and George discussed the problem of keeping watch on Rodriguez, away from Paris. The raid on the estate would not be the end of the assignment, they told their team members.

"This smells like D.C. to me," George said to David. "We were bored as shit there, too."

They took off a little after 4 P.M. The afternoon spread into twilight. It was due to be a no-moon night. In his small space in the chopper, David tested the radiation detectors, to suppress his own boredom. Equipment tests did nothing to dissipate it. The flight seemed longer to him than before.

Finding the bombs was easy, and he was pleased it had been. These men: were they "cutting edge?"

The chopper landed in a gully. The estate was a ten- or twelve-minute drive over narrow and very curved mountain roads. Swiss contacts, five men in all, were waiting for them. The contacts brought a car and van, along with black "fatigues," weapons, with sound suppressors, and American-style night-vision and miniaturized radio equipment.

Two Swiss contact men would stay with the copter as security. The rest would lead the raiders to the estate. The chief contact had arranged surveillance of the estate's main entrances.

George, David, and their teams prepared. The landscape looked like a bizarre, green, two-dimensional world, through the night vision goggles.

Near the entry point David had isolated, the contacts hid the van in a pre-appropriated barn, with a small cottage nearby. David expected guards and security traps, even a fence, close to the road. The far shed would be the first stop, then the stables and storage barn closer to the house. The mansion was not in play: the bombs would not have been stored there.

George's team headed off into the thick woods first, angling to the left. He told David over the headset he and his people had found an electrified, chain link fence, but no guards or cameras. David and his group reached the barrier. He called George: they would cross at the same point.

Meanwhile, David and his men dug a shallow trough. They found a trip-wire below ground level, and clamped it off with wire extenders. One man at a time shimmied under the fence. The two groups split again.

They had seen no guards and heard no noises alien to the forest. David wondered, if they had taken a wrong turn. He heard human sounds at last. About a hundred yards ahead, he saw a structure. There were no guards patrolling. *Maybe they were in mid-rounds*, he thought.

George joined him. The eight men started toward the shed. David sent two men to canvass it. The canvassers reported no guards nearby.

David found conventional locks, but no alarm system on it. A large generator stood beside it, but the machine was cold and smelled of stale petrol. One man trailed him in, while the other two posted themselves safely hidden outside.

The windows were covered with blackout curtains. David turned on a Geiger counter. There were a few rapid clicks as he approached the back corner. In the floor he found a trap-door, more difficult to unlock.

There was a stone staircase, thirty or forty feet deep. To David it looked like a mineshaft. But the walls were smooth, white concrete. David lit a lantern he had in his backpack. As he and his man descended, the Geiger counter kept chattering.

The room was a half-acre large. Perhaps, larger. The light from the lamp faded into deep shadows farther in. The ceiling did not present claustrophobics with any threats, fifteen feet high, with argon lights in steel fixtures.

Part of the place was empty. Thirty feet from the stairs they saw medium- and small-sized crates. As they drew closer, the counter reached a constant clatter. David saw the stampings, "USA" and "U.S. Army," on them.

David picked up one of the smaller containers. It was empty. He ran the Geiger counter over the interior. Clatter continued.

He and his man tried a larger crate. It was empty, too, but the counter did not stop chirping.

All together there were ten or eleven small crates and four or five larger ones. There were many broken boards as well, but nothing else.

"We were too late," David said, as much to himself as to the other man.

Topside, they put their night goggles back on. David locked the trap, and they headed for the door. Before they reached it, David's headset crackled.

"Incoming!" George whispered.

David motioned the other man back to the trap door. He could hear two voices, speaking German and getting nearer.

David cursed himself for locking it. He put the Geiger counter on the floor beside the trap. The voices were getting louder. Already, his man had his sound-suppressed *Uzi* cocked and ready. The lock did not open.

David and the other man put their packs into a cardboard box. Pushing crates away from the wall, they slipped behind them.

The doorknob rattled and the voices were intelligible. It was then he remembered the Geiger counter.

* * *

George repeated the warning to David over his headset. He also summoned his two reconnaissance men.

There was more waiting. The guards had been in the shed for five minutes. How much could there be to a one-story barn?

His recon team called. They were on their way back, and reported the other buildings clear. He told them to stay put. The guards still did not appear.

At the rear wall of the shed, George clamped a small directional microphone on a window. He heard laughing and remarks about "reefer."

The guards finished their "dope break," emerging giddy, their weapons slung.

"Two happy guards. Wait for it," he called to his recon men.

When the guards disappeared up the gravel road, he called David.

"They're gone," David said over the headset in reply. "But

I'm high as a kite."

He and his man rejoined George. "Christ! Those two hash junkies! They're lucky they didn't burn the place to the ground." David told him what they found.

They headed for the stables. The smell of marijuana and hashish still lingered in the cold air. David used a rear door to the building.

It was a functioning horse stable with twenty-plus occupied stalls. If the rest were like the first two horses he saw, David concluded, there was serious *Geld* invested there.

He doubted the owner(s) would endanger those investments with glowing in the dark by stud-time. In the stables, all he heard on the Geiger counter was a typical, low-radiation *TICK*.

They moved on to the two-story barn, a modified A-frame. Loft doors were open on the front, but they were lighted.

Two men came with David. George replaced the lock, after they were inside.

There was unpunctuated darkness. They found hay bales and burlap sacks of animal fodder, but no other animals.

Near a stack of feed bags, they found a trap-door. Its underground staircase was like the one in the shed: dense, cold stone. The descent was as long as earlier. David lit the torch again.

The storage room was smaller, not by much, and similar in construction. This time he found something more substantial.

There were more crates, stamped "USA" or "U.S. Army," many more than had been in the shed. Many differently shaped crates were heavy. He found a grappling hook and pried one open.

It was full of M-16 rifles. He reclosed it and found a Stinger in another crate. Still others were marked, "M-19," "TOW," and "M-3," and marked with British, French, and German Army identifications. David used the Geiger counter, but got the same, less than occasional, *TICK*.

He returned to ground-level, and called George, who had the lock open, by the time they relocked the trapdoor. Once behind the stable, David told George what he found.

"Maybe we should let Rodriguez spook these guys," David whispered. "They might lead us some place interesting. In fact, maybe we should give Rodriguez a little help finding this place."

"If we're lucky, they take out Rodriguez *and* the Iranian," George answered.

"That's what Marbison said, when I floated the idea with him," David whispered. "Back to Paris."

They heard voices getting closer to the clearing. There was loud swearing and cursing in English, as well as German.

Through his goggles, David saw men walking toward the storage barn with the weapons cache. One was an older-looking man, taller than the rest, dressed in camouflage fatigues and leading in both posture and profanity.

David made out, "Goddamn bullshit!" But lost his next remarks, when others spoke. He and George waited until the group was in the barn.

They sneaked up to the back wall of it, found a knothole, and stuck a directional mike into it. David listened.

"Fuckin' bullshit," he heard the same profane voice say. It was an American accent, very Southern.

"I don't give a goddamn, Colonel. Von Markenheim'll hear about this!"

Another voice replied, also from the American South. The voices faded.

David and George returned to their hiding place in the woods. Though it was almost midnight, they decided to watch a while longer. When David looked at his watch again, it read 1:30 A.M.

The group came out. The tall, profane man locked the door. "Satisfied now?!" he said.

"I wish we could tail *them* without getting caught," David said. "Or leave somebody here."

"Anybody in mind, Fella?" George asked.

* * *

Jaime leaned over to the driver, who had picked them up at a meadow landing, near *Solothurn*, Switzerland. He was a Swiss-resident agent for Jaime's service. The helicopter trailed them.

"How far to the next landing strip and churches?" Jaime asked.

"Fifteen kilometers," the driver answered, "between *Zofingen* and *Lenzburg*."

"I hope it's better than the last ones," Jamael said. "I told you we should've stuffed those."

"You know, *amigo*," Jaime said. He was angry at the Iranian, but caught himself.

"As for churches," the driver said. "There are only a few."

"Estates?" Emilio asked.

"One further up in the mountains," the driver answered. "Southwest of Zürich. It's on the other side of the *Hallwiler See*."

They reached the landing field. It was paved and long enough for small, propeller aircraft, borderline for twin-props. There were puddles and patches of ice on the runway.

Over the next two hours they checked churches. None had chimes, only single bells in their towers.

They drove toward *Baden*, then turned southeast to Zürich. They were looking for another airfield, nestled in the *Reuss* River Valley, between two higher plateaus. They could not locate it and called the helicopter to lead them there. That field turned out to have a hard dirt and gravel surface.

Looking for the estate the driver had mentioned, they doubled back toward the *Hallwiler See*, a finger of a lake, west-southwest of Zürich. This they found easily.

The estate had good private security, tall entry gates, fences covered in foliage and hedges, but no signs of guards encumbered with assault weapons, as Jaime expected.

In the small, nearby village, they inquired about the estate. It belonged to a retired American businessman and his wife. The American couple was spending Fall and Winter in Nice and had not been there at least two months.

"Do you think someone else's using their place?" Emilio asked. "Perfect. Like in that classic movie, with Cary Grant."

"It could be, but it doesn't smell right to me," Jaime answered. "Maybe we take a look after we're finished the list. It doesn't have many left."

They turned northeast and returned to Zürich for the night.

They checked into a small hotel, not far from the *Zürichsee*. Jaime called Paris, as earlier arranged.

There had been a surprise development, a cryptic phone call from an English-speaker, offering "interesting information."

"What d'you mean he didn't identify himself?" Jaime boomed. "But he knew my name?! What else?!"

Jaime listened. "That sounds like bullshit! . . . Yeah. He'll call back when? . . . Shit! Yeah. We'll be back in the morning."

"More fucking bullshit," Jamael said. "I'm worried. Our rooms could be under surveillance. The *Sureté*, maybe."

"Or somebody inside," Emilio said, "trying for a private deal with us."

On the flight to Paris later, Jaime felt ambivalence. Despite rainy weather they were in the French capital by noon. The caller was expected to contact them around 1 P.M.

The phone in Jaime's pension room rang at 1:03 P.M. The voice sounded Eastern European to him, Czech or German.

"You're in the market for some special," the caller hesitated, "devices. For a fee, I might lead you."

"Who are you?!!" Jaime asked. "I don't know you for shit!"

"Friends. Let's say the best ones you've got. A little Russian hen in Manhattan," the caller replied, cackling. "She's a friend of ours, too. Real close. Like you." More cackling.

"How'd you find . . ."

"Enough small-talk. If you're interested, Eiffel Tower, second level. Second pay phone from the left, at the café. Come alone. two P.M. Sharp. Tomorrow. Bring half-a-million francs."

"I can't get that much cash together on short notice," Jaime replied.

"How unfortunate. If we see you, we see you. If we don't, you never will know us for shit."

*   *   *

David hung up the receiver, and glanced at the pension with binoculars.

"Well, comrade," the Paris contact smiled. "Did he buy it?"

"He's so ravenous I could smell his froth," David replied.

"You want one of my people to meet him?" the contact asked.

David grinned. "I'll do it. I haven't been in drag for a while. But I want cover. This guy's a rubber cigar. Here's a list of things I'll need."

* * *

The café in the Eiffel Tower was crowded with tourists, mostly American and German, as Jaime waited near the telephones. He had stuck a small "Out of Order" sign on the second phone.

Against his instinct, he left the others at the pension. The postcards he had been browsing for the previous half-hour were boring him, when the phone rang. His watch read 1:59 P.M..

"*M*. Rodriguez?" a high-pitched female voice with a French accent asked.

"Listen carefully. Go to ground level. Wait exactly five minutes. Ascend to the third level. Look for a ravishing brunette in black dress, hat, and veil. *C'est moi.* Hope you're alone. If not, no meet." *CLICK!*

Jaime took the stairs to the first level and waited. His gun was in a concealed pocket in his down jacket.

The top level held Eiffel's original apartment, with its glass windows for public ogle, but not entry. The elevator was crowded, mostly with more tourists.

Jaime looked for the black hat and dress. He took a slow swing around the platform, alternating glances at the apartment, the crowd, and the Paris landscape. Through one room of the apartment he noticed a woman, on the opposite side of the platform, hatted and veiled, with above-elbow gloves. She was watching him. Their glances met.

He hurried around the corner. She stepped aside, avoiding him, as he nearly bumped into her.

"I see you and I share an admiration of *M*. Eiffel's ultimate penthouse," she said in English, calmly, with a quiet French accent. "*M*. Rodriguez, *non?*"

Her haughty, maybe arrogant, self-description was accurate, after all, Jaime thought.

Her body, outlined in a black dress to above-the-knee, with matching hose, *was* "ravishing." Her veil, hanging from a velvet hat, was lightly opaque, revealing a beautiful face, well-made-up and with bright red lipstick. Her perfume was also expensive.

Jaime took her by the elbow to the railing. No one was standing near them, though the tourists were ubiquitously passing.

"My interest in Eiffel's fading. I'm taken with more modern conveniences and devices," Jaime said. "Political devices. And people who provide cartography to them. Perhaps we could discuss the matter over a glass of wine."

"I prefer a position of advantage," she said. "Above the crowd. Also, I prefer to survive encounters of this sort."

"We can't talk here," Jaime whispered.

"We're doing fine," she replied. "Has your cash flow improved?"

"Maybe," he answered. "Is this only a first encounter?"

"*Non*," she said. "A first and final accounting—with me."

"I'm not paying that kind of money," Jaime said, "without verification."

"We do no business," she answered, turning away from him. "Your loss."

He grabbed her arm and brought her back.

"Let go of me," she snarled, pulling away from him. "Or I'll send your manhood to the top of your skull."

Jaime noticed people paying attention to them.

"Darling," he said. "I'm sorry. I want nothing to come between us." The others went back to their sightseeing, nodding their heads.

She straightened her dress. "Better. Shall we resume negotiations?"

* * *

Through a headset, David listened to the conversation from the top of the Eiffel Tower. He was with his Paris contact on the second level, and was dressed in the same ensemble as the woman agent with Rodriguez. The contact had been surprised at what an attractive "woman" David made, especially with the veil over his face.

David was glad the contact talked him into sending one of the contact's female operatives. *Give him the envelope*, David thought.

"How'd your people know about me?" Rodriguez asked.

"My colleague already made that clear. It's not relevant to our current discussion," the woman replied. "We'll take the money now."

"I'll give you ten percent now, the other 90, when I get back. What's to keep me from blowing you off after I've got what I want?"

"You might," she said. "But we know where we can find you. Anywhere. Remember whom we know... ninety-five percent now."

"Twenty percent," Rodriguez haggled.

"Enough," she said. "90%, or I leave now."

"Twenty-five percent," the Cuban replied.

"Bye-bye."

"OK, OK," Rodriguez relented.

"The money, first," she said. *CLICK! CLICK!*

"What do I find in here?" Rodriguez asked.

"Am I your seeing-eye-dog?" the woman snapped. David heard paper tearing.

"It's in French!"

"You were expecting Spanish?!"

"After this is over, I want to meet you out of that lace."

"I never mix business *avec plaisir*," she said. "Bye"

"Don't you mean *a bientot*? I still have to give you the rest."

"You'll be contacted by another colleague. Bye-bye."

David listened, but there was no further conversation. He heard only crowd noises, until the woman's voice said, softly, "On my way out."

On the ground level, David waited for his look-alike in a ladies' room. When finally she came in, he whispered to her, then left, leading Rodriguez on an involuntary tour of the city before giving him the slip.

* * *

As he got out of the taxi, at his pension, Jaime was still cursing his luck. He followed the woman-in-black through Paris, by cab and Metro, only to lose her near the *Place de la Concorde*. He still wondered what she looked like without the veil—or the dress, for that matter. He fancied to himself he would meet her again.

Before returning to his lodgings, he had stopped at the office of a resident-colleague, who translated the paper from the woman. The location corresponded to a stop on Jaime's list. It was an estate outside *Winterthur*.

Back at the pension, Jaime told Emilio and Jamael about the meeting. He omitted his failed pursuit. They would resume their helicopter travel with an aerial view, then a ground reconnoitre, of the estate. They reassured the physicist, who was smoking herself into an uneasy calm. Jaime called their Swiss contact.

By 6:30 A.M. the next morning Jaime, Emilio, and Jamael were on their way to *Winterthur*, Switzerland. They reached the Swiss contact by radio. The rendezvous point was an airstrip.

They located it more easily than Jaime expected. Once landed, they followed the contact's car to the estate. Jaime made a video of it, on drive-bys.

Jaime, Emilio, and Jamael accompanied the contact to a country inn, where they planned their reconnaissance for two nights later.

The next day, the four men scouted the property's boundaries by car. They found several possible entry points.

One seemed especially promising, until the small, otherwise-abandoned cottage across the road from it looked recently used. There was a barn behind it. That night and the following day they reviewed the plan and the geography. The contact provided most of the necessary materiel, including weapons, a Geiger counter, and other equipment. There was only the wait, then, for the operation to commence at 6 P.M.

*   *   *

George listened as the call rang a third time. He was in a telephone stall, outside the village post office, miles from the cottage and the estate. His motor-scooter was outside. The line clicked and a woman's voice answered.

"Put David on," George said, pulling the booth door closed. It was 1:30 A.M.

George briefed his partner. "The morons almost got caught, like the Keystone Kops. See you tomorrow." He returned to his scooter.

The village was dark and quiet. Sporadic street lights dotted the roads. Some houses were lighted. Only occasional pedestrians or vehicles were out.

George rode to the cottage near the entry he, David, and the others had used. He had been splitting time between that shack and the camouflaged "rathole" David and two other agents had helped him prepare in the woods near the weapons barn.

From the woods he observed the estate's happenings. Each night he called David in Paris.

There had been quite a bit of activity on the estate. Trucks had come and gone each day and night. Shipments arrived or departed under armed escort. The loading was well-guarded.

So far he had been lucky. His "rathole" had not attracted any other "rodents." The cottage seemed like it was searched, though not carefully. That concerned him, until he realized Rodriguez and Co. were responsible.

This night George had watched Rodriguez, the Iranian, and two other men do a sloppy reconnaissance of the estate. Laurel and Hardy and The Three Stooges had nothing on these guys and their unintended sight-gags. He diverted the guards, without giving himself away, either to them or to the Cuban. Afterward, he tailed them to where they were staying in the village.

David had told him the rest of the Cuban's people were preparing to leave. They were awaiting Rodriguez' phone call.

It was after 3 A.M. when George arrived at the shack. He slept for a few hours, his scooter and other personal items in the cellar with him. On the trap-door to the basement there was a latch, which George locked before going to sleep.

Overhead footsteps awakened him. He grabbed his automatic pistol and listened. More than one person seemed to be up there. A friendly voice called his name.

"Down here, you son-of-a-bitch!" George said. "You scared the shit out of me!"

"I'm getting your adrenalin on the fast track," David said, when George had joined him. Other agents from the raid were with David. It was mid-morning.

"They got their call," David answered. "They're due here shortly by chopper. Rodriguez'll take them to the 'inn.' Sound right?"

"They're staying at a small *gasthaus*," George said. "Rodriguez and his all-*klutz* orchestra." He laughed. "It was all I could do to keep from popping them."

"You get an 'A' in self-restraint," David said. "At least Rodriguez'll be good for something."

"Leave two guys here," George said. "I'll show you the *gasthaus*."

* * *

Jaime and the contact watched as the helicopter landed. It was carrying his people from Paris, including the physicist. En route to the village, they picked up Jamael and Emilio. Jaime briefed them on the operations.

He decided another reconnaissance was necessary, only delaying the more important operation by a little. He told the physicist of the residual radiation in the storage barn. That information sped her rate of cigarette consumption. Jaime assured her she would only go on the final mission.

They arrived at a storage shed the contact owned, as a staging point. It was a mile-and-a-half from their surreptitious entry to the estate. The contact had brought their equipment to the shed earlier that morning.

Jaime explained the plan on a rough map he prepared. The physicist would wait there with Emilio. It was even more urgent, he concluded, that they "pull the heist." He watched Jamael, who seemed less pleased at the idea of sharing.

They drove to the entry spot after nightfall. The contact parked behind the cottage across the road. The cottage was in the same condition as before: recently used, but not occupied.

They did a facsimile of "the limbo," under the fence then moved on.

* * *

David lifted the hatch to the cottage's cellar. A cell phone call from the "shadow" team assigned to Rodriguez tipped him the Cuban and the others were coming.

George and he emerged and waited half-an-hour. "Give them enough time to get enmeshed," he said. "Then cool that guy."

"Now you're talking," George replied. "I'll put him to sleep from here. With a little luck, none of them'll make it out of there."

David made a call on his cell phone. "Now," he said into it. "Maybe, we should stay," David said to George.

"Let's not be too smart for our own good," George said. "We'll put this guy away and get the hell out of here."

Jaime's man, who was guarding the Cuban's entry point, turned to the cottage, and was speaking into a hand-radio. George and David used a tranquilizer gun on him, and stuffed him into the intruders' van.

"So much for the other ten percent," David quipped, as they sped off on the scooter.

* * *

It was several days since he had seen Samantha Pemberton. After more silence from his microphones, John Marshall decided he should check. He would have looked in sooner, but it had been "open season" on emergencies.

The "bugs" had been silent before, without anything being wrong. However, when she was in Illinois, there was noise, but no talking. Someone, he discovered later, had trashed her room.

SAMANTHA. Did he care for her? Yes, more than his promise to "Old Doc." Protective? Yes. Romantic? Perhaps he had seen too much.... May-October?

It was early afternoon on a regular school day. Dressed in a University maintenance uniform, he faded into the dorm traffic, like when he installed his "bugs" in her room, in August. Picking her lock was also no problem.

The room was lived-in, neat-sloppy. There was organization, but clothes and books were laid around. Her larger suitcase was there, her smaller one gone. The purse he recalled her using regularly was also gone.

Her lobby mailbox was stuffed full. He talked to the on-duty resident-director, telling her he had a work order for a leaky sink in Room 241.

"She hasn't picked up her mail for a couple days," the director told him. Back in her room, Marshall found his microphones in place. He found other ones, but left them alone. In his mind he was grousing again, only this time his anger was real. Unfortunately, he had no time to trace her. He had his "own problems."

XVI

Samantha was looking in the mirror of her new Arden compact, as she reglossed and mummed her lips. Closing the makeup container, she put it into the *Chanel* purse Regina had given her. She still found it difficult to recognize the blonde who was staring back at her. In the background, she heard the jet's engines humming.

A female flight attendant offered another glass of *champagne*. Sam declined. She had already had two with dinner.

Sam had forgotten how the liquor flowed in First Class overseas flights. Never one to doze on air trips, she took the *champagne*, hoping to sleep this time.

She leaned back with her earphones on. She had already seen the in-flight film in Washington, another "hack-and-slash, macho flick," which did not bear a second viewing. The earphones turned into effective earplugs.

Sam thought about Marshall. She remembered what the hairdresser said about her "boyfriend." She wondered if she should call Marshall that; if she wanted to. . . .

She pondered life after this, after she found The Professor and brought him home. *Settle into something "normal"? Boring? Actually, after all this, boring might not be so bad.*

Could she begin to plan? Finish school, finally? Think about graduate school? Law? Career? Even marriage and children? Sin and children? All of the above? Some of the above? With Marshall? Did she want an attachment at all?

Could she manage a career and marriage? Did she want to be on her own for a while, first? Did she still have a responsibility to the Twins? What about a responsibility to herself?

Sam stopped. She was thinking in too many safe, "American Dream" terms. Death invaded her comfortable bourgeois daydreams. Or its penumbra did. Then, there was "The Dream." The quasi-neo-crypto-Nazis. "A little bit of us."

Suddenly, the future seemed to include only the end of this flight. The next sunrise. Paris, five or six hours hence.

Things had gone well thus far. Reviewing her next steps gave her back bourgeois comfort for a time. The Channel Coast. The Calais gap. London overnight. On to Oxford on Sunday, to see "Uncle" Maxim. Stay there, as long as it took.

The *champagne* took over. Sam felt dozy. Her mind was drifting. A light "buzz" behind the forehead.

* * *

He took a stroll to the forward lounge. He passed Samantha Pemberton's seat. She had been quiet, inactive, since takeoff.

She was attractive to him. He had been surprised by her new appearance. If the homing device in the *Chanel* purse had not been working, he would never have recognized her.

Perhaps he would try to pick her up, before the flight was over. *She was probably more approachable,* he thought, *than Regina Foxwirth. Regina would be along, after that. Beautiful, cold Regina . . . Fräulein Pemberton looked beautiful, in her own way.* He almost regretted the assignment. Almost.

* * *

A flight attendant awakened Sam. "We'll be landing in London in about an hour," he said, in perfect "muzak." He handed Sam First-Class perks and offered breakfast.

"Only rolls and tea," Sam replied. She looked over her makeup and did a few adjustments, before the food arrived. Sam was hungry. The *champagne* had worn off, but left no hangover. She slept well and felt refreshed.

Before long, the pilot's voice came over the speaker system. He gave the usual valedictory, with corporate gratitude, mentioning the arrangements for those continuing to Paris. The same flight attendant brought Sam various British and French entry papers. Sam thought of John Marshall again. Had he discovered her absence yet? And there was Bob, too. She felt bad about what she had told him, but she dismissed those regrets.

At Heathrow Airport, Sam took her suitcase, dress bag, and *Chanel* purse and headed off to the plane-change to Paris. She was still impressed at how many clothes she had packed in that dress-carrier. Quite a few of her fellow passengers were going to France as well.

The flight-time to Charles De Gaulle Airport was short. Sam finished filling out her French visa papers before landing. Getting through Passport Control and Customs took longer.

Afterward, Sam caught the *RER* suburban train into the city, to spend too few hours in one of her favorite European cities. She dropped her luggage at the *Gare du Nord* in a locker, and reserved a seat on the next train to Calais, at 2:15 P.M. She continued on by *Metro*.

She always loved morning in Paris. This one was clear and cool, with the sun breaking through the city's smog. She regretted it not being Spring, or having more time, or even having someone else with whom to share the city. Perhaps when all this was over, Spring here. With someone. When this was all over, it would be Spring.

Sam strolled along the *Champs Elysées*, after cashing a few travelers' checks at the American Express office at *11 rue Scribe*. The sidewalks were crowded with weekend shoppers.

Wandering back to the *Opera* district and its shopping areas, Sam spent time in both branches of *Galeries Lafayette* and in *Le Printemps*. The city had not changed much since her most recent visit, though the fast food and high-consumption places along the *Champs* had unfortunately multiplied.

After shopping, she breezed through the *Louvre*. *Such a wonderful escape*, she reflected, as she viewed paintings. These minutes in a favored museum were the only escape she expected.

Sam caught a cab to the *Gare du Nord*. The cab ride reacquainted her with full-bodied adrenalin "rushes."

The train was late leaving. Already Sam abandoned hope of arriving in London before 9 P.M. Before she left the U.S., she made a one-night reservation at a more expensive hotel in the West End, on Kensington High Street.

There were three other people in the compartment with her: an older woman, a woman closer to Sam's age, and a tall, blond man in a leather coat.

Near Calais, before passport checks by Customs, he was replaced by a middle-aged man with grey hair and two attaché cases. The women remained until bus-time to the Hoverport. The crossing was predictably choppy, though the hovercraft made it enjoyable, compared to the boat-train, or "The Chunnel."

Sam fantasized about her fellow passengers. She imagined the first man was an out-of-work Soviet spy, unable to break the "leather habit." The women acted like mother-and-daughter, traveling to London for a plastic money weekend. Or perhaps professionals, with EU meetings in Whitehall. The second man was a hopelessly routine businessman on his way to a premature coronary.

She read the lead stories in *Time* and the *International Herald-Tribune* about unrest in the Balkans and Russia. Russia was in the middle of another constitutional crisis and power struggle. The old-line Communists were active again. The Russian President was due in the West soon, on scheduled visits. *Would she see him during public appearances?*

British Rail from Ramsgate to London was bumpier than the Continental rail lines. The euphoria of Paris had worn Sam out. Though her escape from Washington seemed clean, she felt paranoia again before arrival at Victoria Station.

Oxford the next day. "Uncle Maxim" or "Max" would be surprised, especially since she and The Professor had not visited him in several years. The list of "Must-Stops on Holiday," from The Stash, was not alphabetized. Uncle Max's name was at the top of it.

"Uncle Max" was an old friend of her parents. He was a professor of Political-Economy, a defector from East Germany in the 1970s. He had taught at Oxford since his defection. On Pemberton family trips a stay in Oxford was *de rigueur*. She loved him, like a favorite uncle. If anyone on the list could help her and had a cache of information, it was Uncle Max.

The train from Paddington Station to Oxford was on time. The First-Class bed in the First-Class, West End hotel had been worth it, after airliner and train seats. Despite her *angst*, Sam had rested well.

The ride to Oxford and the still-green-but-leafless English countryside brought back many memories. Sam walked from Oxford Station across the Canal toward Lincoln College to whose faculty Uncle Max belonged. His spouse had divorced him after his defection. He never remarried, though Sam knew he had engaged in unmarried non-celibacy, since that time.

Sam checked into a hotel, a comfortable place with a definite academic afterglow, on the High Street, a relatively short walk from the station.

With the information from her father's files stowed in the hotel's safe, Sam walked to Uncle Max's house. His was "typical English town," as he referred to it, tucked in a row of similar houses, off Magdalen Street near Corpus Christi College.

The housekeeper recognized her, despite the years and the blonding. She hugged Sam warmly, and told her Uncle Max was off on his Sunday morning "stroll-and-stop" in the Magdalen Grove.

"I'll surprise him," Sam gushed, as she headed to the meadows, on the eastern edge of town.

It was fifteen minutes to the Grove, behind Magdalen College. Only scattered human visitors and the deer were awake and moving. She crossed the Grove, toward the River Cherwell, and found him reading under a defrocked tree in the northern corner.

Sam swung from behind the tree, and blurted, loudly, "I should've known I'd find you with your precious deer!"

Uncle Max looked up, startled. "Who're...? It can't be!... Samantha? Sammie Pemberton?" They embraced.

"What're you doing here?" he continued. "How's Tom? Is he with you...? Ah! My little Sammie! Let me look at you." His German accent was tempered by Oxford-English bombardment.

Uncle Max was still the tall, thin, bald, and middle-aged man she remembered. The fringe of hair that rounded his head had turned from grey to white, and more wrinkles showed on his face.

"You've matured well. But your hair was brown."

"I needed a change," Sam replied. "I did this on a lark."

"It becomes you," Uncle Max said, "makes you look more Nordic, northern-European. So, what about your father?"

"Pa's not with me this time," Sam replied. "He's the reason I'm here. Can we go to Addison Walk? I need to talk with you."

"No pleasure trip, is it? Your hair change?"

"I stopped at your house," Sam said. "Bertha told me where you were."

They walked along the Cherwell, till the bridge to the Water Walks.

When Sam saw they were alone on Addison Walk, she said, "I've come for the packet Pa left with you. He sent me for it, for his new book. I've been helping him with it. He couldn't come himself."

"Assuming there's a packet, Sammie," Uncle Max said. "Not saying there is, but if there is, how do I know those're his wishes? He could have written, telephoned, or come himself."

"Do you doubt me, Uncle Max? I'm not a stranger."

"Where're you staying? I assume you're here overnight?"

"At Eastgate... Uncle Max...."

"That's a fine establishment. Have you had breakfast? Let's find some tea. I could use a cup."

In his own library-den, with Bertha, his housekeeper, serving, Uncle Max and Sam found their tea. Bertha excused herself.

"Now, why couldn't your father come himself?" Uncle Max asked. He took a sip of tea, after blowing steam away.

"The quasi-pseudo-family business. 'Very important business.'"

"That Cartel of his, *nicht wahr*? *Gottverdammte* thing," Uncle Max said. "I told him years ago to leave it. Nothing but trouble."

"Pa's working on an *exposé* of it."

"Yes, yes," Uncle Max replied. "I know that. Otherwise, I'd not have agreed. He should have written it years ago."

"Pa was afraid he was being watched."

"You could be, too. D'you expect to pick up all his caches and carry them across Europe? Even I don't know where they all are. He planned it that way."

"He gave me his list before he left," Sam said, blanching at another "grey truth." "But I'm not to carry them myself. Not for long, that is."

"What were his instructions?"

"In each city, I'm to ship similar parcels. By national post, private carriers, like UPS to reliable people in the States, till he retrieves them. I need your help."

"And if he can't retrieve them?"

"By Bob or me."

"If anything happens to you two? Daisy?... or the Twins?"

"No," Sam said, firmly. "The U.S. Government gets them. Friends of his in CIA and the State Department."

"More *verdammte* technocrats!" Uncle Max replied. "Does he expect them to do anything? Especially in our current atmospherics?!"

"He knows a few who'll try," Sam answered. "I met two of them myself."

Uncle Max said, "He told me not to release it to anyone but him, while he's alive. But, if one cannot trust the daughter... We'll go tomorrow. Today we'll spend together. And what's this nonsense of a hotel? You'll stay here."

"I'd love to, Uncle Max," Sam said. "But I think it'd be safer if I didn't this time. Next time, I promise."

He sighed. "Very well. You're as headstrong as your mother was. I could never get her to reconsider things. Your father, too. Stubborn family! But I love you all. Let's take a walk to my den. I've added a few things since you were here last."

The visit to Uncle Max's "den" at the College took several hours. Sam and he reminisced, as he showed her his books and other newer "trophies."

That evening over a more Continental dinner, Sam brought him up to date. Over brandy he confessed a certain love for her mother, though never expecting it to be anything, but unreturned. Sam was surprised, and wondered if his feelings extended to her.

He drove her back to the hotel after midnight. "Ten-thirty. Sharp. I'll pick you up here," he said. "And don't keep me waiting. There's much to do."

The next morning, afraid she would oversleep, Sam awakened at 6:30 A.M. She was nervous, although she did not want Uncle Max to know that.

She looked over the list. Addresses in Vienna, Berlin, Munich, and Salzburg, among others, demanded stops. True to form, Uncle Max was punctual.

At a bank in town, where he kept a safe deposit box, he retrieved a package, wrapped in brown paper, placing it in a shopping bag.

They drove back to his home, but had to park several blocks away. They started for the house, with Uncle Max carrying the bag.

When they were in the middle of Turl Street, Sam heard a car's engine roar. A small, dark car sped toward them. Before she could think, Uncle Max shoved her to the curb.

The car slammed into him and sped off. His body bounced up on the hood and landed against a parked car. Sam got up, her legs throbbing.

"Uncle Max!" she screamed. "Oh, Christ!" she said, as she cradled his head. He was unconscious. Sam felt for a pulse. It was faint.

She lifted him by the shoulders and dragged him to the sidewalk. His head was bleeding. Sam covered him with her coat.

Rushing to a nearby rowhouse, she told the woman who answered what had happened. "I'll ring up the police," the woman replied. "Stay with your friend."

Two police cars and an ambulance with sirens blaring arrived. Sam had Uncle Max's head on her lap, as the emergency team rolled a stretcher to them. He was still unconscious and felt clammy to her.

While the paramedics did their work, Sam told two policemen about the incident. She gave them a description of the car.

"It was no accident!" Sam continued. "He tried to kill us! If it hadn't been for Uncle Max..." She was crying.

One policeman tried to calm her. "Why would anyone want to kill you?" the other asked her. He sounded patronizing to her.

"How the hell do I know?" Sam replied. "Uncle Max was a defector from East Germany years ago."

A paramedic came over to them. "He has serious internal injuries. We're off to hospital." He helped load Uncle Max into the ambulance.

"Please take me to the hospital," Sam said to the policemen. "I want to be with him. He has no family here."

The policemen drove her to John Radcliffe Hospital, in Headington, nearby.

At the emergency clinic, a staff nurse told Sam Uncle Max had multiple, broken bones, a collapsed lung and internal bleeding. The nurse led her to a waiting area, near the operating theatres. The police accompanied her.

"Can you think of a reason someone would want you or him dead?" the patronizer asked. "Seems a bit far-fetched, Miss."

"What had you two been doing earlier?" the other asked.

"He'd picked me up for breakfast at his home," Sam said.

"Is this your parcel or his?" the patronizer asked, picking up the shopping bag next to Sam.

"It's mine," Sam replied. "Gifts for home from Paris. I needed to mail it. I can't believe anyone would want to kill him!" Sam was crying again. "I'm sorry. Can't this wait?"

"'Spose so," replied the patronizer. "We've got a start with what you've told us. Probably won't turn up the perpetrators soon, however."

"I'll call you, when I feel more together," Sam said.

"Keep in touch with us," the other officer said. "We'll post a man at his room. May we see you to your hotel?" Sam declined, preferring to remain at the hospital. "We'll let you know if anything breaks," he told her, before leaving.

Hours passed. Sam felt anger and guilt. The fear, paranoia, and rage she felt after the kidnap attempt returned. Thoughts of death she had on the plane flicked in and out. She was scared, but not ready to quit; she would go on.

"Miss?" the staff nurse, who had spoken to her before, called to her. "These gentlemen would like a word with you."

There were three men with the nurse, two in police uniforms, the third in an ordinary suit. He identified himself, with credentials, as a chief inspector, and reminded her of "Inspector Morse."

During the ensuing interview, the inspector repeated many of the questions the first two constables had. Sam responded with the same answers. He offered her a lift to her hotel and police protection, even though the incident was classified as an ordinary hit-and-run. Again, she declined. The inspector left, after speaking with nurses at the main desk.

Sam decided to spend her time at Uncle Max's house, until she left Oxford. She was anxious to see the contents of the parcel. No need to trouble the police with her departure plans.

Another hour passed. Sam was restless, more agitated than before. Finally, a physician and a nurse, both in surgical garb, came to her.

"It was close," the surgeon said. "But he'll make it. His lung was very badly damaged. His heart stopped once, but we got it started again without a bother."

"May I see him?" Sam asked. "Just a few moments," she pleaded. "He's like my favorite uncle. He has no family of his own here."

"He'll be under heavy sedation," the surgeon replied. "The police asked the same thing. It won't be possible to question him for days."

The surgeon agreed to a short visit. "But you'll have to wear a surgical mask. The Sister here will let you know when it's time to leave."

Half an hour later, the nurse led Sam to a private room on the second floor. The constables Sam had seen with the chief inspector were outside.

The nurse placed a surgical mask over her face, and took her purse and the parcel until the visit was over. Sam was reluctant to leave the parcel with her, but did not want to appear too concerned.

Uncle Max was connected to life support and monitoring equipment, with I.V.s attached to his arms and hands. A nurse watched the monitors.

Sam's guilt felt heavy. Anger was easier, but she could not raise that rage then.

After a very short, too short, time, the duty nurse suggested the visit end. The relief Sam felt at getting the parcel countered her guilt.

At the main admission station, Sam found a police constable, ordered by the inspector to see her safely to her lodgings. He drove her to the hotel and then to Uncle Max's house.

Sam told Bertha about the accident. The housekeeper wanted to see him, but Sam convinced her to wait. Before her cab came, Sam had Bertha place the parcel in Uncle Max's safe in his study.

At the hotel Sam freshened up. As she was gathering clothes and other things, there was a knock on the door. She thought it might be another policeman, with more questions.

It was a hotel clerk with a name tag. She was a red-haired woman, shorter than Sam, with very prominent eyebrows and thick glasses and dressed in a grey suit. "May I have a word with you, Miss?" she asked Sam. "If you would accompany me downstairs, please?"

"What's this about?" Sam replied.

"Your length of stay," the clerk replied. "And the reasons you've been with the police. Only a few moments. Please?" She handed Sam a note and held her finger to her lips.

The note read, "You're being watched. Your room may have microphones in it. Please come into the hall. Liz."

Sam nearly repeated the name out loud. "LIZ??!!" She stuck her head out the door. Except for the clerk, the hall was empty.

"Only a few moments," the clerk repeated.

Sam stepped into the hall and closed the door slowly. "What the hell?!"

"Don't talk. Listen." It was no longer the English hotel clerk's voice she heard but Liz McGonnville's. "You've been followed here."

"Obviously," Sam quipped. "But what're . . . ?"

"I said, 'Listen,'" Liz replied, firmly. "Regina Foxwirth and a man're tailing you. She arrived a day or so ago and met him. He was on the plane with you. You look so different. They must have a homer on you somewhere."

A door to a room down the hall creaked. "As I was saying, Miss," Liz returned to her English voice. "I'm certain we can straighten this out. Downstairs in my office."

A young couple walked past. She waited for them to disappear through the exit.

She and Sam went to a comfortable office, downstairs, near the manager's. "I borrowed this from one of our residents."

"I thought I made a clean escape," Sam said.

"From us you did. I could lay some bullshit on you about not wanting you to go off alone," Liz replied, "which is partly true. Otherwise, we wouldn't be here now. But the truth is I followed Regina here. She'd been keeping tabs on you and is with this guy."

"Mr. Right?"

"Not funny," Liz answered. "He's staying at this hotel. She's not. They mean you harm."

"I think they already tried," Sam interrupted.

"You mean the hit-and-run?"

"How'd . . . ?"

"You're not this naïve," Liz said. "They're after whatever you gather over here, though I find it hard to believe Regina's in on an attempted murder. She wasn't with him."

"But why're you here? And who's 'us'?"

"Hold onto yourself. I work for Washbourne," Liz answered. Then she told Sam her story.

"So, you've been spying on me, too?!" Sam said, angrily. "Won't all you bastards leave me alone?!!"

"Not on you!" Liz said, embracing Sam. "I was assigned surveillance of Regina, who *was* spying on you. Occasionally, I reported your good health."

"Christ!" Sam said, "I don't know whom I can trust anymore. Our introduction. Pre-arranged?"

"I know how you feel."

"How can you?!" Sam said, walking across the room. "I've got nobody. Everyone *else* knows what's going on!"

"I wouldn't be here right now if that were true," Liz replied. "This isn't official. It's as a friend. S.o.p says avoid all contact. So far as my team knows, you aren't here. They didn't know you'd be here. I did. I admire your father. He's got quite a rep in The Agency. Even now."

"Reputation?"

"I shouldn't have blabbered."

"I can't trust you, either," Sam said. "It wasn't the start of a beautiful friendship, after all. Is 'Liz McGonnville' your real name?"

"Most of what I told you is true. A few years removed. I'm actually your age. I just don't look it. I've worked for The Agency since college."

"Are you going to try to stop me?" Sam asked.

"I'm not reporting this. I *am* a friend, even if you don't think so now."

"Can you help me?"

"I'd be disobeying orders if I did," Liz replied. She sounded regretful. "If you were to interfere in an operation, or get too close, I'd have to stop you and have you sent home. Right now, you pose no direct threat of that."

"Somebody's just tried to kill me and almost killed one of our oldest friends. And you won't help me?"

"I'm sorry."

"But you can. Don't you see? You could keep me out of trouble."

"I'd get canned."

"Not to worry. We've got money. We could hire you as a well-paid staffer."

"Government retirement's tough to beat. And once we're in, the Agency never really lets us quit."

"I'd like to know something else. Why'd you introduce Regina to me?"

"I had to protect my cover," Liz replied. "As it is, I blew it after our little talk in the lounge that day." Liz described it. "She could be the one who trashed your room. That spilling incident was all a set-up." She told Sam how she followed Regina.

"Lucky I don't have any of those clothes on," Sam said. "Oh! And the purse! I loved that bag."

"Not to fear," Liz said. "We'll remove the extraneous electronics. The bugs or homers are probably in hemlines, waists, or seams."

"Does your roomie know you're a ringer?"

"Are you serious? She thinks I'm hyperactive."

"Where're you staying?" Sam asked.

"At the Bath House Hotel." Liz gave her the telephone and room numbers.

"Why aren't you staying here?"

"She's my assignment, not the guy. I needed to talk to you, so I made contact with a resident agent who works here. Regina hasn't i.d.'d me. The guy's tall, blond. Nice looking, wears a leather coat."

"I've seen him!" Sam said. She described the train passenger. "Is your hair real? Or Memorex?" Sam asked.

"I could ask the same thing," Liz replied. "It's real. I had it done right after you disappeared. You look good as a blonde, Sam. I always wondered why you hadn't done it before. And I like the clothes, especially that leather skirt. When all this is over, and I get my hair color back, we'll be twins."

"Or triplets, if Regina's not in on the plot. Then again, there were the 'poor Marcoses.'" They both laughed.

"Did you happen to get anything from your friend?"

"Like?"

"Information about your father?" Liz asked.

"We were on the way," Sam sighed another "grey truth." "And while we're near the subject, whatever should we do with Regina?"

"Sit back. I'll lay out the options."

* * *

Later that evening at Uncle Max's house, and alone, Sam opened the parcel. In it she found videotape cassettes, computer disks, and photographs.

She read the notations. They bore Roman- and Arabic-style numerals similar to those in her father's files in The Stash. Some were crossed out in pencil and renumbered. The outlined chapters, poems, etc?.

On Uncle Max's personal computer Sam examined the contents of disks. Documents had been scanned onto them.

She found agreements between The Cartel and various leaders in the Third World. There were manifests for financial transactions and materials, lists of "contractors" and dates beside each name.

Sam watched the lowest numbered video cassette first. The opening scenes were long-distance sequences, with unexpected zooms in-and-out and jerkiness.

They showed dates and arrivals at train stations and airports. She recognized many faces as visitors to her father, like The Baron. There was the Mississippi soldier! There were more famous personages, ones more often in the press.

Through more tapes Sam saw actual meetings of what looked like a board of directors. She saw her father each time. The dialogue was usually in German. As she listened, she heard planning of covert operations in Latin America and Europe.

The Cartel had participated in the Iran-Contra actions, years before, money-laundering in banks, similar to the Bank of Commerce and Credit International ("BCCI"), funneling of arms to rebels in the former Soviet Union and Chechnya, and destabilization of political movements in Africa, Europe, Asia, especially the Middle East, and Latin America.

The next tape began as the first. Sam saw many of the same faces as the others. There were more meetings. Then, without warning, she saw THE FACE.

XVII

As McConneld drove the truck, he nudged Balkovsky, who stretched. It was the night after the raid, 23 October. There were only nine days before the German authorities probably would begin, nationwide, house-to-house searches.

The dead trucker's route took them into Germany, south of *Offenburg*. "If I'm right, the first stop's up ahead. It's a farmhouse."

McConneld turned onto a dirt way. "Hello, Chuck," he said, conversationally. "We're going in." He placed the mini-mike under the driver's seat.

"Do you have the passkey?" Balkovsky asked.

McConneld felt inside his pocket for the poker chip.

The house was a rundown A-frame with a barn behind it. There were low lights showing through the front window curtains. Open fields flanked the house with a tractor in the driveway.

McConneld knocked on the door. An old man in a robe answered.

"*Herr Stoessl, bitte?*" McConneld said. He identified himself as "*Mannfred Freudig*," and showed him the half-chip.

The man closed the door, and reopened it, with his palm out. There was another half-poker-chip, with jagged edges. He asked McConneld for proof of identity.

"*Um Gotteswillen! Wo sind Sie gewesen?*" he asked. "*Und wer ist das?*" McConneld recounted the raid, embellishing their escape. They had hidden out, he said, in an abandoned barn, near *St. Avold*, France. Crossing the border had been chancy. McConneld identified Balkovsky as another of the loading crew.

"*I shall inspect your cargo,*" Stoessl said, heading to the truck, ahead of McConneld and Balkovsky.

"We lost some," McConneld said, "*since we couldn't stop to close the doors, for a while. I almost lost Wolfi here.*"

With practiced coordination McConneld and Balkovsky opened the truck's secret compartment. The old man inspected the crates and their markings.

"We're only a stop here," Stoessl said. "*I guide you to another place in a new truck. Bring yours to the barn.*"

"What happens to mine?" McConneld asked.

"That's my business," Stoessl said, with a tone McConneld interpreted as unchallengeable.

"*Are you coming with us?*" McConneld asked. Stoessl nodded.

Balkovsky drove to the barn. McConneld walked with Stoessl, who probed him.

He wanted more about the raid, McConneld's identity, and Balkovsky. McConneld grumbled responses, short and as final as Stoessl's own had been.

Stoessl opened the barn's high, front doors. He drove a truck through the opening and backed it up to the rear of McConneld's truck. The three transferred the cargo by a crossover ramp on the back of Stoessl's.

When they were finished, Stoessl asked Balkovsky for the truck's keys. Balkovsky refused to give them to him.

"*Tell him what you want done,*" McConneld interrupted. "Wolf's a little stubborn sometimes."

"It makes no difference to me. Park it, yourself," Stoessl said. "Only don't run over anything."

Balkovsky revved the engine, suddenly jerking the truck into the barn. He slipped the microphone nonchalantly to McConneld, when Stoessl was in the cab of his truck. McConneld put the "mike" into his boot.

Stoessl drove. The ride took several hours over secondary and two-lane roads. There was not a hint of the *Autobahn* or other highways.

McConneld and Balkovsky alternated fifteen-minute naps. Stoessl was more talkative than he had been. He asked McConneld more questions about himself and Balkovsky. So far, McConneld's eastern German dialect was holding up.

"Where're we going?" McConneld said. He read road signs.

"*Between Holzheim und Gross-Kissendorf,*" Stoessl replied.

"*I know Kissendorf,*" McConneld said. "*We should've got there* by now. Do we stay there? Or come back with you and help get rid of the truck?"

"Do what you're told," Stoessl answered. "Go where you're told. *Und ask no questions.*" Stoessl said nothing else.

He turned onto a narrow, dirt road, cut between tall woods. The headlights stabbed and wormed through the darkness until they reached a clearing with a large, disheveled barn. The environ reminded McConneld of E-917.

Stoessl honked the horn in a pattern. The barn doors opened, and he drove inside.

The barn's interior was well-lighted and modernistic. McConneld saw a freight elevator on the far side. Men were stacking, packing, and opening crates. Stoessl went to a glass-enclosed office.

The place resembled a small-arms factory. McConneld saw stamped markings from the major NATO armies. But nothing resembled MADM or SADM containers. Stoessl rejoined them, accompanied by another man, from the office.

"*Herr Dorting ist der Chef. He explains what's new to you.*" Stoessl said, before he had the truck unloaded.

Dorting examined McConneld's and Balkovsky's identifications and questioned them. Chuck Channing had generated something for Balkovsky, as well as McConneld, before they left.

McConneld repeated his cover story. Balkovsky played the diffident sidekick, with short, grunt-punctuated responses.

The boss seemed satisfied with their answers. He ordered McConneld to go on a pickup, while Balkovsky was to work there.

"*Can't* Wolf *go with me?*" McConneld asked. "*We've been through a lot in the last forty-eight hours.*"

The boss seemed unimpressed. "*I need him here.*" Balkovsky shrugged helplessly.

Waiting in the office was another man. "*This is who you'll be working with on this run,*" Dorting said. "*I thought you two might know each other. He also used to work for Stasi.*"

Dorting introduced the man as Franz Ostmann. Ostmann seemed to recognize McConneld.

"*You're confusing me with someone else,*" McConneld said. "I worked alone. I stole my file, before reunification, from Stasi headquarters."

Ostmann looked at Dorting. *"Anything else, sir?"*

"You're still going out together," Dorting replied, *"even if you didn't work for East German Intelligence. No harm done, Herr Freudig?"*

McConneld shook his head. *"I'd have done the same thing. Now, if role-playing's over, the assignment, sir?"*

Dorting was sending them to deliver small arms and LAWs to an *"Aktionsgruppe."* Ostmann knew the location already. McConneld would be security. Dorting issued him a MAK-10, with extra clips.

As he left the office, McConneld saw Stoessl driving away. Another, smaller truck pulled into the barn. He and Ostmann waited for it to be loaded, then departed, with Ostmann driving.

They traveled on secondary roads. Ostmann was more social than Stoessl. He told McConneld they were going to a small village near *Ehingen,* southwest of Ulm. He did not care for this particular *"Aktionsgruppe."* He said, *"Smelled too Middle East."*

"Any problem with the village police?" McConneld asked.

"None," Ostmann replied. *"They're on the payroll, too."*

At the village, Ostmann drove to a warehouse. It was on the fringe of town, near agri-storage buildings.

McConneld watched as several men spoke with Ostmann. They opened the doors and Ostmann drove into the building.

More men helped unload the truck. McConneld posted himself just beyond the action, the MAK-10 on his hip. Crates of M-16s, G-3, and other automatic rifles, hand grenades, grenade-launchers, RPGs and LAWs were unloaded.

Ostmann was correct about these guys, McConneld thought, as he heard Arabic passing among them.

"They stink with the Middle East," McConneld said to Ostmann, as they were driving from the warehouse. *"I wouldn't trust them with that stuff."*

"I don't either," Ostmann said. *"But Command wants it."*

After another stop, Ostmann and McConneld continued on to the original barn. Activity was still brisk. There were more men than before.

Dorting told McConneld and Ostmann to nap in a below-ground storage area. He was sending them out again.

McConneld looked for Balkovsky before taking the freight elevator down. He did not find the Russian.

* * *

In his Paris hotel room, David answered the door. Marbison was there.

"We weren't expecting you yet. How long have you been in Paris?" David asked.

"About thirty-six hours. Where're Rodriguez and his people?" Marbison asked. David told him about the ambush two days before.

"You didn't stay, to make sure?" Marbison asked. "Where's George? I'm sure he'll be pleased to see me."

David briefed Marbison on the events of the past several days.

"I'll be undercover after tonight," Marbison said. "Cartel people recruited me, a 'special contractor' for five hundred grand. Euros, that is."

"Nice work, if you get it!!" David replied. "Did you know about this back in Washington?"

Marbison nodded. "But I didn't have the timeframe till after you left. I got the contact-point today. A Left Bank café at seven."

"What about the money? You said you weren't corruptible."

"I'm not. But I didn't say I was cheap. Or stupid," Marbison replied. "I get one-third now, two-thirds after I've finished the job. You might get prizes. Try to keep up, OK?"

* * *

"Show him in," Chuck Channing said to his secretary.

Jack Kinnean came into Channing's office. "Where's your boss?" he asked, plunking down into a padded chair.

"He's unavailable right now," Channing replied.

"Yeah," Kinnean growled. "That's what you said yesterday, Channing! I want to see him. NOW!"

"I'm afraid that's impossible. I don't know when he'll be back."

"Preposterous!" Kinnean roared. "Contact him, if you value your job."

"I'm sorry, sir," Channing answered. "But I don't work for you. When he gets back, I'll be sure and tell him you want to see him. Otherwise, I'll follow my instructions till I'm relieved of duty. Have a nice day."

Kinnean glared at Channing. "You'd better freshen your line. Your boss better, too. You Agency people've never had any imagination." He left.

Channing buzzed his secretary on the intercom. "Please patch me through to Deputy Director Simmons ASAP," he said.

He noted Kinnean's visit on his desk calendar. That made three in as many days, since the 24th. He went over his appointments for the 27th. More "hand-holding" for the Germans. Harvey Barsohn was due. Kinnean would not be the only bad news he had for McConneld when the latter returned.

Somebody named Samantha Pemberton had disappeared, Bill Washbourne told him in a recent phone conversation. He wondered if Kinnean had the "pull" to get him dismissed from the Agency, when his phone rang.

* * *

"The National Security Adviser, on Line One, sir," his secretary spoke to Deputy Director Simmons over the intercom in his Langley office.

"I just got off the phone with Channing," Simmons said. "This is for your ears only. McConneld got a break. He's in the field, undercover, inside Pemberton's Cartel."

"Isn't he too senior to be out there? Why the hell didn't he tell my man that?" the Adviser asked.

"He operates on a need-to-know basis," Simmons replied. "And your man didn't. I'll be back to you, when I have more."

"I want results!" the Adviser bellowed. "If you and your people can't, I'll find someone who can."

* * *

The headline on the front page of the *Frankfurt Allgemeine Zeitung* on the morning of 24 October read, "French Barracks Destroyed By Bomb." Its accompanying story detailed the destruction of a French Army facility outside Strasbourg.

No group immediately took responsibility for the incident. The *Sureté* and the *Deuxieme Bureau* suspected Arab, perhaps Algerian, extremists or Basque Separatists. Three French soldiers were killed in the blast, and thirty more were wounded.

The next day a similar incident occurred outside Trier, Germany. A French Army facility was damaged by a car bomb blast.

In this incident, several civilians were killed, along with four French soldiers. No groups claimed responsibility for the bombing, but German officials stated publicly they believed the events in Strasbourg and Trier were linked.

Le Monde's 26 October lead read, "Turkish Extremists Attack Skinhead Bundeswehr Troopers." In the eastern German city of Cottbus, armed Turks, members of a self-styled militia, raided the homes of skinhead Neo-Nazi leaders, who were also lower-ranking officers in the German Federal Army.

Two of the skinheads were killed, with four others wounded. German authorities failed to apprehend the perpetrators. Members of the Skinhead Movement vowed revenge for the "unprovoked attack on our brethren."

The *Times* of London reported on 27 October the bombing of British military facilities attached to the BAOR, near Bremen. A splinter faction of the IRA claimed responsibility by telephone in London, confirming M.I.-5's own suspicions. Four British soldiers were killed by a truck bomb, eleven wounded.

The *New York Times* reported the same day an explosion which destroyed a nightclub frequented by G.I.s, near Frankfurt. Five U.S. soldiers were killed and another nine wounded, along with twenty civilian patrons.

No group claimed immediate responsibility for the act. U.S. authorities intimated Islamic extremists were involved.

* * *

At the same time McConneld and Ostmann were arriving at *Kissendorf*, a group of technicians, in Hamburg, Germany, were testing large television broadcasting, satellite, and cable hook-up systems. The studio occupied a basement area equivalent to one floor of the tall office building above it. The building was owned by a subsidiary, many times removed, of the Association of International Industrialists, Executives, and Entrepreneurs.

At control consoles, the technical people ran broadcasts and receptions from similar stations in North and South America, and other parts of Europe. The chief technician, a short man in his fifties, supervised the link-up.

"New York, we have Frankfurt, Buenos Aires, and Munich," he said into a console, over the shoulder of another operator. "How're you receiving? Hello, Nice?"

The New York and French responses were affirmative. The chief pushed a button on the neighboring console. Lights under name tags of various cities went and stayed on at once. Around the vast room cheers went up. The chief prepared a quick verbal report for The Baron.

* * *

In the café where they were watching Marbison, George and David sat near the door. It was past 7 P.M. A waiter walked a telephone to Marbison's table. Marbison spoke on it, then got up to leave.

Another man, short, with wide shoulders and shiny suit, sitting alone at a nearby table, followed him.

Outside, they saw Marbison and the other man getting into a late-model Citroën. It sped off toward the Eiffel Tower.

"Here we go again," David said, as they ran to a car across the street. The driver was a fellow agent. The Citroën turned a corner.

"Is it working?" George asked David as he took an electronic device from his jacket. It was beeping regularly, though the sound became more faint. "Speed up," David said. "But not too close."

Their car zigzagged through traffic and across one of the Seine bridges. The Citröen was heading northwest, away from the city. The signal from Marbison's "homer" remained strong, as they followed it into the countryside at high speed. David radioed their surveillance helicopter.

The pursuit continued. The homer signal alternated between faint and strong. The radio microphone crackled. "David. Ari, here. Over." David acknowledged.

"Pick us up. Over," David asked.

"Aircraft rendezvous. Field to your right. Over."

Just then, the receiver David was holding went silent. The signal was gone.

* * *

McConneld felt himself being shaken, as he lay on the thin-mattressed cot. He had stayed at the storage barn for two days after he and Ostmann delivered the weapons. It was Ostmann.

"*Herr Dorting wants us. Another job,*" he said.

They took the lift to the ground floor to Dorting's glass enclosure. Activity was brisk. McConneld did not see Balkovsky.

"*I want you to take these packets to Hamburg,*" Dorting said, "*by train. After delivery, pick up a car and drive to Nürnberg. Ostmann, you've been to the place in Hamburg before. You need to look better.*" He gave McConneld and Ostmann different clothes.

"*Change in there,*" Dorting said, pointing to a small WC behind him.

McConneld went first. The mini-mike slipped from his hand and down the drain of the sink. He did manage to secret his miniature-camera into his coat.

After the clothes change, Dorting handed them train tickets and expense money and called another man to drive them to the station, where they boarded immediately.

En route, they changed trains in *Karlsruhe*, continued on through Frankfurt, and bypassed the *Ruhr* cities. During their passage and stop in Frankfurt, McConneld did not leave his seat.

When they were safely into *Bebra*, he took a walk through the train, without Ostmann, who was sleeping in their compartment. He took the three pouches with him to the WC.

Each was sealed with a wax stamp. Patiently, he used a piece of thin fishing line and a razor blade, shimmying one or the other under the seals.

Inside the first pouch were computer disks and papers, encoded in number sequences and seemingly meaningless letter chains. He photographed the papers from that and the other pouches, resealing the wax blocks and putting the film in a gum wrapper in his boot. McConneld returned to the compartment. Only Ostmann was there, awake.

"*Why did you take those?!*" he asked McConneld. "*I was going nuts!*"

"*Lighten up. Here,*" he said, tossing the packets onto Ostmann's lap. "*I needed a break from your snoring. Stop freaking out. I'm security.*"

When they reached *Hannover*, there was a layover due to a bomb threat on the northern line. When this was cleared, they reached *Hamburg* within the next few hours.

Ostmann took McConneld to a pension he identified as a regular stopover for couriers. The owners were an older couple, McConneld soon discovered, not abashed about telling off-color and nasty ethnic jokes and stories.

The next morning Ostmann led McConneld to a high-rise office building in the business and financial district. On the fifth floor, Ostmann dropped off one pouch, receiving another in its place.

He received instructions to carry it to a location to the southeast, between *Hamburg* and *Luneburg*, along with a map on a paper he read and quickly ate. He did not show it to McConneld before ingesting it.

They rented a car and drove south on the *Autobahn*, then turned southeast toward *Luneburg*. At the village of *Rottorf*, they took a back road.

At a semi-nondescript break in the woods, Ostmann drove a few hundred yards along a dirt and gravel road, and parked.

"*The barn's up ahead,*" Ostmann said, as he got out. He started up the path, with McConneld close. McConneld took a MAK-10 the couple at the pension had given him, from his raincoat. *These people found every empty barn in Germany*, he thought.

The door swung open. A short, fat man in hunters' fatigues answered. He and Ostmann spoke. Inside, it was very similar to Dorting's barn.

There were crates of weapons with NATO armies' stenciling. This place also had a small practice range. Men were firing rifles, M-16s, and *Uzis*, among others, as well as pistols.

Ostmann handed one of the remaining packets to the fat man. In an office similar to Dorting's, the fat man placed disks into a computer. He "scanned" the papers into the computer as well. A printer, behind him, was working.

McConneld read the screen over his shoulder. In German, there was a list of dates, locations, and deliveries for each. The printer was making multiple copies of the schedule.

The last date McConneld noticed was 15 November. From the firing range came a muffled explosion and screams. The fat man hurried from the office, Ostmann behind him. McConneld followed them quickly.

"Fucking American rifles!" someone yelled. Apparently, an M-16 had exploded, wounding the man firing it and another man.

McConneld faded back to the office. He copied the disks from the pouch. The copying times seemed interminable.

He was midway through the fourth disk, when he heard the fat man's voice getting closer, along with Ostmann's. He popped out the copies and stuffed them in his coat pocket, returning the originals to the desk. He was breathing heavily as the fat man came in, followed by Ostmann.

"Perhaps they can save his fingers," the fat man was saying. "Hey, what're you doing in here?" he asked. "Get that greasy weapon off my desk!"

"Guarding the pouches," McConneld replied.

"*He's OK,*" Ostmann said to the fat man.

McConneld picked up the MAK-10 and cradled it. He saw the injured men being carried to a panel-truck on stretchers.

"*Something to take back to Hamburg,*" the fat man said to Ostmann. "*Before you head south.*"

He stuffed papers and disks from the top drawer into the pouch. He resealed and handed it to Ostmann.

They arrived in *Hamburg* in early afternoon. McConneld had no opportunity to examine the contents before they reached the downtown area. Ostmann parked in an underground garage, across from the high-rise.

As they were entering the office suite on the fifth floor, McConneld saw four men in business suits outside large, oak double-doors. He recognized one man immediately. It was Johannes Krattmay: older-looking than when last seen, but no doubt it was he.

McConneld did not recognize two of the others. One looked Middle-Eastern. He heard the third man speaking with a Latin-American accent.

The fourth was also familiar. His hair was shorter than last McConneld saw it. His clothes were more stylish than the fatigue jacket and jeans he had been wearing then: J.D. Marshall.

* * *

Balkovsky put his feet on the dashboard of the truck. Dorting sent him with a crew from the *Gross-Kissendorf* depot. For the next two days the five-man crew ferried weapons to locations in south-central Germany, between depots and *"Aktionsgruppen."*

Their first deliveries were near the peripherals of *Stuttgart*. From there they carried weapons to disparate *"Aktionsgruppen,"* between *Heidelberg* and *Nürnberg*. From *Nürnberg* they headed to a village outside *Würzburg*, where on the second night they checked into a small hotel.

Balkovsky spent that evening in a beer hall. The owner was a friend of the other crew members, and kept the bar open past regular hours for them.

After the fourth round of liter-beers, Balkovsky left for the restroom and a call to the contact-point for his "mole," whose message Balkovsky had given to Yuri Torychenko. When he found a public phone, Balkovsky realized another crewman had followed him.

"Who're you calling?" he asked, slurring his words. His eyes were half-open, barely maintaining that aperture.

"A woman, stupid," Balkovsky replied. "I'm not spending the night with you clods."

"Share?"

"She's married," Balkovsky said. "Her old man's away in the East. Her bed's only big enough for me."

"Won't share with your mates. Selfish bastard." He stumbled to their table, bouncing against chairs and a wall. Balkovsky waited for him to get there, before dialing the number. Despite the hour, the phone only rang once.

"This is Wolf," Balkovsky said. "Is your old man back?"

The female voice replied, "He's only a phone call away, if I need him."

"In an hour. I'm hungry." As Balkovsky hung up the receiver, a hand came down on it. It was the crew chief. Balkovsky repeated the cover story. "She's near Giessen."

"You can't go off," the chief said. "We're rolling before dawn."

"I wasn't clear," Balkovsky said. "She's my woman..."

"Gunter says she's got a man."

"I only told him that, so he wouldn't tag along with me. I hate crowds."

"We all go, or you don't," the chief replied. "We crowd or you crash with us."

"Forget it," Balkovsky said. "I'll call her back and..."

"I want to see her," the chief said. "Are you ashamed of her?"

He turned back for the table, pulling Balkovsky by the arm. "Wolf's taking us on a hunt! In Giessen." They crashed their way to the truck.

"Romeo drives," the chief said.

The woman lived in a downtown rowhouse. Balkovsky had been there since his arrival in Germany, to meet with or leave messages for his "mole."

He parked in an alley and went to the front door, with the other crew members crowding him. The woman answered the door after one knock. Dressed in a nightgown, she was surprised to see the others with Balkovsky. There were whistles and hoots as they saw her.

One man said, *"No wonder you wanted her to yourself."*

"I tried to call you back," Balkovsky said to her. *"But Chief, here, wouldn't let me."*

"We're your chaperons for the evening," another crewman blurted, loudly.

"I don't have enough food for all of them," she said, holding her gown closed tightly across her front.

Balkovsky said, *"It won't be a long night, I promise. You and I'll have another together."* She opened the door for the five men, led by Balkovsky.

When he reached the living room, Balkovsky saw his "mole." The woman joined him, to face Balkovsky and the others.

"You didn't give me a chance to tell you, I had another visitor," she said, embracing the agent.

The crew chief was surprised, after he saw the man. He came to attention, as much as his earlier beer consumption allowed.

"Sir! No idea . . . ! We'll get the hell out! Wolf's in deep shit!"

The agent said, loudly, *"He's a friend of mine. He stays."*

"Yes, sir!" the chief answered. *"Whatever you say."*

"Pick him up," the agent said, *"when you move out in the morning."*

"Anything . . . ?" the chief began.

The agent shook his head and motioned. The crew shuffled quickly out the front door. The woman locked it.

The three watched the crew through the windows before they spoke. The woman poured brandies.

"News, sir," the agent said to Balkovsky. *"The MADMs and SADMs are being distributed to the strike teams. I'm still unable to identify any targets, but the teams're undergoing instruction and intense training with them."*

"Discovered the completion date?" Balkovsky asked.

"15 November," he replied. *"It was moved up once already, and could be moved again. The raid on the farm scared the shit out of Command. They brought in some outside guy to do the SADM training. He's got something to do with the MADMs, too."*

"We've discovered some of the plan," the woman said. *"It's a widespread terror operation. They're targeting the Defence Zone Commands and the Bundeswehr Corps Headquarters . . ."*

"With the nuclear weapons?" Balkovsky interrupted.

"No," the agent replied. "They've assigned those missions to the outside terror groups."

"And the Regulars have the bombs," Balkovsky said. "How many days left before the 15th?"

"Eighteen," the woman replied. "Terrorist attacks have quadrupled since you went undercover. It's already begun."

"Any sign of Thomas Pemberton?" Balkovsky asked.

"He's been at the Board meetings," the agent replied. "They've had him under tightest security, along with the other higher-ups. They're moving them around."

"Can you get to him?"

"I'm not supposed to know," the agent said. "Our compartmentalizing's kept us apart. No overlap."

"We've got to learn the targets for the bombs," Balkovsky said, "at least the main target, if there's one."

"My boss won't confide that," the agent said, "till it's about to happen. We've got some core part to play. They haven't briefed us yet."

"Get to Pemberton," Balkovsky said. "He's our best hope."

"There's another emergency meeting called," the agent said. "My boss'll probably have to be there. Maybe I can tag along with him. He didn't take me to the last one. But that was just a discipline matter."

"We'll meet, when you've seen Pemberton," Balkovsky said. "Signal her," he nodded to the woman.

XVIII

Sam waited in her hotel room for Liz. Earlier that day Liz had gone through the gifts from Regina, finding several tiny homing devices in linings, hems, and seams. Sam and Liz were confident now they had them all.

When she was away from Liz, Sam sent the first cache of information to her father's Jesuit friend at G.U. There were seven different parcels, including dummies.

"The guy's in a room on the third floor," Liz said, as she came in. "Alone, but we've got to move fast. Your dossier said you know how to use this." She handed Sam a 9mm automatic pistol and three clips.

"I hate to admit it," Sam replied, "but I do." She loaded it, pulled the slide back, and put on the safety. Liz loaded a similar weapon.

Liz handed her a small metal cylinder. "This is a sound-suppressor, not a silencer. There's no such thing." She showed Sam how to install it. Sam placed the pistol in her large *Chanel* bag.

"Where's Regina?" Sam asked.

"My people've got her under surveillance at her hotel."

"Have you told them about me?"

Liz answered, "They only know about Regina and her boy. You and I have been over the plan. Don't be nervous. You're a deputy. I'm the sheriff."

"Burglarized, nearly run over by a car, and kidnapped," Sam said. "What's to be nervous about?"

The contact's room was at the end of the hall. Outside it, Sam held the pistol with both hands after releasing the safety. Liz knocked. There was the clank of a lock-chain.

"Pardon, sir," Liz said. She identified herself. "A wallet was turned in to us. We believe it's yours, but we need you to claim it. Won't take a minute, if you don't mind."

The door closed. Sam heard the contact's voice, a fibrous

monotone with a northern-German cadence. "Can't you bring it up to me? I'm busy right now," he said, reopening the door a crack.

"Dreadfully sorry, sir," Liz replied, sounding very stuffily bureaucratic. "Procedures. You understand, I'm sure."

"Bloody English and your 'procedures,'" the contact said. The door closed momentarily, as he released the chain, but did not shut it.

Liz, now holding her own pistol with both hands, gave the door a sharp kick. The door knocked the man to the floor.

"Freeze, slimeball!" Liz said, hurrying into the room. Sam followed and closed the door.

The contact moved groggily. He started to get up. Liz kicked him in the chest. Sam kept her pistol pointed at him.

Liz searched him. She removed an automatic pistol from a shoulder-holster, under his jacket.

He regained his senses, slowly. "What the fuck?!" he said, as he twisted.

Liz sat on the edge of the bed, with the heel of her spiked boot on his solar plexus and her pistol aimed at him. "Sir, we've had a complaint, you see," Liz said in her English incantation. "This young woman alleges you tried to run her down with a car."

"You're not cops!" he replied. "What the fuck're you talking about?!" Liz stepped down with her heel.

The man groaned, loudly. "You bitches!"

Liz dug in again. Another loud groan punctuated the move. "Don't move like that, sir," Liz said. "This lady will feel compelled to shoot. She's not fond of you as it is."

"What do you want?" he gasped.

"Why are you harassing her?" Liz said. "For whom?"

"Fuck you!" he replied. Liz stepped hard with her boot heel. The man screeched. "I don't know! Really! Phone call. Envelope. Five thousand Euros."

"Wasn't that a bit strange? What were your instructions?"

"To watch her."

"And run her down with your car?" Liz stepped again.

He gasped. "Whatever you say! What do you want?"

"Merely that you leave her alone. Or I'll blow your motherfucking head off. Understood?" Liz smiled. She had not broken her English accent at all.

Liz stepped back from him. "As a sign of good faith, get on your stomach on the bed! Nothing stupid now. I don't want you to get hurt."

The man got up cautiously. As he stood, he sprung at Liz who casually stepped aside. He landed on his chest, arms and legs spread.

She kicked his head. "This just isn't your day, is it, sir?" She repeated the blow two more times. His body was limp. She handed Sam her pistol and dragged him to the bed. "Give me a hand!" she said. Together, they swung him onto the mattress.

Liz went into her oversized bag and came out with two pairs of handcuffs and leg shackles. She handed a set to Sam. They cuffed his arms and legs to the bed and Liz gagged him.

Searching his belongings, they found personal items, car keys, extra clips, a locker key, and a small notebook in which he had described Sam's activities.

"We'll call the cops, anonymously, of course," Liz said. "But I'd love to interrogate this guy." She thought for a moment. "I could tip M.I.-5 through local liaison."

"What about Regina?" Sam asked. "Do you think she'll go away?"

"It depends how deep she's in. If I'm wrong and she's really one of them, you'll make another clean escape."

"Are you coming with me?" Sam asked. She wanted Liz for a partner, for now, though there was the problem of her father's "holiday" list.

"I'll see," Liz answered. "Maybe I can pass Regina's surveillance to somebody else. For now, give me the weapon back."

* * *

In her Oxford hotel room, Regina was on the telephone. *"Bad news, Papa,"* Regina said in German. *"That buffoon got himself arrested by the police..."*

She listened. *"From the Oxford police station. He told me the Pemberton girl and another woman incapacitated him."*

Regina felt part-embarrassed and part-pleased at making this call. The arrogant bastard had got what he deserved.

"Yes, I left him there." She nodded, as she listened. "I'll need a new partner... I don't think I know him... How soon?" More pausing. "I'll expect him. Don't worry. See you soon. All my love to Mother. Ciao."

* * *

It was the early morning after their "rousting" of Regina's contact that Sam and Liz took a train to London. The previous night Sam packed and checked out of her hotel. She spent her final night in Oxford at Uncle Max's. Sam felt badly she would not see him before she left. But she promised herself, when this was over, she would return.

After they reached Paddington Station, London, they arranged hovercraft passage to the Continent for later that day.

At the Ramsgate Hoverport that afternoon, before Sam went through Customs, Liz left her. Afterward, Liz rejoined her.

"I cleared my ordnance with our man here," she whispered to Sam, as they boarded the hovercraft. "I'll do the same in Calais."

The ride across the Channel was uneventful. At the French Hoverport, Liz disappeared again. After Sam cleared French Customs, Liz met her on the other side. From there they took a bus to Paris.

In Paris, they purchased train tickets for the *Arlberg Express,* leaving at 10 P.M. that night. They were booked into First-Class sleeping accommodations, to Vienna, by way of Innsbruck.

In the dining room of a self-described sandwich "boutique," they had a quiet dinner. Liz told Sam she had not seen anyone following them since they settled with Regina's "playmate."

"I'm so glad you're here," Sam said. "I needed a friend about now. I have one in Innsbruck, but we can't stop there yet."

"I've squared this trip with my superiors," Liz said. "As far as they're concerned, I'm chasing a lead. If they don't buy it, I may take you up on that job. So sorry, if I made you feel... betrayed."

"It seemed like I was alone, with everyone else's agendas. I wonder what Regina's doing. I hope we've seen the last of her."

"We have. I'm more interested in her boy," Liz said. "It would be fun to see him explaining to the cops that record of your movements."

"What's Regina's angle?" Sam said. Liz gave her a background.

"Funny we never met before," Sam said. "My father and his compartmentalism."

"She's history," Liz said. "What's the plan in Vienna?"

"I have a need-to-know policy."

"You don't trust me?" Liz asked, feigning disbelief. "I'm just yanking your chain."

"I'm lucky I have any links left." Sam recalled her doubts at wanting Liz along. But she needed Liz, as cover support.

On the *Champs Elysées* they caught a cab to the train station. The train departed on time.

The night hours sped and dragged, as Sam dozed and gazed into the shadowed European landscape. Before she left Oxford, she sent her papers and "itinerary list" by special courier service, to a family friend in Vienna. He owned and operated an expensive antique shop in the *Kärntner Strasse*.

As morning matured from sunrise, the train approached the vicinity of Innsbruck. The train was slowing.

"I talked to the conductor," Liz said, excitedly. "There's a train wreck up ahead on the way into Innsbruck. They're diverting us to a branch-line, till they get it cleared. Everything's messed up."

"Did he say how?"

"No, but I had my window open a little. I heard explosions. Muffled, but still nasty. Probably time-delayed devices and plastique. Besides nitro, only that stuff packs a blast like I heard."

A conductor came to her door. He told them they would be delayed at least twelve hours and were diverting to a small village, south of Innsbruck. Buses would take them into the village to arranged accommodations.

"The village's name?" Liz asked, impatiently.

"I believe it's *Mutters*," the conductor replied.

Sam laughed. "I don't believe it!" she exclaimed. "And I said we couldn't stop. You'll love her. Very maternal. Actually, we'd come here sooner or later."

Later Liz and Sam were on the way to the Tyrolean village. When they reached a hotel, where the passengers were being housed, Sam telephoned. Ten minutes later a red, 1970s-vintage Volkswagen "Beetle" pulled up in front.

"Get your bag, and let's go," Sam said to Liz, amid the noise of the hotel lobby. She already left the telephone number with an official of the railway.

"Heidi!!" Sam said. She kissed the driver on the cheek.

"Du hoch, Samantha!" the husky, red-complexioned woman replied. She hugged Sam. "You are *eine Blondine* now?"

"The new me," Sam replied. "Bright, light, and shiny."

"Professor Tom *ist* not *mit* you, *nicht wahr?*" Heidi asked. "Who *ist* your *Freundin?*" Sam introduced Liz.

"I'm here for Pa's package, Heidi," Sam said. "We could use a room."

Heidi sighed, "Is he well? Why did he not come himself?"

Sam repeated the story she told in Oxford, as they drove to Heidi's pension. "I'd have come later," Sam concluded. "This train foul-up's sheer luck. We were—are—on the way to Vienna. I hope I can tell you about it soon."

"You *musst* share a *Doppelzimmer,*" Heidi said. She parked in front of a large, A-frame house. Heidi led them to a two-bed room on the third floor. They joined her in the second-floor kitchen.

"I'll get Professor Tom's *Paket* for you today," Heidi said to Sam. "You don't have to know where it is." She left them.

Sam heard the VW's engine rev, then fade. "After I've had a look at it," Sam said to Liz. "I'll need help, sending it home, with lots of misdirection."

"Will you let me see what's in it?"

"You can see what I see," Sam replied.

Heidi returned, with a cube-shaped box, wrapped in brown paper.

Sam examined the contents, alone. It wasn't that she didn't trust Liz. But Liz had other loyalties. She caught herself in the double-negative.

There were more computer disks and photographs. The photos were 3″-by-5″ and 5″-by-7″ shots of people, with notations. She found one disk, entitled "Little black book." *That sounded like her father's mind,* she thought.

"Heidi," Sam asked. "Do you have a computer?"

"*Nein.* Those *Teufel* are past me."

"Is there a computer store in the village?" Sam persisted.

Heidi handed telephone directories to Sam. The village had changed, but the silicon-chip was still not marketed there. In the larger Innsbruck phone book, Sam found possibilities. "May I borrow your car?" Sam asked.

"I'll drive you."

"I don't want to involve you too far," Sam interrupted.

Heidi shook her head. "I'm already *hier.*" She picked up her purse and keys and headed downstairs.

The ride into Innsbruck took twenty minutes. The beautiful mountains, snow-dusted in spots, reminded Sam of everything that inured her father and her to this place. She needed a taste of those for a moment. Those had been more peaceful times for them, or at least she thought so then.

In town they passed the main train station, and turned onto a narrow, one-way street with shops and businesses. Sam had the computer disks in her purse.

In a computer and electronics store, a smallish salesman, in jacket and tie, helped them. He demonstrated IBM-clones, allowing Sam to try each.

On the final model, Sam asked, if she could try her own disks. She put in the disk, marked "Little black book," and started to scan the contents.

"That's a wide variety of addresses," the salesman said in German to Sam. *"Almost like a customer directory from all over the world."*

"My Christmas card list," Sam replied.

While Liz was talking with the salesman, Sam copied the contents onto the computer's hard-disk. She did the same with the other disks.

When she finished, she dropped her wallet quietly on the floor, kicking it under the desk. Liz and the salesman did not notice. As she was getting into Heidi's car, Sam "discovered" her loss.

Back in the store, alone, she retrieved the wallet. *"I'd like to buy that last computer I tried,"* Sam said, taking out her American Express card.

"Let me see, if we have it in stock, Fräulein," he replied.

"No need," Sam said, quickly. *"The demonstrator felt comfortable. I'll take it."* The salesman assured her of its quality.

"Here's the address in the States where I'd like it shipped, and one in Vienna, where you can send confirmation of shipment," Sam continued. *"Do you send FAXes?"* Again, the salesman was agreeable.

"What took so long?" Liz asked, after they were driving.

"Would you believe it?" Sam replied. "I put it down on a printer. The damned wallet fell inside. Let's send this stuff."

Sam and Liz sent eight distinct packages by post and private express to the U.S. The original package's contents were divided among three. The others were dummies, with blank disks and wadded newspapers.

Heidi drove Sam and Liz to the hotel, where the other passengers were staying. Rail officials told them not to expect to resume their journey until late that night or early the next morning.

Dinner at Heidi's was a simple table of omelets, sausages, and veal. Sam and Heidi recounted earlier experiences, when Sam and her family, or her father, had stayed there.

Heidi told Liz how Sam's grandfather had saved her life. He was an OSS man, attached to a U.S. infantry unit toward the final days of World War II. When the cattle train on which she was being transported to a death camp was overrun by a U.S. column in Czechoslovakia, he found her in one of the cars, crying, under the body of her mother. She was only four years old.

Her family had lived in Innsbruck, before the Nazi *Anschluss*. Afterward Heidi's parents were kept in secret by a Catholic family. Eventually, Heidi was born during the war, and it seemed the family's hiding would spare it from "The Final Solution."

But, as the War came ever closer to Germany and Austria, the Nazis became more systematic in their search for Jews.

Heidi and her family were discovered and shipped to the East. All members of the Catholic family were killed by the *SS*.

After the War, Sam's grandfather arranged for Heidi to return to Innsbruck, to be raised by a family he knew since the early-1930s. She moved to *Mutters* when she married. Her spouse left her, but she stayed in the village. Before he died, Sam's grandfather lent Heidi the money to buy her house. It had really been part-gift, part-interest-free loan.

"Heidi's an adopted Pemberton," Sam said, when Heidi finished her story.

"The Austrian branch of the *familie!*" Heidi boomed. "Now I think you both should sleep, until train-time." Almost like daughters, she shuffled Sam and Liz to their room.

"I see what you meant about 'maternal,'" Liz said, as they lay on their beds. "She means a lot to you, doesn't she?"

"We tried to get her to move to the States with us," Sam said. "But."

"She must've been very nurturing to her own kids," Liz said.

"She never had any," Sam replied. "She thinks of her guests that way. Hers is the biggest 'family' in Austria."

Late that night Heidi awakened them. A rail official had called. The lines were clear. They would be on their way to Vienna within hours.

Heidi drove them to the hotel. "I expect you again soon," Heidi said to Sam. "*Mit Professor Tom. Und Fräulein Liz. Und* perhaps Robert, Maureen, *und* Edward." They hugged tightly.

"Thanks for being a big sister. If I live, I'll be back," Sam said.

Not long after, she and Liz boarded the train. The trip to Vienna seemed longer to Sam than it should, as intermittent rain and sunshine through a white-and-gray skyscape mapped the route. By late morning their train was pulling into the *Westbahnhof*. *The sky was wispily blue by then, with bright Autumn sunshine. A propitious sign,* Sam thought.

She phoned the *Hotel Akademie* on the *Pfeilgasse*, confirming a room for them. They caught Tram #58 near the *Mariahilferstasse,* taking them within foot-travel of the hotel. It was a typical workday in Vienna. The faces on the streetcar reminded Sam of *Prufrock*. Though Vienna's imperial reign ended so many decades before, Sam considered it quite the mixing bowl of ethnicity.

How the Nazis foisted "aryanism" on Austria she never understood. Even today's Nazi descendants were out-of-touch with the ethnic reality of eastern Austria, though, unfortunately, in touch with some of the attitudes there.

At the hotel, Sam felt a wonderful extravagance. It embodied, *"Gemütlichkeit,"* that special hospitality and understated comfort. Next door was the *Studenthaus,* which the hotel ran for traveling and foreign students. Across the street were the *Studentenheim* and the *Hotel Avis.*

From a phone stand in the lobby, Sam rang a number she knew by heart. Liz was in the gift shop, buying something Sam had never seen her use at Georgetown: Dunhill cigarettes.

"Here is Samantha, Wolfgang. In Wien. Did you receive my letter?" Sam asked, in German.

"And your invoice, with explanation," the familiar voice replied. *"Sorry Papa is not with you. Will you be coming by soon for payment? And return of unsold items?"*

"I hope the unsold stuff isn't too big. I mightn't get it in my suitcase. How is your schedule later today?"

"Afternoon's better. I have an appointment for dinner, but I could cancel it."

"Afternoon light's more appealing," Sam said. *"2:30 P.M.?"*

"I look forward to seeing you, Liebe. Same address. Wiedersehen."

Sam rejoined Liz, who was lighting a cigarette. "I still can't believe you smoke," Sam said to her. "Any other secrets you've kept from me?"

"No," Liz replied, exhaling a long stream of smoke. "You don't know how many nicotine fits I went through around you. I almost stopped, involuntarily. But I enjoy it too much."

Sam told Liz about the phone call and her appointment. "Mid-week brunch" and naps followed.

* * *

In a BMW 320i, Regina Foxwirth waited as her new contact checked them into the *Hotel Avis,* on the *Pfeilgasse* across the street from Samantha Pemberton's hotel. Regina held a small receiver in her hand, listening to its monotonous "beeping."

The new contact reserved a small suite, refusing to book two, separate rooms. Her new "partner" was more serious, with no romantic advances to her. She found him physically attractive, but would never admit it.

Still, Regina considered him and the proposed accommodations insufferable. The idea of sharing even a two-room suite with a lower-class German was too much for her. *A "glorified" youth hostel, at that,* she thought.

During the unexpected stopover near Innsbruck, she believed she had lost Samantha and the other woman. Fortunately, they returned to the central hotel. The contact surveilled them, until the train departed.

Regina disguised herself in older-aged, shabby clothes. She felt like she was wearing burlap. *The things she did for her father*, she thought. She wore a long, brunette wig.

The contact returned to the car. *"We're all checked in as a struggling married couple. Is the signal still clear and strong?"* he asked in French. The "beeping" was regular and audible.

"What a pity you didn't manage a microphone, too, in that suitcase," he said, as he unloaded their travel-cases. *"We'll settle in, then check the subjects."*

The second floor "suite" was really a partitioned efficiency without a kitchen.

"Don't worry," the contact said, before Regina protested. *"I'll not contest you for the bed. I'll sleep here on the sofa. And, remember, leave the dangerous stuff to me. Your Papa doesn't want anything happening to you."*

"How long'll I have to endure this?" Regina asked.

"Not long here," the contact answered. *"But we may have to play house on the next stop."*

"Next stop?"

"Mlle. Pemberton's on a junket," the contact said. *"We could be at it for weeks. The information's very important to your Papa. Get unpacked. I want to be out of here in five minutes."*

Back in the car, half-an-hour passed. No Pemberton appeared.

"*I'm slipping into the back for a rest,*" Regina said.

"*No, you're not,*" the contact said, firmly. "*I'm going inside. Watch the entrance. Here are the keys. If they come out, follow them. I'll wait for a call from you.*" The contact pocketed a cell phone.

Regina was put out. She would not have agreed to this if she had known beforehand what it would involve.

The contact came back. "*They're in the restaurant. They should be along soon.*"

Nearly two hours later they had still not appeared.

"*I've had enough of this,*" Regina said, finally. "*I'm going back to that fleatrap. At least it has a bed. Sort of.*"

"*No, you're staying here,*" the contact replied. "*Your Papa said you could be a whiner, without the whine. If you have any questions, call home. Otherwise, sit there, keep alert, and shut up. Please.*"

Regina felt conquered in a way her first contact never managed. She resolved to have her father put this "hired-hand" in his place.

"*There they are!*" the contact said.

Regina watched Samantha and the other woman walk briskly past the *Studentenheim,* and turn the corner to the *Strozzigasse.* She had still not adjusted to Samantha's blonde hair and newer, more stylish clothes. The other woman was wearing a large-brimmed hat, obscuring her face and below which flowed long, thick, and very wavy red hair.

The contact turned the car onto the *Strozzigasse.* Blocks later Samantha and her companion reached the *Auersberg Strasse,* behind the *Parliament* building. Thence to the *Burg Ring,* one stretch of the *Ring Strasse,* an angular semi-circle, anchored at both ends by the Danube Canal. The *Burg Ring* bordered the Hapsburg Dynasty's in-city palace, the *Hofburg.*

The contact pulled the car to the curb and got out. "*Follow. I'll signal you.*" He crossed the street ahead of a wave of cars.

Regina drove the BMW along the slow lane. She felt like a lion-tamer, keeping a Big Cat at bay, and half-expected the car to roar into traffic beyond her control.

At the corner, where the *Opern* and the *Kärntner Rings* meet, with the *Kärntner Strasse* seemingly begotten by their union, Samantha and her companion disappeared into the shopping district, which was the *Kärntner Strasse*.

The contact signaled Regina to join him. He materialized from a crowd, near the first block of shops. *"They're in an antique store in the next block. Call this number,"* he said, handing her a paper. *"Tell them where we are."*

"Whom am I calling?"

The contact said, *"Just do it. Take the car back to the hotel and wait."*

"What'll you do?" Regina asked. She felt anxious, but did not show it.

"Nothing dangerous," the contact said.

* * *

"Wolfgang," Sam called, as Liz closed the door to the antique shop. An older gentleman, dark-haired but grey-templed, in a tweed jacket, entered through a rear doorway. It was framed with thick, paisley curtains and led to an office and storeroom.

"Samantha, wie gehts?" he said, coming around the showcase. They hugged. Sam introduced Liz.

"The envelope you sent me," Wolfgang said, handing Sam a large brown mailer. *"Your package's in the back."*

He locked the front door to the shop, then returned to the curtained doorway. The shop had a familiar smell of expensive mustiness and mildew.

"How's business?" Sam asked, as they entered the disheveled, though apparently organized, office.

Wolfgang shrugged and said, *"You know the high-priced junk business. Everybody but the very rich and the American tourists cut back in bad times. I'm lucky I've got good junk."* He opened a large safe and removed a cube-shaped brown parcel, large enough to hold a centerpiece flower bowl, and handed it to Sam.

She cut the hempy string and opened it. Inside were more computer disks, video and audio tapes, photographs and negatives. *"May I use the equipment?"*

"Help yourself," Wolfgang said, before he returned to the showroom.

Sam put disks into the clone and read for a while. There were documents and reports dated 1985 forward. Liz was leafing through the stack of photos.

"Anything interesting?" Liz asked.

"Lots of incriminating history," Sam answered. "But nothing directly relevant."

They heard the bell on the front door clatter. Liz went to the curtains and peeked through a slit. She saw three men come in. Two wore trench coats, the other a baggy topcoat. They were browsing, when Wolfgang asked them if they needed any help. They declined, and continued their browsing.

A few moments later one lingered at the front door. His back to her. The other two were at the counter, speaking quietly to Wolfgang.

Wolfgang reached into the display case for something. As he did so, one grabbed his head, pushed it against the case, and held it there.

"Where's Samantha Pemberton?" Liz heard him ask Wolfgang in German. The others were now holding *Uzis*.

She took her 9mm automatic from her purse, released the safety, and clicked the slide back. "Better close shop," Liz whispered to Sam. "Trouble."

Sam repacked the box and joined Liz at the curtains.

"Who's that?" Wolfgang replied.

"She's been here thirty minutes," one man said, *"and hasn't come out yet."*

The man holding Wolfgang's head raised and banged it hard onto the glass top.

"Is there a back way out of this place?" Liz asked Sam.

"Yes, but we can't leave Wolfgang," Sam said.

"One of us could hold them off," Liz said, "while the other goes for the cops."

"Why don't we try the phone?"

"Go ahead."

Sam picked up the receiver. The line was dead.

"Are you volunteering to stay?" she said to Liz.

"*You* want to take them?"

"Should I leave the stuff here?" Sam asked.

"*Don't know...what...you're talking—*" Sam heard Wolfgang pant.

"*Fräulein* Pemberton!"

Sam peeked through the curtains. One man was holding Wolfgang in a choke-hold, with a pistol to his head.

"Listen carefully," another said. "Bring what you have, or we'll be forced to kill this man."

Liz aimed her pistol.

"What're you doing?" Sam asked, excitedly. "They've got assault weapons."

"Only stockless *Uzis*. They kick up when you fire, unless you know what you're doing."

"But the other'll kill Wolfgang."

"Then again," Liz said. "They might be scurrying. Either way, they're going to kill us. Get down and feed me refills." She handed Sam her purse.

Sam rummaged and came out with clips. "And you want me to leave you?"

"It's that or we both get nailed. I'll tell you when."

"You have thirty seconds to decide."

Liz fired. Her first shot caught the speaker and sent him crashing backward into furniture. Her next ones were low and shattered glass showcases. She fell back against the lower wall, beside the doorframe.

Automatic weapons fire tore through the curtains, ripped plaster from the rear wall, and shattered the shelves on it. Books and pottery crashed all over the room. The computer monitor on the desk exploded glass and electronic shreds. Another burst followed.

Liz swung into position and squeezed off two bursts. She saw movement from two sides of the salesroom. "Clip!"

Sam tossed her a fresh one. Another burst of automatic fire tore at the walls. Liz reloaded and squeezed off more bursts. "At times like this I wish I'd taken that MAK-10."

"*We'll give you one last chance to save yourselves and the storekeeper*," yelled the same voice as before. "*We'll kill him, if you don't!*"

Sam slid the clips to Liz and searched the desk. She found blank disks, and dumped them into her father's box. She took out the video and audio tapes and did the same with a few blanks she found, taping the box shut.

Meanwhile, Liz was returning fire. Sirens were getting closer.

"Wolfgang!" Sam yelled. "Let me know he's alive! I'll throw the box!"

"Throw the box out, and we'll let him live!"

"You've killed him already, you bastards!" Sam screamed.

"No," she heard Wolfgang's voice gasp. "Don't do it."

"Let me see him! Alive!" She peeked around the doorframe.

With his face bloody, Wolfgang was shoved over the front display case.

"Satisfied, *Fräulein?!*"

"Let him come to us. And the box's yours."

"Throw the box out, and he comes."

"Those sirens're almost here," Liz shouted. "Take what you can get!"

Sam saw Wolfgang disappear behind the counter. Then, one man, using him as a shield, walked the shopkeeper closer to the rear doorway. Ducking behind a column, he kicked Wolfgang toward the room.

Wolfgang fell a few feet from the shreds of the curtain. He began to crawl slowly. A burst of weapons fire tore the tile to his right.

"*We kept our part! Throw out the stuff! Or he's a dead floormat.*"

"Give me cover," Sam said to Liz, who reloaded.

Sam tossed the box, while Liz squeezed off bursts. They both ducked against the walls. Sam heard scuffling noises, then another burst of fire. The bell on the front door jingled.

Liz plunged through the remnants of the curtains, crouching to Wolfgang's left, behind a big armchair. The gunmen were gone.

"*Wolfgang!*" Sam screamed. She rushed to him and cradled

his head in her lap. *"I'm so sorry!"*

"No, no," he coughed. *"I shouldn't have unlocked the door and tried for profit in bad times,"* he said, smiling weakly.

He was bleeding from his right arm. There were no signs of gunshot wounds elsewhere. She helped him up, but he collapsed onto the floor again.

"Come on, Sam!" Liz came over to them. *"If I've gotta answer cops' questions, my cover's gone. Let's see that back way out."*

"Go on," Wolfgang said. *"I'll say it was a robbery, and give wonderful descriptions. They won't last twenty-four hours. I'll close shop till I think it's safe. Go on, but be in touch."*

Sam helped him into a chair. *"You'd better,"* she sniffled, though she smiled a thin smile. *"When they see what I gave them, they'll be back."*

She went into the office, with Liz right behind her, and scooped the contents of her father's box into her *Chanel* bag. As they slipped out the rear exit into an alley, the sirens got their closest and stopped.

They hurried down the alley. Street people were sleeping or lying in small dumpsters or in makeshift tents of cardboard boxes. Sam and Liz went down another alley. They did not stop till they reached *St. Stefan's* Cathedral.

Inside, they lingered. The clerics were preparing for the celebration of All Saints Day, two days away. Sam and Liz casually faded in with a group of Canadian tourists and exited with them.

They found a *Weinkeller* nearby where they plunked into a booth in a back room.

"I need a cigarette," Liz said, panting. She lit a Dunhill, took a very long drag, and exhaled the smoke slowly.

"I don't know how you can do that to yourself," Sam said.

"We've got to figure how they found you. You don't have anything at the hotel you can't live without for a while, right? We can't go back there."

"My new clothes!?"

"Don't panic," Liz said, calmly. "My contacts'll clear our stuff and get it to us. Now are you catching on to this game?! It's not 'no-harm-no-foul.' It's 'all harm-no-foul.' Washbourne told me they didn't think that kidnap attempt in D.C. was Cartel-based.

But these guys knew you by name and what you might be doing."

"Regina?"

"Maybe. Maybe not," Liz said, exhaling another cloud of smoke.

"The first thing to do is get this stuff on its way."

"Somehow they followed you, but I was sure we didn't have tails," Liz said, puffing again. "We went through everything Regina gave you." Sam nodded.

"Well, they've either got another homer on you somewhere, we don't know about." She took another drag. By then the cigarette was down nearly to the filter. "Or they followed us from regular surveillance. Either way they're very good." She stubbed out the cigarette and lit another one.

"Or all of the above," Sam said. "Take it easy on those. I was hoping this'd be a long partnership. I'll get you to quit before it's over."

"Too many more firefights, and I'll be at four packs a day. I've got to work on my shooting. I should've had those crumbs." Her eyes widened. "Ooh! Dizzy. I'm on a nicotine high."

A couple of glasses of wine later they had a new plan. Sam decided to know more from these disks, before sending them off.

Where they were going after Vienna would be affected by the disks. As long as her Dunhills did not run out, Liz said, she was ready for another destination.

By the time they left the *Keller* it was dusk. Sam called her father's friend, on the faculty at the *Universität,* the University of Vienna. He was in his office, and would also help them with viewing and dispatch of the cache. They caught a cab then two trams to the University. While Sam was there, Liz would find them a new place to stay.

During the ride Sam felt guilty. With two family friends nearly killed, she worried about Heidi. Should she go on down her father's "holiday list?" Was there any other way to find him?

Liz left her at the University. In the large stone building, the corpus of the University, Sam rediscovered the friend's office. He was a professor of politics and history, who looked more like an English barrister.

He let her call Innsbruck. Heidi answered after five or six

rings. She sounded like her normal self.

Sam did not tell her about the happenings in the antique store. Heidi still argued with Sam to return home, or at least to hide in *Mutters* with her. Sam refused, but repeated her promise to return there.

She further briefed her father's friend, especially about her "shipping requirements." He led her to a smaller, "writing room," where he often disappeared to work on his articles and books. It was equipped with a computer/printer, stereo/CD-player, and VCR/television combination. He left, and Sam read more disks.

The friend returned with two young men, his student research assistants. They would help her prepare the parcels and bring them to different post offices and private overseas shippers. Before they left, Sam told her friend about Liz and her eventual arrival.

Knowing she would be reading into the night, Sam made sparse notes. When she was finished with disks, she watched a videotape. The tape had segments showing large homes, estates, buildings. The voiceover was in German, her father's voice. It described each structure and its location. They were scattered all over Europe. The other tapes had similar contents. Sam moved on to audio.

These were in French, for the most part, with occasional German, Swiss-German, and Italian passages. Sam recognized her father's voice on these, too. There were descriptions of Cartel "transactions." She fast-forwarded through the tapes, stopping for excerpts.

The professor and his student assistants returned with small packing boxes, tape, and other materials.

Sam made copies of the disks and tapes, with blanks he supplied her. The four prepared the shipments and addressed them. The professor walked his assistants to a car. Sam watched from his office window, as they drove off. She had been at this for over five hours—and still no Liz.

She decided to go to the entrance and wait for her friend. If Liz had still not arrived after that, Sam was ready to accept the friend's office couch offer—alone.

* * *

Inside the University building, he listened to his men report in. He followed Samantha Pemberton to the University, after the gun battle. Dressed in threadbare clothes, he had awaited the women in the alley.

While *Fräulein* Pemberton and the other woman were in *St. Stefan*'s, he ducked into an unoccupied confessional and disposed of his disguise.

At the *Universität,* he found a utility locker room and put on a custodial uniform. He tracked her to a wing of the building. Additional agents joined him, and he sent them to other exits.

Fräulein Foxwirth was safely back at the *Hotel Avis*. She had been pliant and manipulable thus far, more so than her stepfather led him to believe she could or would be. When this phase of the operation was completed, she would be implicated well enough to squelch her arrogant whining, he thought.

* * *

At the designated entrance, Sam watched autumnal Vienna outside. Though the city was an older-peoples' haven, the University district did not quiet into slumber until after midnight, still early by Paris standards, though.

Sporadic "comers and goers" appeared. They had a distinctive "European student" or "professor" look: thin, neat but casual, occasionally disheveled.

This was a side-door arrangement, rather than the main foyer or lobby. Janitorial staff pushed tool carts past her. There were other carts and vacuum-cleaners outside classrooms.

Sam was tired, of either wondering about Liz's tardiness, or dwelling on her father. She decided to return to her friend's suite and entered a long corridor, where two maintenance men in overalls were pushing carts, side-by-side.

"*Entschuldigung,*" she said to them.

They looked back, but ignored her. She repeated her one-word request. Still, they did not move aside.

Great! she thought. *Two wandering minstrels finished for the shift, in no hurry to do anything.*

They suddenly faced and grabbed her arms, holding her tightly. She tried to scream, but a facial blanket of cotton, with a strong medicinal aroma, covered her mouth. The soft cotton was the final thing she felt before she passed out.

* * *

In a taxi to the University, Liz was fretting. Her search for a safe hotel took longer than expected. After that, she met with an emergency contact for her "reload" and refurbishment. That had taken several hours to arrange. In addition to the 9mms, she procured a MAK-10, and extra clips, in a very large *"Vuitton"* bag, given her by the contact.

Liz's cab turned onto the street with the University entrance. She saw three men hurriedly carrying something long and slender, wrapped in sheets, to an Audi double-parked near the entrance. They put "it" gently into the backseat. She recognized one man from the antique shop.

She told the driver to go another half-block, then do a U-turn, after the Audi started away. *"Folgen Sie das Auto,"* she said, excitedly, in German. *"Don't let them notice us."*

"I wanted you to say that!" the driver replied. He dodged the taxi through traffic. The Audi went into swift right and then left turns, away from the *Ringstrasse*.

Eight or nine blocks later the Audi turned left again onto the *Lederergasse*. After four blocks this street changed into the *Strozzigasse*. Liz recognized the area by then, and guessed where the Audi might be heading.

It parked in front of the *Studentenheim*. As it stopped, a new man rolled a laundry cart up to it.

The others lifted the bundle of sheets softly into the cart, then rolled it around the side of the building.

Liz scanned the area with night-vision binoculars. The laundry cart and "crew" had vanished. She found the rear entrance of the *Studentenheim*, and popped the lock.

Inside a dreary, basement corridor she found a freight elevator. Its over-door indicator with old-style brass hands was stopped at the sixth floor. Liz hurried to the level marked,

"Fünftes Stockwerk."

No one else was in the hall. She passed a small directional microphone near each doorway, listening through a headset. Her other hand was inside the *Vuitton* bag, holding a 9mm.

The first doors yielded either silence or quiet German chattering. In a room midway down the hall, she heard a muted mixture of French and German.

Footsteps from inside caused Liz to duck into a utility closet. Different men were speaking German and at least two sets of footsteps passed. The men had been discussing *"the job," "her,"* and *"the tape."*

The room door had not closed. Liz held the microphone through a hole in the closet door.

She heard more German, punctuated by French between a man and a woman. The man's voice was unfamiliar to Liz, but the woman's was not. She knew she had the right room now.

Regina's French was biting, angry, a step removed from quiet, controlled hysteria. The man's replies were commanding, categorical, but not angry.

"You bastard! You never told me!" Regina repeated. *"I'm seeing my father."*

"I need you here."

"You've got what you wanted. You don't need me. What'll you do? Kill her?"

"It depends," the man answered.

"What about the other woman?" Regina said. She sounded haughty now. The hysteria was gone, the anger lingered.

"Don't bother yourself with her. She's of no consequence."

"I don't have any special love for her. But whatever you do, I don't want to watch. You can't make me."

"As you wish," the man said. *"I hoped you'd be stronger. You need a ride to the airport?"*

"I'll catch a taxi," Regina said. *"When this is over . . . "*

"You won't get a plane till the late morning. You'll be back. I'll leave word where we've gone, if we move before that."

"Don't bet on any of that," Regina hissed.

"Your step-father's at the Ulm Estate. He's leaving for Nice on the first or second. Your mother's already in the south of France,"

the man said, calmly. *"You might catch him before he leaves, if you hurry. Otherwise, I'd suggest you fly directly to Nice. Or Berlin, after that."* Liz enjoyed hearing him be so cool, while Regina was losing control.

"You've enough of your fellow trash to keep you company. I'm not staying here any longer," Regina said. *"If you want me, I'll be at the Hilton."*

Liz heard what sounded like a three-person conversation in German, as the door closed. The distinct click of women's heels faded down the hall, with muffled French, especially *"cochon,"* drifting back.

There were more footsteps. She peeked through her microphone hole. A man from the kidnapping disappeared into the room.

Liz hurried down some rear stairs and back to the cab. She handed the driver notes scribbled in German. He was one of her contacts in Vienna. She instructed him, and returned to the closet.

* * *

Regina Foxwirth was on her way to Vienna Airport. The night in the Hilton was an improvement over the *"hovel,"* but it was not as good as she was accustomed.

Her new contact's self-control and insufferable arrogance had been one thing. Unlike his predecessor, his apparent competence and lack of interest in her left her no way to control him. However, kidnapping Samantha Pemberton, drugging and holding her, had been quite another, not that she liked Samantha much, but her step-father misled and lied to her.

Until then she thought she would have done "anything" for him. She realized she was not prepared to go so far—unless it suited her. That time had not come—yet.

Regina had decided to quit this work. She would tell him she never wanted to do anything like this again, and get him to send her to a university she *wanted* to attend. She wanted only controllable men around her.

At the airport, Regina bought a one-way, First-Class ticket to

Stuttgart on Austrian Airlines. She hated flying on that carrier, since of all the nationalized air carriers in Europe, it was the worst. But it had the earliest morning flight. Before she boarded the plane, she called her step-father's estate in *Ulm* for a car to pick her up at *Stuttgart* Airport.

* * *

"Ach, Hans," Regina said to her father's chauffeur. He met her at the arrival gate in *Stuttgart*. *"It's so good to see a friendly face. I've felt utterly abused lately,"* she said.
"You've changed your hair color, Miss?" he asked.
"Mercifully, it's only a wig, Hans," Regina replied.
He took her carry-on dress bag and walked her to a Mercedes stretch limousine, parked in a *"No Parking"* zone. Inside the limo, she freshened herself. She brushed out her blonde hair and did her makeup.

She enjoyed the privacy from the car's darkened windows and curtains. She changed into a long leather skirt-and-jacket suit and a white blouse. She draped her favorite sable coat over her shoulders.

Finished, she lit a Dunhill cigarette, luxuriating in its smoke. The chauffeur handed her a thermos of coffee.

Through the smoke of three more Dunhills and coffee, Regina watched the German countryside go by. She was not used to uneasiness. Her world had always been ordered, comfortable, under control—SAFE.

Her step-father had never refused her anything. She had obeyed his wishes, but she worried about his reaction to her not wanting to go on. He was so accustomed to getting his way.

They reached the estate within an hour. The chauffeur drove the car through yawning, front gates, past armed guards and dogs, and onto the long, tree-bordered road. At the grey-stone castle-like mansion, there were many limousines. A manservant in white coat opened the car door for her and the house's front doors.

"Gnädiges Fräulein, the Herr Baron is in important meetings," he said to Regina. *"I shall tell him you are here, after I fetch your luggage."*

Regina passed through the ornately decorated, marble-floored foyer, to her step-father's study. He had several such rooms in the house, including a large conference room.

That was where she would find him, if she barged in. He usually did not greet interruptions well, but he accepted them from "his little girl," as he had always called her. In this instance, she decided it was better not to.

Usually not a drinker before evening—if at all—Regina fixed herself a truly uncharacteristic *double* Courvoisier and took a long, slow sip. She wanted to drink it all at once, perhaps have another. But she conserved it, like the good liquor-nurse she had always been, always in control. Her step-father did not come for an hour. More Dunhills passed her lips.

She finished the brandy and was pouring herself another, when The Baron came in. Regina stopped long enough for him to greet her with a fatherly hug-and-kiss, which she returned. She poured another brandy and offered it to him.

They toasted each other. *"But a little early for you, not true?"* he asked. *"I was surprised to hear you were on your way home."*

"Who told you? I wanted to arrive secretly."

"People trying to arrive unannounced oughtn't to telephone for a family limousine. Your chore for me isn't finished. You knew my wishes."

"I thought I did," Regina sighed, "until last night. You never told me you ordered Samantha Pemberton...Kidnapped ...Held indefinitely."

"Not indefinitely. Only until our business is transacted. It will be over in a week or two."

"So you admit it? I asked your man if he would kill her. He said, 'It depended.' These're crimes, Papa!"

"Not crimes, my dear. Expedients to smooth business. Insurance."

"Against her father? They're still illegal. That's murder!"

"No one's been ordered to murder Professor Pemberton's daughter. Oh, but don't try to act naïve, Regina!" he said, without raising his voice. *"Legalities have never concerned you before. You know our level of business is not without necessities. Do you think*

I've provided you and your mother the standard of living to which you've become more than accustomed, by playing by every legal nicety? I've bent, even broken the rules before. You and your mother go where you want. Spend what you want. See what you want."

"You've been and are good to us. But Mother had certain resources, before she married you. I do NOT want to go back, Papa."

"You must, my dear. Please don't act faultless. You're in as deeply as anyone. You've done more than your share of illegalities over the years. That wasn't your first break-in, was it?"

"*I won't go back,*" Regina said, firmly. "And I want you to get rid of that second fool you sent to replace the first one."

"Neither alternative can be granted just now," The Baron replied. "You will do as you're told. You've always been too stubborn and headstrong. And remember, you're addicted to your life style. You couldn't live poor, if you had to. Not without the money sewn into the linings of your peasant dresses."

"Please let me out. And send me to some place I want..."

"After this, we'll talk about it. Other things are more important now."

Regina knew she had lost completely. "*You did say you hadn't ordered her murdered, Papa?*" she felt herself relenting. "*It's not that I've any great love for her. I have your promise?*"

"Yes," he replied. "*Now hurry along. I'm very busy. I didn't really have time for this.*" He kissed her cheek. "*You're my prime heir, after your mother. I should've adopted you formally, but you're still provided for handsomely in my will. I shouldn't want to lose you.*"

"*I'll be glad, when this is over,*" Regina pouted. "*By the way, Papa. I was surprised when the new man told me you were either here or in the South of France. I thought you were due in Berlin for a whole month.*"

The Baron did not answer at first. The question seemed to take him aback. "*My, what a sharp little memory you have, Dear. I...uh...had to cancel at the last minute. It's only the end of year conferences. I'll be in Berlin from the 15th of November, instead. You'd better get along, if you want to make the afternoon *plane to Vienna. Or would you rather take one of the Gulfstreams or Lears?"*

By one of her step-father's personal jets, Regina returned to Vienna. She pondered what she should do next, if anything. Until then she had thought of him more as her father, than a step-father. She wanted to believe he would never order Samantha Pemberton murdered.

But he had been right. She was a willing addict of the well-heeled, well-oiled life. And she preferred to keep it that way.

XIX

Otto von Markenheim returned to his conference room. "Sorry for the delay, gentlemen," he said in English, retaking his seat at the head of the long table. "Let's get on with the agenda, shall we?"

Von Markenheim gestured to two men. "These're our newest recruits for Case Blue, Messrs. Rodriguez and Essaid. They've been cleared by Colonel K. himself. An associate of theirs is assisting with the larger devices. In exchange for our support for Latin American and Middle Eastern projects—and other consideration—they'll be working with The Colonel. You're dismissed, Gentlemen. The Colonel's expecting you." The two men left the room.

Von Markenheim acknowledged an assistant to his right.

"*It's come to our attention,*" the assistant said, in German, "*from a Washington source that a spy's infiltrated us. A high-ranking CIA officer, we think.*"

Among those present raised eyebrows, shock, and surprise were ubiquitous.

"*As far as we know, no one in this room,*" the assistant continued. "*But that, too, may change.*" There was a loud, collective groan of ease.

"Steps are already under way," von Markenheim said. "Colonel K.'s taking care of the matter."

"At what level is the spy?" a man on the right side of the table asked.

"Lorry-driver or gunman," von Markenheim said. "*He's seen a few of our outpost facilities . . . On to new business.*"

"Herr Baron," the man to his right continued, "*in view of that fact, should we not cancel Case Blue? Or postpone?*"

Professor Pemberton said, "*We've come too far to quit now.*"

"Thank you, Thomas," von Markenheim said. "We should move it up."

269

"*But we've moved it up once already,*" another man said. "*It's 1 November, less than two weeks before Zero-Day. Can our men be ready?*"

"*The Colonel assures me they ARE ready. The team leaders and their technicians are getting their briefings. Moreover, Stage One's already under way.*"

"*But will the larger devices be ready?*" the man on the right persisted. "*They're not in place, are they?*"

"*On the contrary,*" von Markenheim replied. "*The key ones are in place, thanks to General Tripleleaf. We're keeping the rest for arming work—and insurance.*"

The Baron's right," another man said. "*The future's virtually ours, for the taking. If Colonel K. says we can, I say, let's go.*"

"*Colonel K.'s also assured me,*" von Markenheim said. "*A week earlier wouldn't matter. I suggest we consider that option. We need not reach a decision now. Let's move on.*"

* * *

"Well, that was easy," Jamael said to Jaime, as they got into their car outside Baron von Markenheim's mansion.

"Not as easy as it looked," Jaime retorted. "If it weren't for my connections in Latin America and Africa and my Russian colonel's entrees to Krattmay, we'd never have made it. To think I almost popped the bastard back in Africa."

"It was lucky we dodged that ambush," Jamael said. They reached the gates.

"I owe some motherfucker a shot in the head for that," Jaime agreed.

"I wonder if your doctor's enjoying her new job," Jamael snickered.

Jaime stopped the car at the gates. A guard, with an automatic rifle slung over his shoulder, looked in the driver's window, then waved them on, as the high, brass-colored gates opened.

"I hope she gets the job done in two weeks or less," Jaime said. "Emilio'll stay close to her till then."

"Step on it," Jamael said, "or we'll be late for that briefing!"

*   *   *

In an underground warehouse, beneath a disused farm between *Paderborn* and *Stadt-Oldendorf*, Germany, John Marshall watched as Colonel Johannes Krattmay called the briefing to order. The place reminded Marshall of standard-issue Army depots. It smelled of damp concrete.

"*Achtung!*" Krattmay yelled. "*Gentlemen! This is your introduction to the weapons we'll be using. Pay close attention. Success in this mission depends on your mastering this equipment. You'll receive your individual assignments later. Remember! Less than a handful'll be assigned the main weapons, but you all must be capable.*

"*To maintain security, you'll be provided the appropriate devices just prior to Zero-day. Your briefing officer is Herr John Marshall, formerly of the American Army and MIT. He'll lead you through the schematics of the large, more important devices, and small, less-important, still significant, backup weapons. Please hold questions, until the end.*"

"Open binders to Page S-1," Marshall instructed. The paging noises subsided. On an easel to his left was a large schematic drawing. He also used computer-generated projections.

"*We'll begin with internal layout and design, along with placement of the fissionables. Then, standard triggers and detonators. We're currently working on alternative trigger mechanisms. My previous employers weren't kind enough to supply us with theirs.*" There was laughter.

"*For the larger weapons, that is. The smaller ones came complete. Let's jump over to Schematic 2,*" he continued. "*The close-up of the interior arming mechanisms. Pay special attention to these. Location A is where you place the fissionable packet. Lock it in, in W-45-3 Mark IX devices. Turn to Schematic 5 for the same placement on the W-45-3 Mark XVIs.*"

Marshall spent the next several hours explaining schematics and answering questions about the MADMs.

"*Remember,*" he concluded. "*Placement's easy, if you follow my outline. Setting delayed detonation timers is also easy. BUT, and this is a heavy BUT. This could be the heaviest BUT in the operation. Once you set everything, if you realize you screwed up, you cannot go back and correct it. If you try, you'll set the thing off, by screwing with the anti-tampering back-up. If you fuck up once, don't fuck up the second time. Questions?"* Hands went up.

During the questions, he noticed a messenger talking to Krattmay. The Colonel called over two men, standing guard on the stage, and quietly conferred with them.

Marshall interrupted a questioner. *"Colonel? Anything wrong?"*

"Continue," Krattmay replied, nonchalantly. *"We excuse ourselves."*

Marshall watched them leave. Other men followed them out. He finished with the questions, and continued the briefing.

"Open your third binders. On the Type W-54-etc. small devices. These're more versatile and portable. Their punch is still heavy." He used another projection.

"They can be set for time delay, or radio-controlled detonations. The time delay's good for two weeks. Then they disable themselves. In your materials you've got segments lifted from the Army's own manual and the variations at our disposal. I emphasize the same thing with these, as I did with the bigger boys. Once you've set and locked them, if you realize you screwed up, tough. We don't have the time to cover anti-tampering supersession. Even then, the anti-tampering devices vary. You've got to be acquainted, nut by nut, with the assembly, to know which one's in front of you. Just pack up and get the hell out of there. Let's get to the nuts and bolts."

As he spoke, Jaime Rodriguez and Jamael Essaid came in. They nodded to him and sat in end-row seats.

"You're late, guys," he said to them in English. "But it's not catastrophic. *For the benefit of our new arrivals,"* he continued in German. *"I'll do the briefing in English."*

He did a summary review and picked up again with SADMs. A little while later he declared a break. The Colonel had still not returned. During the recess, Rodriguez and Essaid caught him.

"How's Dr. Pola holding up?" Rodriguez asked.

"She knows her way around a smashed atom," Marshall said. "She's down to two-and-a-half-packs a day. If you come to the lab, you'll go through the blindfold number. Even I don't know where it is."

Marshall resumed the briefing. It took more hours for him to complete the basic SADM indoctrination. The atmosphere in the warehouse was ever-evening, like a casino. Marshall finished the briefing, but The Colonel had still not reappeared.

* * *

In his Frankfurt office, Chuck Channing was examining enlargements from film McConneld left at an emergency "drop" in *Hannover* on 29 October. They showed encoding, on which the cryptographic section was still working.

To another drop, a day after the first, McConneld delivered computer disks. They held past delivery dates, places, and recipients of conventional ordnance, and pending ones up to 15 November. The recipients were identified by initials.

Terror activities had quadrupled in the past two weeks. The car- and truck-bomb "factories" were working overtime.

Channing passed the information to Colonel Barsohn. Coordinated raids disclosed recent abandonment. No weapons or personnel were found. New sites were identified only by code names. There had been no contact from "Mr. Smith," either.

* * *

This had not been his month, McConneld thought to himself: Balkovsky's gas attack, the truck driver's suicide; now, another hit on the head.

"In the dark," literally and figuratively. He awakened, in a closet with a freezing floor and a metal door. His jacket and boots were gone.

He remembered being taken at a depot by The Colonel and his men. He felt a blow on the head, then blacked out. *Was Balkovsky there, too?*

Maybe they mistook him for someone else—but not likely. This could be the final wrap-up. He decided to play ignorant and stick to the cover, till he dropped. Would he do the happy pill?

He heard voices and footsteps. The echoes were sharp. There were jingling sounds at the door. A bolt jerked backward. Light from the hall blinded him.

"Blindfold him!" someone said. Hands grabbed him from both sides and handcuffed his arms behind him. Coarse cloth scratched his face.

"Don't smother him!" the same voice said. "But I want Mr. McConneld to remember his stay with us!" McConneld recognized The Colonel's voice.

"*My name's Freudig!*" McConneld reflexively said, in German. "*It's never been anything else!*"

"Save the bullshit, CIA man!" Krattmay said, in English. "We know all about you! We won't kill you yet. After you tell us everything, you'll beg for it."

"*My name's Freudig! I don't know what the fuck you're talking about!*" McConneld shouted in German. Hands spun McConneld.

Too many years of this stuff, McConneld thought. His brain was still doing laps around the room, after his body stopped.

The hands led him into an elevator, then through a noisy area with more voices. Outside into the cold, he was pushed into a car.

His head cleared a little. Hold out till the SEALs or Rangers located him. But how could they? He wanted to kill the bastard who fingered him. If he got out of this, he would find the double and pop him—or her. Have pistol, no wait. If . . .

The drive was short. Hands hustled him from the car. He was shivering: a shirt never cut it in European Autumn or Winter.

Scuffled across dirt, asphalt, he was carried over a raised threshold, then to warmth. More loud noise, but different: machinery, like turbines. Through a doorway? Soundproof room and echoes. Dumped in a chair. Blindfold yanked. More lights.

McConneld squinted. When he could see again, there was Krattmay. The Colonel leered at him, then slapped him across the face.

"Back with us, McConneld?" Krattmay cackled, then slapped him again. "We'll do soft, then hard."

"*I don't know what the hell! . . .*" McConneld said in German.

"You don't understand," The Colonel said. "The game's over. Come clean, and you get a merciful end. If not, messy and painful. Tell me who's your contact? Where're your drops? Scheduled drop-times?"

McConneld persisted with his German denials. The Colonel repeated the questions in English. McConneld made general denials. Slaps across McConneld's face followed.

"How much do you know about my organization?" The Colonel asked. "What've you passed to your Control?"

"*My name's Freudig,*" McConneld said, out of breath. "*Ex-Stasi, recruited by your people. Don't know any McConnell.*"

The Colonel smacked him back and forth. "You'll tell me everything," The Colonel replied. "Get the LSD. They used to say this would 'blow your mind.' We sell it in the States to anxious college students. Hold him."

McConneld saw Krattmay squeeze the air pocket and a bit of fluid from the hypodermic syringe. From behind, hands and arms held McConneld tightly to the chair. He felt the cold plunge of the needle, pain.

"I use a smatter of heroin and mescaline with the LSD," The Colonel said, after he finished. "After that, I'll give you a taste of truth-drugs."

After the injection, McConneld alternated between narcotic high and fear. Whenever someone moved, he saw swatches and stripes of colors in their wakes. Each movement was a single frame, in outrageous colors and ultra-slow motion.

He was exploring a bizarre, tissue-like cavern. Ganglia swooped down, grabbing at his throat. He was with a much-younger Balkovsky. A loud voice called. A god. He hid behind a ridge of red muscle. The voice was relentless.

From nowhere a concussion threw him over the ridge and into a wet red ravine. He bit down hard on a tooth on the right side of his mouth. He felt euphoric, then blacked out.

* * *

"*Is he dead?*" The Colonel asked his man, who was using a stethoscope on McConneld's chest.

"His heartbeat seems faint, very erratic. He could be dying."

"Give him something," Krattmay said. "If he doesn't come to, dump the body and bury it. I'll be in Vienna. You know how to reach me."

* * *

On a delivery with his group, Balkovsky saw his "mole" again. The agent was with men in combat fatigues, though he himself wore street clothes.

The mole surreptitiously stuffed a paper into the General's hand. The note read in German, *"Must see you. Big news."*

Balkovsky meandered to a staircase, near the warehouse's elevator. The agent joined him. They went down the stairs to the sleeping quarters.

"Our people took a prisoner at the Kissendorf depot early this morning," the agent replied. *"He's supposedly a CIA infiltrator. The Colonel's been interrogating the guy, using heavy drugs. I don't know how long he can hold out. I heard The Colonel refer to him as 'O'Connel,' or 'McDonald.' Some Irish name."*

"Oh shit!" Balkovsky said. "Where are they holding him?! Can you get away?"

"A power plant, within driving distance of here," the agent answered. "But I thought you didn't want to be missed."

"We've got to get him out of there or kill him," Balkovsky said. "Do you have a car?" The agent nodded. "How soon before you leave?"

"Right away, but you'll be missed. I could vouch for you again..."

Balkovsky said, *"I don't want you involved. Drive me by. I'll take it from there."*

"I've vouched for you once already. That crew-chief's bound to recall."

"Play it straight. If they catch me, you want my head as much as they do. On a related matter, have you been able to get to Professor Pemberton?"

The agent replied, "S*ince the CIA man was discovered, secu-*

rity's unbelievably tight. At best there's only a slim chance I can."

One at a time, the agent and Balkovsky left. His chief did not seem to notice his exit.

The agent drove off alone, while Balkovsky started into the woods nearby. Half-a-mile away, Balkovsky reached the road and found the agent waiting for him. They were off to the plant.

* * *

Somewhere between Never-Never-Land and the Rabbit Hole, Sam found herself. She heard a *pooka*, speaking particularly guttural German, calling to her in a room, underground, with moss wallpaper. She dove into a portmanteau and pulled it closed, womb-like.

Her father's voice? Marshall's? The Nazi's? The German changed to French, then Italian, then back to German. But it was Swiss-German. Germans, holding their noses, mocking the French, forcing German through their nostrils. The darkness faded into more light. The *pooka* faded, too.

Another voice was speaking German-accented English, then French-accented German. A woman. REGINA! Sam turned around. No one.

Now she was at the University. Which one? She saw grey stone, columns, arches. Vienna, or Washington, or Boston? She was in a lecture. The teacher was her father, but she could not hear him.

Sam closed her eyes, then reopened them. She saw a grey ceiling, crying out for repainting. Its dirty splotches blurred into grey Rorschach tests.

She craned her neck and head forward. She was alone. There were voices, low and irregular, probably in the next room.

Leaning on her arms, she tried to get up. They were tied to either side of her, like a bed crucifixion. Something coarse scratched her wrists, as she tugged. Her legs were spread, tied to the lower bed frame.

Had she been raped? She felt her clothes. They seemed tight and intact, but there was no guarantee.

Whoever "they" were: more faceless abductors with drugs. She cursed her father, but realized she came looking; it was her own fault.

Voices were louder. She lay back, and closed her eyes. Her body felt limp. The Rorschach tests from the ceiling turned a rainbow of colors. With the vertigo, the mental acceleration, it was not hard for her to pretend unconsciousness. A door opened. Someone was speaking more guttural German, talking about her! She needed light. Her eyes opened uncontrollably: they were in business for themselves!

One voice said, *"She's looking at me! Give her something!"*

Another replied, *"Don't worry! We gave her enough to keep her out for days. She can't really see you, Colonel. She's in her own dreamland."*

Through jellied eyes Sam saw the Nazi officer from her dream.

"Keep her, till you hear from me," he said. *"A week or two. You can reach me in . . ."* The voices trailed off into murmurs. The door closed, with no more murmurs.

* * *

"Are you sure it's her?" Liz McGonnville asked the agent.

He called her away from the stakeout of Sam Pemberton's abductors. Liz and the man were speaking in a room off the lobby of the Vienna Hilton.

"She matched the description you gave us," he answered. "She checked in alone, under, 'R. Flannery Armstrong,' with a passport to match. She hasn't been out, and has had no visitors. There has been heavy phone traffic to France."

"I'm going up," Liz said. "Stay in the background once we're there." Regina's room number was 404.

In the stakeout room, Liz bunned her hair and changed clothes to that of a room-service waitress. Checking her 9mm, then placing it in one pocket with a sleep dart-gun in the other, she wheeled a serving cart to Regina's door.

"Room Service, Gnädige Frau," she called, in German. There was movement inside. The door opened slightly.

"*I didn't order anything,*" Regina answered. "*Take it away! You!?*"

Liz reached up with the pistol. "Why, Regina! Where's that expensive toilet-training of yours?! Not going to invite me in?"

Regina tried to close the door, but Liz was ready. She rammed the cart against it. Regina fell to the floor. Once inside, Liz hurriedly closed the door.

"I should've known," Regina said, getting up slowly. "The hair fooled me. What do you want?"

"I want Sam back," Liz replied, "alive and in one piece."

"I don't know...."

"Cut the bullshit, Regina," Liz said. "I saw the snatch."

"Then you know where she is. Go take her yourself," Regina said, contemptuously. She lit a cigarette and inhaled deeply.

"Your cronies'll kill her, if we're not fast. You'll get us in."

"The hell I shall!" Regina said.

"You two-faced bitch! Watch my lips," Liz said. "If anything happens to Sam, I promise I'll kill you."

Regina's eyes widened, with genuine fear. "I didn't know about this."

"You didn't know about the hit-and-run in Oxford?!" Liz asked. "We're nearly killed in that antique store? You've got NO credibility, lady!"

"I didn't!" Regina protested. It was a vulnerable, pleading indignation Regina was showing. She semi-circled Liz, approaching the door. "But you can't force me to help you!"

Liz cut Regina off from the exit. "I could. But dragging you kicking and screaming won't help me. Remember, you won't be able to hide. I'll find you anywhere."

With that, she took out the dart-gun from her other pocket and shot Regina with a tranquilizer/sleep drug.

Regina wavered, then collapsed. Liz ushered her colleagues in from their surveillance room. Together they bound and gagged the unconscious Regina. When they were finished, Regina lay belly-down, width-wise across the center of the bed. Her hands were tied by a cord, running under the boxspring, and thence to her bound feet.

As a final touch, Liz called the front desk, impersonating

Regina and requesting she not be disturbed for the following twenty-four hours. She also put the "Do Not Disturb" sign on the doorknob as they were leaving.

"Should we Pamper her?!" Liz's other colleague asked. "I guess that depends?"

"She's been pampered enough already," Liz said. "That's her problem."

The surveillance men remained at the Hilton. Liz changed clothes again and left for the *Studentenheim*.

XX

On the morning of 2 November, *The Times* of London reported in a banner headline a bomb explosion at the headquarters of the British Army in Northern Ireland. Twenty-seven British soldiers were killed and fifty-nine wounded, in what Whitehall called the bloodiest day for the British Army in Northern Ireland since the Good Friday Peace Accords.

Militant splinter factions within the IRA claimed responsibility for the attack by telephone to Reuters. The callers indicated the attack was in reaction to the continued negotiations between the IRA leadership and the British Government. A spokesman at No. 10 Downing Street denounced this "most barbarous act, when peace could be within sight once more."

* * *

Balkovsky looked at the fourteen faces, around the table. "*Questions?*" he asked them in German. Blueprints lay on the tabletop.

"*How much time before the guards pass by?*" one man asked.

"*Twelve minutes,*" Balkovsky said. "*The delivery lorry's got to be on time. There's no other way out. These show where we disable the alarm systems.*"

"*Are the German authorities in on this?*" another asked.

"*I'm not doing shit with them,*" Balkovsky replied.

"*What happens, if we can't get him out?*"

Balkovsky sighed. "*We kill him. Let's not dwell on that. I only hope the diversion works. Are you ready, Achim?*"

The man beside Balkovsky nodded. "*If I were a theist,*" Balkovsky responded, "*I'd pray for you.*"

* * *

Still in his blackened closet, McConneld rolled over. A cold draft from under the door smacked him semi-awake. His head throbbed; his neck was stiff.

McConneld heard footsteps approaching and turned to avoid the light, as the door opened. Hands pulled him to his feet. "*Halten Sie ihn!!*" a new voice shouted.

A hand pulled McConneld's head up by his hair. There was a cool sensation on his arm, then the intrusion of a hypodermic needle.

"Good to see you with us again, Herr McConneld!!" the new voice continued. "Your friends are on the way to rescue you. After we deal with them, we'll be back to finish with you. For now, you'll sleep."

A rag was stuffed into McConneld's mouth. Tape was strapped tightly across it. More tape flattened his ears, on the way around his head. His captors left him lying on his stomach, trussed like a steer in a rodeo event: hands and feet bound behind his back and tied together.

* * *

Balkovsky looked at his watch. 7:27 P.M. The scheduled food delivery truck, their means of escape, would be leaving by the front gate of the power plant in thirty-three minutes. At 8:01 P.M. four of his men were due to open fire with assault weapons, LAWs, and grenade launchers near the front gate.

He and the men from the briefing were concealed outside the fence at the rear of the compound. Balkovsky identified two weak spots along the perimeter, from the plans supplied by his mole.

Four men would disable or obfuscate the alarm and surveillance systems. The remainder, with Balkovsky, would make their ways through a place less accessible to the guard patrols.

Over his headset came a message. The surveillance system had been neutralized in their area. Balkovsky and his men cut through the fence.

Their destination was "Building 9," a storage and generator building, providing the plant's own power. McConneld was held on an underground level. Another message crackled over Balkovsky's headset. Achim reported more guards deploying near the front fence. Balkovsky and his team found Building 9, disposing of the three guards near the entrance. Inside, Balkovsky led the way, past turbines and smaller generators, downstairs to the subterranean levels. In two-man teams they spread out, searching rooms and offices. They disposed of more guards, but did not find McConneld.

There were three more levels. Balkovsky checked his watch. 7:45 P.M. *So many levels, so little time*, he thought. The next one held spare parts and replacement generators, but no holding area or rooms.

The third had cubicles and closets. But halfway through it, Balkovsky saw no guards or other personnel. He decided to skip to the final level. There were seven minutes before the delivery truck would arrive at the exit gate.

In the final hall, to his right, he heard voices in German. He sent two men to the other side of the concentric corridor, while he and the rest leap-frogged toward the conversations. One of his men tripped over an electrical cable and smashed into trash cans. The German chatter stopped.

"Karl? Helmut? Who's there?" someone called in German.

Balkovsky dove behind a wall. Weapons fire tore at the concrete. Another of his men landed beside him. Across from them in the opposite corridor, his remaining men were returning the fire.

"Four of them!" the man who joined Balkovsky told him.

The opposite wall was raked by fire. They turned around the corner, Balkovsky kneeling, the other man standing, and opened fire in quick bursts.

"Where're Horst and Gerd?" Balkovsky shouted, as he ducked behind the wall. *"Cover me!"* He jumped across the open space. Gunfire trailed him.

"Two of you, down that way. This corridor circles around behind them. Find Gerd and Horst!"

Balkovsky and the third man returned fire. The enemy fire did not slow down. *"They must have a fucking ammo dump!"* Balkovsky said.

Suddenly, farther ahead, he heard unremitting fire. There were no ricochets. *"Gerd?! Horst?!"* he yelled.

"What d'you want, Alex?"

Balkovsky peeked around the corner. Up ahead he saw his four men standing over bodies on the floor. *"Four minutes! Move your asses!"*

"This door's locked," a man called from the other end. He chopped the door open with a fire ax. McConneld was lying on his stomach, motionless.

Balkovsky cut McConneld's ropes with his stiletto. Two men carried McConneld. As they reached the stairwell, a freight elevator was coming down.

"Why walk, when we can ride?" Balkovsky said, positioning himself and his automatic rifle to fire when the elevator doors opened.

The rest, including the two carrying McConneld, spread to either side of the metal doors.

The doors opened quickly. In the split-second he had, Balkovsky saw two more guards and a man in a white lab coat with a physician's bag.

He did not hesitate. The impact slammed the three men back against the rear of the car. Balkovsky and the men with McConneld rushed on, shoving the bodies aside. His other men took the stairs.

"On the way!" Balkovsky said into the microphone of his headset. 7:58 P.M. On the ground floor, Balkovsky was the first outside. The delivery truck was due to pass that exit. Truck headlights appeared to their left. The truck slowed, blinking its lights. As it inched along, the men with McConneld shoved him into the rear and jumped in. Balkovsky was the last.

The rear doors slammed, and the locking bolt banged into place. The truck picked up speed, then stopped.

8 P.M. There was an explosion, then another and another, along with shouts, and bursts of automatic weapons fire. The truck sped off.

"Is he still breathing?" Balkovsky asked.

"Seems so," replied a man, attending McConneld. *"But he's drugged."* He put on a stethoscope, and listened to McConneld's

heartbeat. *"Regular, but very reduced. Without knowing what they gave him, anything else is too risky."*

"The stuff in here might give us a clue," Balkovsky said, handing him a physician's bag. *"It belonged to our friend on the elevator."*

* * *

McConneld opened his eyes. He instinctively squinted, before looking at the surroundings. It wasn't a dream! He was on a mattress, wearing pajamas.

The room door was unlocked. Looking out cautiously, he saw a man, seated across from him, reading a magazine. The man glanced over, calling to someone down the hall. McConneld scurried back to bed, pretending to be asleep. He heard the door open.

"Get up, you bum! Don't sleep the day away!" It was Balkovsky.

"Christ! You're the most beautiful sight I've seen in days. Where am I?!!"

"A sympathetic clinic, an hour from Frankfurt," Balkovsky replied. "We got you out last night, from a power plant south of here." He sat on the edge of the bed.

"I owe you one. My head feels like someone ran over it with a tank," McConneld said, slumping onto his pillow. "Rusty treads and all. How did you find me?"

"I'd rather not say," Balkovsky said. "My physician identified whatever they used on you and gave you a reagent. You've been asleep for eighteen hours."

"Shit! We've got to get to my office!" McConneld said. "When The Colonel took me, he knew everything. There's a leak somewhere. You, for instance, broke me out, to cover yourself."

"I think you're still stoned," Balkovsky replied.

"I'm blabbering," McConneld said. "Where're my clothes?"

"Trashed. Try the new ones in the closet. But you can't announce yourself."

"I'm not barging in," McConneld replied. "The spy thinks I'm dead. It's time for an Agatha Christie finale."

"Any suspects in mind, *M. Poirot?*"

"A few, but..."

"You'd rather not say at this time?" Balkovsky sighed.

* * *

"What the hell?...sir?" Chuck Channing said, as he answered his apartment door. McConneld and Balkovsky pushed past him.

"It's two A.M.! Uh, good to see you, sir. If I could see you." He was bare-chested, with pajama bottoms on.

"As far as anyone else's concerned, I'm not back," McConneld said, pointing a 9mm pistol at Channing.

"What the...?!" Channing said, raising his arms.

"Miles to go before we sleep," McConneld replied. "Don't take it personally, but as of now, everyone's under suspicion." He told Channing about his capture and interrogation.

"You don't suspect me, do you, Fearless Leader?" Channing asked.

"Your reaction won you points. But I'm not counting anyone safe. Call Harvey Barsohn. I want him at the office in three hours."

"Do you trust *him?*" Channing motioned to Balkovsky.

"In an odd sort of way, I do," McConneld said. "Start accusing people, Old Buddy, and you'll lose the points you've racked up so far."

"Any other invitees?" Channing asked. "What do I tell Colonel Barsohn?"

"Tell him whatever you want. Just get him there," McConneld answered. "That aide of Barsohn's. What's his name? Martin? And that pinhead, Kinnean. Did Deputy Director Simmons send a pouch for me?"

Channing replied, "It's locked in your safe. I went through it. It has copies of travelogues, date and appointment calendars. Other stuff."

"Was anybody with you when you went through it?"

"As a matter of fact, your secretary. She and I cross-referenced that major's files with the pouch."

"One for you, Chuckie Boy," McConneld said. "Before we came here we called and Langley told us about the pouch. We also rifled someone's apartment, and found this." McConneld took another pistol, a .45 automatic, from his jacket. "Got any blanks?"

"What do you want with that?" Channing asked.

"I'll explain on the way. Now make the calls."

"But don't you want to know what we found, when we compared that stuff?" Channing asked.

"I think I can guess, but tell us on the way," McConneld replied. "After you make the calls."

* * *

5 A.M. McConneld, Balkovsky, and Channing were in Channing's office. McConneld's secretary was also present. Colonel Barsohn and his aide were waiting downstairs. Jack Kinnean was on his way.

The secretary brought Barsohn and the aide in. McConneld took out his pistol as Channing frisked both men. They both were carrying 9mm pistols.

"Drop your drawers, Harvey. We have one more party guest to go."

Later Channing's desk phone buzzed. Kinnean was on the way up. McConneld was behind the door, pistol drawn, as Channing let Kinnean in.

"What.?!" Kinnean said. "I thought you were..."

"That I was what? Sit down! All of you." Channing, Barsohn, Martin, and Kinnean spread around the room, silent.

"You can't treat us like this!" Kinnean protested. "Put that gun down."

"As much as I hate to say this," Barsohn said, "Kinnean's right. Put the gun down, Buck."

"I can't do that," McConneld said, "till our little unmasking drama's run its course. Please take notes." He motioned to the secretary, who sat at Channing's desk with pad in hand.

"Where the hell've you been?" Kinnean asked. "I kept trying to see you, but your boy here never let me in the loop."

"You weren't supposed to be," McConneld rebuked Kinnean. "Where've I been, you ask? One of you knows, and he's a double agent. Harvey, Chuck, and Martin. You all knew I was undercover and my cover name."

"I didn't know," Kinnean interrupted. "Who's this 'Mr. Smith'?"

"May I introduce General Alexei Balkovsky of Russian Intelligence?" McConneld said, quickly.

"A Russian? You trust a Russian before you trust your own people?" Kinnean asked.

"That's right, Chump," McConneld replied. "You three couldn't know where I was, 'cause I lost the mike early. But you were in on my plan. I'll start with you, Harvey. Our dead major was your direct subordinate. And Service retirement's not as good as a Swiss bank account full of cash, is it?"

Barsohn protested, "He wasn't under my direct command over here. He reported to the IG's Office, European Command, or Investigations."

"That's cosmetic, and you know it, Harvey," McConneld said. "Martin could've been your third man. Records show trips the major took to Washington. You could've passed classified material to him, for your buyers. Or maybe he reported to you."

"That's a lie!" Barsohn yelled. "That bastard was the traitor, not me!!"

"Someone sold me out to The Colonel!" McConneld shouted back. "The major's dead. You're the smartest, enough to run a network from inside DIA. You could've gotten the transfer codes for the nukes, for your friend, The Colonel. Birds of a feather."

"This is bullshit! Only God knows why you're fucking with me!" Barsohn shouted. "I hadn't talked to that major, since he was shipped over here!"

"Suppose I told you," McConneld said, "I've got travelogues and calendars, proving you met with him all over the States and foreign stops?"

"Forgeries! Bullshit! Just one problem with your theory. The guy who sold you out will still be loose."

"I've found the guy," McConneld said, walking to the desk. He kept the pistol aimed at the four men.

"Security?" he called, loudly. Three uniformed marines came into the office, with their 9mm pistols drawn.

"Colonel Barsohn's under arrest for espionage. Sorry, Martin, guilt by association. I'll be down to start the paperwork."

Barsohn grumbled, "When the truth comes out, I'll make you eat shit for this!" He and Martin preceded the marine guards out.

"I'm glad *that's* over," McConneld said, putting his pistol on the desk. With his handkerchief, he wiped his face.

"You really believe Colonel Barsohn's the traitor?" Channing asked. "Does this mean you don't suspect me anymore?"

"And me?" Kinnean asked.

"You're safe, Chuckles," McConneld replied. "You're too colorful for a double. Gray little men, with no flair. Or... Fanatics, burying themselves like bureaucrats. Right, Kinnean?"

"What?" Kinnean replied, startled. "I'm no fanatic."

"Oh, but I think you are. Or rather, you were, when you came in with the first wave in 1981. How many more of you were there in that entourage?"

"What're you talking about? You got your man. You said so."

"Harvey? He's no more the double than my pet Doberman. You are."

"But I didn't know where you were! You admitted that."

"But you did," McConneld said. "Chuck Channing told Mr. Simmons, who told your boss. Your boss thought nothing of it, when you asked him. His good 'right-hand,' he called you. You slimy bastard. I'll enjoy watching you fry."

"But you've got proof on Barsohn."

"I said, 'Suppose.' But on you, I do. Your Washington offices kept wonderful records. Guess what we discovered. Chuck?"

"Same places, same dates as our major, back many years," Channing said.

"Coincidence. Nothing more. My jobs've always involved traveling all over the world. So I was in the same cities."

"There's an old saying in Vegas. Once is coincidence. Twice is happenstance," McConneld said. "Three times—enemy action."

"I'll beat it in a court of law."

"This ain't a court of law, boyo," McConneld said. "I wonder what the good old marine general'll say about this."

Suddenly, Kinnean pulled a .45-caliber automatic from an inside pocket. "I'll tell you how many of us there were, in the '80 Revolution.' That's what we called it. Loads. Too many for you to find or stop. We're buried so deep in the bureaucracy, and elsewhere, it'd take underground nuclear tests to bring us up. The old fool had no idea how helpful he was. He thought he was in a movie."

"Don't be a fool! You won't get a hundred yards," McConneld said, reaching for his gun.

"I'll take you with me and finish what The Colonel fucked up."

"Think you can get away from here, do you?" McConneld asked.

"I'm not even going to try," Kinnean answered. He laughed. "That marine idiot. So far up his ass, he needs a glass navel to see the sunrise. We're surrounded by enemies, welfare mothers, and bums wanting a handout. Our current boy-toy we've got now. Such a sympathetic regime in the good ol' W.H. A little terror goes a long way."

"Do you think we'll sit back and let that happen?" McConneld asked.

"You won't have a choice," Kinnean spat back. "Our public doesn't give two shits what happens. Take away their rights, and they won't know the difference, as long as you do it slowly. You play on their lovely fears of each other. Keep them divided and fed. Scare them with terrorists . . . and anthrax."

"Is your boss involved?" Channing asked.

"That moron? No, but I'll only say this. The Nazis *weren't* so bad. They got carried away, is all. AND good combustion won't be wasted this time, either. I'm only sorry I won't be here."

Kinnean rested the muzzle on his temple, and pulled the trigger. His head was thrown sideways by the force of the powder discharge. He collapsed, with the gun hitting the carpet beside him.

"Goddamn it, Chuck! I told you to put blanks in that thing!" McConneld said, hurrying to Kinnean's body.

"I did! Who expected the idiot would try to kill himself, instead of us?!"

"Call an ambulance!" McConneld said to the secretary. "You bastard! You aren't getting off so easily!" He held Kinnean's head, which was bleeding from a burned spot on the temple.

"I hope Harvey and Martin've got a sense of humor. Call Security, Chuck."

"He did more damage with the blank," Balkovsky observed. "The concussion of the powder explosion probably caused an implosion inside his brain."

"Another lead, shot to hell," McConneld said, shaking his head.

* * *

After his showdown with Kinnean, McConneld put in a call to CIA-Langley, to Deputy Director Simmons. "No question," McConneld replied in response to his superior's incredulity. "That stuff you got me clinched it. He's in a coma. Medics don't know if he'll survive. Before he pulled the trigger he was raving about 'good fire' not being 'wasted' or something."

"That'll get the National Security Adviser off our backs. Did your man implicate his boss?" Simmons asked.

McConneld summarized Kinnean's remarks. "It'll be fun telling him," Simmons said.

"Let me," McConneld said. "After the jerking-around he gave us, I've earned the shot at him."

"He's yours," Simmons replied.

* * *

"Your call to the National Security Adviser," McConneld's secretary told him over his desk intercom.

"Good and bad news, General," McConneld said. "Good stuff, first. We've leads on some of the stolen weapons. Also plugged a major intelligence leak at your end."

"Who was it? How high up?"

"You're sitting down, aren't you, General?" McConneld enjoyed being the "newsboy" for that headline. He wished he could have seen the Adviser's face. "I don't fucking believe it!"

the Adviser said. "Where's your proof?"

McConneld told him. The Adviser did not interrupt him.

"If that gets out, I'll be ruined," the Adviser said. "It'll be a black eye for the Administration."

"Not only the Administration. If it gets out, you won't play the violin for any self-respecting Georgetown matron again."

"What buys your silence?"

"You get off our backs and run interference for us. Do that and your violin career's safe. Don't and you might as well take that Stradivarius apart one splinter at a time. You'll spend your time collecting your Corps pension. If I were you, I'd check everyone who came into Federal service during the '80s, early '90s, and '00s. You've got lots of moles and sleepers to dis-inter. How about it?"

"I don't have much choice, do I?"

"Not unless you planned an Aspin-exit."

"You'd better . . . I mean, I hope you're successful. I'll help at this end."

"That's better, General. On that note, don't let me keep you from those background checks. And, if you need any more hand-holding, try your wife."

* * *

Channing came rushing into McConneld's office. It was later the same day as McConneld's conversation with the National Security Adviser.

"Another unscheduled message from Tom Pemberton!" Channing exclaimed. He handed McConneld a paper. "A public house, outside *Weimar*. He used the same men's room trick as before."

McConneld read the message. It was a copy of a much smaller original. Water stains ran the entire length of that side. Splotches on the right side were probably letters, rinsed out by the water.

The first line stated, "Berlin—trigger—15 N." The two or three letters after the "N" had disappeared in blue ink-blots.

The second and final line read, "2—Re——" After the "2" was a blue blur that looked like it could have been "4," "8," or "9."

There was a diluted blue streak following the "e." McConneld guessed six or more letters had been washed away.

"The original's on its way. Local control faxed us that, as soon as he got it. If you'll notice," Channing said. "It's in plain language, not code."

An hour later the original arrived. Cryptographic/analyses sections, even with computer enhancement, had been unable to identify the missing parts.

"Crypto says he must've used an old Flair," Channing said. "There wasn't enough impression in the paper to recover."

"At least we know Berlin's the starting point. We can go on the assumption he meant 15 November. Twelve days from now."

* * *

In a remote laboratory in deep, southern Bavaria, near the Swiss border, John Marshall and Dr. Pola were discussing detonator schematics. Jaime and Jamael were due, with The Colonel.

"But given the safety devices built in, that design might not generate critical mass and the necessary chain-reaction," Dr. Pola said, nervously. "My hypotheticals have indicated this block, here, dampens the buildup to critical mass. Even if we use our approximation-detonator package, the miniaturized computerization controls can't be overridden, without the codes."

"Trust me on this one, Doctor," Marshall replied. "If we use a computer feedback, we'll mirror-image the control circuits and fake them out. That'll jerry-rig the override problem. Uncle Sam always prepares against the most exotic threats and misses the simple ones. It'll have to be done manually, upon arming."

Pola lit a cigarette and puffed furiously, while studying technical materials.

Marshall whispered, "You have more important things to worry about. You don't really think they're going to let us live, after we finish this, do you? Don't be naïve."

He found her assistants. Three were working on computer simulations. Four others were working on an MADM with his own assistants. She instructed them to run the model Marshall suggested and others.

Jaime and Jamael arrived, blindfolded, accompanied by The Colonel's men. The Colonel was not with them.

"This is no way for Colonel Krattmay to treat us!" Jaime said, as they removed the blindfolds. "Doesn't he trust us?"

"The Colonel doesn't trust anyone," one man snapped. "He distrusts some people less than others."

Emilio joined them. The three left for a time. Marshall restarted his non-scientific conversation with Pola.

"They'll *need* us. Each requires individual fusing solutions," Pola replied. "And there's always the radiation hazard. They can't afford to arm too long before. I'm doing my job. You'd better do yours."

Dr. Pola's assistants returned. "*Frau Doktor,*" one said. "The model you gave us checks out. According to the computer, it will override the safety systems and allow critical mass and detonation."

Pola turned to Marshall. "Nice job," she said. "Too bad we can't test it first. All we need now are the plutonium triggers."

"They've already got them," Marshall whispered. "It makes you wonder if they need us any more, doesn't it, Doctor?"

* * *

"Are you out of your fucking mind?" Emilio asked Jaime.

They were in a restroom down the hall from Pola's lab. "They won't notice one of their bombs is missing?"

"Things'll be in such an uproar," Jaime said. "Or we'll relieve a team of its package. Either way, we get what we want."

"What about Marshall? And Dr. Pola?" Emilio asked.

"Fuck Marshall," Jamael said. "He's working for them."

"We'll take the doctor with us," Jaime said.

"It'll be tough," Emilio said. "Dr. Pola wants me nearby all the time."

"Who's in charge of who?" Jamael asked. "Tell her to chill."

Jaime agreed. "If you can't, keep up her cigarette supply. But watch for my signal and be ready to run."

* * *

In the conference room, at his estate near *Ulm,* Baron von Markenheim, Colonel Krattmay, and The Cartel's board of directors discussed the raid on the power plant.

"*I assure you all,*" Colonel Krattmay said in German. "*He wasn't inside long enough to learn anything. He only saw a few storage installations, never the nukes. Whoever his rescuers were, they were well-armed. Our people're out of there. If the Federal Police follow-up, they'll find nothing.*"

"*How can you be sure?*" asked a member to von Markenheim's right. "*You didn't know of the spy, till our Washington source reported it. And I might add, that source's dropped from sight. Do we have any word on him?*"

"*He was last seen in Europe,*" The Baron said. "*No further information.*"

"*The Americans are no closer than when we stole the weapons,*" Krattmay said. "*Everything's going according to plan. It was a minor scare to keep us on our toes.*"

"*A spy in the organization is not a 'minor scare,' Herr Oberst,*" another man said to Krattmay.

"*This bickering's getting us no place,*" The Baron interrupted. "*We discussed the matter. Are we all agreed? Any of the Board believe we ought to postpone?*" No hands went up. "*Colonel K. suggested we go ahead of schedule.*"

"*But my section won't be ready,*" Professor Pemberton said.

"*Thomas,*" von Markenheim replied. "*You assured me. Your last reports were sound and needed only updating.*"

Pemberton answered,"*But some unforeseen events in the financial markets recently have made it imperative to revise. Not to mention political events in Central America, here, and the Middle East.*"

"*How long?*" von Markenheim asked.

"*We had no problem with the original date,*" Pemberton replied. "*It'd be tight, but we could be finished.*"

Von Markenheim said, "*You'll be ready by the new date.*"

"*Otto,*" Pemberton said. "*All our economic and financial follow-up depends on this. Otherwise, we won't control or countervail events, especially U.S. actions.*"

"*A chance like this comes only once in a generation,*" von

Markenheim said. *"I'll not lose it, because some junior analyst couldn't get his report in on time. No more defeatist talk or delay, Thomas. 'Otherwise' does not exist. I also need to talk with you, alone, after this."*

"So," von Markenheim continued. *"In the vein of new business... We must consider the new date. Colonel K...."*

At the head of the table, Colonel Krattmay used a diagram. *"I propose the 8th of November,"* he said.

"But Herr Oberst," one man to von Markenheim's left interrupted. *"That is only five days. Perhaps Herr Professor Doktor Pemberton is right."*

"No question we're ready," Krattmay replied. *"I anticipated a problem, after the spy, and planned accordingly. The larger devices are now operational. Thanks to General Tripleleaf, the key MADM's emplaced. It needs only activation and its timer.*

"Our first and second waves are ready and in place. The rest can be within 2 to 4 days. They're waiting for the signal. We'll only need to place the detonators and timers a day or two ahead. We'll be safely and far enough away."

"If Colonel K. says we're ready," another man further down the table said, *"that's enough for me."*

"There could be a bonus in it for us," Krattmay said, with a half-smile. *"We might knock off our principal Russian obstacle."*

"Who?" went up from the table, like a chorus.

"The President," Krattmay replied. *"He might be on a surprise visit to Berlin!"*

There was murmuring around the long table. One by one, heads nodded in agreement. Even Professor Pemberton offered no further resistance.

"It's settled," von Markenheim said. *"Colonel K's recommendation is adopted. Case Blue commences on 8 November."*

The meeting continued with area reports and more routine matters. Finally, it went into Committee-of-the-Whole and working groups.

"I shall return shortly," von Markenheim said. *"Thomas?"* He called Professor Pemberton. They left the conference room by the high, oak doors, with Colonel Krattmay. The Baron led the way to his study.

"Wait outside, Herr Oberst," von Markenheim said. *"I'll call you, if and when I need you."* Once inside, he fixed both of them a brandy.

"To Case Blue," von Markenheim toasted. Both men sipped. "Several days ago we discovered a leak in the organization," von Markenheim said.

"That's shocking!" Pemberton said.

"It was shocking," von Markenheim said, sternly. *"Especially who. I'm speaking as a friend of your father's. One also bearing the responsibility of wealth."*

"Me?" Pemberton exclaimed. "I don't know what you're talking about, Baron! I haven't been away from you and the Board."

"Don't embarrass us both by lying, Thomas. We have proof."

"Something conveniently manufactured by Colonel Krattmay?"

"No. By you," von Markenheim said.

"Impossible, my dear Baron," Pemberton said.

"Our agents in Vienna picked up a cache of information, from an antique store in the Kärntner Strasse. Does that sound familiar?"

"Should it?"

"It could only have come from you. Also, your daughter, Samantha, was picking it up, before our people got it away from her. Our people have her, in protective custody."

"Protected from what?"

"From anything unfortunate. But I wanted to ask...?"

"I've often tried to imagine what this scene would be like, Baron. But I never thought you'd ask me why."

"This is a friend of your family talking, Thomas," von Markenheim said. *"With the duty of great wealth..."*

"Your habit over the years of supporting extreme right-wing regimes, neo-Nazis, Nazi war criminals, Baron..."

"Is that the world you want, Thomas. One without order? The world of hungry little nations, eating each other up? We offer the world order and stability."

"Thanks, if that's stability, I'll take chaos, Baron."

"I'm persuaded you were stalling, Thomas. Your work really is complete. But please consider your daughter's well-being. And act prudently."

"How'd you define that?"

"We want to know about your activities, the locations of any caches of information. For whom or what purpose you're storing it..."

"There are no other caches," Pemberton replied. "I stored that one as insurance."

"Against what?"

"The day you had no further use for me and decided to terminate me. Or my family. Or both."

"You and I were both insured, then, Thomas," von Markenheim replied, after downing his brandy. "*Unfortunately, your policy's been canceled. We want the information. If you tell us, I give you my word on two things. Your daughter will be unharmed...*"

"And the second?"

"Yours will be a merciful death."

"And if I refuse?"

"I can't guarantee Samantha's safety."

"You'll kill both of us anyway. No deal, Baron. Call your bully boy and let's get this over with. With or without mercy."

XXI

Liz McGonnville listened, as her colleague briefed the six-person team, in a pension three blocks from the *Studentenheim*. The pension was a "drop" for the local network, whose Control had assembled the team. It was nearly a day since the kidnapping, but Sam was still being held there.

Liz's colleague, doing the briefing, would lead the mission. He had more experience in anti-terror operations. Liz would participate and observe, though she had wanted to lead the raid herself.

The briefing continued. "You two hit the windows simultaneously. When we hear the glass, we're in the doors. She's in the interior bedroom, probably drugged."

Liz spoke to a ninth man. "Doc, I need her lucid."

On the way, Liz radioed the surveillance unit. The report was: no guards in the hall, two to four men inside with the subject. Once Liz and the team were in place, the surveillance agents would act as cover against any new arrivals.

On site at the *Studentenheim,* the team, including Liz and the doctor, went in by the delivery door. The roof men reported in-position and were ready to rappel into the windows. Liz followed, as the advance men and the leader snaked their ways up the staircases. The sixth floor hall was vacant.

As the men positioned themselves, Liz's headset crackled a warning. Earlier visitors just entered the lobby and were on the way up.

Coolly and calmly, Liz ordered the surveillance team to delay or "dispose" of the new arrivals.

* * *

Sam opened her eyes. The room was still. It had stopped spinning. She tried to sit up, but barely raised her head. Voices were getting closer: more German. She closed her eyes.

"*It's time to shoot her up again,*" one man's voice said, as the door opened. The darkness of her eyelids brightened.

"How much longer d'we keep her?" another voice retorted. "Why not kill her and be done with it?"

KILL! The word, like a cold, invisible hand, grabbed Sam's heart. Adrenal fear was clearing her head.

As she felt the shock of an alcohol wipe, she heard glass smashing. Two black-clad intruders wrestled with two other men. The intruders knocked the others unconscious. From the next room, Sam heard more commotion. There were sound-suppressed gunshots.

"Can you walk, Miss?" one intruder asked, as he untied her.

"Barely," Sam heard herself say in a gruff whisper. "Help!"

Two more black suits came in. One was carrying a heavy climbing rope, coiled over a shoulder. He tied one end to the bed frame and dropped the rest through the broken window. "We've got company."

One man gently tied Sam's hands together with a handkerchief and draped her over the back of another. He carried her to the window ledge, and backed himself and her down the rope.

The autumnal air spurred more adrenal fear. The jerky descent on the rope was better than "speed." A sudden bump and stop. He ducked under her hands and untied them. Other hands hurried her away. Sam felt the weakness of medication before anesthesia: wanting to speak, unable to. She blacked out.

* * *

"Sam? Wake up!" Sam thought she heard Liz's voice through the haze. She felt jostling and vibration. She rolled her head from side to side.

"Sam, it's Liz. How d'you feel?"

Sam's brain was spinning inside her skull, then changing directions. "Where?" *Was that rasp really me?*

"Doc, can't you give her something?"

"Not without knowing what they've given her."

"You're safe," Liz said. "They had you in the *Studentenheim,* across from our hotel."

"Going home?" Sam rasped.

"Somewhere safe," Liz said. "Easy. Not too fast." Sam sat up slowly.

"Got an aspirin?" she asked. "My head's doing backward somersaults. Ooh! Try that with a hangover." She held her forehead.

"How about it, Doc?" Liz asked.

Sam felt something bitter on her lips. She opened her eyes, to see Liz forcing the bitter taste into her mouth. Liz was wearing something black. She explained the events of the previous twenty-four hours.

"Regina fingered you," Liz said. "She wouldn't admit it, but she did."

"You've talked to her?!" Sam was excited. "Take me to her!" She leaned into a squatting position, slowly, painfully.

"Relax. We'll see her, as soon as I'm sure you're all right."

"I'm all right. We've got to see her! Now! OOOHHHH, my head!"

"OK, OK," Liz said, rubbing Sam's shoulders and back. "Take it easy! Herb! Tell your man to drive us to the Hilton."

* * *

As they walked through the Hilton lobby, Sam leaned against Liz, who had changed to street clothes in the truck. She guided Sam to the elevators. Sam had short dozes on the way. Through sleepy squints, Sam saw Liz speaking with three men.

"The subject's asleep," one man said to Liz. "Use this. It'll wake her up."

Liz led Sam down the hall and unlocked a door. A bedside lamp was on, as they came in.

Sam saw a dark shape, lying across the king-sized bed. She slumped into a chair. "Give me a minute, before you wake her."

Liz rubbed Sam's shoulders and neck, with a quick, hard massage. The aspirin dulled her headache the smallest bit. She could have used ten pills instead of two.

Liz broke smelling salts under Regina's nose. Regina stirred slowly. Her blonde hair draped her head and face, like a ragmop. Regina opened her eyes and cursed indecipherably through her gag.

"Calm down, Regina," Liz said, half-soothingly, "I'll take the gag out, if you don't try anything stupid. The room's soundproof. Screaming won't help you."

Liz pulled the handkerchief down. Regina tried to spit out the wadding. She moaned, with a wet wad hanging from her mouth, then screamed. She squirmed on the bed. "Let me go, you bastards!!"

Liz took out her Baretta and let Regina see it. "I'm not afraid to use this, Reggie Baby," Liz said. "Ask Sam."

"She's dangerous," Sam blurted. "She'll do you."

Regina became pale. "Please, let me go?!" she whimpered, loudly.

"That's better," Liz said, looking at Sam. "She's all yours."

Sam's mental brass-and-drum-section had settled into dull ache. Her anger kept her attention away from the headache. "Where's my father?"

"I don't even know him," Regina answered.

"Why don't I believe you?" Liz interjected.

"Where's The Baron?" Sam pursued.

"I shan't tell you," Regina replied, "even if I knew. Which I don't."

"When'd you see him last?"

"You tell me," Regina said.

"A few days ago," Liz said. "You flew to see him."

"So, you know," Regina said. "He's not there. I don't know where."

"Think long and hard," Liz said, "before you answer my next question. Where will he be later this month? Or next week?"

"I shan't tell you."

"But you do know, don't you, Regina?" Liz rejoined, quickly.

Regina turned her face, burrowing it into the bedspread.

"Regina," Sam said. "Did you try to kill me in Oxford? Was that you?" Regina shook her head.

"You're a lying sack of shit," Liz said, "and in this up to your pretty little bleached roots. We'll turn you over to the English cops: attempted murder, conspiracy to commit, lots more. Better hope Sam's friend doesn't die. That's capital murder. You're looking at grey-stone days till your roots match the walls, with deep, ugly wrinkles overrunning your face. Your partner's already spilled on you by now."

"I had nothing to do with any of that!" Regina screamed.

"Tell it to your lawyer. You'll have the best, I'm sure . . . or will you?" Liz dropped her voice.

"I'm innocent! He asked me to watch Samantha and follow her. Nothing else."

"Who 'he'?" Sam asked. "The Baron?" Regina nodded.

"Even over here? Didn't you think that strange?"

"No," Regina replied. "I worked on industrial espionage cases for him before."

Sam asked, "'Industrial espionage?' That's what he told you?"

"You've had at least two partners," Liz asked. "If you're only supposed to watch, what do you need them for?"

"I reported to them. I pointed Samantha out."

"In other words, you fingered her?" Liz said, quickly. "That's called conspiracy and aiding-and-abetting. That gets you a slightly diminished sentence, but still a sentence."

"What do you want from me?!"

"Answer Sam's questions," Liz said. "And maybe we forget all about turning you in. Keep this up, and you're on your way to old and shriveled."

"I can't!" Regina pleaded. "It'd be the end of me. He'd cut me off."

"And *I'll* kill you, if you don't," Liz countered. "What you mean is, it'd be the end of your cushy, jet-set life? You have to ask yourself: Do I want to go now, or later? Or slowly, in the gray-rock motel?"

"I'm innocent! I didn't do anything wrong!"

Liz said, "The joint's full of innocent people. And The Baron'll know where to find you. People die in prison every day."

"Give her a chance, Liz," Sam said. "Regina's a smart girl. She knows how to land on her feet."

"I can't tell you. I don't remember!"

"She's had her shot," Liz said. "We'll plough your brain with drugs, like your playmates did to Sam. *Then* we'll throw you to the cops."

"Give me a chance! I don't know! I can't remember!"

"You've had too many already!"

"Where's The Baron?" Sam repeated.

"I don't know for certain," Regina said, whining.

"Then, tell us what you do know, for certain," Sam said.

"No, I can't!" Regina bawled. "Really, I can't! It'd be the end of me!" Regina's makeup was running down her cheeks.

"Sorry, Regina. You're not trying hard enough. OK, Enforcer, do it!"

Liz started screwing a sound-suppressor onto her pistol.

"No! Wait!" Regina pleaded. "My step-father's due in Berlin later this month."

"When?!" Liz demanded.

"Around the 15th," Regina panted the words. "He was supposed to be there the whole month, but he changed his plans! I don't know why! Really! It's the usual meeting. Samantha knows what I mean."

"See? It wasn't so hard, Reggie," Liz said. "Lie back and relax. Uh, well. Relax."

"Where he goes, so goes my father. I can collect the cache, while we're there."

"What about me?" Regina asked, meekly.

"I'm working on it," Liz answered. "How about shaving your head bald for collaborating with the enemy? Actually, you'd look good as a baldy."

Regina shrieked, "NO!" Then, she cried.

"She's got to come with us," Sam blurted.

"Are you crazy?" Liz asked. "She's *our* animal, I grant you. But she could still do something stupid."

"We own her now," Sam said. "If she screws up and we turn her over to his people, The Baron will probably order her killed."

"I'll have to bring somebody along, as a babysitter," Liz said. "She can't be left alone. I might have to explain upstairs, which means I have to disclose you, Sam. Either way."

"But she'll know where her step-father is. We shan't, without her."

Liz agreed. "But if she's any problem, I'll pop her and walk. S-H-O-O-T. Understand?"

Regina nodded, nervously. "But you've got to protect me. I'm not telling you more, without assurances."

"My guy will be your bodyguard, but your hair's still got to go."

"Would you stop that, Liz?" Sam scolded.

"Why?" Liz asked. "I think she'd look great bald."

"I want to be sent home to the States," Regina said, ignoring further threats to her mane. "I wanted away from this mess. He wouldn't let me."

"You're not in a good bargaining position," Liz said. "You'll do what you're told. Or else."

"After you've got what you want, then what?" Regina asked.

Liz shrugged. "I figured you had trusts somewhere."

"My mother and I'll have to disappear," Regina said.

"I don't have to deal with this," Liz said. "We don't need her that badly."

"Perhaps I could help," Sam said. "We all might have to disappear. Remember, Regina. You're with us now."

Again, Regina nodded. She was pale, vulnerable. This was the first time Sam had seen her this way. Even the lasagna's candor had not lasted so long.

"I'm going tomorrow," Sam said to Liz, "with or without you. I need Regina, but, if you don't let her go, there's not much I can do."

"This'll probably cost me my career," Liz replied. "But we're sisters. I'll see to arrangements."

"For four?" Sam asked. Liz nodded.

They stayed in Regina's room that night. Liz and Sam shared one bed while Regina remained attached to the other, though a little less uncomfortably. Agents from the surveillance detail took shifts, watching Regina.

Liz arranged train reservations to Berlin for the next morning, 9:40 A.M. She chose a member of the surveillance team as Regina's security man.

Sam slept the uncomfortable sleep of nightmares. She was back in the room. She was back in the cave. Darkness. Death. Stench... Nazis. The Nazi officer. The face in the room. Close. Too close. She sat up in bed suddenly. The night lamp was on. Liz was lying beside her. Regina was snoring.

"Are you all right, Miss?" Regina's security man asked. Sam sighed, lying back down.

Around 8 A.M., Sam and Liz left the hotel, with Regina and her new bodyguard. Liz ordered their luggage from the *Hotel Akademie* brought to the train station. They had adjacent sleep-compartments with Regina and the guard. Regina looked bored, occasionally uncomfortable, but no longer dangerous.

Once in Germany, Federal police searched each compartment and everyone's luggage. Liz and the security agent identified themselves as U.S. Army CID, plainclothes, escorting witnesses to Berlin, and disclosed their pistols.

The Germans were satisfied with their credentials, less pleased with their weapons. Liz produced authorizations for the arms, and the police hemmed-and-hawed, but left them with their 9mms. There had been sabotage of rail lines in the vicinity. The German authorities had increased security.

"We'd better get off at the next station," Liz said to Sam, after the police were gone. "If Regina's playmates caught up with us, or any of those *Bundes*-boys were on their payroll."

The next stop was *Passau*. They detrained, and Sam was relieved to see the Federal police remain onboard.

She booked First-Class seats to *Stuttgart*, by way of *Munich, Augsburg,* and *Ulm*. They had to wait in the *Passau* station an hour for their new train. Liz telephoned agents in those three cities.

"My step-father's got a place outside *Ulm*," Regina said. "But I'm certain he's not there any longer."

"I'd love to check that place out," Sam said.

"Are you out of your frigging mind?" Liz interrupted her. "There's a time to confront and a time to avoid."

"I didn't say now," Sam protested. "Maybe Regina can take us on an unannounced tour, after Berlin."

"Not likely," Regina huffed.

* * *

Back in his *Ulm* estate's library-study, Baron von Markenheim was working on urgent details, personal and otherwise. He returned soon after the board meeting and Professor Pemberton's apprehension. There was a knock on the door.

"Colonel Krattmay," the chief butler said to him. The Colonel entered.

"Bad news," The Colonel said. "Someone's taken Fräulein Pemberton."

"*Gottverdammtes!!*" von Markenheim shouted. "*Are we a sieve?!*"

"We may have a lead to her whereabouts, but it's thin."

"At least her father won't know," von Markenheim huffed. "You still have him at the airfield, nicht? Any success?"

"Not so far, but I'm waiting to get him to my own place," Krattmay said. "How much longer before you can leave?"

"Soon," von Markenheim replied. "The General's due. I'm glad when this shuttling will be over!"

* * *

On the train to *Stuttgart,* Sam and Liz alternated naps. Liz relieved Regina's guard, before her own snooze. Near *Augsburg,* the train slowed, then stopped on a siding for over an hour. There were distant emergency sirens.

European sirens. Sam shivered whenever she heard them, though she recognized the irrationality of her reaction: World War II movies and the *Gestapo*. She was sorry the siren sounds survived the first *denazification* of Europe.

A conductor came to the compartment, apologizing for the delay. There had been a bomb-induced derailment up ahead. Alternate travel would be provided to the nearest station.

But a while later the train started again. It did not stop, until *Ulm*. There would be a delay, before it would continue to *Stuttgart.*

Against Liz's advice, Sam took a walk. After repeated assurances from the chief conductor that the train would not depart for at least two hours, Sam left the immediate vicinity of the platform.

As she was leaving the station, she felt a tap on the shoulder.

"I couldn't let you go off alone," Liz said to her. "I left my man with orders to go on to Berlin, if we missed."

They found coffee across the street in a café. While they were waiting to cross back to the station, Sam saw a man escorted to a nearby limousine.

His was another face of recent acquaintance. It was the face of the Nazi soldier with the Mississippi accent, but older. She went pale and nervous.

"What's the matter?" Liz asked. Then, Liz caught Sam's stare. "Well, I'll be damned! What the hell's he doing here?!"

"You know him?!" Sam asked.

Liz replied, "That's Lieutenant General Tripleleaf. He was with Air Force Intelligence and DIA long before me. But you can't work in Intelligence without hearing about him."

Sam pulled Liz back from the curb. "Tell me more. I saw him, in pictures my father had."

"He was big-time Air Force, probably on his way to Chief of Staff, or JCS Chairman. Then Reagan signed the INF Treaty. He resigned in protest and publicly called Reagan a Comm-symp—'Communist Sympathizer.' I heard he was operating as an arms dealer and international businessman, but I thought he was mostly in the Third World. Not Europe."

"Let's find out where he's going," Sam said, excitedly.

"Are you crazy?" Liz said. "Didn't you want to get to Berlin?"

"You heard Regina. The Baron's not due for a few days. Let's grab a cab and follow him," Sam said.

"This guy's got nothing to do with your father," Liz said. "You don't value your freedom much, do you?"

"Don't go philosophical on me, Lizzie," Sam replied. "Are you with me?"

Liz pointed to an older, dark-blue Mercedes, further down their side of the street. The driver pulled around parked cars and stopped beside them.

"This is my contact here," Liz said. "Remember my calls?"

Liz asked the driver for a cigarette. He produced a fresh pack of Dunhills and let her keep it. "*Suppose it'll sleet tomorrow?*" she asked him, in German.

"*It only sleets here, when Hell freezes over,*" he answered. She explained the assignment, through puffs of smoke.

The limousine drove off. Its route led away from the city, to smaller, country roads. Traffic was slim, but enough to keep a buffer of cars between the limousine and them.

"*Where are we?*" Liz asked.

"*An area of farms and estates,*" the contact said.

Up ahead the forestation thinned. There were patchwork fields, bordered by groves. The limousine turned right.

Liz's contact sped up. They passed an estate's entry gates, with high, iron fencing, stone columns, and guards. Liz caught a flash of the limo up the estate's driveway. On a stone column, there was a brass plaque, engraved, "*Karin H. II.*"

"*Do you know whose that is?*" Liz asked.

"*By a quirk I do,*" the contact replied, and identified the owner.

"She said he had a place near *Ulm,*" Sam said.

"*Double back,*" Liz said. "*I want to watch that gate for a while.*"

"Now who's not in a hurry?" Sam asked Liz, in English.

"This connection's too important," Liz said. "*Could we get in there to take a look?*" Liz asked the contact.

The contact replied, "*I'll reconnoitre and see.*"

He did a U-turn into a traveler's clearing, shaded and off the road, several hundred yards from the entrance. Carrying electronic binoculars, he left them.

"*They've got patrols along the perimeter,*" he said, after returning. "*And electronic surveillance. We're not getting in without a reconnaissance-in-force.*"

"No time now," Liz replied. "Later. After Berlin." As Liz was speaking, she saw a car leaving from the gateway.

"*There's the limousine,*" the contact said, from behind the binoculars. They followed.

"Maybe this was a wild goose chase," Sam said to Liz. "He wasn't in there very long. We don't even know, if The Baron's with him."

"I'll bet next month's pay he is," Liz said. "We're going to find out, one way or another."

"We've missed our train by now," Sam said.

"I'll get us to Berlin," Liz answered.

They pursued the limousine back to the *Autobahn*. It took the entry ramp, marked *Augsburg*. The limo exited toward *Gunzburg*. At *Gunzburg*, the car turned north again.

Sam saw and heard planes close by. The limousine took an access road, marked with an airfield sign, and passed through a checkpoint. The airfield was a public, municipal facility, a former military field, the contact told Liz. When they reached the checkpoint, the contact asked a guard to direct them to a charter service.

On the way Sam saw the limo parked in front of a building, with a large sign on its roof, "O. v. M., AG." There were private guards nearby, automatic weapons over their shoulders.

There were different-sized aircraft, bearing the same name as the building. A twin-engine turbo-prop, with no company markings, was warming up. With the contact's binoculars, Sam watched the entrance to the building. The contact went inside the hangar.

Liz wanted a closer look. She left Sam in the car. As she neared the O. v. M., AG terminal, a guard came over.

"*What are you doing here?*" he shouted in German. The limo driver was coming, with another guard.

"*I'm looking for an air charter service,*" she answered. "*The gate guard told me to come here.*"

"*He's mistaken,*" the first guard said. "*Try over there.*" He motioned to the hangar Liz had passed.

The limo driver asked what the matter was. The guard explained, using more respectful tones than he had with Liz.

"*But I don't understand,*" Liz said. "*If it's wrong . . .*"

"*We can call the gate,*" the limo driver said, patiently. "*Perhaps you merely misunderstood.*" He offered to escort Liz to a phone in the lobby.

"*You're right,*" Liz said, quickly. "*I'll try over at that other hangar.*" She walked away.

Liz glanced over her shoulder. The two guards were following her, but not seemingly trying to catch her. The plane's engines were revving now. Its front door was open, its ladder extended.

The contact turned the car around and pushed the rear driver's side door open. Liz dove in. *"Make a pass of that terminal,"* Liz said to the contact.

He zoomed the car within feet of the limousine. The limo driver jumped onto the hood of his car.

The contact sped the Mercedes behind the terminal and came back around. Sam saw six or seven men walking toward the plane. They stopped, apparently startled.

Sam recognized The Baron, General Tripleleaf, and The Face. There were guards with assault rifles at the ready. The remaining man she also recognized. Her chest felt icy and tight. The man's arms were bound behind his back. He was being led by the guards. "Stop! Stop the car!" she screamed.

"We can't!" Liz shouted. "They're already shooting!"

Sam heard thuds against the car, as they swerved.

"Get your heads down!" the contact shouted, as he floored it. The checkpoint gate was open. They sped through it.

Sam screamed, "I could've saved him! Can't we go back?!!"

Liz replied, "You're talking crazy, Sam!" Liz said, hugging her.

Sam was crying. "I'm sorry, Pa! I'm sorry! I'm sorry!"

"We'll save him," Liz said to Sam.

The contact pulled the car into the woods and stopped. He rolled his window down. *"Do you hear that?"* he said, finally.

A helicopter was coming closer. The contact opened the trunk and handed Liz a G-3 assault weapon and took one for himself. *"Are you checked out on one of these?"* he asked. Liz nodded.

"You have a pistol?" Liz asked. *"She's an expert with an automatic."*

"A crying civilian?" he looked skeptical. *"What the shit!"* he said. *"We can use every hand. Does she speak German?"*

"Fluently," Sam replied, in kind.

"Then, here," he said, handing her a 9mm Baretta.

"What're these?" Sam asked, picking up a clip of ammunition she did not recognize.

"Rubber bullets," the contact replied, *"for incapacitation. Take a few of these,"* he said, handing her standard clips.

Sam put the clips in her coat pocket and nonchalantly picked up two clips of the rubber bullets, pocketing them as well. "What's the plan?" she asked, loading the pistol.

"Wait here. Give the heli time to miss us. Then on."

The sound of the helicopter was louder. The contact pulled a dark-green-and-brown tarp from the trunk and covered the car. Sam crouched beside it. Despite her coat, she was shivering. Failed. Guilty. But she did not let herself cry any more. No dignity in that.

She would have another chance to accomplish her missions. She took a very deep breath, sucking the tears back from the edge.

Liz came back. "We saw a few cars," she told Sam, "probably hostile. The helicopter circled across the road."

"Where's your guy?" Sam asked.

"Keeping an eye out. He's steady and good."

"Nice try." Sam smiled sadly.

Liz said, undeterred, "They're likely on their way to Berlin."

"I screwed up!" Sam said, fighting back the tears again. "He needed me. I failed him."

"The only thing you failed to do," Liz scolded, "was get killed. I'll not listen to any self-pitying bullshit, Sam! We'll get him out of this. You just wait."

The contact rejoined them. "*I didn't see anyone else,*" he said. "*I knew we shouldn't have made that last pass.*"

"*It's too late to say what we shouldn't have done,*" Sam said. "*Let's get to Berlin.*"

"*They'll be watching the Ulm station,*" Liz said. "*We'll have to make other arrangements again.*"

"*I'll drive you,*" the contact said. "*I've got a cover business in Berlin. We'll change cars.*"

"An extra day or two won't hurt anything," Liz said. "At least we know Regina was on the level. Really, Sam. Everything's going to be all right."

"I wish I could believe that," Sam said, sighing.

They uncovered the car. The contact repacked the weapons in the trunk. They were leaving, when they heard the distant barking of dogs.

Sam watched behind them. She saw no cars, no dogs, no one.

From there, they headed northeast to *Nordlingen*. In a small residential garage, attached to a "drop-house," in that city, they left the Mercedes, for a late-model VW.

They were off again, this time for Berlin, by way of *Stuttgart, Schweinfurt, Weimar,* and *Potsdam. No express, only a milk run,* Sam thought. She wanted one, after the airfield.

* * *

In his office in the new administration building of the *Bundeswehr's* II Corps Headquarters, northeast of *Augsburg,* the Corps commander's aide was reviewing a final report for his boss. The report covered the status of the II Corps HQ's relocation to its new *Augsburg* facilities. The aide was happy at the removal from the *Ulm* area. The *Ulm* base was old, despite additional construction over the years. As a young officer years before, he had his first staff assignment there. But he held no fond memories of *Ulm-lager.*

The mobile corps headquarters had also begun operating in this locality, weeks before. How the whole change had not collided with the recent American Operation Move-up, he did not know. The general was on leave and not due back till 18 November. That was over two weeks away.

But the aide knew his superior. He would be back ahead of time. Nothing was scheduled, until after Christmas. There had been some dispatches about possible house-to-house searches from the Defence and Interior Ministries. They had not been marked "Urgent," and he received no response on his request for confirmation. He took the initiative to copy them to the Defense Zone Command in Munich. *Damn nuisance,* he thought. *No reason the Home Defense Command people couldn't handle those. That was what they were paid for.*

XXII

At a small inn near The Colonel's "safe-houses" in Switzerland, Jaime, Jamael, and Emilio were planning their own theft of an SADM. This safe-house was across the lake from the laboratory, where Pola and Marshall were working on the MADMs.

"So, we don't know *when* the bombs're being distributed?" Emilio asked.

"I've discovered where one team'll be holed up, after they get theirs. It's a village, south of *Stuttgart. Neuffen.* The stayover's a farmhouse, outside it."

"Did you get directions, too?" Emilio asked.

"So much to do, so little faith," Jaime replied. "Their computer system gave me that tidbit. Their system's encrypted against outsiders. All I needed were the passwords."

"It sounds too easy," Jamael said. "They're setting us up."

"Just 'cause you're paranoid, doesn't mean *they're* not out to get you. Your instincts are sharp, though," Jaime replied. "But it's also our best shot."

"If I didn't know your luck," Emilio said, "I'd say you're a suicidal maniac. But you got more fucking lives than a cat on speed."

Jamael said, "When we don't report, they'll put out the word."

"I'm tired of your goddamn whining!" Jaime said. "Are you in or out?"

"If it's a trap, I'll never let you forget it, especially after they kill us."

Jaime outlined the operation from a computer-generated map, with hand-drawn notations. "I've already got ship transport arranged. After we get the bomb, we sit tight till the Cartel deal's over," Jaime said.

"What about the Doctor and Marshall?" Emilio asked.

"I told you before," Jamael said. "Fuck Marshall and her."

"I agree with Mr. Fatal here," Jaime said, "but only halfway.

We can't write off Dr. Pola. Make a break with her, by 11 P.M. on the 4th."

"How many are in the team we're burgling?" Emilio asked.

"Three tickets to cancel. Tops," Jaime said. "You get to the lab and stick with Pola." He suddenly felt in his pockets. "Shit! I lost it! Code stuff, to get us in with the bomb group. Hey, *amigo*," he said to Jamael. "Look in the car around the driver's seat? Look for a piece of paper in Spanish." Jaime cracked the door and watched the Iranian go down the hall stairs.

"That wasn't the only bomb team I placed," Jaime said. *"I located others. We try for them ourselves. As far as J. goes, this is the only one."*

"One thing," Emilio asked, as they were leaving. "What do I do, if I can't get Dr. Pola out?"

"Use your best judgment," Jaime replied. *"Terminate, if you have to."*

At the car they found Jamael being held by four other men.

"What the hell're you assholes doing?" one man asked, in English, with a heavy eastern-German accent. He oversaw security for trips to the lab, and was an important subordinate of The Colonel.

"The house's driving us NUTS, *amigo*!" Jaime said. "We needed *choocha*. Know what I mean? We didn't want an audience, when we were unwinding!"

"Get back to the house!" the East German growled. "Keep it iced for another week, or I'll shoot it off next time! We make sure you get back." He assigned a man to ride with them, while he and his other men followed.

"We'll have to pull this on our own," Jaime whispered to Emilio in Spanish.

When they reached the house, Jaime and Jamael stayed there. Emilio was brought to the lab.

Over the next day, they saw Emilio or Dr. Pola at the house. On "chaperoned" visits to the lab, they saw only the physicist. They did not see John Marshall.

On one visit, the East German security man stopped them. "We have a briefing at the house tonight," he said. "6 P.M. Don't be late! If I come looking . . . !"

Back at the safe-house, Jaime reviewed the plan. He also thought about the Russian in New York. He missed her, her touch, her feel, her immense power to hold him relentlessly. No woman had captivated him so, even across thousands of miles. After this was finished, he would find and love her again.

* * *

The dark grey concrete walls stank of mildew. This small warehouse basement room, in the French hills southeast of Saarbrücken, was crowded and smoky, as the meeting began.

"The Colonel regrets he couldn't be with us tonight," the briefing officer said. Behind him, John Marshall waited his turn.

"I'll give each team its instructions," the briefer continued. "Information is on a need-only basis. You won't discuss this with anyone else but me and the other members of your team. No exceptions. No friends, no women, no wives. Understood?"

The audience shouted back an affirmative reply.

"You're the best," he continued. "All volunteers and as ready as we can make you. Be vigilant. You must not fail!

"There'll be a final review by Herrn Marshall. Then, I'll see each of the six team leaders one at a time. None of you'll know if you're the first-team or the back-up, till you receive your device. If you have not received it within the next seventy-two to ninety-six hours, yours is back-up. There'll be no further contact, unless we need you. Stay at your area at least four more days after those ninety-six-hours. Unforeseen things happen.

"After this, you'll be returned to your wait-stations. Your device will be delivered to you. Wait for the signal! If for any reason the signal doesn't happen, return to your waiting area. The device will be collected from you. After your missions, those who go, you'll disappear, according to the routes I'll give you at the time I designate your targets."

Marshall went over his arming checklist. There were few questions. His briefing took less than half-an-hour. The briefer met each team leader in a small enclosure at the back of the room. After another hour, the final team was gone.

"I'd be obliged for a ride to the airstrip," Marshall said to the briefer.

They went by helicopter to a small, private airstrip with a single runway. A two-engine plane flew them to another remote strip, northwest of *Erfurt*. From there another helicopter flew only Marshall to an isolated helipad, closer to *Gottingen*. He was met by car, and taken to another dingy, grey basement, in a seemingly disused barn.

Another briefing of six teams followed. This briefer exhorted his troops, as the earlier one had, but was more shrill. After listening to him, Marshall's own adrenalin was making him shaky. He gave his rote, faster this time. The briefing officer was faster at assignments, than the first.

An hour later Marshall was on his way to a similar briefing farther west. This time it was on the Dutch side of the common border with Germany.

Marshall had one more to do, before he returned to the vicinity of the lab on 5 November. He still had not determined its precise location. With these briefings and the time frames, he knew he could not dawdle.

* * *

In the study at his villa outside Berlin, Baron von Markenheim awaited a visit from Colonel Krattmay. It was the day after The Colonel dropped him and General Tripleleaf off in Berlin, en route south-southeast with Thomas Pemberton in custody. The butler announced Colonel Krattmay.

"You wanted an update," Krattmay said. "*Our ground and air search teams didn't turn up anything. So far, no other security problems have surfaced. The final briefings are under way. The terror groups are doing exactly what we wanted them to, and they're getting our ordnance safely. The Western militaries are on alert, but the attacks are spreading them out real thin.*"

"Any reaction from Washington?"

"There won't be," Krattmay said, "*not in time, anyway. By the time Case Blue succeeds, some factions will still be finding out it happened.*"

"*Plans for afterward,*" von Markenheim said, "*are finalized. Consolidation won't take long. It will be like the first time. It makes me feel young again.*"

"Has the Board made any leadership decisions?"

"I'll take it temporarily . . ." The Baron replied.

"I was hoping for something more permanent. For both of us."

"*Patience, Colonel,*" von Markenheim chided. "*You'll get your chance. Our eastern friends'll take care of cleaning up the mess. We've got much more in common with them after all.*"

Krattmay agreed, "*So many years of enmity, so much we could've done together. Only polemic and rhetoric separated us. The skinheads'll have had their usefulness, too, like the SA. But they're expendable.*"

"I'll be glad to be rid of them," von Markenheim said. "*Young hotheads. They don't know who their real friends are. Compliments to you on the change of date ploy, as rehearsed.*"

"And I'll take care of our friend Tripleleaf before he gets too troublesome," Krattmay said, smiling.

"Not prematurely, remember? You're sure there's time to get word out?"

"I'm testing a leak. We shall kill two birds with one message."

"I'll see you, as planned, before the 8th?" von Markenheim asked.

"Bet the fortune on it," Krattmay replied, before leaving.

Von Markenheim made calls to *Ulm*, elsewhere in Bavaria, and Switzerland, before lunch and a nap.

* * *

The evening of 4 November Jaime and Jamael watched a film in the basement theatre of the safe-house till 8 P.M. The dozen or so other men in the theatre with them were "heavily into gore."

Each man had a single drink of vodka. The Colonel left orders no one was to have more than one. The bartender was enforcing the rule.

Jaime and the others slipped from the loud, smoky lounge, to his third-floor room where they changed clothes. This night was their breakout. They would "borrow" a car and drive to *Neuffen*, with their secreted weapons, tear-gas grenades, and masks. Earlier that afternoon they saw Emilio and the physicist at the lab. Emilio had the dummy weapon casings Jaime had had her and Marshall make.

Around 9:45 P.M., they climbed across the neighboring roofs. Two blocks away they found an old BMW 320i with the keys in the ignition. Jaime was about to close the driver's door when a hand dragged him out.

"I knew you assholes were up to something!" It was the East German security man. He kicked Jaime in the belly. "The Colonel distrusts you less than he should."

"You're out of your fucking mind!" Jaime retorted. "We're on a trim hunt."

Jaime was pushed against the car and frisked. A hand reached under his jacket and removed his pistol. He saw Jamael across the car roof.

"The Colonel was satisfied with your connections. I wasn't," the East German said.

Jaime's arms were handcuffed behind his back. As Jaime and Jamael were led to the mouth of a nearby alley, Jaime heard sound-suppressed shots. The two men beside him and Jamael crumpled. The East German and his remaining man spun around, their weapons drawn.

Jaime and Jamael scampered behind a car. There were more shots. The East German and the other went down. Dr. Pola, Emilio, and another of Jaime's agents came from the alley.

Emilio searched the East German's body for the handcuff keys. He released Jaime and Jamael.

"I overheard the security man talking about you. I reached Carlos."

They dragged the four bodies to a garage nearby. Inside, they stuffed them under a tarpaulin.

Emilio's vehicle was an old VW bus with antique paint and smudges. "Where did you get this piece of junk?" Jamael asked.

"Carlos picked it up. We borrowed license plates, too."

Jaime looked at his map with a penlight. "We've got 160 kilometers to cover," he said. "It won't be long before they know those clowns are missing. I want to have the toy by then.

Doctor, how're you holding up?"

"Good," she answered. "But I'm dying for a cigarette."

"You're about to meet your first tactical device," Jaime said. "We'll get your nicotine level up before that."

* * *

His team leader might be able to play hours of solitaire, but he couldn't. He had sent the recognition signals on schedule and wondered when the return signal would arrive. There had been nothing so far. The damned farmhouse was putting him to sleep, without really trying.

He caught himself dozing, and woke up his relief, even if it had only been three hours. He went out on the house's front porch and lit a cigar.

On his third puff, from behind, he was gripped around the neck. Kicking wildly, he sensed himself being lifted. He flailed with his elbows. Something sharp pushed into his chest. It was the last thing he felt.

* * *

"Put him in the bushes," Jaime whispered to his man, Carlos.

Jaime pulled the pin on a tear-gas grenade and lobbed it into the farmhouse. With his mask on, he went inside. Jamael was with him, also masked. The opacity of the gas reflected his light back at him.

A door into the next room was shut. Jaime kicked it open. In his right hand he held his pistol. An unexpected blow struck his wrist. He dropped the gun. Someone pulled his mask off. Another blow struck him in the chest. He fell against a wall.

Returning kicks at the dark shape in front of him, he landed one, hard, solid. The shape fell back, but retaliated with its own jump-kick. Jaime ducked to his right, coughing. The shape slammed into the wall, bouncing backward onto the floor.

Jaime leaped onto the sprawled shape. They battled. The other landed a close kick into Jaime's right side. Pain spread across Jaime's chest.

"Roll right, Jaime!" It was Emilio. Jaime lurched. He heard sound-suppressed shots. His opponent collapsed beside him.

Another skirmish was taking place near the door, he realized. Through the pain, he felt for the flashlight.

Jamael and Carlos had another man, a much bigger one, on his back. Everyone was coughing.

Jaime stumbled to the front door, tears pouring from his eyes. His choking became more violent. Outside, the others joined him, dragging their captive.

"Do him!" Jaime whooped out the words. Quiet shots followed. He tried to breathe deeply. His coughing was spasmodic. The coughing aggravated his ribs. Jamael gave him his gas mask from the house. Back inside, they found a backpack with an oval casing. In a canvas bag they found the "packet."

"Get the van," Jaime said to Emilio. The others carried the packs. Emilio drove up, Doctor Pola with him.

With a radiation detector Emilio had stolen from the lab, she checked the containers. The clicking became frenetic and loud as she ran the rod over the smaller one. She removed the contents, with Emilio's help, and examined them.

"I hope your own rads're low. You've got your wish," she said to Jaime, finally. "God help us. New members of the nuclear club, Havana and Tehran."

*   *   *

Marshall arrived at the Bavarian lab in the afternoon of 5 November. The Colonel was waiting for him. He led Marshall to an office on a level below the workrooms. The Colonel was anxious for Marshall's report. It was the first time Marshall had seen Krattmay show any emotion at all.

Reserving his own misgivings, Marshall gave a quick description of the meetings. When he finished, The Colonel asked only general questions and called men to join them.

"Goddammed son-of-a-bitch!" The Colonel suddenly shouted. He slapped Marshall across the face. "Cut the charade!" Krattmay's men held Marshall.

"What the fuck's doing?" Marshall recoiled after the blows.

"Your playmates've disappeared, along with the physicist," Krattmay answered. "That Cuban prick and his sidekicks killed four of my best men, before he escaped."

"I swear!" Marshall said. "I didn't know what they had in mind."

"They were your friends."

"Like hell!!" Marshall shot back. "We spoke, after they joined up."

"You're a lying asshole!" Krattmay yelled. "I'll teach you to fuck with me!"

Marshall struggled. "You came to me! I didn't seek you out! *You* recruited *them*! Now I'm the patsy?!"

One of the guards moved to hit Marshall, but Krattmay stopped him. "Let him finish," The Colonel said, "then beat the shit out of him."

"You guys fucked up and trusted those clowns!" Marshall said, surprised at the reprieve. "Now you're out good troops and I'm elected the fall guy!?"

"We might be out more than that," Krattmay replied. "We found tampering with our computer system."

"A boom-wafer?!" Marshall asked.

"Funny *you* suggest that," Krattmay said. "A team stopped sending its check in signature. Either way you're dead."

"You're wrong!" Marshall yelled. "How many ways can I say it?! I did what I was hired to. You don't want to pay. That's it!"

"And the physicist? She's disappeared, too," Krattmay said.

"She's working for you," Marshall said. "She was straight—with you—and me. Rodriguez probably kidnapped her."

"That's neither here nor there," Krattmay said, finally. "*Take him across the lake and keep him there. Then fly him to Wannsee 2 after that.*

"Put him with the other. Interrogate, but don't kill him, unless he gives you no choice. I'll join you in a few days, after Blue. I'm claiming the pleasure of terminating both of them."

"You're making a big mistake!" Marshall said. "You need me. If something goes wrong."

"Take him," Krattmay said, dispassionately. His men dragged Marshall from the office.

* * *

Telling McConneld he would meet him in Berlin, on 5 November, Balkovsky drove to a farm outside *Hof*, northwest of *Bayreuth*. Before McConneld's rescue, he relocated the woman he visited while undercover. He considered removing her from the field entirely, but she was too valuable an agent.

The woman ushered him into a back room of the farmhouse. The mole was there, looking more apprehensive than Balkovsky had seen him.

"They've moved up the date. The Colonel's taken a new prisoner to his own country home. Scuttlebutt said a Board member, spy," the mole said. *"He's waiting to deal with him, till after the operation."*

"Professor Pemberton? Other things?"

"I haven't seen him. Teams have their SADMs. The MADM teams're on the move, too. They brought in an American to do the briefings, an expert who was with the American Army."

"Was he in on the original job?" Balkovsky asked.

"I don't think so. The Colonel already tied up the loose ends. The new guy only came in the last two weeks. There's talk about 'a bonus.' No idea what that is yet."

"I wonder," Balkovsky said.

"You got your man out OK? That little caper really pissed The Colonel off," the mole said, smiling. He loosened up. *"He reported to The Baron, who never takes bad news well, even from The Colonel.*

"Everything WAS tight. Now, it's tighter. If The Colonel were around, I probably couldn't have made it here."

"Better be ready to bolt," Balkovsky said. *"I'll need to know anything new, immediately."*

* * *

Marshall's guards hurried him from the black limousine to a small cabin-cruiser on the Swiss side of the lake. He was groggy, after being locked in a closet. His hands were tied behind his back. Cuts and bruises on his face burned.

His captors shoved him into the boat and set off. He felt

something hard against his cheek. *"Nothing smart, Shithead!"* someone next to him growled.

The night was moonless and dark. He saw lights from a far shore. The cold air and wind numbed his facial wounds, as the boat sped up. The waters were rough, as winds whipped up waves on the lake.

The others in the boat were not ready for the turbulence. They were falling side-to-side, even over Marshall's legs, as the white crests pushed the boat right and left.

"I'm gonna puke!" Marshall groaned. He toiled to his knees, but was knocked down. *"Let me up, asshole! You want a floating john?!"* He put his head over the port side and feigned a vomiting spell.

"Stupid fucker!" someone laughed behind him.

Marshall fell backwards. In the darkness, he slipped his ropes under his legs, till his arms were in front of him. He faked another upchuck.

"Sit down, shithead!" the growler said, tapping him on the back. *"Hey!!"* Marshall abruptly threw his hands, ropes and all, around the growler's throat. He jammed his knee into the small of the man's back and pulled.

The growler grasped at the coarse hemp, choking. Marshall tugged harder, until the man's body dragged them both down. He grabbed a lifebelt from the floor.

"What the fuck!?" another yelled.

Marshall kicked the man backward and dove off the boat. As he hit the icy waters, he heard shots behind him. His dive took him skimming across the surface. He released the lifebelt, grabbed a breath, and plunged deeper.

From above, there was rumbling. A light beam spread over his head. It passed back and forth.

Cupped-handed, he pulled hard to keep himself below the surface. His lungs tugged for air. He swam to his right, away from the sound. He surfaced and gasped in more cold air.

The boat was in front of him, heading away. But then it turned left. Lights passed toward him. He ducked, but the frigidity put him into ultra-slow-motion.

"There!" someone shouted. Bullet wakes popped around him.

Marshall gulped air and dove. He felt a push against his leg. Then, sensation was gone. No time to think. Kick! Kick!

The rumbling passed overhead, then faded. The waters churned, spinning him like a buoy, adrift. He pulled upward with his hands and broke the surface again.

The boat was farther away. There was automatic and assault weapons fire. The boat zigzagged and headed off. Marshall watched as its lights became a disconnected beacon. Only its motor-harmony was audible. Then that, too, faded.

What he could feel of his body screamed in pain. The rest was silent. Last call as an ice cube, he thought.

To his right, he saw lights and heard chugging. With what little energy he had, he swam toward them. Something skimmed his face. The float.

"*Over here!!*" he shouted. The wind deflected his words into his face.

A light snaked toward him. Marshall clutched the float, trying to dog-paddle. The chugging came closer. Waves bobbed him like a fishing lure.

Marshall felt something bigger than the cabin cruiser coasting nearby. Waves bounced him more violently.

A rope fell out to him. He twisted up in it and felt himself being pulled and bumped into an object, large, hard, solid. Hands hauled him from the water. I'm dead, he thought, as he passed out.

XXIII

BERLIN. A place of past frustrations and future hopes. Of nonconformity, tolerance, and Cold War-clichés, in one geography. The Wall had collapsed. Or imploded. So had clarity.

As the contact, Liz, and Sam reached the *Berliner Ring,* the suburbs and the city were sealed in a grey drizzle, fog, low visibility. Haunting shapes were recognizable, as friend or enemy, only at close range.

A metaphor for the "post-Cold War World," Sam thought, from the backseat of the VW. She was sorry she had missed Checkpoint Charlie's departure.

Berlin had been special for her: visits with family, or she and The Professor, solo. There had also been times of lone adventure in discotheques, cabarets, museums, theaters, and clubs, but not like the danger she now faced.

From Weimar, Sam had reserved a room for 6 November for herself and Liz in a comfortable, family-run pension. She reserved it under the name in the British passport the contact provided to her, but called back from a roadside stop and cancelled. The contact and Liz convinced her to stay at a safe-house he kept in central Berlin, in the *Tiergarten* District.

But first, Liz wanted to pick up Regina and the bodyguard. They were to be at a hotel near the *Kurfürstendamm,* or *Ku'damm,* one of Berlin's main drags. At the front desk, Liz asked for "*Herr Liegnitz,*" the agent's cover.

The clerk indicated, with regrets, that no such gentleman was registered there. She also found no messages left for Liz.

"Something's very wrong. I'll see you to the safe-house," Liz said, as they were leaving the hotel. She lit a Dunhill.

"I'm going with you," Sam said, hurriedly.

The contact drove to *Bahnhof Zoo,* Berlin's main station. Regina's train had arrived despite unscheduled stops and other problems. But Liz and Sam found no *Herr und Frau Liegnitz.*

They did, however, retrieve their own luggage. Sam was relieved. Her new wardrobe symbolized a touch of freedom, under the oppression of these experiences. If time allowed, she wanted to add to it while in Berlin. She also had her father's cache to collect.

"*Better check in with Local Control*," she said to the contact, after finishing a fourth cigarette. "You can't come, Sam. *Drop her at the safe-house.*"

The house, a drab end of a drab row, had the newness of postwar materials and the oldness of rehashed design. Its furnishings were as bland as the exterior. But there were books and a color TV with VCR. Liz had the contact reissue Sam the Baretta.

Sam "vegged" on German morning television. She watched news clips of the Russian president's arrival for a short, personal, and spur-of-the-moment visit with the Chancellor. Liz and the contact returned several hours later.

"No word from Regina's baby sitter. He's *incommunicado*," Liz said. "Or dead." She puffed on yet another Dunhill.

"Let's not get maudlin so early," Sam said. "You're going to smoke yourself to death before my eyes."

"It's the job," Liz said. "Agency personnel are on alert. Stay put, till we get back."

"There's plenty of stuff in the kitchen," the contact interjected.

"Food and television. How boring!" Sam said, reflexively. "May I step out, Mother, or will the maid be in with tea?"

"Behave yourself for once," Liz rejoined, as she and the contact left.

Sam loaded the pistol and did another tour of the house. She collected books from upstairs, innocuous mystery stuff.

Alone again, she fought off "what-if" and guilt, but they won. Her father as prisoner subverted her. More helplessness, frustration, anger at herself, at him, at The Baron, at others. Without Regina, she didn't know how she would find The Baron, or her father. But she must find him.

She needed air and light, space in a crowd. Despite Liz's quasi-order, Sam decided to go out. Before she was ready, Liz and the contact returned.

"I'm glad to see you did as you were told," Liz said. "In other good news, my guy played musical trains, dragging Regina from station-to-station. They ended up in Nice. The bad boys were on us again. Now *we* retrieve, while *you* stay."

"But."

"No," Liz said, firmly. "After we've got Regina—and the alert has passed—we look for your old man."

"That'll be too late," Sam replied, anxiously.

"I don't think so," Liz answered. "But that's the way it is. Otherwise, I take my lumps and turn you over to my people."

"They can't force me to . . ."

"No more babe-in-the-woods stuff, please. Do as you're told. I'll be back ASAP."

"Yes, Mother," Sam said. "You can count on your little girl. I shan't embarrass the family."

* * *

Marshall opened his eyes. His face burned, but he felt briskly warm. He was in a bunk, with wool blankets, wearing coarse underwear and long-johns, not his own. The smell of pipe smoke was strong.

Across the small wooden room sat an older man, in shabby wool clothes, puffing. *"You are finally awake after a day,"* the man said, in Swiss-German, *"and alive on my fishing boat. I saw them shooting at you. Police?"*

Marshall shivered. *"Dangerous criminals. Thanks for saving my life."*

The man waved off Marshall's gratitude, as if to say "Don't mention it." *"Are you Jewish?"*

Marshall shook his head. *"But I'm still their enemy. Have you helped others?"*

"Jews and Israelis. Those bastards come from that house down the See, nicht?"

"Who are you, Captain?"

The man handed him a coffee mug, without answering. On his exposed wrist Marshall saw a tattooed number.

"What can I do for you? Do you need money? I could arrange a gift."

"Save your money, Mister," the man replied. "There's nothing I need. My father escaped here. Sobibor. I've had a full life."

"Were you with him as a kid? Or was that Auschwitz or Treblinka?"

"A new pipe," he said, finally. "A trip to Israel is too much to ask."

"I've got some pull," Marshall said. "I can get you the best pipe in Jerusalem. Can you put me ashore quietly on the German side? I've got to get to Frankfurt."

"When my son's up," the man said. "He'll get you where you need to go." He gave Marshall work-clothes.

"I don't even know your name," Marshall said.

"My father's name was Liebman. Enough questions. Rest." He left the cabin, a large cloud of smoke trailing him.

Marshall finished his coffee. He dressed and lay in the blankets again. The cold of the lake water was still with him. He would tell CIA a tale of one MADM—and of his help to make it so. Omit that part? But tell them of the Cuban physicist.

He would have to get to France after Frankfurt, to track down his colleagues. It should not be too hard to find them, then back on The Colonel's trail.

* * *

At a bar near their Paris hotel in the early-morning hours of 6 November, George and David waited for a contact at a back table. They were through their first round when she arrived. After recognition responses, she joined them for a Scotch-neat. She was tall, with brown hair.

"One of my people's been killed in Berlin," she said, after a second swallow. "You're off your current assignment. I'm sending you both up there."

"We're expecting hot info," David said, "from an informant. We can't leave."

"You be there by 0700 tomorrow," she said, firmly. "Our man was inside a Neo-Nazi terrorist organization. He was found a few hours ago near the *Spree*, with the top of his head . . . I want the bastards who did it."

"We're on independent status," David said. "Our informer's on real hot stuff. A big Nazi covert thing, too. We don't know your operation from Adam."

"Your original orders are overridden," she interrupted. "I cleared it with Central. They cleared it with West. You've got till first light. If he no-shows, leave an address for him. Thanks for the Scotch, gentlemen." She left.

"Your man Marbison's out of luck," George said. "It's been two weeks. I gave up on him when we lost the plane."

"Now who's playing by the book?" David asked. "You just don't like the guy."

"You're not going off half-cocked," George said, downing his drink in one swallow, "without me."

* * *

Disturbed by his "mole's news," General Balkovsky reached the U.S. Consulate on the *Clay Allee* in Berlin's *Zehlendorf* District, on the evening of 6 November, two days later than planned. He had spent the time in hastily called "meets." None confirmed the mole's info, but they did not disprove it, either. Still brooding, "Mr. Smith" was shown to McConneld's offices, where McConneld, Channing, and Colonel Barsohn were at work.

"I was worried," McConneld said. "Are you Security for that impromptu?"

"My subs are," Balkousky said. He relayed what the mole told him.

"Let's go over what we think we know," McConneld said. "Nazis or neo-Nazis, led by Krattmay, got the bombs, and are backed secretly by von Markenheim and his Cartel. The ties are deep enough we couldn't dig them up for years. Berlin's the target." He stopped. "If there are twenty targets, it could take ten days to get the bombs issued. Right, Harvey?"

"MADMs're too big. Maybe discovered on the way," Barsohn replied. "They must be in place and ready for arming."

"We're only talking fifteen or so possible targets," McConneld continued.

"But your man said 'Berlin's the target,'" Barsohn said. "If the General's right, that can't be."

"Are we dealing with a 'madame' or a back-pack here?" McConneld asked.

"I'd opt for an SADM," Barsohn answered, "less risks. The bigger, the more chance of discovery, or radiation detectors. The cores give off high rad readings."

"They're banking on us thinking that way," McConneld replied. "But we can't discount either one. 15 November's the day. It makes no sense for Nazis to waste Berlin. It's sacred ground to them."

"It wasn't always like that," Channing said. "Berlin wasn't pro-Nazi during the '20s and early '30s. Communists and Nazis were killing each other for the streets. Remember *Cabaret*? The western half hasn't exactly been a fascist state for the last forty-plus years, either."

"I *worked* that room, remember?" McConneld said.

"If they kill our president," Balkovsky interrupted.

"Why use a nuke?" McConneld replied. "There would be too much damage to the *Vaterland*. They've got conventional stuff out the wazoo. Besides which, von Markenheim's Cartel's in the international arms trade. That job'd only take a Stinger at the right time and place, or an LAW. With all the loose nukes floating around the former Union . . ."

"They might not get him with conventional stuff," Balkovsky said. "Doing it abroad, with one of yours . . ."

"They've obviously had this planned for a year or more. Your boy only decided within the last two or three weeks to make the trip," McConneld said. "He's a lucky bonus, but not the main show."

"Remember, guys," Barsohn said, "the bombs they've got are low yield and pretty clean. There will be collateral damage, but not excessive amounts. The detonation area's safe within days."

"What's 'not excessive'?" Channing asked.

"If they blame these terror nutsos and us, they'd be able to explain away the damage," Barsohn said, ignoring Channing's question.

"Did you tell the Germans about Pemberton's message?" Balkovsky asked.

"No, but they've got their suspicions," McConneld answered. His secretary came in, handing him an envelope.

"It's from my German opposite number," McConneld said. "They've initiated roadblocks and checkpoints into Berlin, Munich, other cities. I guess that 1 November deadline was flexible, not only symbolic."

"If we're dealing with an SADM, the Germans will have to tear every vehicle apart. They can't keep the press at bay. And, if it's already in the city..." Barsohn said.

McConneld looked at a copy of Pemberton's message. "Berlin—trigger—15 N," he read. "Trigger. Tom's always a careful writer. If he said, 'trigger,' whatever they plan here gets a big snowball rolling."

"Without knowing the other targets," Balkovsky said, "the only way to stop it would be to prevent it here."

"Can we at least locate von Markenheim?" Barsohn asked.

"He and his'll be light years from it," Channing suggested.

"But I want every man we can spare on that connection and the streets," McConneld said. "Concentrate them on government and military buildings and facilities. Anything official and public."

"We can't do that without tipping the Germans," Barsohn said. "We have to let them in on this. Berlin's too big a place, figuratively and literally."

"Do that," Balkovsky said. "And you lose my source. I'm not sacrificing him for Germany. The Colonel will kill him."

"Be reasonable, Alexei," McConneld replied. "We've got to trust them."

"You do. I don't," Balkovsky said. "We do it ourselves, or Moscow-here-I-come. That was our agreement."

"I could have you detained," McConneld said.

Balkovsky replied, "But that doesn't get your answer. We've lost control of them. The only way to regain part of it is to make them indebted to us into the next generation. They save themselves, and they'll think they can do without all of us."

"I can't agree with your analysis," McConneld replied. "But you're not going to budge, are you?"

Balkovsky shook his head emphatically.

"I'm probably going to regret this, but I can't afford a resumption of the Cold War," McConneld said. "No Germans. But, if you don't come up with something in the next forty-eight to seventy-two hours, I'm breaking our deal. What did that jackass Kinnean spout?"

Channing read from a notepad. "Nazis good for something ...Dirty stuff....Control them...Good combustion...not wasted...Sorry not here for it."

"I thought he said, 'Good fire.' 'Good fire won't be wasted.'" McConneld said. His secretary repeated most of what Channing had read. "Also, something about 'this time, too,' or 'this time, either.'"

Channing reread Pemberton's last message. "It looks like it could've been '24,' '28,' or '29,'" he said, finally.

"It could be a date, like '15 N'," McConneld said. "'20-something'? Do a computer search. Is there any way you can get your man back to Moscow, Alexei?" Balkovsky shook his head.

* * *

In the rundown basement flat he used for many years as a "weigh station," near the center of old "East Berlin," Colonel Krattmay waited with Heinz Friederich. It was nearly 11:30 P.M. 6 November. General Tripleleaf was due at midnight.

Both men were dressed in dirty, work-overalls and mud-caked boots, and had scraggly beards. They had moved into the flat earlier that day and looked like two of the thousands of construction workers, rebuilding the eastern section of the city. The Federal police's roadblocks and checkpoints succeeded their arrival by twenty-four hours. Everything The Colonel needed was in the city already.

He and Friederich had shaved each other's heads to the completely bare skin an hour before. The Colonel called the full balding a "cheap, *incognito* measure."

Krattmay had not briefed Friederich on the location of the materials, or this mission. As far as Friederich knew, they had another, ordinary rendezvous. He had also not told Friederich the exact starting date for *Case Blue*.

"I wish he'd get here," The Colonel said, stroking his vacant scalp. "It reminds me of Namibia. Remember?"

"Do we really need him along tonight?"

"He's the liaison. No General, no contact."

"When will you brief me on the new stuff?"

There was a knock on the back door, which opened into a small yard and alley. Friederich exchanged pass-phrases with the as-yet-unseen visitor, before opening the door. General Tripleleaf came in, alone, dressed in a business suit.

"Good haircuts," the General said. "I'll pop for the wax-and-polish, if you want. Have you gotten a call yet?" Friederich shook his head.

* * *

From his regular rounds in the sub-basement heating and power facilities, the guard-technician looked at his watch. It was midnight, 6 November. In the control panel for the new furnaces, he disengaged an integrated circuit from its board.

A red light lit up on the panel. He knew this was also happening in the main security control room on the ground floor of the old structure.

Replacing the cover, he completed his rounds and returned to the guards' station. The phone was ringing.

"Station A... Yes, sir," he said. He listened. "Not when I inspected. I'll be back to you." He had coffee, and called the control-room back.

* * *

The General answered his cell phone while in Krattmay's basement flat. "What kind of problem?" he asked in German. "Shit! Will it complicate things? OK, I'll be there, as fast as I can. Show time!" he said to Krattmay, "as planned."

Krattmay and Friederich's vehicle was an enclosed panel truck, with an electronics contractor's logo on the sides. Tripleleaf passed them in his Mercedes 450SL. The route took them along the *Allee Prenzlauer*, onto the *Karl Liebknechtstrasse*, and, finally, to *Unter Den Linden*.

The General's car turned right onto *Otto Grotenwohl-Strasse*, before the *Brandenburger Tor*, the Brandenburg Gate, and headed north. After only two blocks, he turned left onto *Reichstag ufer*, and pulled to the curb, nearest the *Reichstag* building, the seat of the German Parliament. Uniformed guards approached his car. Krattmay saw others heading toward the van.

"*Our meet's the fucking Reichstag?*" Friederich whispered to Krattmay before the guards reached them.

"*You may not park here,*" a uniformed guard said to Krattmay. The man carried his G-3 automatic in his hands.

Tripleleaf was out of his car, speaking with the guards.

"*We are here to repair environmental controls,*" Krattmay replied, calmly, in German. "*It's an emergency call and got us out of bed for this shit! Some bigshot ... !!*"

"*They're with me,*" Tripleleaf said. "*Here are my clearance and authorizations. It's bad enough I'm here. The goddamned project manager's drunk.*" Tripleleaf handed an officer his i.d. and clipboard.

The officer examined both. He left them for a guard station on the side of the building. He returned and gave Tripleleaf his things back.

Tripleleaf, Krattmay, and Friederich followed the officer to a basement entrance. They were patted down after coming through a metal detector.

"*Funny looking tools,*" a guard said to them, as he searched Krattmay's and Friederich's toolboxes.

Krattmay said, nonchalantly, "*You can't put a crowbar into an integrated circuit the size of your fingernail.*"

The guards led them to the security control room, where Tripleleaf spoke with the night supervisor. He called the guard-technician, who originally confirmed the malfunction and escorted Krattmay and Friederich.

"*It's good to see you again, Schmidt,*" Krattmay whispered to the technician.

Schmidt replied, "*Everything's ready. I'll help you unpack.*"

Once in the sub-basement, he led them to a construction storage room, with wooden crates stacked floor-to-ceiling on one side. The floor was littered with plaster dust and construction waste. Schmidt and The Colonel laid out large, clean plastic sheets on the floor.

They opened medium-sized crates and boxes. The Colonel cradled small electronic and other components from each. There was one large item, rectangular, overweight for its size, which Krattmay and Schmidt lifted from its packing case together.

"You'll have to help us," Krattmay said to him, "when the time comes."

He led Krattmay and Friederich to a large, apparently newly installed furnace, one of several in the huge, concrete room. This one had not been fired up as yet. Schmidt and Krattmay carried a larger component, and Schmidt helped them remove a cover panel on the furnace.

"We're here to arm, aren't we, sir?" Friederich asked, trying to contain his incredulity. "Why no clue?"

"Come in, both of you. I'll need your help." Krattmay picked up small tools, and climbed into the furnace.

In the dark, steel enclosure, Friederich could not see what his superior was doing. The Colonel turned on a lantern. The furnace was not so cramped, as one might have expected. They could stand, without stooping or crouching. It was like a large walk-in closet.

They worked on either side of a tall rectangular pillar, which abutted the furnace's back wall. When they had the pillar loose, they dragged it from the furnace wall and leaned it beside its erstwhile content.

"What's this made of? Lead?" Friederich grunted. Friederich saw an ordnance casing, heavy, olive-drab, curved and roundish. In an erect position, attached by steel braces and supports was an MADM, like the one at the lab. This one seemed smaller than the lab specimen. There were cover plates, which Krattmay directed them to remove.

"Schmidt, I'll call, when we need you. See that we're not disturbed," the Colonel said. He ran his thumb across his throat.

Friederich followed Schmidt through the opening in the furnace wall and returned with the components, except the largest one.

"Here's hoping the computers are right." The Colonel picked

up a few smaller components. *"Give me the flashlight here,"* he said to Friederich.

He placed two of the tinier components into spaces, which seemed specifically made for them. *"I thought these are our improvisations,"* Friederich said. *"They look made-to-order."*

"It helps to own the company that makes them. Give me more light on this."

Krattmay worked patiently, emplacing components and adjusting both them and the internal elements of the device. The work went slowly. Krattmay's adjustments seemed endless.

"Now I know why neither side ever used these things," Friederich said, exasperatedly. *"By ready-time, you'd be overrun."*

With Schmidt's help, Krattmay and Friederich fitted the final, heavy component into its place. Krattmay locked it in, and adjusted the controls on a panel.

A red-lighted, LED digital panel with multiple windows came on. Krattmay set the first window for "08-11-15-00-00." He set the second one, below it.

The final one had smaller, multiple windows. He set the sequence, "5-3104-4-200-1-1306-5-7214-245," among the nine readout windows and fitted two keys into locks, similar to the locks on vending machines but more detailed. He turned them simultaneously. The second LED window began ticking.

"Marshall was right," Krattmay reflected, watching the chronometer functioning. *"Maybe he was telling the truth, after all."*

He closed the covers on the device, except one. This he left half-open. On the LED read-out panel, he pushed a small inconspicuous button below the third set of windows with an awl. A sequence of red, yellow, and green pinpoint lights, one of each color, came on below the window, bearing "245."

Unrolling copper wire, he connected it to an electrical pack/detonator and a ball of plastique. Krattmay attached the wires to contacts in the half-open compartment and closed the panel. The three men replaced the cover and bolted it.

They closed the furnace's outside panel, cleaned up, and headed to the guard's station, by way of the control panel Schmidt had earlier sabotaged. Schmidt replaced the integrated circuit.

Krattmay said to him, "*Our people have to be out by 0800 the morning of the 8th! Now, where's the WC?*"

Schmidt took him, while Friederich waited at the guard station. Schmidt returned without Krattmay. Ten or so minutes after that Krattmay joined them.

"*See you as planned,*" he said to Schmidt, before they returned to the control-room. "*We have chores to finish,*" he said to Friederich.

Tripleleaf was calmer. "*Next time, wait till morning! I got a reception later.*" The three men were out quickly.

At Tripleleaf's car, Krattmay whispered to both men, "How 'bout a celebration? We'll take a chopper."

"It's two in the morning!" Tripleleaf said.

"Big shit!" Krattmay replied. "How often's an occasion like this come along? We can patch up our differences, since Pemberton was responsible for most of that. And we can toast the New Dawn, too." Friederich joined Krattmay's cajoling.

"What the hell!" Tripleleaf said. "We'll meet back at that basement!"

At the apartment, Krattmay and Friederich showered and changed clothes. As they were leaving, Krattmay took a long glance around the room. "*The room that's launched a thousand operations,*" he said.

"New and better ones are ahead, sir," Friederich replied. "*Do we need to celebrate tonight? Really?*"

"*I thought you told the General . . .*"

"*I was backing you, sir,*" Friederich said. "*I'm spent. You don't need me.*"

"*You're on me. That's an order,*" Krattmay whispered.

From Tempelhof, they flew to Leipzig aboard one of Tripleleaf's corporate jets. They arrived at an airfield northwest of the city and took a limousine, which was waiting for them, to a restaurant/hotel. The restaurant staff was equally prepared for their arrival.

"You had this shindig planned," Tripleleaf said to Krattmay.

"Only tentatively," Krattmay answered. "This is hired hands' night out. I ordered champagne. *Dom Perignon '53*, a sumptuous meal from soup to nuts. It's courtesy of The Baron."

"Too bad Otto isn't here," Tripleleaf said. Krattmay agreed.

When a waiter brought the first bottle of champagne, Krattmay insisted on opening it, away from the table. He poured three servings into finely stemmed, tall crystal glasses and dropped tiny white pills into one glass. Bringing it to the table, he handed it to The General.

Tripleleaf started to hand it to Friederich, when Krattmay stopped him. "No, No! The first glass rightly belongs to the man, without whom our enterprise would never have been possible. You, General." He handed Friederich another glass, and repeated the toast.

Tripleleaf emptied his glass in one swallow. The three men threw the glasses into a nearby brick hearth, where a fire was burning robustly.

Krattmay poured another round. Waiters brought the first course and another bottle of champagne. The three ate and drank, with course-after-course delivered by the waiters, on cue.

Krattmay and Friederich kept their liquor intakes modest. Tripleleaf took advantage of the wine cellar. Krattmay had forgotten what a high alcohol tolerance The General had.

Midway through the beef course, Friederich leaned over to Krattmay. *"Even without the booze, sir, I'm losing it. I've got to excuse myself. Did you reserve rooms upstairs?"*

"Why so itchy? Enjoy. That's an order," Krattmay replied.

"I can't believe Blue's finally underway," Friederich whispered. *"I expected to be wired. Instead, I'm falling asleep."*

Tripleleaf noticed them talking to each other. "No secrets from a friend, Boys!" he boomed. "Tell Uncle Wally all about it!"

"I've gotta get some sleep," Friederich said.

"The party's just starting!" Tripleleaf said. "At ease, Boy. Have another!"

"I need you with me," Krattmay said, firmly, in German. *"Let your hair down. It will be the last chance for a while."*

It was nearly 6:30 A.M. After glasses of Port and cigars, the General seemed unaffected by his substantial liquor intake. But, as they were leaving the private dining room, he tripped, fell on his face, and did not move.

Krattmay and Friederich picked up the heavy-set man and sandwiched him between them. He stirred a little, but did not wake up.

"I've been expecting this," Krattmay said, as they struggled to the elevator. *"We have a suite upstairs for this eventuality."*

Inside the suite, they deposited the sleeping Tripleleaf into a padded chair with wooden arms. He flopped over its back. *"The great General Walter Tripleleaf, USAF,"* Krattmay hissed. He removed packages of ace bandages from a nearby drawer.

"Secure him, before he wakes," he said, handing one to Friederich. *"Follow your orders, Captain."*

Krattmay tightly bound Tripleleaf's legs to the chair legs. Friederich tied his wrists to the arms. When Krattmay was satisfied Tripleleaf could not escape, he wrapped strips of duct tape over Tripleleaf's mouth and around his head.

The General had still not roused. Krattmay broke smelling salts beneath Tripleleaf's nostrils and jammed them in deeply. Tripleleaf's eyes opened, wearily, almost dreamily. He became more alert and showed a mixture of fear and anger. Finally, Krattmay stepped back from his prisoner.

"So," Krattmay said. "I'm a 'candy-assed yes-boy,' huh, Fatman?!" He slapped Tripleleaf across the face numerous times. "You stupid bastard! To think you'd ever be one of us?! Ideology without national pride." He cackled.

"It's nationalism, stupid! Did I forget to mention, you'd been convicted of treason? I hope you enjoyed your last meal. This is the execution. The Baron sends regards." Tripleleaf's expression changed to terror.

"Remember that first toast? Yours had an excruciatingly painful poison. It will look like suicide, with an appropriate note. To be sure you don't screw this up, I'm giving you a little ol' shot."

With a syringe and needle, Krattmay injected the contents into Tripleleaf's arm. "I'll give The Baron your best, when I see him."

Before they left, Krattmay put a *"Nicht Stören!"* sign on the doorknob. He smirked, as he closed, then locked, the door.

XXIV

Chuck Channing came from the computer and communications center with printouts. He had worked there for hours, despite repeated calls from McConneld. "Lots o' shit here!" Channing said, dropping the pile on a desk. "Even Archives stuff. If we start with the War, there are no November dates they'd want to celebrate and no victories that month for the first three years. After that, it was slow, then fast, meltdown. Stalingrad, *Supercharge,* or *Torch* weren't things they'd cheer about." Channing noticed Balkovsky grimace.

"Avenge, maybe?" McConneld asked.

"The dates're still wrong. Before and after, but no 15ths."

"Perhaps that's too literal," Balkovsky said. "Maybe 15 November isn't tied to any previous event of the same date."

"These clowns're students of history. Whatever's planned is tied to an event," McConneld rejoined.

"The General might be right," Channing said. "I don't recall the 15th being significant. Pre-war, there was *Kristallnacht.* 9 November '38. That doesn't seem important enough, though."

"Start at the takeover," McConneld said. "Early '30s, wasn't it? '32?"

"30 January '33, actually," Channing said.

Channing gave them a history of the period, including November 1932 elections, failed coalitions leading up to Hitler's appointment as Chancellor and the February 1933 elections Hitler called as a bluff.

"He must have won those February elections," McConneld observed.

"They'd locked up the opposition or killed it by then, like a Soviet election. Sorry, General."

"Times have changed," Balkovsky said, blandly.

Channing reviewed the 1920s. "There's the Munich *Beer Hall Putsch* in '23, 8–9 November, coinciding with the anniversary of the Proclamation of the Republic." Channing described Hitler's abortive attempt to topple the Bavarian Government.

"Close," McConneld said. "If Alexei's right about a new date, that one might be in play."

"In Munich?" Barsohn asked.

"Maybe, maybe not," McConneld replied. "Let's go over other November dates from that perspective."

"There really aren't any," Channing said, "except the end of World War One. And we've already covered them."

"We're missing something then," McConneld said. "A riot in Munich. The Armistice ending World War One."

"But the Versailles Treaty," Channing said, "which was really what Hitler and the Nazis hated, wasn't signed until May and June 1919. Germany was blackmailed into signing by the British blockade, which hadn't been lifted, despite the Armistice on 11 November."

"That's close!" McConneld said. "Eleven... fifteen."

"The question is," Barsohn said, "close to what?"

"Government overthrow," McConneld said. "Back in D.C., when Washbourne suggested that, I rejected it. Now..."

"Absurd!" Barsohn said. "They'd never pull a coup off today. Ostensibly spontaneous, without a massive public uprising? The logistics alone would sink them, along with a hostile population."

"Don't forget what they've got to power it off," McConneld said, "that Hitler and his boys didn't have in 1923. They probably have more in's to the German Government and Security apparatus than we know."

"Then Pemberton's wrong," Barsohn said. "Munich *would* be the trigger. Things happened there in November, not here."

"Not altogether accurate," Channing corrected. "Things happened here, too, at the end of World War One. Chaos. Opposing factions killing each other. Liebknecht and Luxemburg assassinated by the *Freikorps*. Communists proclaimed a rival government, which was later suppressed by an unholy alliance between the Social Democratic President and the *Freikorps* leaders. Berlin was not quiet or uneventful."

"But not Nazi things," Barsohn countered. "And 15 November sure as hell isn't Hitler's birthday."

"But the German defeat was more than significant to them," Channing replied. "The 'stab-in-the-back' myth got started then, sort of like some of your Army colleagues said about Vietnam. 'The politicians stabbed us in the back at home. They didn't let us win it.' Sound familiar?"

"What's Vietnam got to do with it?" Barsohn seemed puzzled.

"The spectre of a lost war," Channing said, "thought by some as winnable."

"We can debate cause-and-effect after this is over. That wasn't the case in World War One," McConneld said. "They were bled white."

"We're talking *myths* and public perceptions here," Channing said. "Myths that were more powerful than reality or truth. The German High Command did everything to perpetuate the myth. The generals wouldn't even ask for the cease-fire. They yukered civilians, who later took the rap. The guy, who signed for Germany, was killed in the streets a couple years later."

"Let's get back on track, Professor," McConneld chided. "Recap."

"A possible coup, set for 15 November," Channing said. "Berlin's the trigger for a full-scale takeover, tied to the 11th."

"But if I were they," Balkovsky interjected. "I wouldn't move it up four measly days. I'd move it up more. They know we're on their trail."

"The 15th's only eight days away," Barsohn said. "Do you think it's underway?"

"As we speak," Balkovsky replied.

"That still leaves us with where," McConneld said. "What the hell does '2—Re—' mean, I wonder?"

* * *

The shore line was dotted with nightlights, as the small motor launch slowed. Marshall crouched, as the captain's son cut the engine. They were approaching a village's dock area, where other boats were tied up or anchored.

Marshall had considered being dropped off on any beach along the German side of the lake, but did not want to explain himself, without passport, identification, or money. The young man slid the boat alongside an auxiliary pier and tied it to a piling.

"*Thanks,*" Marshall said to him. "*This is the end of the line for you. I don't want you getting hurt. I owe your father.*"

"*You don't know your way, sir,*" the young man replied. "*I can help.*"

"*Sorry, kid,*" Marshall said. "*The people I'm dealing with will kill, as look at you. Let's keep your family tree growing.*"

The young man made no move to return to the boat. "*I've helped others my papa's saved. Why're we wasting time? We can borrow a friend's car.*"

"*I'm not getting through,*" Marshall said. "*I must get going—alone . . . How old're you? Eighteen?*"

"*Twenty, sir. I want someday to go to Israel.*"

"*A patriot, huh? OK, kid, you lead—for now. By the way, where are we?*"

"*Hagnaua,*" the young man answered. "*We can get to Friedrichshafen easily. A friend lives near here.*"

The captain's son took Marshall through narrow streets, to a basement flat where his woman-friend lived. Over Marshall's protests, she volunteered to drive, rather than only lending them her VW. Thinking he could discourage further help, Marshall told them his actual destination. The captain's son shoved him into the backseat. They headed northwest, with the woman pushing the VW to the top of the speedometer.

She was bubbly and funny: a perfect complement for the young man, who was too serious, Marshall reflected, like himself. At first, she seemed content with driving him to *Stuttgart*. As they reached that *Autobahn* exit, she continued on, north—to *Frankfurt*.

Though Marshall considered losing them at a rest stop near *Karlsruhe*, he resigned himself to their presence. How else could he have gotten to *Frankfurt*, without money, credit cards, or larceny? Besides, with the speed the woman was driving, he doubted he could reach *Frankfurt* any faster by jet. He already decided to get the young man to Israel, after all this was over.

When they reached *Frankfurt,* it was around 2:30 A.M. They cleared the roadblocks into the city. Downtown, they found the

U.S. Consulate. Marshall told them to drop him at the next block.

"*Thanks again, kid,*" Marshall said, as he slammed the passenger door. "*I'll take it from here. Now, get lost!*"

He was half-surprised when the woman, without protest, sped off. Marshall watched the car disappear into the diminished traffic. Marshall crossed the street to the block, across from the Consulate's main entrance, near a call-box. He had one thing to do, before he went inside.

* * *

"You're alive!! Where the hell are you?!" David yelled into the receiver. He had been semi-conscious, but was suddenly awake when he recognized the caller.

"We'll catch the next flight. The main *Lufthansa* counter," David said. "Marbison's resurfaced!" he said to George. "The guy's like a cat! We're going to *Frankfurt*."

"Frankfurt?! What about Berlin?"

"Fuck Berlin. For now, anyway," David said, putting his trousers on, before realizing he was briefless. He hurriedly dressed in more comfortable order. They were packed and in the hotel's lobby in five minutes, then a cab to *de Gaulle* Airport.

* * *

"I'm telling you!" Marshall repeated, less calmly than the first three times. "I've got to see the Agency OIC. IMMEDIATELY! The security of the Free World's literally in the balance!"

"Of course it is, but I'm sorry, sir," the Consulate guard said. "No one's here to help you. If you come back during regular business hours, I'm sure there'll be someone who can."

"Cut the shit, Junior. You've done your duty with the non-denial denial. I know the manual on these cadences," Marshall said. "Who's your O.D.? Call him or her at home!"

"I'm sorry, sir," the guard said, calmly. "Without some kind of identification, you'll have to come back when we're open."

"I'm not going till you get your Agency man in here!"

"If you don't leave, sir, I'll have to call Security." He motioned to the two on-duty Marine guards behind them. "I'll also ask these men to escort you from the building."

"That's the most intelligent thing you've said," Marshall shot back. "Call Security, by all means. I probably know him."

A tall man, in business suit and i.d. card hanging by neckchain, came to the lobby. Three marines were with him. "What's the trouble?" he asked.

"Christ! It's you, Jack Manley!" Marshall said. "Am I glad to see you!"

"Jesus! What're you doing here?!" Manley exclaimed, embracing Marshall.

"I heard you retired!" Marshall said.

"They couldn't do without me and offered me a civilian job," Manley replied. "It's better than being a couch potato on pension."

"You? A couch potato? I've got to see the Agency OIC. When I say URGENT, I'm not close to the half-of-it."

"I'll vouch for this guy," Manley said to the desk guard. Manley led Marshall to an office down the hall. Marshall told him about the MADM, omitting his own work in arming it.

"Jesus Christ! Those goddamned things!" Manley said. "We'd better call Corps-HQ or CENTAG. The new Agency OIC is just over. Washington sent somebody special, with lots more personnel, a while back, too."

"The way things've been going, they've scampered already. Who's this D.C. guy?"

"A big fish. The Agency people buttoned it up." Manley made phone calls. "He's in Berlin," Manley said, when he finished. "His name's McConneld. Let's get the OIC in here first."

A little later a dark-suited man joined them. Manley introduced him as Frank Billings, Agency OIC. Marshall repeated the story to him. "I'd better alert the Germans," Billings said.

"What about the big guy in Berlin? McConneld?"

Billings called the U.S. Consulate. "Office 3104," he said. "Can you locate Mr. McConneld for me? Emergency."

"Mr. McConneld?" Billings identified himself, and explained

the situation. He listened, then hung up. "You're on your way to Berlin," he said to Marshall. "Mr. McConneld is anxious to see you."

"He wants me right away?" Marshall asked. "Can you rustle me up identification? I've been a non-person for days. I've got one other thing to do first. Jack, you got a phone book? Or the number for *Lufthansa?*"

* * *

It was late night, early morning of 6-7 November in a disused warehouse near the *Wilhelmshaven* docks. Jaime, Jamael, Emilio, and other members of the Cuban's team were playing cards, in an office, partitioned by wooden dividers.

Dr. Pola was staying at a pension nearby. She had gotten sick from the smell of the place earlier that day.

"Where the hell are my guys?" Jamael said, nervously, after dropping out of the latest hand. "They better not have gotten themselves picked up!"

He glanced out an exterior door, then returned to the office and the poker game. "I should not have let them go," he lamented, picking up his cards.

"Funny thing about that, *amigo*," Jaime said. "I still remember that shit you gave me in New York. Now wasn't the time, or words to that effect."

"A couple of them said they'd kill you," Emilio said, "if you didn't let them out. Maybe you didn't have a choice. Deal me out." He left, for a washroom on the other side of the warehouse.

Moments later there were knocks on the outside door. The raps were repeated.

"I'll get it," Jaime said. "My hand sucks. It's probably your guys." He counter-knocked, and unbolted the door. A lone man came in.

"Nadim?" Jamael said, as the new arrival came in. "Where're the others?"

He started to answer rapidly in Persian, then switched into English.

"I told you assholes to stay together," Jamael said, angrily.

"We stiffed a couple whores, at a bar and brothel," Nadim said. "Their pimps are after us. We fought and ran. The other guys were heading for another joint."

"Get them back here!" Jamael ordered. Nadim left.

Minutes later, there were more knocks on the door, soft like Nadim's. "The idiot probably forgot something," Jamael said. He unbolted and pushed the door open. It closed, without anyone coming in. "What the?! Nobody there." He stuck his head out. Suddenly, his body was motionless, then fell flat.

Jaime jumped up from the table. Before he reached the door, figures in black clothes and ski masks and armed with stockless *AKM*s rushed through the doorway. Jaime counted thirteen in all, and they were speaking German. Two stood over Jamael. The rest fanned out. They relieved Jaime of his automatic and rounded up his men.

Another man joined Jaime's guards. "Where is it?!" he yelled, in German-accented English. "We want it! Now!"

"What?" Jaime replied, calmly.

"Don't play dumb with me, scumball!" the man yelled. "I'll waste all of you and tear this dump apart!" Another black-clad man spoke with the leader.

"Where's your other man?" the leader asked Jaime. "Games? OK, let's play Beat-the-shit-out-of-the-dummy." He slugged Jaime in the abdomen. Jaime doubled over, to his knees. "Want to play some more?!"

"I told you . . ." Before Jaime finished, the leader kicked him in the face.

Men went into other parts of the warehouse. Jaime was held upright by the arms.

"Round two of our game," the leader said, punching Jaime in the abdomen again. "Where's the package?!"

"Don't know." Jaime gasped. Two more punches landed. The second felt like it knocked his front out his back. The men sent to search returned.

The leader said, "Tell me, or you'll watch your men die, one at a time." He cocked his weapon. "How about you?" He pointed it at Jaime's man, Juan.

"*Don't tell him, man!*" Juan said, in Spanish. "*He'll kill us anyway.*"

"Bad advice, friend," the leader said. "I'll kill you if he doesn't."

Jaime gasped, "Not losing you, man. Promise you won't kill..."

"Sure. Why not? Ready to talk?"

"Trap door." Jaime exhaled. "Office." The men holding Jaime let go. He fell to his knees. Through the pain, Jaime heard crashing sounds and German voices.

"Smart boy," the leader said. "It better be the truth!"

Two men joined the leader. One stooped over, holding an oversized backpack. The other held a smaller knapsack. The leader examined each.

"Score!" he said. "Sorry we must steal-and-run. But we must see a man about a price. We'll take that useless lump over there with us, for insurance." He pointed to Jamael and yelled orders. The men near Jamael picked him up by the arms.

"Sorry! I lied!" the leader said. He pointed his weapon toward Juan and fired.

Jaime heard a second burst of fire. Several of the raiders fell to the ground. The leader shouted more orders. His men returned fire. Others carried the components and wounded comrades out. The raiders backpedaled, firing bursts and retreating to the door. They disappeared one at a time, until the leader was the final one out.

* * *

"You idiot!" Jamael said, as he got into the two-and-a-half-ton panel truck, near the warehouse. "You nearly fucked it up!"

"Sorry, sir," the raid leader said, as the truck drove off. "But we did get the device. Tehran will be pleased."

* * *

Jaime heard footsteps coming toward him. "*You all right?*"

It was Emilio. "*Juan's messed up pretty bad. I think he'll live, but we better get him to a doctor. You don't look so good yourself.*"

Rest a minute. Don't try to get up . . ."

"That you, opening up? Thanks. They took Jamael," Jaime said, softly.

"Yeah, ain't that a shame, either way," Emilio said.

Jaime tried to stand, but fell down. Emilio helped him. *"I'm going to enjoy this. Help me back to the office."* He stumbled on, with Emilio supporting him.

"Here's the transmitter," Emilio said. Jaime nodded.

Emilio placed a small, but powerful radio transmitter on the table. He adjusted the frequency, plugged in push-button controls, and handed them to Jaime, who pushed the button.

"Lucky thing," Emilio said, *"you had Dr. Pola cook up that dummy model for those dummies."* They both laughed. In Jaime's case, the joy was painful.

"That's what they get for underestimating a Cuban," Jaime said. *"Now only Habana's the new club member."*

* * *

The early edition of the *Wilhelmshaven Allgemeinezeitung* on the morning of 7 November reported that a delivery truck exploded in a residential neighborhood, not far from the harbor.

Few details were available at press-time, but a source in the local police suggested it was part of the ongoing wave of terror attacks, reaching unprecedented levels in recent weeks.

The explosion damaged nearby homes and vehicles. An exact death toll was unavailable, but another police source on the scene, observing the devastation, noted the count could reach more than a dozen. No survivors of the truck had been found.

* * *

At Baron von Markenheim's estate, outside Berlin, in its library-conference room, an important meeting of the Cartel's Board had been convened, as scheduled. It was mid-morning, 7 November. After reports and preliminary discussion, Colonel Krattmay arrived. He briefed them on the "demise" of General Tripleleaf and other progress, since his previous report.

"Your address to the nation, Herr Baron, on our network will be at 0900," one man said to von Markenheim. "On the 13th..."

"Why a five-day delay?" another man asked.

"I thought that was clear," von Markenheim said, patiently. He explained that much time was needed for "consolidation," and the "Cincinnatus Idea."

"The Chancellor will present no special difficulty?" The Baron asked.

"He'll have been with the rest," Krattmay replied.

"Please review the operational elements of the plan," a Board member to von Markenheim's right said.

"The initial occurrence," Krattmay said, "will signal our other representatives to complete their deliveries. When those have been suitably serviced, our contacts in appropriate regulatory and military positions and their units will consolidate our preeminent profit and market position. Our individual service representatives will also be approaching and disposing of competition with a hands-on style."

"And if the initial signal is not given?" the Board member persisted.

"Our representatives will abort deliveries and return the merchandise to pre-arranged pickup points, where we'll retrieve and store it for another opportunity."

"And the Americans' response, if we gain, as you put it, our 'preeminent market position'?" another Board member asked.

"They'll be too busy explaining how their merchandise was stolen and used by known terror groups," Krattmay answered. "Besides, their government is in sympathetic hands now."

"You're certain we're safe here?" another asked.

"Perfectly," Krattmay replied. "Everything's in motion. One small detail's being taken care of today."

"A moment like this," von Markenheim said, "allows for some retrospective reflection. As much as I revered The Führer, he had one major failing. He didn't know how to consolidate his gains. To wait out his enemies. He was always in too much of a hurry. I would never have told him that to his face. Me, the wet-nose. But we'll not make that mistake. So, meine Herren." The Baron smiled. "After tomorrow, within three days, Germany will again *be ours. And after that Russia and Europe. It should be. We own enough of it."*

"*The only parts of the world that really matter,*" Krattmay added.

* * *

From the doorstep of the *Frankfurt* Consulate to *Tempelhof*, John Marshall was in Berlin in under two hours. An Air Force fighter, with priority status, carried him to Berlin. He was met there by a chauffeur and Mercedes limousine. After exchange of code words, the chauffeur let Marshall into the Mercedes.

Waiting for him inside was another Agency type, Charles Channing, who showed Marshall his credentials. Marshall nodded wearily. The cold lake and lack of sleep had caught up with him again.

"Mr. McConneld's sorry he couldn't meet you. I'll debrief you first," Channing said. "Then, you'll brief Mr. McConneld."

"Look, kid," Marshall said. "You better take me straight to him. Things're about to get hairier." He repeated his story.

It was not long, before they were at the Embassy. Channing led Marshall to a suite, a Restricted Area of the building.

They entered an Operations Center, where Channing introduced McConneld and several other men, among them a "Colonel Barsohn," and a "Mr. Smith." The latter looked familiar to Marshall, but he could not quite place why.

"Well, well, well. So, Mr. Marshall. We finally meet," McConneld said. "The only reason you're here, and not locked up in cold storage."

"Could you rephrase that?" Marshall said, quickly. "I spent a night in Lake Constance and almost ended up a *Leder*-pop."

"You have something I need," McConneld continued.

"Don't come on to me like that, Pal," Marshall said, recoiling. "I've had two real bad days, and I'm looking for someone to take them out on. My first choice isn't available."

"I saw you with the fucking Colonel!" McConneld replied.

"I was undercover!" Marshall said. "You don't have time to question my ancestry. I'm here, aren't I? We got a real problem."

"Sorry, I probably can empathize with you more than you realize."

"I overheard they took a spy."

McConneld nodded. "But I've got to know something. Why *were* you following Samantha Pemberton back in D.C.?"

"That shit again?!" Marshall said. "I told someone named Washbourne. Can we move on? By the way, how is she? Sam, I mean."

"She gave her surveillance the slip back in D.C.," McConneld said. "What've you got?"

Marshall felt mindless as he repeated his story. "There's no guarantee they're still there," he concluded. "I tried to delay, as best as I could. The guys working there weren't idiots."

"You're a friend of Tom Pemberton, right?" Barsohn asked.

"He wouldn't tell me details," Marshall replied. "'Really big.' That's all he said. Felt like I was talking to Ed Sullivan."

"How do you fit into all this?" McConneld asked.

"Old Doc and I go way back," Marshall replied. "I've been helping him on The Cartel for years. But he's been selective with info, even with old friends. He said he was planning a big exposé."

"That's it?" McConneld asked. "An exposé?"

"Obviously not all," Marshall replied. "If he's deliberately undercover for you.... Surprised I know your arrangements?"

"That son-of-a-bitch!" McConneld said, grimacing, "is playing every angle. You know where he is or has his information?"

Marshall shook his head. "I said he was selective. Get inside. Get out with info and me intact. Stop the bad guys."

"The Colonel got in the way of the plan?" McConneld asked.

Marshall nodded. "What have you got? I'll try to help."

* * *

DeGaulle Airport, 7 A.M., 7 November. *"Madames et Monsieurs, Lufthansa Flight 403,"* the public address system called in French.

George and David had been waiting for it, since their early-morning arrival from the hotel. The plane was crowded, the flight uneventful. Only the landing in Frankfurt, delayed by a bomb-scare on the ground, took longer than it should have.

At the *Lufthansa* ticket desk there was a problem: no "Marbison." Checking messages, David found something. "Forwarding address. 'U.S. Embassy, Berlin.'"

"Looks like we're going to be good little boys and follow orders after all," George said. "I always had a feeling he worked for American Intelligence."

"If he does," David said, "he's the most inept agent I've ever seen. He's a lot of things, but inept's not one."

XXV

On the afternoon of 7 November, after the meeting at The Baron's estate, Colonel Krattmay, with Heinz Friederich along, took a whirlwind inspection tour of farms and other sites near and far from Berlin. They were abandoned, as expected.

He also saw to details and last-minute contacts unavailable before that. The Colonel seemed jumpy, Friederich noticed, but later returned to normal.

They traveled by helicopters, panel trucks and cars, changing vehicles every few hours. The Colonel seemed, by instinct, to find the village or town where the next vehicle was, each with registration in one of his aliases. Friederich thought it odd that his boss had not told him, but The Colonel had operated that way before.

By late evening, they were finished. They had covered hundreds of kilometres around northeastern Germany, especially southwest of Berlin.

After what Krattmay described as the "second-to-last chore," he took a *Transit road* exit, south of *Leipzig*, heading toward *Weimar*, then to secondary and tertiary roads. From one of these he eventually turned the truck onto a slushy, mud-and-dirt road, leading into an evergreen forest. He pulled the truck into a ravine and drove along a narrow trench. Though the mud and snow slowed them, the truck's four-wheel drive kept them from getting mired or stuck. Krattmay finally stopped the truck.

"I've got something to dump," Krattmay said. *"This is a good spot to bury it. This won't take that long."*

Krattmay handed Friederich a pick and shovel. He took a shovel himself, and, with a kerosene camping lantern, led Friederich further into the woods.

Friederich did not see any signs of human development. *"What's so important and worth this much trouble?"* he asked.

Krattmay stopped in a space between two tall conifers. "*Dig a nice big hole. I need to go back to the truck.*"

The glow of the lamp turned the snow and ice bright silver and glass sculpturesque. It was harder than Friederich expected, with an ice-coating, like the tundra's perma-frost. Whatever his boss wanted to bury, it must have already been in the truck.

After fifteen minutes, the Colonel had not returned. Friederich thought about looking for him, but kept digging. The hole was already over a meter deep. He heard branches rustling and footsteps.

"*Colonel?*" he called. There was no answer. He called again.

"*Yes, Captain?*" Krattmay asked, from the darkness to Friederich's right.

Friederich sighed. "*What took so long?*"

"*I overestimated myself,*" Krattmay replied. He came into the lantern's arc. "*I might need help getting it from the truck.*"

"*How much deeper should I go?*"

"*Another meter'll do,*" Krattmay answered. "*Need a break?*" Krattmay asked. He replaced Friederich. Another half-hour passed. The hole was nearly two meters deep.

A light snow began to fall.

"*Great!*" Krattmay said, acidly, when he noticed. "*This is good enough. Help me out, will you?*" He reached out his hand. When Friederich took it, Krattmay gave a sudden tug. Friederich lost his balance and fell prone into the hole.

Friederich rolled on his back and looked up. Krattmay was silhouetted by the lantern, out of the hole now. In his right hand was an automatic pistol.

"*What . . . ?!*" Friederich said.

"*My final chore of the evening,*" Krattmay replied, coolly. "*It was obliging of you to dig your own grave.*"

Friederich said, standing up, "*Have you lost your mind? I'm with you!*"

"*With that Russian general, you mean. I've been letting you feed him what he could find out otherwise. But as neat and tidy as the present scene is, I want you out of there. I never kill a man, unless I'm eye-to-eye with him. Get up!*"

Krattmay stepped from the edge. Friederich climbed out slowly.

"*You little bastard!*" Krattmay continued. "*Of all the sleaze to sell out to. How much did they pay you?*"

"Nothing," Friederich said, his hands in the air. "*So you know! Fuck you! I was raised to hate you and your kind, you psychotic, self-hating perverts.*"

"Shut up, you little bastard!" Krattmay shouted. "*One more word, and Tripleleaf's death'll look like a mercy killing.*"

"*Generation after generation,*" Friederich jeered. "*Get rid of your grandfather, your old man percolates. Get rid of him, and you bubble up. Lots of Africa, thousands of corpses later . . .*"

"*Shut up!*" Krattmay shouted. He fired. The snow in front of Friederich popped with the slug.

Friederich lunged across the space between them. He grabbed Krattmay's pistol hand. The gun went off.

They tumbled into the hole, their arms locked together above their heads. Krattmay pulled their arms to waist level. They rolled in the mud. Friederich felt the muzzle on his hip.

The gun discharged again. Pain blasted across his right side and leg. His resistance was weakening. He struggled to push the gun away from himself.

The Colonel was smiling. "*Now I'll finish you, you little bastard!*" his hot breath hissed into Friederich's face.

That look, that arrogant smile. From somewhere outside himself arrived strength Friederich had not had before. A shocked look came over the Colonel's face.

Friederich squeezed his hands. This time he felt only the concussion and recoil from the blast. Krattmay's face was vacant. Friederich squeezed again. Krattmay's face tensed, then was blank. Friederich yanked the pistol away from the Colonel's hand and clawed his way out of the hole. His hip felt like the leg was only hanging on by its outside skin layers. There was oozing down his leg.

A dark stain was spread across Krattmay's chest. There was no steam from his nose or mouth. The Colonel's bald head, resting in the mud, had brown smears on it. Friederich could hardly believe Krattmay was dead or dying.

Friederich limped to the truck, stopping several times. There, he tore rags, and tourniquetted his hip and leg, as best he could. Fortunately, the truck was an automatic. He could drive left-legged.

He drove from the ravine, but the truck swerved, like a motorized pendulum. He remembered not seeing any farmhouses nearby. Even if there were, the Colonel's people could be there. He felt like someone was holding a branding-iron on his hip.

Hunched over the steering wheel, he tried to stay alert. He was back on hard pavement. So far, he had not seen other vehicles.

A little further, another vehicle passed him, from the opposite direction. He considered turning around, stopping it, but decided to keep going, as long as he could.

Back on the *Transit* road, he pressed as hard as he could on the accelerator. *Kilometers to go ... Colonel dead ... Bomb ... Stop the Bomb!*

"*Else,*" he murmured. If he could reach the farm near *Hof* ... *If ... Contact ... General ...*

* * *

It was evening, on 7 November, at McConneld's command center in Berlin. McConneld & Co. were working, while Channing was back at the computer center.

Marshall had been debriefed for many hours. He described the full sequence from his recruitment by The Cartel, through work in Bavaria and north Europe. On maps he localized the areas where he believed the lab, etc., were. He also related the SADM briefings. The Cartel's people were careful about their locations. Marshall recounted the bomb-arming lab and the people working with him: Europeans, mostly, with impressive physics and commercial-use expertise; the security measures to and from the lab; and the house across the border where they stayed.

After that, he detailed Cartel business over the previous decades. McConneld had always suspected elements of the U.S.

Intelligence field of being involved, but he could never prove it. Marshall's information, some of which sounded as coming from inside other agencies, confirmed those suspicions: arms and materiel, cover organizations and dummy and off-shore corporations, Third World wannabe dictators and experienced tyrants, assassinations by "special employees or contractors."

They reviewed Channing's historical records. Marshall pointed out a few dates he remembered from The Professor as significant, but they were a hodgepodge of World War I, Interwar, Nazi Era, and World War II dates.

Something The Professor told him about another date eluded him. Try as he did, he could not recall it.

"We better head south," McConneld said. "Any ideas? Harvey? Al?"

"I've been in touch with Corps HQ down there," Barsohn said. "They'll lend us troops and helicopters."

"You go clunking around, you'll spook them," Marshall said. "These guys're fast and slick. I never realized how many hiding places Germany could have, till I hooked up with them."

"Amen to that. Got a better way?" McConneld asked.

"Black-Bird flights with high-altitude radiation detectors?"

"Negative so far," Barsohn said. "But we haven't been so localized before."

"Now I remember," Marshall blurted. "The Cartel higher-ups have a fixation with 8 November. That's why they have their year-end meeting here. They call it the 'Month of Sorrows.' Before reunification, they held it on this side of the Wall or in Munich."

"If they're here themselves," Barsohn said. "That would put the kibosh on Berlin. It must be Munich."

"But remember Tom's message," McConneld said. "If it's south, what's 'triggering' what? Do we know Tripleleaf's whereabouts."

"I still think they're after my President. That's the trigger," Balkovsky said.

"And use a nuke for that?" Barsohn asked. "Even then they might not get him. And your government's reaction?"

"Harvey, what're the blast and firestorm areas on the

weapons they've got?" McConneld asked.

"Air-blast or underground?"

"Ground-level," McConneld answered.

"On the MADMs, probably blast area radii between a quarter-mile to a mile, depending on terrain, etc. Firestorm, maybe two to three. We're not dealing with Hiroshima."

"Where'd The Cartel usually meet?" McConneld asked Marshall.

"*In* Berlin, itself. These guys only go First-Class and lots of security, before they say a word," Marshall replied. "Secret, but in plain view."

McConneld had personnel check major hotels for regular conventions, especially those requiring added security, with or without the official name.

"If they were outside the city, Harvey," McConneld continued, "could they be safe from even the biggest MADM?"

"Unless there's a radiation problem," Barsohn said. "As I told you before, these are clean, with less collateral damage. They could be nearby and not get hurt."

"Berlin could still be in play?" McConneld asked Barsohn.

"Theoretically," Barsohn said. "With a coup, they'd have to be nearby."

"Any way to locate The Baron?" Marshall asked.

"He was last seen boarding a private plane at a small airport. Near *Ulm*," McConneld said. "That was three or four days ago. None near Berlin. He could be halfway to Borneo by now."

"One thing I learned about The Baron. He supervises everything, though he's buffered with plausible and complete deniability," Marshall said. "Find him, and we find the opening gambit."

"Tom Pemberton was also sighted, apparently a prisoner, at the same place," McConneld added. "But The Baron's a sacred cow with the German Government. He can do no wrong, as far as they're concerned. We need evidence on him beyond ANY doubt."

Barsohn said, "Assassinating Balkovsky's president fits with discrediting us, especially with *our* nuke."

Channing came in. "No one knows where Tripleleaf is," he said to McConneld. "He's not in Mississippi or his offices over here. Nobody's talking."

"Christ!" Marshall said, unexpectedly. "Now I got it!" He pointed at "Mr. Smith." "You're Major Balkovsky, KGB. I remember you from Laos thirty years ago. I almost popped you! Nothing personal, you understand. Orders."

"What a memory!" Balkovsky said. "Not many people knew I was in Laos."

McConneld's secretary brought in a large envelope. "A messenger delivered this, sir," she said. It was addressed to "John Marshall, c/o U. S. Embassy."

"Anybody know you're here?" he asked Marshall.

"Oh! Could it be?" Marshall said, wide-eyed. Inside was another envelope with a Berlin hotel's address and sheets of paper, signed by one "nephew."

"Get me a car?" Marshall felt more awake than he had in hours.

"We need you here," McConneld said.

"Don't be a brass lemming," Marshall said.

"Chuck, go with him," McConneld said. "We'll need Mr. Marshall when we leave for the south!"

"He'll only slow me down," Marshall snapped. "Please get me the car. I said 'please.' And two building passes."

"Absolutely not!" McConneld said. "Don't drag anybody here."

"Not just anybody," Marshall said. "It'll cost you nothing."

He drove to the Grand Hotel, where he found his "nephews," in Room 817.

"It's about time you guys caught up," Marshall said. "I've arranged for you to come to the Embassy with me."

"We were afraid you were dead," David said.

"I'm sure you were broken up about that," Marshall said, nodding at George.

"Actually," George answered, "it would've upset my partner, so I cared. At least we know your real name now. That is, maybe we do."

"It's my name," Marshall said.

"Where'd you get that code name?" George asked.

"Later," Marshall said. "I promised a man I wouldn't be long."

* * *

Channing hung up the receiver. "Marshall's at Reception with two guys."

"Bring them up yourself, Chuck," McConneld said.

Channing returned to McConneld's private office with Marshall. He left the other two in the hall with a Marine guard.

"You didn't have to bring the muscle," Marshall said. "They ain't gonna steal the hallway. I'll vouch for them."

"And who vouches for you?" McConneld asked.

"You," Marshall snapped back. He detailed his work with them, the places they discovered, omitting affiliation.

"Bottom line, shall we?" McConneld said. "Who do they work for?"

"In the introductions," Marshall said. "We wouldn't want them to see the Big Board. Not yet, anyway."

Marshall brought in the men. "This is David Arad," Marshall said, "and George Cohn, of the *Mossad*."

"I figured," McConneld said. "Otherwise, you'd be at Reception. Now that you're here, I'll ask you to stay."

"No problem," David replied. "You'll want us checked out."

"We're also here on a job," George interrupted. "One of our people was murdered a few days ago."

"I saw that in a report," McConneld said. "German Intelligence and the police are working on it."

"We like to do things ourselves," George said.

"Don't mind George," Marshall said to McConneld. "He's naturally obnoxious, but he grows on you after a while."

"Did your report mention," George continued, "our man was greased after infiltrating a secret Nazi organization here in Berlin?"

"The report didn't," McConneld replied, "but I pursued. If you'll excuse me, I've got something to take care of. Chuck, entertain our guests, till I get back."

An hour later McConneld returned. "Messrs. Arad and Cohn're squeaky clean," he declared. "I'm told you're reliable, dedicated, friendly, courteous, kind. You caught us on our way south.

"Chuck, I want you to stay here," McConneld continued.

"Coordinate things. You coming, Al?"

"I'd love to," Balkovsky said. "I've got a few errands first, though, with our people on the presidential party."

* * *

At his out-of-the-way hotel, Balkovsky received a message, from his connection on the president's security team. In imperative code, it instructed Balkovsky to meet the sender at a small restaurant in the eastern suburbs of the city.

In workmen's overalls, he left by the hotel's service entrance and took the *S-* and *U-Bahns,* cabs, and finally rented a car, before reaching the meet. He trusted McConneld, but not all U.S. Intelligence. As for German counter-intelligence, he was sure he already disclosed his presence to them, by trips to McConneld's office. This journey had to be different.

The restaurant was in an older, greyish building, probably a private home or small apartment house, before it was graced with standard, commercial German cuisine. His security contact was finishing a dinner of *Bratwurst,* potatoes, and *sauerkraut.* He was a grey little man, a piece of *déja vu* from the Soviet past.

"You're late," the contact said, in German, through a mouthful of sauerkraut. *"You've got a date in Hof."* A message had arrived from Balkovsky's relocated agent.

"How? You're not in the circuit."

"Extraordinary times," the contact said. *"It sounded urgent. I hope it still is."*

"I'll need to see the president, when I return," Balkovsky said. He ducked into the WC, where he lost the overalls. He left the restaurant by the kitchen entrance.

From Berlin he headed on a *Transit* road south. In the vicinity of *Dessau,* a city about one hundred kilometres southwest of Berlin, there was a major backup due to a large traffic accident. After an hour covered only five kilometres, Balkovsky continued on a secondary road. This, too, was crowded, by other escapees from the *Transit* road traffic jam.

* * *

McConneld & Co., minus Channing, left Berlin around 8 P.M. by helicopter. Balkovsky could catch up, or wait in Berlin, though McConneld doubted his colleague ever loitered or lingered anywhere.

At another airbase near *Frankfurt*, they were joined by their ground-troop assistance. Rangers, Special Forces, and other elite troops were assigned, under Colonel Barsohn's overall command. Barsohn briefed the unit commanders, as Marshall described the region to be covered.

He, McConneld, and Barsohn divided the Lake Constance region into 12 sectors. Helicopters with sensor equipment and troops were assigned to each. Gunships would escort troop carriers to any position, requiring a closer recon. They would also be on call, if any position needed "softening up" before troops landed.

Barsohn specially requested heat and radiation sensing equipment. Recon ships would do wide sweeps of their assigned sectors, to detect any of the bombs' core materials, before ground searches were under way.

When the expedition was complete, McConneld et al. continued southwest, in the general direction of Lake Constance. There were separate flights, with different initial headings, to mask what it was: an air-assault, in-being.

Marshall was concerned about the "congestion." "I hope you don't spook them," he said to McConneld. "If the eighth's the day, they're in transit."

Within an hour-and-a-half sweeps of a fifty-kilometer arc of the northern shore of Lake Constance were underway. McConneld and Barsohn decided not to set roadblocks. Barsohn had arranged higher-altitude aircraft recon and oversight, with sensing equipment for anything escaping the area.

As it was, McConneld knew he could conceal these activities from the Germans for only a short time. Then, the Germans would protest not being consulted or involved. If he found some or all bombs, the German protests would be hollow. If not, most operations were a mixture of luck, percentages, and conjectures. Still, he could also not afford to break his deal with Balkovsky. The Russian had the best chance of providing further info on the enemy's plans or the whereabouts of the bombs.

* * *

The detours cost Balkovsky more hours. Along the secondary roads there were also Federal Police and *Heimatschutz* roadblocks.

Balkovsky used the U.S. identification McConneld gave him to get through them, almost as easily as his old KGB i.d. did during the days of the East German regime.

Back on the *Transit* road northeast of Leipzig, Balkovsky was slowed by more traffic delays and roadblocks. At one stop, by flare, he saw bombed-out vehicles: cars and a trailer lorry. As he passed the exits for Leipzig, he glanced at his watch. It was after 1 A.M. Leipzig was only the halfway point between Berlin and *Hof*. Further away from Leipzig, the roadblocks were more intermittent. But there were more traffic slowdowns and accidents. He did not reach *Hof* until 3 A.M.

He made one short stop, before heading to the farm. There he picked up a 9mm automatic pistol and ammunition from another of his agents.

Balkovsky arrived at the farm around 5 A.M. To the side of the driveway leading to the farmhouse was a panel truck, crunched against a tree. Taking out the 9mm, he approached it. It was abandoned, with blood on the windshield, floor and seats. There was a dark stain in the snow, close to the left door. The contact Else's car was missing.

The house was dark. The backdoor was unlocked, but no one was inside. In a beer stein, prearranged as a message drop, he found a scrap of paper with only, *"Every hour,"* in German.

An hour passed. The sun was rising over the white, snowy field in front of the house. At the stroke of 7 A.M. the telephone burped its twin-sized rings. It was Else.

She was at a hospital in *Bayreuth*, about 45 kilometers, southwest of *Hof*. She had taken his "nephew" there.

He had been seriously wounded and lost a lot of blood. She hoped the *"message on"* Balkovsky's *"answering machine found you well."* The latter phrase meant he should come immediately.

Balkovsky took the *Autobahn* to *Bayreuth*. He reached the hospital after 9 A.M., as there were more roadblocks. From offhand conversation with Federal police and *Heimatschutz* personnel, he learned there had been terrorist activity in and around *Bayreuth* within the past three days.

Else was waiting for him in the main lobby. Her usually lustrous eyes were underlined in natural gray and fatigue. She was pale and had no makeup on.

"He suffered a head injury," she told Balkovsky. "He's lost much blood. His hip and thigh are shattered. He might lose the leg. The blood loss alone could have killed him. They thought it best to isolate him."

Her cover story was that, while Heinz was visiting her, a crazy foreign man came to the farm and held them at gunpoint. He seemed on-the-run. Heinz fought him for his gun. It went off. He pistol-whipped Heinz, after he got the better of him.

"The hospital staff called the police," she continued. "They're upstairs, outside Heinz's room, waiting to talk to him."

"I hope they don't see the farm."

"They want a description of the gunman. This is what I gave them." She handed Balkovsky a slip of paper with phrases on it.

"If he talks to you, before me, get those to him. I was hoping he wouldn't wake up before I could tell him."

"Any idea what he wanted to tell me?"

"Only fragments at best. Bombing, the Colonel dead... Berlin. Something about a general."

"Me?"

"I don't think so."

Else led Balkovsky to Friederich's room on the fourth floor. Uniformed *Bayreuth* policemen and two detectives were there.

She introduced Balkovsky as Friederich's "Uncle *Willi*." Balkovsky spoke in Eastern German dialect and produced corroborating German identification, forged, he brought with him from Moscow.

The police detectives asked about Balkovsky's background, his relationship with his "nephew." They were curious about how he discovered the injury and arrived so quickly.

Else explained "Uncle Willi" was an old friend of hers, too.

They seemed satisfied, but still wanted to talk with Friederich.

The on-duty physician told them there was no change in Friederich's condition. Balkovsky asked to see his "nephew." Though cautious, she did not see harm from a short, quiet visit by a relative and a close friend. The detectives asked to be present.

"There's time for that later," she replied. *"Let the uncle see him first."*

Balkovsky found Friederich, with his head bandaged, a "tent" around his side, and intravenous tubes attached to him. His face had been beaten.

Friederich unexpectedly opened his eyes and grabbed Balkovsky's arm. His glance was distant, but alert. He pulled Balkovsky closer, with surprising strength.

Balkovsky stooped over, close to his face. *"Thought you were incommunicado, Comrade."*

"No time...Colonel's dead," Friederich said, shallow-breathed. *"Bomb...Set...Go off..."* Friederich closed his eyes, his grip weakened for a moment, but he pulled Balkovsky back.

"8th...Berlin...Berlin...Reichs," he gasped. *"Reichstag..."*

Balkovsky was excited. He held Friederich's shoulders. *"Today!? In the Reichstag Building?"* he whispered. Friederich nodded, slowly.

"When?! When's the bomb set to explode?!" Friederich did not answer. *"What time?!!"* Balkovsky leaned closer. *"What time?!"* Friederich had passed out.

"I'll try to awaken him," Else said. She sat beside Friederich and spoke gently to him. She patted his cheeks. He did not stir.

Finally, reluctantly, she slapped him hard. Again. And a third time. He moaned. She spoke to him. His eyes opened.

"Can you hear me?" Balkovsky asked. Friederich nodded.

"What time's the bomb due to go off?" he asked, slowly.

"Fifteen...Hundred...Hours," Friederich whispered. *"Stop!...Please...Stop them!"*

"Where did they put it?"

"Im..." Friederich closed his eyes.

"Where?" Balkovsky repeated, quietly.

"Im...Heizraum...Kessel..."

Else told Friederich the cover-story. After that, Friederich fell asleep.

"*He probably won't remember,*" Balkovsky said to her. "*How did his head get shaved?*"

Else shrugged. "*During the operation?*"

Outside, Balkovsky and she excused themselves with the police, claiming to return shortly.

Balkovsky offered to drive Else back to the farm. On the road, he thought out loud. "*Charter a plane . . . Get back to Berlin. Where's the nearest airport I could get a charter?*"

"*There are two of them, one northwest, the other southeast. Take your pick. They're about the same distance from here.*"

"*I'll see the president and get him back to Moscow, before . . .*"

"*Aren't you going to try to stop it?*"

"*No,*" Balkovsky replied. He was composed.

"*General, you can't be serious,*" Else said. "*You can't let this happen.*"

"*We'll make sure this time. Lay waste to the place,*" Balkovsky said. "*Break Germany up and keep it under control. The bastards have to pay.*"

"*But millions will die!*" Else said, pleadingly, "*on both sides. That's not why I worked for you, to be an accomplice to mass murder!*"

"*Don't be overly dramatic,*" Balkovsky said. "*You're a professional. You follow orders, no matter how distasteful or ugly.*"

"*Even professionals need reasons to believe,*" Else replied. "*I'm no mercenary. The past's dead. So are the people you're talking about. Let the dead rest. We've got the future to worry about.*"

"*I am. I don't want them to happen again.*"

"*If you stop this . . .*"

"*It's only a matter of time, before they try again. They're on the rise. If they don't succeed now, they'll be back. But if we let them think they've won, then crush them . . .*"

"*That's not the future I want. You have the power to prevent it. YOU have that power.*"

"*I've been too far, to change now . . .*"

"*I've got a confession. I've loved you* all *the time I've worked for you,*" Else said. Balkovsky was startled.

"Yes, I knew before this operation," Else said. *"Should I apologize? ... You're no mass murderer. Nor an accomplice to murder. You've short-circuited Fascism and the Right your whole career. Don't become one of them, hateful and murderous."*

"I'm under orders. I'll try, of course, but, if I fail, so much the better."

"You mustn't fail," Else said, *"because I love you."* She kissed him, hard and deep. *"I don't even care you're married."*

"You don't know me," Balkovsky said, pushing her away. *"You can't possibly know me, let alone love me ... "*

"Go ahead, then, with your hatred, bitterness," Else said. *"Throw me away. And the future. You know how Heinz feels."*

"Heinz is my agent," Balkovsky said. *"He doesn't get paid to think, or feel."*

"He's more than your agent," Else answered. *"He's your son, if not a legitimate one."*

"Christ! Is there anything you don't know about me?! How about my underwear size?!"

"In Russian or Western European sizes? You're partial to French shorts."

Balkovsky turned more ruddy than usual. His ears blazed at the tips. *"This is our chance to keep them down for generations."*

"At what cost? Your son? Me? I'll go to the Germans myself and expose you. I'll tell them everything."

"You don't know enough to hurt us," Balkovsky said.

"They'll have you, an accessory before and after the fact."

"I can't let go. I'm too close. And you won't say a word to anyone." He took a dart gun from his inside pocket and shot her. She was quickly unconscious, lying against the car door.

"It'll be a whole new world, when you awaken, my dear ... Sorry, Son. For your Grandpapa," he whispered.

* * *

0600. Southwestern Germany. First light was not far off. McConneld & Co. were in a helicopter, near the western end of Lake Constance. They were on their way to a mobile command post in a field near the lake shore.

"That's a roger, Big Duke," Barsohn said, over his headset. "Bogey in Sector 6 was negative," he said to McConneld.

"You're sure it wasn't across the lake?" McConneld asked Marshall. "In Switzerland?"

"There weren't any checkpoints when they first brought me in," Marshall said. "Only after we went back and forth to the safe-house."

"We picked up their trail, ourselves, a while back," David said to McConneld. He described his and George's reconnaissance of General Tripleleaf's Swiss estate. "Undeniably trace radioactivity."

"We're not going to find them," Marshall said. "In daylight, we'll be a little obvious."

"Call it 'maneuvers,' and keep going," Barsohn snapped. "EOD does it all the time."

"Give it another five or six hours," McConneld said. "If we haven't heard from 'Mr. Smith,' I'll head back to Berlin. Harvey, keep on here, till you hear from me. Marshall, you and your friends're free to stay or come back with me."

"If it's all the same to you," Marshall said. "I never had much affection for that lake anyhow. In the meantime, let's try one lead, a certain fisherman, who saved my ass." He gave Barsohn the general location of Liebman's boat. "Pass me that nightscope, would you?"

Fifteen minutes later Marshall spotted a boat, sitting at anchor near *Hagnaua*. The chopper radioed, confirming it was Liebman's. With the chopper hovering, Marshall was lowered by rope. The old man was on deck.

Marshall arranged for Liebman to lead them to the vicinity of Krattmay's safe-house and stayed aboard during the crossing. The chopper haunted the boat like a moon shadow on its wake.

Liebman showed Marshall where he and his son plucked him from the water. Not long after that, Marshall thought he identified the dock, from which he was loaded onto the speedboat.

The sun was up over the lake by then. By the time the chopper set down on the Swiss shore and Marshall rejoined McConneld and the others, with Liebman in tow, it was after 8:30 A.M.

After locating the house, McConneld had the pilot land the aircraft a few kilometers away.

"What about the Swiss authorities?" Marshall asked.

"No time," McConneld said. "We'll be finished when they would have arrived."

Colonel Barsohn called in units. The air cavalry was on the way.

* * *

Sam woke to the sounds of German early-morning TV. She had passed out on a couch in the living room and was numb as to how many days she had been at the house. Each was more deadening than its predecessor. In the kitchen for a glass of iced tea, Sam glanced at a wall calendar. *It must be the 8th. 8 A.M. on the 8th*, she thought, sipping her tea.

Two days had crawled by since Liz's First Commandment. Sam committed only one sin against it, a walk around the neighborhood the previous day.

She was being unbelievably good. It was sickening how good, she thought. Until this adventure, that had been her role, the good girl, *"la mademoiselle,"* the steady daughter, the big sister, the obedient little sister.

But after the transatlantic leap, that changed: an extended period of brash, sauce, and naughtiness. This quasi-pseudo-forced house sitting was a throwback to her old *persona*. Damn Liz for reinstating domestication.

Time to reassert that rebellion, that independence. She would renew memories, plant seeds for new ones. The weather was encouraging the break from cabin fever.

She changed clothes, to an unwrinkled skirt and blouse and the sweater she already had been wearing. Another errand, the dry cleaner's, either that or pull out the American Express cards and switch to shopping-mode. They were not mutually exclusive. She would do both.

Sam walked to the *Turmstrasse U-Bahn* station. From there she rode the subway to *Zoologischer Garten*, then changed for the *Wilmersdorf-Ku'damm* stop. Though during the Berlin equivalent of rush-hour, her trip did not take long. Even under democracy, the Germans knew how to make the trains run on time.

XXVI

In cover near the house to which Liebman led them, were McConneld & Co., and three twenty-five-man squads of U.S. Rangers. The property bordered the lake, with access by road. The house was a grey-stone, provincial structure, with large windows and doors. Straggling smoke dribbled from its chimneys.

Marshall recognized it. It was closer to the water than he thought. His captors could have marched him to the dock. "Lazy bastards," he laughed.

"Alpha and George, in position," Colonel Barsohn's radioman said, softly. "All's quiet. Bravo's got the boat dock covered. All boats disabled."

"Call the road-detach," Barsohn said. "Alert us to any new arrivals . . . Order to Alpha and George, move in."

The U.S. troops did cover-infiltration to the house, like an urban SWAT team expecting snipers. The house showed no signs of lights or life. McConneld and the others followed, with Barsohn and his radioman, leading.

Crouched, the radioman listened to his head-set. "Inside, ground floor, sir," he said. "No hostiles encountered." The ground floor and cellar were secure, entry to the second and third floors in progress. From troops who reached the attic, the radioman received a concluding message: All secure, no one found.

McConneld and the others rushed in. Soldiers were doing a full search. The fireplaces were piled with smoldering ash and debris, contents not fully burned, but singed or blackened.

"We got the right place," Marshall said, seeing the mess the troops made.

A sergeant brought Barsohn something. "Sir, my guy found this in a bathroom." It was a crumpled American Express receipt from an establishment in *Ahrensdorf.* Though smudged and faded, he read the date as 6 or 7 November. The name seemed to be "Audran Arnold."

He called McConneld over. "Where the hell is *Ahrensdorf*? Somebody bring me a map."

"Looks like a seven to me." McConneld repeated the name. "That name rings a bell."

An aide to the operational commander brought a laptop computer. He typed *Ahrensdorf* in and waited. A map of Germany appeared on the screen, followed by a side-bar with village names.

McConneld said, "Harvey, I need a com-link with Channing."

To the operational commander Barsohn said, "Call Green-4. It's got a mini-sat, doesn't it?"

A UH-53 helicopter landed. Soldiers from it set up a small satellite communications station in the snow. McConneld soon had one answer from Channing in Berlin. The name was an alias.

"That bastard again!" McConneld said. "That gives us confirmation of his whereabouts. What day did he take you?" he asked Marshall.

"After briefings," Marshall said. "Time ran together. Probably the fifth."

Finally, Channing had a second answer. It was a roadhouse inn in a village twenty-five kilometers south of Berlin. McConneld ordered agents there at once.

"Berlin *is* the place," McConneld said. "We've got to get back there now. Harvey? Marshall?" Both men joined him.

The UH-53 ferried them to a Huey transport helicopter. En route, McConneld received another message from Channing. Preliminary investigations with the roadhouse staff indicated "Audran Arnold" was a "bushy-haired Englishman," with a British passport. He checked in, in the very-late-hours of 6 or 7 November and left a few hours later.

"Not twelve hours ago," McConneld said to Barsohn. "Can't this thing go any faster?" Barsohn asked for an ETA from the pilot: 1345 Hours.

* * *

General Balkovsky arrived in Berlin after 11 A.M. by chartered plane, with a sleeping Else along. The drug he used on her could last till late afternoon.

At *Tegel* Airport, he caught a cab to one of his safe-houses. There, he bound and gagged her, before heading to his embassy, to meet with the president. He planned to collect her after that.

He phoned for the meeting, prior to leaving. Another taxi trip, interspersed with cab changes, and he was at the embassy residence.

The President was a late riser. This was a particularly late sleep-in, after a long night-and-morning of state-carousing with German officials. Dressed in a bathrobe, he joined Balkovsky in the state-visitors' suite. The President poured himself a drink, downed it, and poured another.

"Mr. President," Balkovsky said, impatiently. "*I've discovered an assassination plot on your life.*"

"*Evidence?*" the President asked, sternly. Balkovsky told him about Friederich. "*Solely against me?*"

"*Not solely, but you're an integral part of the plan.*"

"*I've heard things about you, General.*" The President poured Balkovsky a drink, "*Looking for Nazis under every bed.*"

"*You've talked to Minister Torychenko,*" Balkovsky replied.

"*Before I left Moscow, he recommended relieving you of this assignment.*"

"*What grounds? Incompetence?*"

"*Too much competence. Overzeal. Something like that.*"

"*The Minister's a friend. Friends disagree,*" Balkovsky said. "*The organization behind it is an executive/covert operations branch, with the 'Association of International Industrialists, Executives, and Entrepreneurs.'*"

The President interrupted. "*My unfavorite capitalists.*"

"*The Minister told me our dealings with The Cartel were winding down. He's concerned our government's been infiltrated by both organizations.*"

"*Where're you going with this, General? Picture, please.*"

"*I recommend you return home. Immediately. Urgently,*" Balkovsky said.

"*I'm good at knowing when someone's bluffing—or lying. Whatever these people are planning, you* will *prevent it. I don't care what it takes.*

"I don't run from a fight, General, even when the tanks come out. I'm not running now." The President emptied his glass. "The Chancellor's a proud man, but he honours a debt. We'll accrue this for later. With this Chechnya nonsense, we couldn't deal with a military threat anyhow. If you'll excuse me, General. I've got to get over a Tsar-sized hangover before my speech."

Balkovsky melded into an exiting maintenance crew, on lunch break, 11:50 A.M. At a busy lunchroom-cafeteria blocks from the residence, he broke away, when the group queued up.

As he made his way through the lunch crowds on the streets, his mood turned angry, ambivalent, uncertain. He needed time.

Get to the airport in time... Prevent the explosion... Get back to Moscow. Perhaps, the president was expendable. Pick up Else. Call McConnell... Go back to *Bayreuth,* pick up Heinz. Would his spouse like to meet a new, old member of the family? So much to do. Or *not* do. And so little time to decide.

* * *

A busy morning of *Wunder*-shopping was at its climax, as Sam had tea in a café on one of the commercial tributaries of the *Ku'damm*. The *Wilmersdorferstrasse* was next with its clothes, shoes, and perfume. On *Fasanenstrasse* she browsed upscale shops and antique stores.

Nice to forget the mess, if only for a few hours. Sam decided to bring her goodies back to the safe-house, before retrieving her father's Berlin cache. It was the only one, whose location she remembered by heart. What if Liz were at the house? Wing it.

Passing a newsstand, she saw front-pages, announcing the Russian President's address to the *Reichstag* that afternoon. A chance to see him in person! Even a glimpse! After her father's stories, the Russian intrigued her.

In the windows of an electronics and camera store, the VCRs' consensus was between five and ten minutes after noon. Not enough time, she would go straight to the *Reichstag*. She bought a decent pair of binoculars, first.

Catching a bus to *Bahnhof-Zoo*, Sam placed her new clothes

in a suitcase-sized pay locker. She transferred to a #100 bus, which ran up *Die Strasse des 17. Juni* and *Unter Den Linden* to *Alexanderplatz,* past the *Brandenburger Tor* and the *Reichstag.*

Sam got off at *Ebertstrasse* and the *Pariser Platz.* It was only a few blocks' walk north from the *Brandenburger Tor* to the parliament building. This day there were police barricades, preventing motor traffic. Large crowds were milling around, on and off the sidewalks.

Another block away, barricades cordoned the crowds from the *Reichstag* grounds. The building was usually open for tours, even permanent historical exhibits. She walked the southern periphery of the police lines. The radius included the *Platz der Republik* and other green-spaces, surrounding the *Reichstag*'s own block. The Germans weren't taking chances with this guy's life, Sam thought.

Sam reached the metal rails of the barricades. Uniformed police and other, camouflage-dressed troops patrolled the lines.

The binoculars made her feel claustrophobic with the *Reichstag*, close enough to see faces. She hoped the Russian President would enter that way.

*   *   *

The lunch crowds were in full swirl around Balkovsky. The north German cold did not reduce the number of people on the streets. Almost like an American city ... Or a Russian one.

He imagined the aftermath of the mushroom. BLAST. FIRESTORM. RADIATION. Most of these people dead or dying.

Many seemed too young to have known the War. His father's War, really. But one casualty in it made it HIS WAR. The Bastards. Been fighting, hating them for that. Till The Wall came down. Not his wall. Mortar, cold stone, the slabs in his wall were intact.

The President changed that. Ordered him to tear his wall down. Stripped him defenseless.

Was there strength in vulnerability? The President sought invulnerability, too. The Chancellor's savior.

He wanted Balkovsky to be Germany's savior. Of all countries! Them owing their lives to him! They owed their freedom to his father and other Russian soldiers, dead and alive, though that was hard for them to accept.

What delicious and ironic revenge! Them owing their futures to him. Play on their guilt for another generation! Perhaps the person-on-the-street would not know it. But his or her leaders would!

It was too irresistible! He would follow orders. Time to find McConneld. *Else.* He would release her after it was disarmed and make it up to her.

12:30 P.M. The President was due to speak in an hour or two. Balkovsky caught a cab to the U.S. Embassy.

From Reception, he had Channing called. Channing brought him upstairs. "Where're McConneld and the others?" Balkovsky said, quietly to Channing, on the way.

"Still down south," Channing replied.

"Get him back now!" Balkovsky said. "I know where the bomb is and when it's set to go off!" Balkovsky told him what Friederich had said.

"I think I know what Tom Pemberton meant," Channing said.

*   *   *

"Roger!" the crewman said into the mini-microphone of his headset. "Sir? Emergency message from ComCen, Berlin."

Barsohn took the crewman's headset, and listened. "Holy Shit!" Barsohn said. He ordered the pilot to head for *Rhein-Main* airbase.

"Your Russian friend came through," he said to McConneld, then relayed the message. "We'll change aircraft and take EOD. I'll arrange for advance teams."

"Christ!!" McConneld said. "If EOD can't disarm in time?!"

"A C-130'll stand by to carry it the hell away," Barsohn said.

"So much for the test ban treaty," Marshall said.

Barsohn spoke with Command at *Rhein-Main* airbase, requesting three C-130 transport planes for them, along with EOD teams. He requested other EOD teams be dispatched directly to Berlin.

"Will you tell the Germans?" Barsohn asked McConneld. "Or do you want me to?"

"I'll do it," McConneld said. "Patch through to Channing and Berlin."

Barsohn had the pilot reestablish contact with ComCen, Berlin and asked for their ETA at *Rhein-Main*. The pilot expected to be there within fifteen minutes.

McConneld had a conference call with Channing and high-ranking German officials. He described his plan. He was informed there were already barricades around the grounds. He told them to pretext it as a drill or conventional bomb scare.

He advised against their moving the bomb, even if they found it before he or EOD's arrived. Both Barsohn and Marshall said it probably was booby-trapped.

He listened. "Get him out! . . . What?! . . . Shit!"

"Get who out?" Marshall asked.

"Balkovsky's President. He's there to give a speech."

On approach into *Rhein-Main* another call came from Berlin. It was Channing and a German official on another conference call.

The Russian had been informed. He told his hosts his future and the *Reichstag*'s were intertwined, irretrievably, "Like their nations."

"What a time for a case of the Stupids!" Marshall said.

At *Rhein-Main,* McConneld and the others met EOD teams, fully equipped and loaded. Other teams were already en route. The switch to a C-130 took a very few minutes. They were back in the air and on the way to Berlin, with prearranged landing clearance for *Tempelhof.*

* * *

Outside the *Reichstag,* Sam was impatient. The November cold was sharp. The police and the peripheral guards announced by loudspeakers that the crowds had to move back and disperse. The Russian President had cancelled his speech. People near Sam refused to leave, but the approach of a squad of troops, armed with assault rifles, convinced them to vacate.

The crowds gave way on the *Ebertstrasse*. A small convoy of U.S. Army vehicles drove toward the barricades. They slowed, as the police opened the obstacles, and continued to the *Reichstag's* rear entrance.

Sam drifted down the *Ebertstrasse,* with the crowd. For thirty yards from the police line were different utility trucks, gas, water/sewer, electrical repair and maintenance. Men working seemed unperturbed by the mass, mess, and chaos around them.

Several manholes were opened. Makeshift enclosures at street level covered them. Crewmen lingered nearby or at the trucks.

From many yards away, Sam casually glanced at a crew from the Sewer and Water Department. Beside one of the trucks she saw a face that caused her to stop suddenly. Dressed in overalls and a European-style worker's jacket, he took off his hardhat to mop his brow. He was bald.

But his face. The Face. From the photographs. From the dream. She tried to get a longer look at him with the binoculars. As quickly as she focused, he had disappeared and did not reemerge. More people pushed past her. The police were hustling the crowds farther from the vicinity of the *Reichstag*.

The police and troops were setting up barricades along the curbs on the *Ebertstrasse,* south of the original ones. Sam got caught in the rush and was pulled another block down *Ebertstrasse*. She tried to break free, but the human suction was too much for her.

Finally, at the *Brandenburger Tor*, she was spewed from the horde. She tried to return up *Ebertstrasse*. The crowds were wave-like and too tall for her to get another look.

She crossed back and lingered at the western side of the *Tor*. Crowds seemed to be drifting toward the Russian embassy, on the next block, beyond the *Pariser Platz*.

Even on an emotional repast the mental ghosts haunted. Was it The Face? At the airfield? Or transference? Back to Freud with dreams and wishes? This time a daylight, urban mirage? She would never know, if the ghost-in-the-dream and the workman were one.

* * *

The flight into *Tempelhof* took over an hour, with congestion over Berlin, despite the priority clearance. McConneld & Co. were met by Channing, Balkovsky, and German civilian and military officials in Mercedes limousines and sedans.

The EOD teams followed in camouflage-painted trucks and HMMWVs. It was a short ride from *Tempelhof* to the *Reichstag*.

Marshall took a front seat in the limo carrying McConneld, Barsohn, and some of the Germans. The convoy headed north on the *Mehrings Damm*, bearing left onto *Stresemannstrasse,* then right onto the *Ebertstrasse.*

On the final leg of the drive, Marshall watched the crowds. The multitude of faces reminded him of Ezra Pound's "petals on a wet, black bough."

Near the Brandenburg Gate, Marshall seized a glimpse, like a super-fast shutter speed, of a blonde woman, standing at a barricade. Familiar. Could it be? "Pull over!" he said to the driver.

The driver veered to the curb and waved the vehicles behind them on.

"What the hell're you doing?!" McConneld asked.

Marshall jumped from the passenger door, as the car was rolling to a stop. *"GO!"* he yelled, as he slammed the car door. The limousine sped away.

Marshall jogged along the crowd, back toward the Gate. He ducked under a barricade and melded into the crowd, fighting his way along the sidewalk.

He came up behind what he thought was the same blonde woman. Up close, he tapped her on the shoulder. She looked back at him, with annoyance.

"Oh, shit!" She turned quickly away.

"Sam?!!!" Marshall yelled. "What the hell?"

She did not answer. Instead, she pushed her way along the barrier.

Marshall hopped the railing and trotted, until he was beside her again. Grabbing her by the shoulder, he turned her around.

"What the hell are *you* doing here?!!!"

"Leave me alone!" she said in German. *"I don't know you!"*

A policeman came over. *"Is this man bothering you,*

Fräulein?" he asked.

"*Yes,*" she answered.

The officer reached for Marshall's elbow. Marshall pulled out identification McConneld had given him, before they left for Lake Constance.

"I'm with that convoy that just went through," Marshall said. "This woman's wanted in connection with an ongoing investigation. You understand? I need to take her with me."

"Sorry to have interfered, *mein Herr.* Anything I can do to help?" the officer asked, handing Marshall the i.d.

"I'll take it from here," Marshall said, clutching Sam's arm again. "Up the pavement, if you don't mind?"

The policeman ushered them along the first twenty yards, across the street. They were now on the *Reichstag* side.

Marshall waved him off, dragging Sam from the *Ebertstrasse*. They stopped near the Soviet war memorial and its park. "That was a shitty little trick! Now, why are you here?!"

"You don't have much imagination, do you?!" she replied.

"Your old man," Marshall bellowed. "This ain't no joyride!"

"I don't know why people say you're stupid," Sam said.

"I'm telling you," Marshall said. "Get your ass the fuck over to *Tegel* and get you and it on the next plane out of here! You've got to!"

"I'm not going!"

"I don't have time to mess with you!" he said. He lowered his voice and spoke into her ear. "This whole fucking city could be gone by three! Vaporized! Fire-stormed!"

"Bombed?!" she asked, excitedly.

"That's putting it mildly," he said. "If you don't go now, I'll take you with me. Even in all this, McConneld would find time to send you to the States under armed guard. At least you'd be away from here."

"Oh, God! You do care!" Sam exclaimed.

"Right," Marshall said. "We'll tell our kids we met at a nuclear bombing. Love at first blast. Your old man would never forgive me if I let you be immolated by a nuke."

She kissed him on the lips. "But where'll I go?"

He held her away from him. "I don't have time for this. Anywhere but here! Paris's great!" He jogged her to a street and flagged a cab.

"How shall I find you, after this blows over?" Sam said. "Let me rephrase that... If you make it?... I mean..."

"U.S. Embassy, Berlin, Room 404. Give them Ext. 429M," Marshall said to Sam, before shoving her into the taxi. "*Flughafen Tegel! Am schnellsten!*" he said to the driver, throwing him a 100-Euro bill.

On his way to the *Reichstag*, Marshall found the same officer as before. He helped Marshall through the police lines. Security men stopped Marshall, as he and the officer reached the building. After Marshall handed his i.d. to them, they took him to the rear entrance.

Squads of German troops were on duty. Nearby were U.S. Army and *Bundeswehr* trucks and HMMWVs, including radioactive materials disposal vehicles.

He and Channing joined McConneld and the others in the sub-basement. EOD personnel were at work, clearing the corridors, running radiation readings, and searching.

"In the '*Heizraum, im Kessel,*'" Balkovsky said to McConneld.

"The furnace room's down this hall," a German official, in army fatigue gear, said to McConneld, in English. "Recently new furnaces were installed. The entire heating system was replaced."

The furnace room was a huge, high-ceilinged affair with a number of large, and tall, individual furnace units. An EOD crew isolated one unit, with prefabricated shielding panels.

An EOD officer spoke with Colonel Barsohn. "There are no signs of it ever being fired up," he was saying.

Marshall explained the override arrangement and the arming/detonator materials he and the physicist developed. "If I know that son-of-a-bitch, he booby-trapped the thing."

The EOD officer ordered X-ray and other examinations with portable X-ray machines, fluoroscopes, and other heat and radiation detectors. Results confirmed all but the unfired furnace were functioning according to design. The cold furnace showed a large impenetrable container inside it.

"When's this pup set to go off?" the EOD commander asked.

"Fifteen hundred hours," Balkovsky answered, quickly.

The officer said, "It's thirteen-twenty-eight now. Thirty-five minutes, max, to deactivate, and have a safety margin."

"A plane's at *Tempelhof*," Barsohn said. "Carry on."

EOD personnel used specially trained K-9s to detect plastique or similar conventional explosives. The dogs discovered no explosives around the furnace's casing. EOD men slowly removed an access door from the exterior.

Marshall panned the furnace's interior walls, until he found a large, apparently lead rectangular housing, bracketed to one wall. He shone his light for an EOD man, who preceded a dog into the chamber. The animal sniffed methodically around the interior perimeter, got up on its hind legs, and sniffed the column. Halfway up, the dog rubbed its nose and whined.

"It must be plastique," the EOD man said. "Pal's never been wrong."

Marshall discussed the situation with the EOD commander. "Ice that sucker first," Marshall said. The commander agreed.

"What've you got?" Marshall asked.

"Liquid nitrogen," the commander answered. "We pack it in a prefab enclosure. Density of the lead will slow down the freezing rate. We'll compensate."

"Get me gloves, will you?" Marshall asked. "I'll be the primary."

EOD personnel built a thermal "blanket," on the outside wall of the furnace, and a containment enclosure around the housing itself. When the "blanket" was finished, the technicians pumped liquid nitrogen through self-sealing holes, and monitored the temperature inside the "blanket."

After one minute, a technician told Marshall the exterior casing was ready. Marshall and three EOD personnel drilled out the bolts and brackets on the casing. When the last bracket was dislodged, the four men, wearing industrial strength clothing and gloves, lifted the shell from the furnace wall.

Marshall peeked behind it. He found nothing attaching the casing to what it was concealing and recognized what was before him. "Chill it out," he said to his colleagues.

They replaced the containment enclosure, sealed it, and

resumed liquid nitrogen treatment through the self-sealing holes. The temperature inside the enclosure reached several hundred degrees below 0 within another minute. Marshall used a micro-sensor to read the surface temperature of the MADM casing. It matched the enclosure's.

Marshall and the others drilled out the screws on the cover plates, with hand drills. Marshall took them off one-at-a-time.

Under the third one he handled, he found a wire assembly, detonator/electro-pack, and plastique.

"Christ!!" he said. "Here's hoping the nitrogen's slowed the electrical impulse. Two pairs of hands here on-the-double!"

The other EOD men crowded beside him. At his signal, they each, simultaneously, snipped one electrical connection between the plastique packet and the contacts on the MADM.

Marshall closed his eyes and held his breath, as they did. He detached the booby trap from the cover and handed it to an EOD man.

"Stay on your toes," Marshall said. "This bastard could've set another of these in here." He finished the remaining covers, finding no more mini-bombs or booby traps. In the meantime, the third EOD man told Marshall the plastique packet had been safely disarmed.

"So much for the easy part," Marshall said. "Get the serial number."

It was engraved on a metal strip, below one of the LED read-out panels. "The CO's relayed it," the third EOD man told Marshall. "We'll have the anti-tamperproof override code soon."

"I recognize my embroidery," Marshall said. He looked at one chronometer, frozen on "8-11-13-53-39." Another LED read, "8-11-15-00-00."

"Replace the cover, and maintain nitrogen," Marshall said.

The EOD commander ducked his head inside. "About ten more minutes," he said, "before we consider disposal by air. How're you doing?"

Marshall replied,"I may do this for a living. Doctor Nuke, at your service. Get Colonel Barsohn for me, will you?"

The commander's head disappeared. Barsohn looked in.

"Mr. OIC," Marshall said to him. "You make the call. I think I can disarm this sucker, but I'll go beyond the safety margin. We could stop now and move it to *Tempelhof*. But we'll have less than an hour's flying time."

"If the liquid nitrogen doesn't keep it suspended for an indefinite period, sir," an EOD man said. "If it does, we've got unlimited time."

"You got a Bikini Atoll in mind?" Marshall rejoined.

"The South Atlantic, sir," the EOD man replied, without hesitation.

"Or?" Barsohn asked.

"I go for broke. With these guys," Marshall said.

The EOD commander peeked his head in. "It's one of the missing weapons. I've got the code," he said. He gave the color and number sequences, for the first tamper-proof control, to Marshall.

"Go for it," Barsohn said, calmly.

Marshall and the EOD men went back to work. Marshall plugged a small, numbered key-pad into a slot beneath an LED window and three lights, colored red, green, and yellow. He punched in the code the EOD commander gave him.

The colored lights began to blink. Marshall used a thin screwdriver to push a recessed button below the lights. He tapped in a code sequence, akin to Morse Code. One by one, they went off.

"Remember, sir," one of Marshall's EOD men said. "The plug-in components in those upper compartments have to be removed in precisely the right order. One of us will have to help you. In the left side block, it should be 4-1, simultaneous, then 3, alone. Then, 2."

Marshall inhaled deeply, as he worked on the locking screws. With a sort-of "1-2-3-go," cadence, Marshall and the EOD man lifted the two components from the slots. There were wire connections to each, which also had to be detached simultaneously.

Fortunately, they were modular, like phone equipment. Marshall and his EOD assistant watched each other's speed of removal.

Marshall continued with the next. More painfully slow extraction followed. The EOD man concluded with the fourth slot.

"We're past fail-safe," Marshall heard the EOD commander say quietly from behind him.

They went on to the right compartment. "At least you guys aren't getting predictable," Marshall said, after the EOD man told him the progression. He sighed a shallow sigh, when they finished this phase.

What remained was taking out the detonator package. They had to release the eight screws in proper order. The EOD commander fed them the sequence. Marshall and his partner on the "componentectomy" alternated with the other two EOD men.

When the last screw was withdrawn from its shaft, Marshall attached hooked rods to each corner of the pack. With each man taking a rod, they pulled gently in unison. The pack began to slide out.

"Three more men in here!" Marshall yelled. "On the double!"

The EOD commander, Colonel Barsohn, and a third camouflage-fatigued figure hustled in. The new arrivals helped Marshall and the others, as they lifted it from the compartment.

"Hold it!" Marshall said, suddenly. "Wires! . . . One black, one red."

"Don't cut them!" an EOD man said, quickly. "It could cause a short! You'll have to detach, the way we did before."

"Won't the nitrogen slow that?" Marshall asked.

"Maybe," the EOD man said.

"Two guys get under it, piggy-back," Marshall said. "I need a light and the longest fucking screwdriver you've got."

Two soldiers crouched in, with tool chests. Marshall reached behind the detonator pack and into the compartment. "Shit!" Marshall said.

"Is that like 'oops!'?" Barsohn grunted, from under the pack.

"Third and fourth wires back here," Marshall said. "Any suggestions?"

"What colors?" the EOD commander asked.

"Near as I can tell," Marshall answered. "Brown or purple. And green."

"It should be green. Go green," Marshall's erstwhile EOD assistant said. "Remember, sir. You must remove those in the correct order. Otherwise, you'll detonate the device."

"You mean I'll blow us to Hell?!" Marshall asked. "You're a balm and consolation."

Marshall pushed the screwdriver into the compartment and latched the lugnut wrenchhead over the nut with the green wire. The nut was very tight, but Marshall loosened it after a few seconds. The wire slipped off.

"What's next?"

"Should be purple," came the answer from beside him.

"There's that word again, 'should.'"

"It alternates, sir. Sometimes red, sometimes purple."

"Give me a time on this, while you're at it," Marshall said to the EOD commander, as he left.

The commander returned. "My guy's right," he said. "Purple's next. Then, red. Then, black."

"Sure?"

"To be honest, records show only three colored wires on this device," the EOD commander answered.

Marshall said, "Which one didn't they have?"

"Black."

"You're assuming it's an add-on?" Marshall said. "Any possibility the sequence could be altered manually?"

"There's always a possibility," the EOD commander said, "especially with jerry-rigging like this. What're you going to do?"

"I'm assuming this bastard wouldn't be satisfied as an add-on," Marshall said. "I'm taking the black one off next."

"If you're wrong!" Colonel Barsohn interrupted.

"You called it," Marshall said. "My gut says this is it."

"That better not be indigestion you're feeling," Barsohn said.

"Time?" Marshall asked the EOD commander. "How's temperature?"

"1444 Hours. Climbing rapidly!"

Marshall went after the nut on the black-wire connection. It was looser than the first. He reached wooden forceps to the wire and slipped it off.

Nothing happened. Marshall sighed the longest sigh of his life, up to that time, as sweat poured down his face.

The others in the furnace with him gave out a loud cheer. "Let's hear it for guts!" Barsohn said.

Marshall finished with the purple and red wires. The detonation pack was now loose from the MADM.

He and three EOD men carried it to a flat-bed dolly. Marshall leaned against the wall, drained, and soaked from the inside.

McConneld & Co. congratulated him. "You age a little?" McConneld asked.

"Only three centuries or so," Marshall replied. "Anybody got some Scotch? I could use a triple!"

Colonel Barsohn ordered a full radiation and detector search of the building.

"Only nineteen to go," McConneld said. "But we found it without them."

"Back to Square One?" Balkovsky asked. "Just make sure they know *who* discovered it and saved their asses. Present company included, naturally." He sounded very New York-ish again.

"Time to face the Germans," Barsohn said. "What about The Baron, The Colonel, and their all-boy orchestra?"

"One's dead," Balkovsky said. He told them Friederich's story.

"Shit!!" Marshall said. "I wanted to cap him myself!"

"Join the club and get in line. When?" McConneld asked.

"Within the past twelve to eighteen hours," Balkovsky said.

"Either way," McConneld said. "No direct link with von Markenheim. The Germans will never buy it. We'll have to establish a connection ourselves. And right now, there's only one man who can do that."

Word came from the Chancellor that he wanted to see Marshall and the others right away. Aides escorted them to his office suite.

This was the first time Marshall had seen the German Chancellor, close up. Through his interpreter, the Chancellor asked for the man who defused the bomb. Looking obviously relieved and cautiously ebullient, the Chancellor hugged Marshall tightly.

"*I never thought you were this emotional,*" Marshall said to the Chancellor in German.

Balkovsky whispered to Marshall, "Tell him who found the location."

McConneld quickly told the Chancellor about the Russian's

role. The Chancellor seemed happily surprised at a Russian's involvement, adding, "*I thought this was an American monopoly!*"

At his order, his aides arranged for champagne and lunch. Flanked by security guards, caterers arrived with, poured and distributed the first round of champagne.

The German leader toasted McConneld, Marshall, and Balkovsky. Then, everyone tossed his glass into a large, nearby stone fireplace. Another round was distributed.

"*Thank my President, too, when you see him,*" Balkovsky said, after the second round was gone.

Several rounds of toasts later, the Chancellor's mood turned surprisingly somber. He asked McConneld about progress on recovering the remaining weapons.

"*We're real close,*" McConneld assured him.

"*You have access to me. Whatever you need, just ask,*" the Chancellor said. "*Do you know who the culprits were?*"

"*We do,*" McConneld said, "*though we're not prepared to disclose yet. We're putting an air-tight case together. But I'd recommend that the truth of today be kept secret. The press and the public must never discover what happened today.*"

"*Agreed,*" the Chancellor replied.

*　　*　　*

"*This'll be fine right here,*" Sam said to the taxi driver.

She was in her second taxi, since seeing John Marshall. She rode the first to *Tegel*, where she bought a ticket. The flight was due to leave at 2:35 P.M.

Now, Sam was on her way to claiming her father's Berlin cache. This one he left in a safe deposit box in a branch of the *Berliner Bank*.

In the bank, Sam identified herself and produced a key. It had come from The Stash.

The customer service executive led Sam to the vault, where, together, they opened her father's box. Inside was a box, containing 3 1/2″ disks and photographs. The disks were labeled with year-dates.

"*May I use one of your computers?*" Sam asked the bank official.

"*Natürlich, Fräulein,*" the executive replied. She showed Sam to an unoccupied work station in the main lobby.

Sam started with the earliest-dated disk. Immediately, a dialogue box, showed on the screen, requesting a password.

"Bastard!" Sam murmured to herself. She typed in distinct words and phrases, like the ones she discovered back in Carbondale, but none worked. It was The Stash all over again.

Frustrated, she tried another disk. Another dialogue box appeared. Three more disks and three more dialogue boxes later, she was ready to quit.

Sam looked at the photos in the folders. They showed landscapes and houses, with and without people. Each photo had a name and four-digit number, beginning with "19—." All told, there were over fifty photos.

The first picture in the top folder was an over-water shot of a mansion, probably from a lake. Along the bottom white border, hand-printed in small lettering, was "*Wannsee II.*"

She knew the area, known as *Wannsee,* in the Berlin metropolitan area, but had never seen a house like this there. It seemed to be sitting by itself, surrounded by woods and mountains.

The first disk she tried, too, had the same number as the "*Wannsee II*" photo. She kept the pictures in the order she found them, noting the numbers on each.

Eight other photos had the *Wannsee* photo's number, but different titles. There were shots of the same mansion from several vantages.

She put the first disk in again. When the dialogue box reappeared, she typed in "*Wannsee.*" That failed, too. Then, she added the Roman numerals. The dialogue box disappeared. *All that Classical education has paid off,* she reflected.

The first image was a digitalized photo of the mansion, scanned onto the disk. Headings ranged from "Location" to "Title." Sam skimmed text and maps with areas of Switzerland, and other photos, with the same number as the mansion's. She saw her father, The Baron, and other men, among them, The

Face. He was standing on a dock, dressed in fishing gear and holding a large fish, with that same mansion behind him.

It was 2 P.M. She brought the box to the bank official, and asked for it to be shipped. The bank official was happy to oblige. Before Sam left, she packed the cache and addressed it to the priest at Georgetown University. Sam caught a cab to *Tegel*. She remembered her new clothes in the locker, but scolded herself for thinking of superficial and trivial matters.

The plane took off around 2:45 P.M. As it turned westward, Sam looked at the city. She closed her eyes. Images of Hiroshima, Nagasaki, and A- and H-Bomb tests flashed. So, too, did Robert Oppenheimer's comment on witnessing the Trinity test. She felt guilty about escaping.

XXVII

Sam was in de Gaulle Airport a little after 5 P.M. and looked at late newspaper editions. Paris was Paris, though a bit more dangerous: there had been a *Metro* bombing. No sign or sound of a Berlin conflagration. Marshall must have saved the day. Her guilt at having escaped waned.

The next *Swissair* to Zürich did not leave for two hours. Sam bought a ticket to Zürich and one from Zürich to Berlin for the very late night of the 10th. From the information she had, she could find what she was looking for in that time.

She browsed in a bookstore, purchasing newspapers, a Swiss road map, paperbacks, and pad and pens. She picked at a dinner in a non-Americanized, fast-food place.

While she ate, she studied the map, especially the area southeast of Zürich. Her father's travels had taken them there many times over the years. *If it weren't already snowed-in*, Sam thought...

Later, in the flight lounge, Sam scanned the newspapers. Stories covered the Russian President's visit. Due to a temporary health problem, his speech at the *Reichstag* had been postponed a day or two. There were photographs of the crowds, waiting along the *Ebertstrasse*. Sam looked for herself.

She tried to be interested in the remainder of the papers, even reading bridge columns, but the feel of layover time persisted: wasted time, unstoreable for later. Sam started a paperback, mind-candy mystery fiction.

Sam planned her next moves. Get a hotel. Rent a jeep or LandRover. Buy snow- and/or camping-gear. Her American Express bills would be humongous after this trip. She'd be paying her father for years.

She caught herself. She *would* be paying him back, she insisted, not his estate.

Flight call and boarding began early. Time passed more

quickly. So did the flight.

Clear of the plane by 9:30 P.M. Sam rented a LandRover from a car rental booth in *Zürich-Kloten* airport. It was the last available.

She reserved a room at the *Hotel Leonhard* and drove into town. The hotel was not far from the main train station. She mapped routes to *Willerzell* and the *Sihlsee*, a lake southeast of Zürich.

She also called an antique store not far from the hotel. The owner's surname, this phone number, and a shop's trade-name were in her father's Berlin papers, under a notation, "Weapons—Discreet." There was also a code-exchange noted.

The owner was in. Sam identified herself and used the first code remark. He replied as expected, and they arranged to meet the next day.

The next morning Sam shopped. At a winter-wear and sporting goods store, she bought a thermal ski suit, hiking boots, and camping gear. She did not rent ski equipment. Only the higher elevations showed much snow, so far.

Around noon, she drove to the antique store. Baroque furniture and other durables crowded the interior of the shop, with display cases toward the back. A bell chimed her arrival. From behind curtains that covered a doorway, a man in his mid- to late-50s emerged, with the expectant look of a salesperson about to wait on a customer.

"*I called yesterday*," Sam said, in German. "*I'm Samantha Pemberton.*"

Sam placed the broken piece of a key from her father's Berlin cache on the counter. The piece had been taped to a page with this shop's name and address.

"*That's interesting,*" the shopkeeper said. He reached in his pocket, coming out with a key shaft, and matched it to Sam's.

"*Now, Fräulein Pemberton,*" the shopkeeper said. "*How may I help you?*"

"*I know from my father that you can fulfill certain merchandise needs otherwise unavailable . . .*"

"*What're we talking about. How big?*"

"*Two automatic pistols. Extra clips and ammunition. 45s or

9mms, preferably. I'm fully trained," Sam said. "Pop saw to it. And a few electronics. Can do?" Sam handed him a list. "How much?"

"Child's play," the shopkeeper said, after reading it. "Since I know your father, it depends on how soon. Mode of payment..."

"A few days. Not more than a week," Sam answered. "Cash, of course. I'm not flipping you my American Express card."

"I'll cut you a deal," the shopkeeper said, "'cause I owe your father a lot. Thirty years ago he risked his neck to help me escape East Germany. Helping you's the very least I can do."

"I've got to go away soon. Two or three days, at the outside. Then I'll be back. Maybe you can help me." She described her father's disappearance and the situation. "If I find it, I might find someone who knows where he is."

"Do the authorities know?"

"CIA does. They told me to stay out of it, but I wasn't waiting for word he was dead."

The man laughed. "You're your father's daughter, all right. I can get you 9mms. And the other stuff you mentioned..." He stopped, as though thinking. Then, "Everything for 2,000 Swiss Francs or 1,500 Dollars, American."

"I'll give you $2,000, American," Sam said, "if you help me find this." She took out a photograph of the mansion and a map, showing him her guesses.

"If we leave right away," the shopkeeper said, "we might find it before nightfall."

"You're in, then?"

"Easy enough work. Antiques're slow right now. Call me Klaus."

"We can take my Rover. It's outside."

"We'll take my four-wheel-drive. Are you checked out on anything larger than a pistol?"

"Shotguns, rifles," Sam answered. "Hunting stuff, mostly."

He rejoined her shortly, in coarse corduroys and a flannel shirt, with hiking boots. "You'll look less conspicuous. Man and woman traveling together." He locked up the shop and turned a "Closed" sign on the door.

"I've got a friend in real estate down south," Klaus said. "She's *reliable and knows how to keep her mouth shut. Maybe she can help us."*

Klaus used the highway on the western shore of the *Züricher See*, past *Thalwil* and *Horgen*. At *Wadenswil* they stopped in a real estate office. Klaus' friend, *Evangelein*, was in her late fifties, well-presented in dress, hair, and makeup.

She maintained files and descriptions of the more expensive homes and estates in the area. *"If I don't have it in my file,"* she said, in a soft, though firm tone, *"it doesn't exist."*

Sam showed her the photo, and told her where she suspected it of being.

Evangelein said, *"I recognize it. That property was sold three years ago. I remember, because it brought a fat commission to one of our competitors. It was the one that got away from us."* She stopped midway through a binder. She turned the volume around for them to see.

There were pictures of the mansion and grounds from different vantages. One was similar to the photo Sam had, but closer. *"The estate rests beside the Sihlsee,"* Evangelein said, *"on the western shore. A girlfriend of mine was the sales agent. The buyer just walked in and paid cash. All very quietly done. I wouldn't know the details, if I didn't know her."*

"Wasn't that suspicious?" Sam asked.

"Oh, no!" Evangelein said. *"Especially since the old oil money started thirty years ago. She figured he was eccentric or a front for someone. She tried to maintain contact with him afterward, but he never returned her calls. It's very secluded. The fence was rebuilt, and there were more guards than the former owners maintained."*

"Who were the previous owners?" Sam asked.

"As I recall, they were from an old German industrial family. Very wealthy. They liked their privacy." Evangelein gave them directions.

From *Wadenswil* they followed secondary roads to *Birchli*, on the western shore of the *Sihlsee*. Sam noted from her map there were campgrounds nearby. South of *Gross*, where the road took a turn and led to a bridge across the *See*, they found the estate.

They could see the mansion, high enough on a hill that it was visible over the trees. A gravel and dirt road, branching from the highway led between tall banks of conifers and evergreens. There was no posting.

The road wound through forest for several hundred yards. At that point there was an intersection. The crossroad, also gravel and dirt, in either direction was unsigned.

The way straight ahead was signed and posted. In German, it read, *"Private road. No trespassing!"*

Klaus turned left, followed the road till it ended in a clearing, which bordered the shoreline and the beach. Klaus parked beside the trees. The forest receded from the beach all along the coast.

They could see the mansion again. It presided over the *See*, from its hill. There were boat docks, but no fences or enclosures along the shore.

"Your friend does like his seclusion," Klaus said, finally. *"I want to try something."*

Klaus and Sam drove to the forked intersection and turned left, onto the private road. This road ran another several hundred yards.

Ahead, Sam saw large gates, uniting high fences. She glimpsed guards and dogs lingering there.

"Get in the back," Klaus told Sam, *"under the blankets. Hurry."*

She slumped between the seats, across the floor and covered herself with the coarse wool. The vehicle slowed, then stopped.

"Hi," she heard Klaus say.

"What're you doing here?" It was a rough, provocative response. *"Didn't you see the sign, you idiot?"*

"What sign?" Klaus said. He sounded confused.

"The No Trespassing one, Idiot!"

"Oh, that one! I did see it. But I was hoping you could help me. I seem to be lost. I must have taken a wrong turn."

"What're you looking for?" More anger and impatience.

"Willerzell," Klaus said.

"That's on the other side of the See. Go back to the road. Turn right. Over the bridge. Past Euthal. Willerzell's after that. Now, get out of here!"

"May I turn around?"

"*Back up and get going!*"

The vehicle started in reverse and ran for several moments, before it stopped. "*You can come out now,*" Klaus said. "*I can't say much for your friend's hired hands. Good help is so hard to find these days.*"

Sam peaked between the seats. "*He's no friend,*" Sam said, sweeping her hair from her face.

"*How're you getting in there?*" Klaus asked. "*It would take an army.*"

"*I'll worry about that later,*" Sam answered, settling into the front seat. "*I'd say you earned your money.*"

"*You want help? Later, I mean?*"

"*Just the hardware,*" Sam said. "*I can take care of myself.*"

Sam looked at the map again. "*There's another road south from Euthal.*"

"*It runs past the southeast end of the See and across the Sihl. Are you thinking what I think you are?*"

"*Only a look,*" Sam said.

"*I hope you know what you're doing,*" Klaus said. They were at the intersection. He backed onto the road to the lakeshore.

"*But let's try this way here.*" Sam pointed to the road they had not taken.

* * *

McConneld and Co.'s euphoria had not taken long to wear off, though the Russian President joined them for the Chancellor's lunch. They were back at work at the Embassy, after that.

Waiting for McConneld were messages from Deputy Director Simmons. The National Security Adviser had also phoned.

McConneld called Simmons. The Deputy Director congratulated McConneld, telling him "the highest political circles" were anxious for and confident of a swift "mop-up" of the operation.

"Mop-up?!" McConneld said. "We're at Square One again, Mac."

"I'll tell them you're making progress," Simmons said. "And, Buck? Call the National Security Adviser. He's been driving me nuts, since we got the news. This is his version of an apology."

Later, McConneld was on-line with the Adviser. The accolades were flowing from the receiver. *Please!* McConneld thought. *I can't handle all this sugar! Especially from you!*

"And there's someone else here, who wants to talk to you," the Adviser said, finally.

Another voice came on the line. "This here's the President. Just wanted to extend my own congrat's on a job well done." He became effusive, with praise.

McConneld had not spoken in such a personal way with this president before, only in meetings or brief social functions. But the Office and its aura still held something special for McConneld, despite who might be the occupant. He found himself wordless.

"You there?" the President asked, when McConneld had not replied.

McConneld rediscovered speech in a raspy throat. He thanked the chief executive and briefed him. McConneld featured Marshall, Balkovsky, and Barsohn, along with the EOD teams in his narrative.

"I'll see y'all get medals for this," the President said, "except for the Russian. Well, maybe I can swing something for him, too. I'll want to see you at the White House, when you've finished cleaning this thing up. Soon, I trust. VERY SOON. Any of the other gentlemen there?"

McConneld handed the phone to Barsohn. Lunch or dinner at the White House, he smiled to himself and he didn't have to make a campaign contribution, fortunately.

Their night was otherwise a late one. Sleeping quarters were arranged in the building for them, including for Marshall and Balkovsky. They took shifts, working in twos and threes.

They reviewed files, reports, and field dispatches. The most recent reports had not disclosed the whereabouts of either von Markenheim or Tripleleaf. Terror attacks throughout Western Europe had not stopped, though they seemed more intermittent, for the previous twenty-four hours.

Meanwhile, the EOD search of the *Reichstag* discovered nothing further of an explosive nature. The building received its clean bill and would reopen. Either way, the Chancellor and the *Bundestag* had serious legislative sessions each day and evening for the next three weeks.

"Where're your two chums?" McConneld asked Marshall at one point.

Marshall shrugged. "I don't own them. I only rent them."

"Here's how I see it," Colonel Barsohn said, at one point. "They fucked up. They know it."

"And they know we know." Channing interrupted.

"And they know we know they know," Marshall further interrupted. "We're all so knowledgeable." His voice trailed off.

"They're sitting on nineteen weapons."

"That could be painful," Marshall interrupted again.

"Would you get serious?" Barsohn retorted.

"I'll try, Harvey," Marshall said. "But you're a great straight man."

"They've got three options," Barsohn resumed. "First, they can sit tight and do nothing."

"In which case, we get no weapons back," McConneld said.

"I don't read these guys like that," Barsohn said. "Second, they could set one off, in retaliation for our stopping them. Or, third, they could wait for another opportunity."

"There's another possibility," Marshall said. "They could surrender. But I wouldn't count on it. I picked up a few things, while inside. They'd eat the fissionables and glow, rather than do nothing indefinitely."

"The problem with your second option," Balkovsky said, "is we'll have no warning. Highly plausible and what I'd do, if I were they."

"In the third," McConneld said. "We expect it. That one's D.O.A."

"Been there. Done that," Marshall said. "Didn't anybody hear me?"

"It's time for pre-emptive action. We should hit Markenheim's estates," Barsohn said. "You said he was always in charge of any operation. I'll bet they're the storage sites."

"He's never that close," Marshall said.

McConneld interjected, "No matter what the Chancellor

said, he's got constraints. Without proof of von Markenheim's direct involvement, we can't raid the homes of one of the country's most illustrious citizens and industrialists."

"What about that source of yours?" Barsohn asked Balkovsky.

"He's in no shape to talk, let alone testify. I'm lucky I got what I did."

"Are you sure Krattmay's dead?" Barsohn asked.

Balkovsky nodded. "No way to find out where."

"We should try now," McConneld said. "His body might tell us something."

"It's probably been covered by snow," Balkovsky said.

"Then, we *are* at Square One," McConneld said, "waiting for another misstep. Only one man...But we don't have a clue where he is."

A staff person brought Channing a file. "Maybe not entirely clueless," Channing said. "You might find this a start. Slim, but a start." He handed it to McConneld.

"Why didn't we get this sooner? Who brought her in?"

"McGonnville. She and another agent've been debriefing her," Channing answered.

"Tell McGonnville I want to see her right away," McConneld said. "Slim, all right. Slim and arrogant."

* * *

Liz McGonnville arrived at the Embassy forty-five minutes after receiving McConneld's summons. She left Regina in debriefing and interrogation. Liz told McConneld and an Army colonel about Regina's escapades since Washington. She omitted Sam Pemberton.

"She's been a low-grade informant-spy," Liz concluded. "She pinpointed some of her step-father's haunts."

"Any near here?" McConneld asked.

"Not that she knows," Liz answered. "She expected him to be here this month, but he changed plans."

"I'm still not clear why she suddenly picked up and left D.C.," McConneld said. "But The Baron did change plans, after a long, regular history. Why?"

"As a lead, it is VERY thin," the Army colonel said. McConneld introduced him.

"Ever see her old man?"

"She visited him once," Liz answered. She told him where. "And I saw him, too." She described the airport adventure. "There were others I didn't recognize."

"I read your report of that," McConneld said.

"Anyone else?" Barsohn asked.

"General Walter Tripleleaf. Thomas Pemberton. Pemberton was a prisoner. They led him to a plane."

"At least he's still alive. Maybe," Barsohn said. "Where's that again?" Liz repeated her guess.

"Chuck, call the Interior Ministry," McConneld said to another man. "Get a list of all airports, airfields. Anything purporting to operate planes in that area."

"Chuck" went to another side of the operations room and was on the phone for five or ten minutes, before returning. "They're faxing us a copy, momentarily," he said. "Six or eight possibles."

"Tripleleaf's out of sight, remember?" Colonel Barsohn said. "So is von Markenheim. This sounds like a shell-game."

"No hard evidence to link the Baron or Big T to the bomb," "Chuck" said.

"I don't expect von Markenheim confided deep stuff to Ms. Foxwirth. But she might know things she doesn't realize. Bring her in," McConneld said.

Liz walked to Regina's debriefing room. On the way, she pondered her next job. She'd need one, when Mr. McConneld found out about Sam and her own complicity. She wondered if Sam were serious about that offer. Wherever Sam was.

* * *

The Frankfurter Allgemeine Zeitung reported in a special edition for the afternoon of 10 November that German Federal Police had conducted nationwide raids of the offices and homes of known and suspected neo-Nazis and their organizations.

A government spokesman announced the raids, carried out

under the auspices of the federal Office For The Defense Of The Constitution, were intended to reduce the recent waves of terrorist attacks. Hundreds of suspects were in custody. The spokesman indicated this round of raids had been planned for months.

He refused comment on whether further raids were planned or in motion. However, he did not discount the possibility of future federal action of this sort.

* * *

"This should be Willerzell," Sam said to Klaus, as he slowed the vehicle. *"Let's find that other campground."*
"Do you want to go back to Zürich this evening?" Klaus asked. *"Or look for a place to stay around here?"*
"I'm not ready yet," Sam replied. *"We might as well go back."*
Sam studied the map. The small road she cajoled Klaus into taking, after the encounter with the estate guards, was a shortcut to the road to *Euthal*. They followed it south. It ended in *Weglosen*. There were cable cars to a camping area on the *Ibergeregg*. Other, smaller roads were not on Sam's map.

Klaus and Sam drove north. From the road, they could see the mansion. "The warlock's castle," Sam murmured.

In Zürich, at her hotel, she packed what one would need for a camping overnight. She was interested in projecting the illusion, not the reality.

The next morning, after reaching the *Sihlsee* area, she took the road which ran along the eastern bank of the *See* between *Egg* and *Euthal*.

South of *Euthal*, she turned onto the mud and gravel shortcut they discovered the previous day. There was an area of fence, viney and neglected. It seemed a ready opening. Sam noted its location and continued to the *See*.

The dead end at the *See* was where Sam stopped, as Klaus had. From a nearby dock, unassociated with the mansion, Sam rented a boat and took a ride up the *See* past it.

There were only a few obvious guards around or near the estate's docks. Her ski suit kept her toasty, though her face did burn from the cold wind over the water.

Back in her Rover, Sam drove toward the *Egg-Weglosen* road. The best place from which to watch the comings and goings at the estate seemed to be the entry road. She would stake out the estate, until she had to go back to Zürich for her flight. She hoped the guards had been lulled into complacency by the excessive solitude.

Sam parked along the tree line near the *See* and watched the intersection with her binoculars. It was nearly 11 A.M., when she settled into her vigil. Her flight was scheduled to leave *Kloten* in twelve hours, getting her into Berlin during the early-morning of 11 November.

The hours were numbing. Sam sipped coffee from a thermos. Then, it was Cokes from a cooler. Her thermal suit still kept her warm enough, though her face was frosted at times.

The same covered jeep left and came back multiple times. The trips were not time-patterned. Each seemed to have two riders. Sam checked her mirrors. The area behind her remained blessedly vacant.

The afternoon droned on. The jeep's unpredictable appearances became less frequent. As dusk was materializing, the jeep appeared once more. There were three regular-sized Mercedes cars and one limousine with it.

Sam waited more hours. No other vehicles came or left. As 8 P.M. passed, Sam suspended the stakeout and returned to Zürich. At her hotel, she left her camping stuff and the Rover. She had rented both the room and the vehicle for a week each.

Before leaving her hotel, she reserved a room at the Berlin *Savoy Hotel*. Then she took a taxi to *Kloten*. She was checked in for her flight with two hours to go.

Her thoughts shifted among her father, John Marshall, and The Face, more so the first two, but the last kept intruding, like a cerebral ferret nibbling away at the other synapses. Inter the ferret. Banish him from the pathways.

"Mr. Face," in Berlin? If so, why? If it weren't... Sam wished she had had time to prove it to herself. Till she confronted the real Mr. Face, as she knew she would, that question would haunt her. The confrontation would come. But when?

Then there was Marshall. He had saved her life. Again.

Did he love her? Did she love him? Wasn't that why she was going to Berlin? For an answer, one way or the other? Instead of staying NOW, staying until she found her father safe? If she even could find him there...Was that the place?...For some things?...

She dozed. In her haze, she saw images of her father, Marshall, others. The images faded, blurred, refocused, different colors, black and white. Mr. Face in the sewer. Oh, No, Mr. Face! Her father in that airport. Her father, a prisoner in the sewer. In the sewer. *Marshall, Marshall, where are you?*

Sam felt someone shaking her gently. *"Fräulein? Der Flug,"* an airline employee spoke to her: boarding time. The Paris mind-candy fiction helped the flight pass.

When the plane broke from the night cloud-cover, Sam glanced onto a deceptively quiet and peaceful Berlin. Nice to see it still there, Sam reflected.

She was not clear of *Tegel* until after 2 A.M., 11 November, even though she did not have to wait for checked-luggage. She took a cab to the *Savoy*. She registered under the name on the British passport from Liz's contact.

In her room, exhausted from the past two days, she fell asleep, before her body heat warmed the sheets.

Sam awakened before 7 A.M. that morning. It was a restive, not a restful, sleep she slept. As she was dressing, she decided to stay that night at the hotel, before hooking up with Liz. Or should she? She needed to get back to Zürich ASAP. *Would Liz be a problem?*

Her plan for that day was simple: reclaim her new clothes and pin down Marshall's feelings, before Zürich. But she would not go to the Embassy in person, the better to avoid Mr. McConneld. An hour later she was back at the hotel with her purchases. From a phone outside the hotel, she called the U.S. Embassy and asked for Marshall in her best North-German accent.

"429M...He hasn't come in yet. Something I could help you with?"

"It's personal," Sam said, sounding pouty. "He promised me

breakfast, when he hurried away."

"Care to leave a message?"

"Tell him his *Liebchen* from the War Memorial Park wants desperately, needs desperately, to see him," Sam replied. "I'm waiting breathlessly at the *Savoy*. He's so *beautiful!*"

"*Liebchen*...At the *Savoy*...A number where he can reach you?"

Sam gave her the British passport name and the hotel phone. Sam returned to her mind-candy fiction.

* * *

Marshall arrived at McConneld's office around 8 A.M. Channing handed him a pink message slip. "Some German called for you," Channing said. "Can't you keep it tucked till this is over?!"

Marshall read the message. At first, the caller's identity stumped him. Then, "the War Memorial Park" struck.

"Just somebody I picked up. I thought I'd dusted her off," he said to Channing. "Tell McConneld I'll be back. Taking a cell phone, if you need me."

At the *Savoy's* front desk he asked for Sam's room number and found his way to it. His knock was greeted with, *"Who is it?"* in German.

"Your *Liebchen* from the War Memorial," he replied.

The door opened a slit, then wide. Sam pulled him into the room and slammed the door.

"What're you doing back here?" Marshall asked, still off balance. "I told you to take a holiday."

"Holiday's over," Sam said, "when I knew you and the city were safe. All I want now is to see you out of your clothes."

"What an offer!" Marshall said. "How can I refuse? Is that the only reason you're back?"

"Don't you know why?"

"Hum a few bars."

"I had to know...if you really loved me."

"Was I that obvious?" Marshall asked.

"Yes and no," Sam said. "I was hoping."

"Or the other way around? Deciding, if you love me," Marshall asked.

"Why, you self-centered jerk!"

"I'm not the one who came back and pulled a bonehead play. You're lucky McConneld wasn't in."

"It's the only way you gave me to find you."

"Besides making me look like some yo-yo, who couldn't keep it tucked," he said.

"What'd you tell them?"

"'Just somebody.' Nobody serious."

"Just somebody. Nobody serious?!" Sam repeated.

"Let me rephrase. No one they had to worry about."

"And you?"

"I was always worried about you, you silly little tweeb," Marshall said. "I never thought I'd hear myself say this to any woman. I love you."

They embraced tightly. Sam kissed him, hard on the lips. "But I'm old enough to be your father," Marshall said, when their mouths parted.

"Well, maybe a *young* father," he said, after she kissed him more times. He kissed her back.

His body felt good to her. His touch. Sam had needed that hug. *Don't let go,* she thought. "Oh, John! I think I've loved you since that first night."

"When I didn't need to be there? Remind me not to cross you. You could beat the shit out of me. But maybe we should get to know each other, before we go farther."

"Oh, God!" Sam laughed. "The iconoclast is old-fashioned!"

"Maybe I am," Marshall said, sounding a little defensive.

"You've been spewing a lot of 'maybes' in the last minute," Sam said. "I don't want maybes. I want yeses." She let go of him, walked over to the bed, and began unbuttoning her blouse.

XXVIII

Sam was playing with the hairs on Marshall's chest. "I always wondered how it felt," she said, exhaling a deep breath. "S'won—der—ful!"

"You know how long it's been, since I was with someone I really loved?" Marshall sighed. "Eons. Millennia. Longer than I can remember."

"Did you ever smoke? Afterward?"

"You know you're a little off-the-wall sometimes," he said. "I hate fucking tobacco."

"I wouldn't want intercourse with it, either. You're an amazing man, though! Multiples in such a short time!" Sam said.

"Us old men savour it. You're fantastic, too! I wanted to keep up with you and give you that special feeling, the first time." He kissed her softly on the forehead.

Sam looked into his eyes. "I wanted you, Darling. I wanted you so much! Thank you."

Marshall reached to the nighttable for his watch. "Shit!" he said. "It's after nine, already! McConneld'll wonder what happened. Got to get back."

"Can't we seal this with a quiet breakfast?" Sam said, somewhere between pleading and whining. "Are you hungry?"

"I was."

Sam grimaced. "I didn't mean that way."

"Famished," Marshall said. "Hell! The security of the Free World can survive without me a tad longer. Let's go."

They dressed quickly and left, hand-in-hand. Sam wore a new unitard jumpsuit, a down coat, and thigh boots. They took a taxi, to a café with Einstein's name, near the *Nollendorfstrasse,* Sam remembered as a good breakfast place.

Seated at an out-of-the-way table, Sam took Marshall's hand in hers. She kissed it gently and rubbed it on her cheek. "I needed this," she said.

"So did I," he said, stroking her skin.

"With Pa gone God-only-knows-where, I've felt adrift. I've had to be *Ms. Self-sufficient*, but I always had that safe family haven. My world's changed."

"Welcome to reality, Sam," Marshall said. A clock across the room cuckoo'd 9:45 A.M.

"But there're still things I prefer to do alone," Sam said.

A waiter took their orders for Continental breakfasts. The hot tea and rolls tasted particularly good to Sam.

"I've been adrift for a while myself," Marshall said.

"Can I tell you a secret?" Sam asked.

Marshall leaned closer to her. "Is this 'Top Secret' or just 'Hush-Hush'?"

"Nothing like that," Sam said, lightly slapping his hand. "You've been on my mind so much lately, you were in my dreams last night. And the night before."

"Off that track for a moment. I meant to ask you where you went, after I threw you in that cab."

"Paris. I remember looking down on this city. These terrible images. Mushroom clouds. Then, after we landed—late, by-the-way. Not by-the-way, we landed late at *Charles de Gaulle*. I found no signs of 'Berlin Obliteration, Film-At-Eleven,' so I figured you'd saved it. Can you tell me anything about that?"

"Afraid not. Not yet, anyway. I was glad you were safe. Of course, seeing you in that crowd . . . Imagine my surprise! And that dirty trick you tried with the cop."

"I said I was sorry for that," Sam replied, feeling a blush.

"I guess I might've done that myself. Found any leads to your father?" Marshall asked, after a sip of coffee.

"Nothing," Sam answered. "I was about to ask you that question."

"Another big zilch," Marshall said.

"Pa," Sam said, sighing a sad sigh. "I love him and hate him at the same time right now."

"Don't hate him too much," Marshall said. "He's doing what he thinks is right."

"It's funny. You and Pa, both, were in that dream," Sam said, excitedly. "And this one guy. I saw his face in Pa's pictures back home." Sam then related the dream she had had on the plane from St. Louis to D.C.

"That's grisly," Marshall said, when Sam was finished. "Were there names or captions on the pictures?"

"All I recall is how cold his face and his eyes were. Deliberate. Calculating. Like he'd kill without blinking." She described his various uniforms from the many black-and-white pictures.

"Our Army?"

"I can't say for sure. That's the way my subconscious works. I'll see somebody or think about something, and, BOOM! There he/she/it is in a dream. But it usually takes longer than a day or two. That's what's so strange about these last few."

Marshall looked quizzically at Sam.

"I know it doesn't make much sense, but I never expected you or anyone else I'd seen recently in a dream so soon."

"Was this cold-faced guy in the dreams with me the last few nights?" Marshall asked. Sam nodded.

"Well, you said you'd seen him months ago? Sounds more like your pattern. You have been more stressed out."

"Perhaps," Sam said. "But that's just it. I saw someone who looked like that guy."

"The guy in the picture?!" Marshall interrupted. "When?"

"That same day I saw you. As a matter of fact, near where you caught me. This person was a ways off. I tried, but I didn't get a second look at him."

"Tell me more about him."

"He was bald."

"How could you tell? It was cold. Wasn't he wearing a hat?"

"He had a hard-hat on, but took it off to wipe his forehead and face." Sam described the scene and the work crew.

"It must've been someone else," Marshall said. "For one thing, if it's the guy I believe it was, he's dead. And even if he weren't, he would've been miles from Berlin by then. He'd done his work already . . . unless . . ."

"Unless what?"

"Unless he wasn't dead. He wasn't finished at all. Show me where you saw him?"

"Remember where you grabbed me?" Sam asked. "Up the street. A big man—er—'Person-hole'. In the street."

They took a cab to the *Brandenburger Tor*. Marshall asked the driver about "hardware" stores nearby. On the way, the driver stopped at a small electronics and tool store. Marshall came back with three flashlights, a large and two smaller ones, crow-, pry-, and roll-bars, a miniature sledgehammer, screwdrivers, and other tools in a big canvas tote. The cab continued to the *Brandenburger Tor*. Marshall had the driver drop them, north of the Gate and its esplanade.

Sam looked around for the leftovers of the crowd barricades and stanchions. "I was near that light pole," she said. "In fact, I know I was. I recall that poster."

She hesitated. There was more than one utility cover. She closed her eyes, trying to recreate the scene in her mind.

"The truck, his truck, was back this way." Her mind's eye scoured more.

"How d'you know it was his truck?"

Sam described the temporary enclosure that covered the hole. "He disappeared into it and didn't reappear. I got caught up in stuff. You showed up, and I didn't have time to breathe, or think."

"How about the kind of truck?"

Sam thought for a moment. "It wasn't gas. Or electric. I recall *Wasser* on the truck."

Marshall dodged cars, looking for the metal covers. The first one he came to was gas. Cars were honking, as he bobbed along the right-hand pavement. Sam was behind him. "In the ballpark?" Marshall shouted to her.

"Closer to the curb, I think," she replied.

Marshall sprinted across another traffic lane. He found an oversized metal cover, with the name of the Berlin Water and Sewer Company on it.

"Think this is it?" he called to Sam, who caught up with him.

Sam scanned her memory again. "I think so," she answered. "But I can't be absolutely certain."

"There are no absolutes in life," Marshall snapped. "Please bring me the tools."

Marshall pulled the phone from his pocket and punched in a number.

"McConneld, please." He waited. "Then, let me talk to Channing." More waiting. "Channing?" Marshall told him to check on work crews for the 8th and gave him the cell phone number.

Marshall made another call. *"Herr Arad's Zimmer, bitte*...David? Oh, George. It's me. Where's David?...When's he due back?...Good. Get your asses over here!" Marshall told him where they were and pocketed the phone.

A few minutes later his pocket burped out several rings. "Channing? McConneld back yet? Where the hell is he?!" Marshall listened. "Get them back! If I'm right, they're on a wild goose chase. What else've you got?" More listening. "Like I thought. I'll call you back." He replaced the phone in his pocket. "Channing says McConneld and Balkovsky headed south with a search crew two hours ago."

"Balkovsky? Who's that?" Sam asked.

"Nobody you'd know," Marshall said. "Channing said the Water Company didn't know anything about a crew that day. They repaired a sudden main-break a couple weeks ago and re-inspected last week. Re-inspection's not due till next month."

Marshall pushed the end of a crowbar into a thin space between the iron cover and the frame and pounded it with his new hammer. His crude lever in place, Marshall felt the stress through his arms and shoulders. The cover barely lifted.

"Hold this, while I get another in place," Marshall said. "Don't let it pop out."

Sam held the bar tightly. Through her gloves the freeze of the metal penetrated. The wind from the cars chilled her face.

Marshall repeated the process with the second bar. Sam felt the pressure and pushed as hard as she could.

"Push harder!" Marshall exclaimed. "On the count of three, push together! Ready?" Sam nodded. "Push!" he shouted.

The weight of the cover pulled at Sam's whole upper body. Marshall's face was red. The cover rose.

"I'll keep it up," Marshall said. "Slip this under!" He shoved an iron roll-bar to her with his foot. Slowly, the utility hole yawned open.

Passersby and pedestrians were stopping to watch. Marshall fed them a story in German about Sam's losing a necklace down the hole. Several people offered to help, but Marshall waved them off, while he caught his breath.

A car in the curb lane, driving slower than other traffic, passed them and pulled over. Its flashers went on. George and David got out. Marshall introduced them to Sam.

"What's she doing here?" George asked.

"Helping me," Marshall said. "I'd appreciate if you kept her presence to yourselves."

"What's the real story?" David asked.

"I think the Colonel's still among us," Marshall said, "regardless of what Balkovsky's source told him. I believe Sam saw him the day we disarmed the MADM."

"Where'd you see him?" George asked Sam, who described what she saw.

"But what the fuck was he doing here?" George asked. "He activates the Bomb. Then hangs out nearby? He's fanatic, but that doesn't figure."

"Unless he knew it wouldn't go off," Marshall said. "Unless we were supposed to find it."

"Decoy. Diversion," David said.

"... Intended to cause us to drop our guard," Marshall said.

"Maybe I'm dense," George asked. "Diversion from what?"

"Another bomb or bombs," Marshall said, "set to go off later and trigger what they got cooking. There's been a drop in terror attacks in the past seventy-two hours. Maybe it's the lull before the storm."

"You think he set it down there?" David asked Marshall.

"It's a calculated risk," Marshall said. "But, yes, I do. He had to wait till the last minute and knew he couldn't place it *in* the building."

"What if we don't find whatever it is?" George asked.

"Either I'm wrong or this city's toast," Marshall said.

"D'we know what we're looking for?" David asked.

"Something relatively small or a couple small somethings," Marshall said. "We could be dealing with another MADM, but I don't think so. An SADM'd do the job, as well, maybe more neatly."

"There you go with 'maybe' again," Sam interjected.

"I'll call Channing. I need to know one more thing." He used the cell phone. "Channing, you're the history man," Marshall said. "Anything significant about today, 11 November, from the Nazi viewpoint? Don't take too long. We may not have much."

A police car slowed and pulled behind David's car. "Great!" George said. "What do we tell these clowns?"

"Let me handle it," Marshall said. "We'll tell them the truth, but only some. Sam, put your hood on." He left them, to speak with the police.

The driver was the same officer who intervened between him and Sam. The other officer set up orange rubber stanchions to shield the hole.

"Everything's cool," Marshall said, after he returned. "They understand we've got to work quietly."

The phone in Marshall's pocket rang. "That's got to be it!" he said, excitedly. "Grab ahold of every guy you can and get over here!" Marshall told Channing where they were. "Cops mark the spot. I'll let you know."

* * *

Channing pushed the call-disconnect button of his phone console, then speed-dialed. "Communications? Channing. Raise Mr. McConneld. Tell him to get back here as fast as possible!"

In the situation room, he spoke with Colonel Barsohn and relayed orders for certain operatives to meet him near the *Reichstag*. Colonel Barsohn collared his own people, as well.

A buzzer on Channing's phone console went off. It was the secretary, telling him that Agent McGonnville and a visitor-in-custody had arrived.

"Keep her in Room 401A, under guard. Send McGonnville in," Channing said. "McGonnville! Good! I need everyone I can get. You're on me," Channing said. He phoned for cars.

"Where're we going, sir?!" McGonnville asked. Channing told her. "What about Ms. Foxwirth?"

"She can keep," Channing said, as they left.

Thank God! Liz thought. *A little more government-pension-time built up!*

* * *

"Once more into the breach," Marshall said, looking into the dark pool that was the utility opening.

"What about her?" George asked.

"She stays up here," Marshall said.

"You need all the eyes you can get," Sam replied. "Don't quibble. Let's go!"

"It won't be pretty," Marshall warned.

"What has been, this trip?" Sam rejoined.

Marshall went first, lighting the way for the others. He gave flashlights each to George and David and kept a larger one for himself and Sam.

The stench, overwhelming as it was, reminded Sam of the cave in her dream. "Maybe you don't need my eyes after all," she said.

"I told you so. Now you're in," Marshall said. "Shit 'n' all."

He ran his light over the walls and floor nearby. The old, grey concrete walls were wet, with slime shining the beam back at him.

"This must be north," Marshall said, pointing the light up the shaft in front of them. "He'd get the bomb as close to the building as he could."

"But definitely not inside," David said.

"Been there," Marshall said. "Done that, before you arrived."

"After the first one, it would be the safest building in the country, right?" Sam suggested.

"You're brilliant," Marshall said, "and beautiful."

"Finding this is going to be the wildest luck!" George said.

"Quit yammering!" Marshall said. "That call from Channing. 11 A.M., eleven November. 11-11-11. That's when the Armistice took effect. The Original Stab-in-the-Back got launched. It's after ten now."

"What the hell're we looking for?!" David asked. "What do these things look like?"

"New concrete or closure," Marshall said. "Brick. Anything." Marshall described SADMs, oval-shaped, backpack-sized. "I doubt he left it or them in the open. You guys pan the walls."

They started up the high-ceilinged shaft. There was a brick access-walk, beside the sewer flow-way, which was like a canal. Sam heard scurrying and chattering sounds ahead of them. Marshall led, as they walked single file.

"How far to the *Reichstag*?" Sam asked.

"A thousand to fifteen hundred feet, maybe," Marshall said.

"What if it's in the drink?" George asked.

"We're sunk," Marshall said. "Think positive thoughts, George."

"Jews saving Germany," George said. "Israeli ones at that. Positive enough for you?"

Marshall pierced the long darkness before them with the torch light. The walls looked old and untouched, the only parts of Berlin that survived war.

"How far do you think we've gone?" Sam asked.

"A couple hundred feet," Marshall said, "give or take."

Something ran over Sam's feet, and she shrieked. Her back was cold, as she felt her heart start back up.

"It's only rats," David said. "They're more afraid of you than vice versa."

"They must be petrified," Sam said.

They came to a perpendicular tunnel, to their right and left. Marshall ran his light over a pipe that crossed the water canal, the only access to the shaft to their right.

"You two go that way. Yell if you find anything. And, George?" Marshall said. "Try not to fall in the shit."

"Fuck you," George said. He reached the opposite access-walk.

"I've got a feeling this is the branch line for the *Reichstag*," Marshall said to Sam, after they turned left into new darkness.

Sam heard the rush of water up ahead and to her right. There was splashing, as well.

Marshall shined the bright beam over the walls, but with only one flashlight, the search was slower.

"We've got to have walked a quarter mile by now," Marshall

said. "We're probably right under the damn *Reichstag*. We must've missed it."

"Now who's being negative?" Sam scolded.

Suddenly, to their right, as Marshall shown the light, Sam saw two newly rebricked sections of the far wall, separated by at least ten feet. The mortar between the bricks was still very clean, in contrast to the stuff around them.

"Holy shit!" she gasped. "You think?"

"About the right sizes," Marshall said. "That's got to be them." He shouted to George and David. Sam heard running footsteps as light beams dribbled toward them.

"Take a look!" Marshall said. The other two men ran their lights over the wall, meeting Marshall's. "Do you have tools that can break concrete?"

"I'll see what I can do," David said.

"Leave one of your lights and bring me my tools from topside. I left a baby-sledge," Marshall said. David handed him a flashlight, before he and George left.

"How are we going to get over there?" Sam asked.

"We may have to swim," Marshall said. "But maybe German efficiency'll bail us out again. Look around for anything like a plank."

Sam walked further down the shaft. With the flashlight beam in front of her, she was looking for rats as much as for boards.

"Find anything?" Marshall called.

"Not yet," Sam answered.

She scanned the path. There was commotion echoing behind her. She guessed the other two had returned. She walked back to Marshall, plankless.

"German efficiency of another sort," she said. "Isn't cleanliness next to Germanness?"

"Now, you've got to get out of here," he said to her.

"I'm not going," she called.

"I don't have time for this," Marshall yelled.

"So let's stop shitting around," Sam said.

She threw off her coat, wrapped the flashlight in it, and tossed it across the water. It landed on the opposite walkway with a thud. Sam took off her boots, threw them toward the coat, and jumped into the water. She did not feel for the bottom, and paddled, miraculously not swallowing water.

"You little fool!" Marshall called.

Sam reached the other side. "I'll hate myself in the morning, but I'm not leaving you," she said, pulling herself onto the stone edge.

She kept breathing through her mouth, not wanting to know her own stench-level. She put her coat and boots back on. With the flashlight she looked over the new brickwork.

"Assuming there's a morning," Marshall said.

He handed the cell phone to David, before taking off his jacket and boots and throwing them to the other side. He did a racing dive into the water.

"I must look and smell like shit right now," Sam said to Marshall, after he joined her. "I'm burning these clothes when we get out of here."

"It's only a little shit. Throw me the tools," Marshall called to David.

"You want us over there?" David asked.

"One of you," Marshall answered. "I want the other to call Channing and get an update. Better go topside to do it."

David threw the canvas bag across to Marshall, who let it land on the ledge.

"Age before beauty, old buddy," George said. "I'll get on the phone." He took the cell phone from David and hurried away.

"I owe you one," David said, as he took off his shoes, overcoat, and suit-jacket.

"McConneld will go ape-shit when he sees you," Marshall said to Sam. He surveyed the two jigsaw-edged sections of newly replaced brick-work. He took out a long screwdriver and a push-bar.

"As long as you're here," Marshall said. "Run the light over the borders of this new stuff."

"What're you looking for?"

"Any sign he booby-trapped these things," Marshall answered.

Sam heard a splash and more water thrashing behind her.

Then David was dripping beside them.

"There could be seismic devices to prevent tampering, too," Marshall said.

"Almost like an inertial guidance system?" Sam interrupted.

"Very good!" Marshall replied. "Where'd you learn about that?"

"I read a lot," Sam answered. "You know, you can be a condescending jerk sometimes."

"What did I say?" Marshall asked. Sam did not answer.

"Well, anyway," he continued, "any vibration and the things detonate anyway. I could use a stethoscope."

"Will high-sensitivity mikes do?" David asked.

"You know they would," Marshall answered.

"George!?" David shouted down the shaft. There were running footsteps. David told him to bring electronic equipment from the car.

"What about chipping out the older bricks on either side?" Sam asked.

"You know, you have a first-rate mind for this work," Marshall said. "Good idea, except that, if I were he, I'd set them in a small, self-contained chamber, inside these sections. Even if we tried your idea, we'd run into an interior wall. We're running short of time. Hold the light over here, Sam."

Marshall centered her hand and the beam on an older section of mortar. He carefully scraped over it. The mortar granulated easily into loose, sandy powder. Sam could feel dust in her mouth and spat.

"I'm causing you to pick up all sorts of nasty habits," Marshall said. "Your father will never forgive me. By the way, you'd better keep that hood on your head. Even with that hair, McC'll recognize you." Not long after, Marshall removed his first brick. With the flashlight he peered through the slit.

"We have to get more out, before I can see anything," he said, handing it back to her.

With gentle strokes of the screwdriver, he swept more mortar. Eventually, he had three more bricks out, forming a diamond-pattern. His hole was a row-and-a-half away from one of the replaced sections.

Marshall reached his arm into the opening carefully. "I feel something all right. It's metallic and cold, but I can't tell what it is."

Over the next minutes he removed brick-after-old-brick. When he was finished, he was another row closer to the new stuff.

"I don't feel any wires attached to this older stuff," Marshall said to David. "Take a screwdriver and do the same thing I'm doing."

Sam held David's flashlight. The two beams, pointing in opposite directions, reminded her of a marquee's lights on opening night. Her arms were cramping. Despite the coat, the wet unitard was chilling her, too.

It was not long, before David had a hole in the wall, the shape of a parallelogram. He looked into the opening. "Looks like there's something dark-colored in there," he said. He handed the flashlight to Sam and extracted more bricks.

There were footsteps, clattering and reverberating from the tunnel, to Sam's right. She saw George as the footsteps echoed to a stop.

"I got the mikes in plastic baggies," George said, "in case they land in shit."

Turning from his soft demolition work, David signaled his partner to throw the packet to him, and he caught it. He unpacked small electronic equipment. David handed Marshall several items. Each man returned to his respective chores.

Marshall reached inside the opening with a small microphone. He listened through a receiver.

"Nothing," he said, after a minute. "David, how's yours?"

"Nothing here either," David answered.

"It's probably the exterior walls of the enclosures," Marshall concluded. "Somehow we've got to get inside."

Sam heard voices and commotion from the tunnel-shaft from which George had reappeared.

"David?" Marshall said. David looked over through a faceful of brick and mortar dust.

"If anyone asks, she's one of your people, got it?" Marshall said, nodding toward Sam.

"Don't worry," David grunted. "I'll clue George."

"Marshall?!" It was Channing's voice, calling from down the shaft. Lights and more noise were getting closer.

"Who's with you?" Marshall yelled back.

"Colonel Barsohn. Our people. There are more on the way."

"Is McConneld with you?" Marshall asked.

"He and Balkovsky didn't get back yet."

"We need liquid nitrogen," Marshall yelled. "Lots of it."

Sam flipped her hood over her head, hunching her shoulders, as she watched the new arrivals join George on the access-walk.

"Who's with you?" Channing asked.

"David and another of their people," Marshall answered.

"What the hell's this all about?" Channing and Barsohn blurted, in unison.

"SADMs," Marshall replied. "Two of them, we think. Behind this new brick-work." Channing whistled loudly.

"E.O.D.?" Barsohn asked.

"No time," Marshall said. "If I'm right, these suckers are due to go off at 1100."

"That's why you asked me," Channing said. "11-11-11. They must shoot craps."

"That's only twenty-six minutes from now," Barsohn said. "We don't even have time for a requiem, let alone evacuation. That son-of-a-bitch fucking fed us a lullaby, with these as the real sleeping pills!!"

"How far're you now?" Channing asked. "What d'you need from us?"

Marshall described the situation and their progress. "Have your guys search the walls up and down here," Marshall said. "I'm banking on these being the whole show. But there's no telling if that scumbag set more."

Channing and Barsohn detailed their people to check beyond Marshall's position.

"I need a couple more hands, lots of liquid nitrogen, and protective gear. Nothing fancy. Whatever works," Marshall replied.

"Where the hell are we going to get liquid nitrogen now?!" Channing asked. He sounded exasperated.

"Hospitals," Marshall said. "Most have supplies on hand.

Call the damn Germans. It's their city. The nitrogen should take out even our own anti-tampering devices inside the packages. The bastard's probably got these things booby-trapped, too."

"McGonnville?" Channing called.

Sam peeked from under her hood. She could make out Liz's face by the flashlights on the far side.

"You, Gordeen, and Thompson, go topside and get on the horn to the Germans." Channing repeated Marshall's request. "Tell them to land it by chopper in the middle of the *Ebertstrasse*, if they have to! Just get it here! On second thought, I'll go with you."

"And a bridge," Marshall said. "I don't think you want to come the way we did."

"There's got to be access to your side," Barsohn said. "We'll see what we can do and a comm-link with EOD." He headed off after Channing.

Marshall and David resumed their work. In a few minutes they each had openings in the older sections, through which they could climb. The metal they felt earlier were sheet-metal walls, reaching up to the ceiling of the internal chambers. Outside the metal, brick-work rose from floor to chest height, as an exterior lining for the metal. Marshall hoped the metallic walls would be good insulation for the liquid nitrogen's freezing action, if they could not access the chambers.

He attached mini-mikes David gave him to the metal wall and listened. He heard only slight echoes of the noises in the tunnel. He left the mikes in place, but climbed out.

As Sam crawled the light over the new mortar, Marshall looked and felt for any sign of sensors or electronic contacts hidden in it. The troughs between the bricks were smooth, as they normally would be.

"David?!" Marshall called. "Do you hear anything?"

"Just background sounds," David replied.

"Check the mortar," Marshall said. He described what to do. Sam helped David.

"Nothing," David said, shortly.

"We've got to risk cracking the front stuff," Marshall said. "We'll start at a corner and work inward."

Each man chipped the mortar from the lowest corner, where the old and new brickwork met. Marshall found this to be stiffer and more resistant to disassembling. Finally, he felt his screwdriver break through, seemingly to air.

Channing and the others returned. "Liquid nitrogen's on the way," Channing called. "German bomb disposal is also due."

"Time?" Marshall asked.

"1041 hours," Colonel Barsohn said. "Contact established with EOD. We're piping it down by wire, to avoid atmospherics."

Marshall saw camouflage-clad soldiers with Barsohn working on electronic equipment. They had floodlights set up, too.

"That's a roger," he heard one say.

"I need something to insulate the interiors. Old mattresses. Anything dense and thick," Marshall called to Channing. "And don't let anyone strike a match. There may be gas leaks."

"I already took care of that problem," Channing said. "The Germans said they've got dampening equipment. We scrounged stuff from a construction site. We'll have a bridge to you in no time."

Sam heard footsteps and clattering, approaching Channing's position. More camouflaged figures appeared, carrying lengths of planking and wood poles. They shoved the poles across the water, like makeshift tree branches spanning a creek. Planks worked as a floor over the poles.

Meanwhile, Marshall removed his first new brick and found no wires connected to it. He worked his way brick-by-brick along the edge of the newly replaced facia. This was slow, as the newer mortar had set well.

"Where the hell's this famed German punctuality?!" Marshall called. He removed the last new brick in the outer row, with no booby traps thus far.

"They'll be here," Channing replied.

"I can't freeze *and* disarm two of these things in two minutes," Marshall said. "David, how're you coming?"

"Almost got the right row out. No surprises so far," David said.

"Can you get your hand in? Reach inside," Marshall instructed and did the same. "Feel anything?"

"Nothing but air so far," David replied.

Marshall rubbed his hand methodically over the inside surfaces of the bricks next to him. They were clear. He moved to the next row. Again, nothing.

"I'm removing the next row," Marshall said. He pulled Sam and the light closer to him.

"John," Sam whispered. "I'm really frightened! Are we going to die?!"

"Not if these ten digits still have their magic," he said.

"I should've listened to you!" Sam whispered. "I don't want to die!"

"We're not going to, damn it! That is, if the damn Germans ever get here." Then, shouting over to Channing, "Where the fuck are the Germans with that nitrogen?! Time?!"

"1044," Barsohn answered.

"Got tools! We need more hands over here!" Marshall said.

Four people in camouflage-uniforms hustled across the pole-bridge. "Where do you need us?" one asked.

"Start at the bottom corners on both," Marshall answered. He described procedures to them.

Two new arrivals each helped David and Marshall. In the next moments, they had their first bricks out and were working on the whole row. They, too, encountered no wires or booby traps.

Marshall finished his second. He pulled Sam's hand, till the beam shown into the opening. Cautiously, Marshall stuck his head through the crevice.

Sam put her hand inside the chamber, squeezed her head in behind it, and passed the light over the walls. She thought of the Catacombs, as she watched the room unfold. But this one had sheet-metal side walls, with none of the Old World charm.

Marshall guided the beam to the ceiling and the floor. Propped on a heavy-looking wooden frame was a thick, oval-shaped, olive-green disk. It reminded Sam of a poo-poo pillow with a thyroid condition. In a dark-sort-of-way, she had to laugh, though she did so quietly.

"That's it!" Marshall whispered. He guided the light over the immediate area, gently squeezing Sam's hand as he did. He saw no wires or connections between the SADM/frame and the bricks.

Marshall said to the people helping him, "We can take these out faster!" He told them what he saw. With crowbars, they ground the mortar out. Before long, they had the rest of the new brick-work removed.

Now, Marshall could see the SADM straightaway. "David?!" he called. "We got a live one at twelve o'clock!"

Barsohn joined them. He whispered into Marshall's ear. "I'd prefer your man over there not be disarming our weapon."

"Are you serious?" Marshall murmured.

"Maybe he's your best pal," Barsohn continued, "but he's still a foreign agent, even if an ally."

"Probably our best ally," Marshall whispered over his shoulder. "You want your guys to supervise?"

"I want our people to do the work," Barsohn said. "I don't want anyone without clearance even breathing on those innards."

"Oh, like they don't have their own?" Marshall said. "Let me tell you, Colonel. I'd trust that guy with my back. Not sure I'd trust too many others that much, but this is hardly the time for loyalty oaths!"

"Who the hell's this?" Barsohn interrupted, pointing at Sam. Sam pulled her head into the hood as far as she could.

"Another one of theirs," Marshall said. "David and George's. I wish I had a twin to work on that one, but I don't. I didn't know you were a brass lemming, Harvey. Lighten up. Time?"

Barsohn sighed loudly. "1047."

"You'd better check your search-teams," Marshall said. "God forbid, there's another set-up like this, and we missed it." Barsohn left him.

From the traveled end of the tunnel Marshall suddenly heard noise and spoken German speeding toward them. "The cav's here!" Channing shouted.

A rush of German battle-dresses reached Channing and the others. From the amount of noise and the lights, Marshall guessed this was a twenty- to thirty-person squad. Two or three of the newcomers spoke with Channing, who pointed to Marshall. Marshall, in turn, beckoned them. Six came over the pole-bridge, one-at-a-time. With their arrival the access-walk was getting crowded.

From Channing's side of the tunnel the Germans pushed what looked like an aluminum mobile footbridge across the canal. When it was secured, other men rolled tall cylinders on handtrucks to Marshall's side.

"Here's your nitrogen," one of the Germans said to Marshall. *Kapitan Oberdorfer*, Federal Police."

"What've you got for an enclosure?" Marshall responded.

"Uh . . . Prefabricated. Something like a very small closet, or box."

"We need two of them," Marshall replied. "Can do?"

"Can do," Capt. Oberdorfer said, holding his thumb up. He called to his men on Channing's side of the canal. Some carried small rectangular slabs over the bridge.

"Highly dense and insulated plastic," he said to Marshall, "with interior insulation, as well."

Marshall checked with David, who, with his U.S. assistants, had the other chamber open. It was explosively equipped, too.

"At least the bastard's predictable," Marshall said. He conferred with Captain Oberdorfer. "I want your people to enclose no farther than thirty centimeters from the package, but don't touch. Then, freeze."

"Don't worry. My men are very experienced with demolition removal," Oberdorfer replied. "Can do."

"You've only dealt with this kind in practice," Marshall said. "How long will it take to freeze?"

"Ten to twenty seconds," the German answered. "Maximum."

Marshall loved prefab-anything. Within two minutes the Germans had his SADM contained and were pumping in liquid nitrogen.

"Time?!" Marshall called to Barsohn.

"1053," came back the answer. "The comm-link's wired over here to you," Barsohn added. "The line's open, if you need it."

"Ready?" Marshall asked Capt. Oberdorfer, as he put on protective clothing and gloves, which another German had brought him.

"Another five seconds."

"David?" Marshall called. "You ready?"

"You're flying the airplane," David answered.

"Here's hoping I haven't used up my nine lives yet," Marshall mumbled to himself, as he climbed into the chamber.

* * *

In the conference room of another of his villa/estates, this one near Hamburg, Baron Otto von Markenheim was in the company of The Cartel's Board of Directors. He seldomly used this home, though he had owned it for over forty years. He and the Board decided to relocate there, despite The Colonel's assurances they were safe from the effects of the blasts, at his more-frequented estate outside Berlin. It was nearly 11 A.M., 11 November.

"Well, *meine Herren*," The Baron said. "*I can now tell you that our plan for the coup is on schedule. That is why I had champagne brought in.*"

The men around the large conference table looked at each other, surprised. "*But, Herr Baron, 8 November was the date . . .*"

"That's what I wanted you to believe," The Baron replied. "*The real date is today. I am expecting confirmation that it's begun, as planned, in a very few minutes. As soon as our other teams are alerted by modem, cell-phones, and Internet that the Reichstag has been destroyed, they will deal with their individual targets . . . Foreign and Defence Ministries, Military Staff, Home Defense and Corps Commands, and so forth. Numerous executive actions will be carried out once the word goes. Our contractors are in place.*

"*We shall be the only organized force to reassert order. And our people and their allies in the Bundeswehr will then seize control of communications, political, military and other facilities, to stave off anarchy and complete breakdown from this dastardly international leftist, terrorist conspiracy.*

"*My broadcast is rescheduled for tomorrow morning. At that time, I shall express my deep regret at the savage and barbaric acts of the past twenty-four hours, especially at the deaths of the*

Chancellor and his government. I'll explain why I'm stepping forward to restore order, while disclosing the origins of the weapons, and the identities of those responsible for this attempt to destroy our nation.

"Between the General's involvement and the source of the devices, that should discredit and neutralize the Americans and NATO. Our terrorists will harass Allied and American command facilities. We have people in all the military mobile command structures, who will immobilize any responses.

"We'll blame terrorists and leftist organizations. It is the last gasp of a dying ideology, to keep itself off the dustbin of history. We've proof of the Terror Network's involvement in the occurrences of the past month. Our people will accept this, our act of faith.

"It is still true. If you repeat The Lie long and loud enough, people will believe it. It worked with their grandparents and parents.

"Germany will be rightfully ours. Again. Of course, we've enough of those lovely devices to deal, finally, with Israel. Thoroughly. Or anyone else, who gets in our way."

He stood, and raised his glass. All the others did the same. *"To our imminent victory! Sieg Heil!"*

They drank. Then, several Board members toasted The Baron. Von Markenheim looked at his watch. It was 10:52 A.M. He could hardly contain his excitement. *The Führer's spirit was about to rise again.*

* * *

Marshall had the Germans remove the top of the containment enclosure, leaving the sides and bottom in place. Fog seemed to emanate from the SADM itself.

On the inside of the box they had attached a thermometer. They set up a spotlight on a tripod overhead, turning the small room into a well-lit stage.

Marshall ran his gloved hands lightly over the SADM, feeling for the lock and latch. On one side he found them. He also found the serial number on the outside of the casing, and dictated it to Barsohn, who was leaning through the opening in the wall.

"It checks out as one of the stolen weapons," Barsohn said, after a minute or two.

"What about the immediate vicinity here?" Marshall asked.

"My guys haven't found anything else," Barsohn replied. "It looks like this is the whole party."

Marshall carefully disarmed the lock, using the double-click system and released the latch. Lifting and holding the hinged, top cover, he examined the contents.

The fissionable materials package occupied the center of the disk. Two small, parallel LED readout windows showed red numbers. The top one was set on "11-11-11-00-00-00," while the other was frozen. Marshall knew that it normally would be ticking away, with the red characters in the two right-hand slots appearing and changing so fast that the numerals would seem to collapse into one continuous blur of perpendicular and parallel lines.

It was as he suspected. The Colonel had set the anti-tampering device. The bastard was listening to his lectures. "Tools?!" Marshall shouted. "I need a screwdriver, a wrench, and two extra hands!"

The U.S. soldier, who helped Marshall before the Germans arrived, also suitably dressed and gloved, held the anti-tampering device. Marshall disconnected the bolts and screws from its detonator. They cradled it out and handed it to two Germans.

"How's the baby's temperature?" Marshall asked.

"Rising," a German answered.

"You've probably got four to five minutes, with that stuff," Barsohn said.

"Thanks, Mother," Marshall replied.

"I just thought you'd like to know," Barsohn said.

Marshall went into the other chamber and instructed David in what to do. He supervised, while David opened the lock and latch and disarmed the anti-tampering device.

Marshall returned to his own work. He found the links, attaching the fissionable packet and balancing it in the casing. "Ask them if there's a special sequence of removal." He waited, while Barsohn transmitted the query.

"They said no. This is like any you're acquainted with," Barsohn said. "You should be able to pick up and remove the packet without any hassle. Remember, the contacts are underneath the packet."

Marshall grasped the fissionable pack with both hands. Slowly and carefully, he started lifting it out. As he did, he saw a small wire bend up from the back of it. He stopped and lowered it into its niche.

"Fuck!" he exclaimed. "There's a wire that doesn't belong here! David! Don't pick up the pack yet! The bastard's thrown us his own booby trap!"

Marshall had the Germans re-administer liquid nitrogen, but he left the SADM lid open this time. David's SADM was treated the same way.

"Time?!" he called to Barsohn, when they were finished.

"1057!" Barsohn answered.

"Give it to me each thirty seconds," Marshall said.

The Germans reopened the bomb casing. While three of them lifted, then held the fissionables pack slightly above its compartment, Marshall worked at the back of the SADM, where the wire materialized.

"1057.5!" Barsohn said.

Another man held a light for Marshall, as he traced the wire. The gloves made it difficult. He crawled his two fingers past the terminal and another with its wire.

"1058!"

Marshall called for two pairs of razor-sharp, plastic wire-cutters. Oberdorfer brought them to him. Marshall explained that they would simultaneously snip the wires, then have the others lift the packet from the casing.

Oberdorfer and Marshall bent over the SADM and reached the wires. Marshall guided first his, then Oberdorfer's to their respective targets.

"1058.5!"

Marshall took a deep breath. The back of his neck was cold and wet.

"Go!" he said, suddenly.

In the next second his cutter broke through the wire. The three men holding the packet lifted it abruptly from its cradle. It came out unfettered.

Marshall glanced into the compartment. Lying near the contacts was a small lump of plastique with detonator and battery pack.

"The bastard!" Marshall said. "He wired it to go off, if the bomb's disarmed!"

"1059!" Barsohn boomed.

Marshall rushed to David, nearly tripping into the water on the way. After opening the enclosure, he found a similar arrangement connected to the packet in David's SADM.

"1059.5!" Barsohn called, as Marshall and David snipped the wires on the second booby trap. Two other men, holding that packet, abruptly yanked it from its concealed contacts. Marshall closed his eyes and held his breath.

"1100!"

A long, deafeningly silent moment passed. Marshall exhaled so hard he felt like a deflating balloon.

"Christ! You did it!" Barsohn shouted.

"I guess eleven's my lucky number!" Marshall blurted, not sure why. But it sounded good.

David seized him in a bearhug. After David let go, Marshall stumbled to the unbricked cavity in the wall and slumped through to the tunnel.

The scene was chaotic. Celebrations and clean-up collided. The tunnel was a ready-made sound chamber, with the noise able to deafen even the dead. But through it, order emerged. Marshall watched teams pack the fissile components, followed by their oval containers.

Marshall looked for Sam. She was leaning against the tunnel wall, past the crowd. He lumbered to her, arms outstretched, and kissed her gently and long on the lips. "I'm getting too old for this shit!" Marshall whispered. "How's it feel to be the savior of the Western World?"

"Heady," Sam answered. "But I'll take a raincheck on the credit angle, till I have Pa back in one piece."

* * *

There was a knock on the conference room door. Baron von Markenheim had a phone call in his study.

Alone in his library-study, von Markenheim took the call on a line marked, *"Scrambled."* It was from one of his well-situated sources in the Federal Ministry of Defense.

As he listened, von Markenheim's smile turned to disbelief, then anger. He told the caller to "submerge," then signed off. He pushed a two-digit, speed-dial number on the console. When his call was answered, he spoke one phrase into the receiver, *"Prevent and retrieve."*

Returning to the conference room, he gaveled for order and instructed everyone to be seated.

"Gentlemen, something has gone awry," von Markenheim said, quickly. *"The Reichstag is still standing. I recommend we adjourn."*

XXIX

McConneld and Balkovsky landed at Berlin-*Tegel* around 12:45 P.M., after receiving Channing's message. Their chopper had developed engine trouble. The pilot diverted to *Rhein-Main*, where they changed aircraft and continued on. Back at the Embassy, they found Channing and Barsohn, who briefed them on Marshall and the SADMs.

"Well," McConneld said, finally. "Three down, seventeen to go."

"Good plan," Balkovsky said. "We don't find the first one, they go forward. We find it, they still go forward."

"Where's Marshall now? And how did he know they were there?" McConneld asked.

Channing said, "The Germans are strip-searching the sewer system. I think they have an *HSK* unit on it."

"And my questions?" McConneld pursued.

"I thought I answered the second, Chief," Channing replied. "He believed he'd be more useful 'in-the-field.' Or maybe more aptly 'gone-to-ground'."

"'In-the-sewer,' as't'were? Well?" McConneld persisted.

"He said he'd tell me, when he got back here," Channing said.

"Well, get him!" McConneld said. "And how about that Foxwirth woman? Did McGonnville bring her in?" Channing told him.

"I'll see her," McConneld said. "McGonnville, too. Is she in?"

"No," Channing replied. "But I can get her here, no problem."

Half-an-hour later, Marshall arrived. "Heard you did another boffo job," McConneld said to him. "Sorry I missed it. How'd you know they were there?"

Marshall thought for a moment. "I didn't, not for sure. Then I recalled something I forgot on 8 November. Remember when you let me out? I'd seen a guy working in the street, who looked like the Colonel. But I only got a glimpse of him."

"A street worker?" Balkovsky asked.

Marshall told them Sam's version, *sans* Sam. "Besides, we thought the Colonel was dead."

McConneld said, "How'd you put those things together?"

"Something about the whole scenario on the eighth," Marshall said, "was gnawing at me. It seemed . . . well, too easy. Now, admittedly, the guy I saw was bald."

"Bald?!" Balkovsky interrupted. "My source's head was recently shaved. My source was with the Colonel, when he armed the first bomb."

"So, I mightn't have been far off-base," Marshall continued. He described the events after that.

"And they brought another agent with them," Barsohn added. "Right?" He looked at Marshall for confirmation.

Marshall said, quickly, "But David and I did the work."

"I thought I saw you hugging that other agent afterward," Barsohn said.

"Just a friendly gesture," Marshall said. "Don't worry, Harvey. I didn't drop any state secrets."

"What's that all about?" McConneld asked.

"A small disagreement between Harvey and me," Marshall said. "He was skittish about David disarming the SADM."

"A matter of Clearance and Security," Barsohn said. "I still think you were wrong."

"The important thing is the job," McConneld said. "Make nice, kids. If the Colonel's not dead, we've got to track him."

"But, how?" Channing asked. "This is up there with, 'when-everything-you-know-is-wrong.'"

"He used at least one alias in the past week. I want all of them run down with credit card companies, commercial establishments, anything. Germany, France, Switzerland, Austria. Throw in Britain, for good measure."

"That could take weeks," Channing said.

"Maybe Ms. Foxwirth can help us," McConneld said. "Find the most recent photo we've got of Krattmay. Try Langley or Interpol. If we tie him to her step-father, we may have something the Germans, including the Chancellor, will swallow about von Markenheim. Maybe."

Channing went to the computer and communications center. Marshall asked McConneld about his earlier absence.

"Alexei decided to let me talk with his 'source.' We were also going to locate that airfield, where McGonnville says she saw Tom Pemberton. We can still do that."

A young man McConneld knew as a staff analyst, in shirt-sleeves and tie, delivered files to McConneld. "Well, well! Look at this! That heating renovation, on the *Reichstag*? A large, *general* contracting firm handled it. Guess who, buried in holding companies and dummy corporations?"

"Von Markenheim?" Barsohn asked, anxiously.

"I wish. Close, but no brass ring," McConneld said. "None other than Walter Tripleleaf, USAF, Retired."

"Who's also dropped from sight," Marshall said.

"They must've used him as a front," Barsohn said.

McConneld continued, "There was an emergency malfunction. An electronic glitch a night or two before the first bomb. The same General Tripleleaf made a house call with the repairmen. According to this, he stayed upstairs with security, while they went downstairs."

"How's that help us?" Barsohn said. "It sounds like it implicates our side, as silent partners, or incompetents."

"True," McConneld said. "But we knew of the connections between Tripleleaf and The Cartel, even if we can't prove them beyond a reasonable doubt."

"Wouldn't it be lovely, if we could?" Marshall asked. "Certain people in Washington would kill to keep those from coming to light. They'd protect Tripleleaf, and themselves, to the death."

Channing returned. "Langley faxed this," he said, handing McConneld a reprographic. "It's over ten years old. He may not look like this anymore."

"Till I saw him a few weeks ago, this was how I remembered him," McConneld said, looking at the grainy reproduction. "Call McGonnville in, too. And let's have Ms. Foxwirth."

Marshall chose to listen to the interview from the next room. Regina Foxwirth arrived, accompanied by two Agency men.

McConneld decided on the light touch for Ms. Foxwirth: no

hard tactics. From McGonnville's preliminary, he expected no trouble. He showed her the photo.

"I've never seen this man," Ms. Foxwirth replied.

McConneld asked, "Never with your step-father?"

She answered, "My step-father kept us away from most of his business associates, but not all."

"Please understand," McConneld said. "We'll give you the best protection possible. Your step-father won't know information came from you, if you cooperate."

"That's what Elizabeth said," Regina replied, "after the indignity to which she subjected me. But I really do not have anything I can tell you."

"Start with your leaving D.C.," McConneld said. "Why so abruptly?"

"Didn't Elizabeth tell you?"

"You tell us," Harvey Barsohn said. "Then we'll all know if she did."

"My step-father sent me to Georgetown to keep tabs on Samantha Pemberton. I was to report to him, through a contact man, who was a despicable person, I must say."

"I'm sure," McConneld said. "But why'd you stop?"

"I didn't," Regina answered.

"You left Washington, didn't you?" McConneld asked.

"So did she," Regina replied. Regina told McConneld her experiences, since leaving, including Liz McGonnville's treatment of the first contact and herself. She detailed her conversation with The Baron about Samantha.

"I told Elizabeth I needed protection for myself and my mother," Regina said. "She told me I'd have it. Then, on the way to Berlin, we kept having to switch trains. It was dreadful. Elizabeth and another man came and got us."

"If I told you your step-father wasn't at any of his estates or his yacht, where do you think he might be?" McConneld asked.

"I'm certain I do not know," Regina said. "He was supposed to be in Berlin this whole month, but changed plans. Have you checked his offices, his home near *Ulm*, and the ones up here? Or, actually, in the nearby countryside?"

"Why, yes," McConneld said. "He's not in any of those places."

"Then I can't help you," Regina said. "He has others but he never uses them."

"Such as?" Barsohn asked.

"One near Hamburg," Regina replied. "I can't remember the last time he was there. It's in my mother's name, but it's really his. Like all his things, he lets one have the privilege of use for a time. I haven't been there in at least seven years. And I don't think Father was there then."

"I'd like you to go with these gentlemen," McConneld said, motioning to Channing and Barsohn. "And, give them a list of your step-father's homes and haunts, as you recall."

"Has he disappeared?" Regina asked, sadly. McConneld nodded. "I always suspected this would come," Regina said. "'Spose I did not want to believe it. I've thought of him as my father."

McConneld walked her to the door, with Barsohn, Channing, and her two escorts, accompanying her. He felt sorry for her. The past months had apparently stripped away her reputed arrogance and unassailable quasi-pseudo-self-assurance.

"I know nothing. I see nothing," Marshall said, in a semi-German accent after coming back.

"It was worth a try, anyway," McConneld said. "So Samantha Pemberton's definitely over here somewhere? No surprise, I admit, but it sounds like McGonnville's well aware of this. How 'bout you?"

Marshall said, "No clue. When she lost your people, she lost me, too. I had my own problems."

"I'm interested to hear McGonnville's story," McConneld said, "though I'm sure the Colonel's aliases will also keep us busy."

Through the afternoon, McConneld, Channing, and other staff contacted major credit card companies with requests. McConneld left only once, with Channing.

That was for a briefing with the Chancellor, Foreign and Defense Ministers, and other high-ranking German officials. Once more the Chancellor was beyond grateful. At the same time, though, he was frustrated and angry that his country, and Berlin specifically, seemed like a live nuclear minefield. He casually commented, when this matter was resolved, he would press

Washington on the possibility of having those weapons withdrawn from Europe.

When McConneld returned, there were other congratulatory messages from Washington, particularly from the White House, awaiting him. "Is McGonnville back in?" McConneld asked, after his phone conversation with Washington.

"She hasn't checked in," Channing said. "She's in the field, without contact."

"Pull strings," McConneld remarked. "Get her in here!"

When the responses to McConneld's and Barsohn's inquiries began flowing in, there were hundreds of credit card charges, very far apart, geographically, on the same dates. To promising ones, agents were sent.

"The bastard's laid red herrings all over," Barsohn commented.

That night and the next morning came and went, with more leads to be pursued, but no breakthroughs.

"You know what day it is?" Channing said to McConneld, after returning from yet another briefing with German officials.

"Barely," McConneld replied. "We're close, real close, and the son-of-a-bitch is always one slither ahead. I need a shower."

"Have you seen a paper lately?" Channing said. "I thought you might be interested in this," Channing said, handing him a newspaper. "Take a look at the bottom of the front page."

"American General Found . . . Apparent Suicide," McConneld translated, aloud. "General Walter Tripleleaf?!!"

Balkovsky and Marshall read over McConneld's shoulder.

"Why didn't we get this?!" McConneld said. "Wake up Harvey Barsohn, Chuck. He's down the hall on a cot."

The general's body was discovered by staff in a Leipzig hotel the night before. A maid found the body in an upstairs suite, reserved under Tripleleaf's name. From the body's condition, authorities estimated, he had been dead three or four days.

Channing returned with Barsohn, while McConneld was reading the story. McConneld handed the paper to Barsohn. "Yet another literally dead end."

"Poor maid!" Marshall said. "He must've been real funky by then!"

"I want to hear what the Interior Ministry and the Federal Police have," McConneld said.

"The Germans reported it to the military attaché at our Consulate in Bonn," Channing said. "He reported it to Washington and saw no connection with us."

"Next stop, Leipzig," McConneld said.

"I figured you'd say that," Channing replied. "A chopper's at *Tegel* for us."

* * *

Sam awakened early on the morning of 12 November at the Savoy, alone. She needed the space and time and had the answer she wanted. She also decided not to reprise her stay with Liz, having so narrowly avoided Mr. McConneld.

Marshall dropped her at the hotel the day before, when they finally escaped the leftover jubilation in the Berlin sewers. He also told her to "stay put." She was happy to shed her filthy unitard, discard it, and take a long, hot bath.

She stayed close to her room, having her meals there and leaving only once, to call *Swissair* from a pay phone and to shop for a replacement unitard. She booked a seat to Zürich for the next morning.

Her flight left *Tegel* at 8:10 A.M. and arrived in Zürich by 10:30, where an ATM supplied cash for her purchases from Klaus. She was back in her Zürich hotel room by 11:30 A.M., and phoned him. When she arrived at the shop, the atmosphere was basic musty-antique and quiet. No customers were in the shop.

He led her to a rear storage room, where he unpacked two Baretta 9mm pistols, a stockless *Uzi*, clips for each, sound suppressors, ammunition, and miniaturized listening devices.

"*Ah, good! Both kinds of ammunition. How much is all this?*" Sam asked. "*I didn't bring enough cash for this much stuff.*"

"*Everything, but the Uzi, is as agreed,*" Klaus said. "*The Uzi's a gift. It cost me next to nothing. I had a hunch you might need it. Know how to use it?*"

"I'm a fast study, though I do know it kicks up. Now you've made me feel like a heel," Sam said. "I was going to ask you for another favor. I don't feel right."

"Ask," Klaus said.

"Could we get floor plans for that house on the lake?"

Klaus thought. *"The nearest town's civil center might have them. If not, Evangelein could be of help. Call me after five P.M."*

Later, at her hotel, Sam packed her camping equipment. Having left the weapons with Klaus, she would pick them up when she returned later that evening. When she called Klaus, he had what she asked for. She drove to the shop.

"How'd you get them so fast?" Sam asked, as Klaus showed her old maps of the estate, and four distinct sets of drawings.

"An old friend," Klaus replied. *"Not Evangelein. Another expatriate, who's a civil servant now."*

Sam examined the illustrations. *"These are two different houses."*

Klaus replied, *"He did a little digging and found the original house, which was hundreds of years old, burned about twenty-five years ago. It had been rebuilt inside many times, as you can see. The previous owners built on the same site and kept the same shell and architecture. Notice the dates in the lower right corners. And look at this, on this map of the grounds."*

He laid a larger map on the counter. *"There seems to be a tunnel or viaduct, underground, leading up to the house. It shows on the older plans. See?"* Sam compared the map and drawings.

"But it doesn't show up on the newer ones," Klaus said. "There's no way of knowing if it's still there. The old owners could've had it closed up."

"It's worth a look," Sam said. *"The new people might not even know it's there. Where's an entrance?"*

"According to this, there are control points in different places. The first's predictably at the See. Another one here."

"May I take these with me?" Sam asked.

"Of course," Klaus answered. *"But I can't let you go alone."*

"Thanks, but I can take care of myself. Let's settle up. I need time to study these."

Klaus instructed her in the care and use of the Uzi. Before

Sam left the shop, she and Klaus loaded magazines. Later that evening, she drove to the *Sihlsee*, as a dress rehearsal.

* * *

At an improvised helipad on the outskirts of Leipzig, McConneld, Channing, and Balkovsky were met by representatives of the local and Federal police. The Interior Ministry arranged it, as a result of McConneld's phone call. This time Barsohn remained in Berlin as liaison. Marshall also stayed there.

The police officials drove them to the hotel, where the body was found. The suite was sealed. A police inspector, in charge of the investigation, briefed them on the preliminary conclusion: suicide.

Tripleleaf's body had been lying on the bed, with a bottle of Champagne, one glass with Champagne and other residue, and a bottle of liquid on a nighttable. He was fully clothed, with no apparent signs of a struggle. There had also been a note, found in an antique portable typewriter on a desk.

"*Initial indications,*" the inspector said, "*are the stuff in the bottle was a slow-acting poison.*" He read from an early report. "*We're still waiting for full autopsy results. It looks clean.*"

"A little too neat," McConneld commented. "Why take something slow?"

"Who knows?" the inspector replied. "*I've stopped trying to understand the suicides' minds.*"

"Anything else in the room?"

"*No luggage or belongings. Only the things in his pockets and the stuff I already mentioned.*"

"*I'd like to see the body,*" McConneld said.

"*It may've already been turned over to your Army,*" the inspector said. "*Otherwise, it's still in our morgue.*"

"But you're still waiting for the final autopsy report," Channing interjected.

The inspector said, "*Soon after we reported it to your people, someone from your Army called to arrange a pick-up. They were dispatching investigators of their own.*"

"You interviewed the staff?" Channing asked.

"*My men did,*" the inspector answered. "*He checked in late. Actually, early on the morning of the 7th, alone. He reserved the room for four days, had a late dinner, and paid by credit card. Lots to drink. He must've had, what I believe you Americans call, 'a hollow leg.'*" The inspector laughed. "*He put a 'Do Not Disturb' sign on the door. No one saw him after that, until his body was found.*"

"How did he arrive?" Channing asked.

"*By limousine. But we haven't been able to trace it yet.*"

"They did what they came to," McConneld said. "*The newspaper didn't say anything about a note. May we see it?*"

"*Your consular people recommended not disclosing that. It's at the station,*" the inspector answered. "*It was not very illuminating. He was very depressed. We found his fingerprints on the typewriter and the bottles.*"

"You did a full search?" McConneld asked.

The inspector nodded. "*You can see that, too, when we're back at the station.*" Resealing the room, the inspector and his men drove McConneld & Co. to their offices. Among Tripleleaf's personal effects were a wallet, keys, money, credit card stub, other usual, unnotable items. The typewriter was a small electric portable, with case.

The note read, "I'm leaving because I've disgraced myself and my family."

"Brief and to the point," McConneld observed. "*You saw the body?*" He asked the inspector. "*No abrasions? Bruises?*"

"*I didn't examine it closely, but what I saw didn't seem to indicate violence or third parties.*"

"*All these were from his room?*" Channing said. The inspector acknowledged. "*Do you know where this was found?*" Channing held up a small piece of flat aluminum, roughly an inch long and shaped like an hourglass.

"Not really. I could ask my men."

Channing dropped the metal piece onto his superior's open palm. McConneld recognized it: a clip from an ace bandage.

One detective recalled finding it, stuck in a drawer. He brought it on a whim, but believed it was left from an earlier occupant.

The inspector called the morgue. The General's body had been surrendered to "representatives" of the U.S. Army, escorted by an Interior Ministry official.

"Sorry for the inconvenience," the inspector said, after he informed them. *"I'm certain you can track him down with them."*

While they were at the station, the inspector received a draft of the autopsy report. Tripleleaf's body still contained residue of ingested food and amounts of the poison. His blood-alcohol level was high. The report showed no conclusive proof of *"foul play,"* but did note his face had several bruises and abrasions on it. Its conclusion: "Cause of death was myocardial infarction, ultimately due to self-inflicted ingestion of a toxic agent."

McConneld and Co. did perfunctory thank-yous, and were driven back to the helipad. They were in Berlin, after a refueling stop, within a few hours.

Back at his offices, McConneld contacted the U.S. Command and German Interior Ministry. Each pled no knowledge of reclaiming the body.

"Very neat," McConneld said. "No muss. No fuss. And he's on the bottom of a river drinking dung."

"He was hit all right," Channing said. "Ace bandages are an old Mob trick. They leave no marks on the skin." He and McConneld briefed Barsohn and Marshall on the results of the trip.

* * *

McConneld's secretary came into the command and operations center late in the evening of the 12th and found him working with Barsohn and Channing. "A courier from our London embassy is waiting to see you, sir," she said. "He said it was urgent."

The secretary showed the courier into McConneld's private office. The courier identified himself, as McGill Hopkins, special assistant to the U.S. Ambassador in London. Hopkins reminded McConneld of the standard-issue State Department assistant: perfectly dressed, perfectly coifed, perfectly educated, and perhaps poor-but-proud.

Hopkins carried a letter for McConneld from the ambassador. He knew its contents and explained the purpose of his visit.

An English barrister had contacted the ambassador, through friends in M.I.-5 and -6. A meeting was arranged among the barrister, the ambassador and her assistants, including Hopkins, and ranking Agency officials at a safe location outside London, that afternoon, 12 November.

The barrister, a secret, legal representative of General Walter Tripleleaf, brought with him a sealed attaché case. The general had instructed him weeks before to bring the case to the U.S. Embassy in London, in the event that Tripleleaf died, no matter what the cause of death. When he learned of the general's death from the newspapers that morning, he retrieved the case, whose contents he had never seen, from safekeeping and had his friends schedule the meeting.

The ambassador contacted Foggy Bottom, which, in turn, notified Langley. Deputy Director Simmons, at Langley, recommended contacting McConneld.

At the meeting with the barrister, the ambassador examined the contents. She did not disclose those to him, Hopkins noted, but she seemed preoccupied with them.

She dispatched Hopkins, first, to brief McConneld and arrange the transfer. A special courier would arrive, with the material, when the ambassador received word of Hopkins' meeting with McConneld.

The letter reiterated what Hopkins told him. The ambassador mentioned she had had a background check done on the barrister. He was well-respected in the legal community, with contacts in reliable political circles.

The ambassador requested that McConneld corroborate Hopkins' contact in Berlin by faxing the phrase, "Leafy green vegetable matter," to her residence and included her private number. The Berlin Consular staff confirmed it.

Channing came back with a faxed response from London. It read, "Vegetable order en route. God bless the Third Air Force."

"That's the ambassador's response," Hopkins said. "The courier arrives by Air Force flight at *Tempelhof* late tonight."

* * *

It was nearly midnight, 12 November, as McConneld, Channing, and Barsohn waited in an Embassy limousine. It was parked on the runway side of the semi-circular terminal at *Tempelhof.* A U.S. Air Force Tri-star was taxiing toward the terminal.

The front door opened, and the exit ladder dropped into place. A man in a winter coat and two uniformed marines deplaned.

When they met, McConneld verified his and the others' identities, as did the man in the coat. He was the courier. He removed a leather pouch from its handcuff-grip on his wrist and handed it to McConneld. The courier gave McConneld two keys. He and his escorts returned to the jet.

On the way to the Embassy, McConneld removed the contents, an attaché case. The case had a broken wax seal on the center lock. "Holy shit!" McConneld exclaimed. "Home run! Look at this stuff!" He handed pages to Channing and Barsohn.

Barsohn said, after reading them, "We got the bastards!" Channing agreed.

McConneld said, "They don't know the s.o.b. left this."

"They may not try to reposition things now, anyway," Barsohn suggested. "Things are too hot."

"He was taking a big chance," Channing said, "if this fell into the wrong hands. I'm surprised he didn't encrypt it on disks."

"Maybe he was old-fashioned," McConneld said. "This confirms he was murdered. He figured something might happen, when they didn't need him anymore."

"He's having the last laugh," Channing said. "Another old, dead bee."

At the Embassy, Barsohn contacted AFCENT and requested Special Forces and Ranger units, helicopters, and EOD personnel, as well as follow-in airborne troops.

"SEALs! Damn it!" McConneld said to him, while he was still on the phone. "I want SEALs!" He gave Barsohn a particular name. Barsohn requested and was assured SEAL personnel were available.

"I'm in," Marshall said, after McConneld told him about the

papers. "And, if you don't mind, I want David and George along." McConneld did not object, nor did Barsohn.

Meanwhile, McConneld and Channing, with the help of additional staff, plotted the locations from Tripleleaf's papers. The places mentioned were spread over Germany and Switzerland.

There were five in all. The first was outside a town called *Wildershausen*, southwest of Bremen. The second was in the *Rothaargebirge*, an area of rough terrain and hills, east of the Rhine. The third location was in the *Pfalzer Bergland*, another hilly area, on the west side of the Rhine and north of *Kaiserslautern*. The fourth was in the *Altmuhltal* region, between *Nürnberg* and Munich. The final one was near a small town, named *Euthal*, in Switzerland.

McConneld and Barsohn requested "Black-bird" reconnaissance flights, by SR-71s. These were ordered, though the SR-71 fleet had generally been put in "cold storage," years before. Dumb thing, McConneld believed. He liked that plane.

Barsohn received calls-back. One was from AFCENT. They were drawing on SEAL teams from CINCLANT, Norfolk, and two other East Coast bases. Those teams would arrive in Germany within hours. The other assets he requested would be ready very soon as well.

McConneld was as pleased as the situation allowed. For the first time, he felt ahead of the opposition.

They did preliminary planning for the raids. Various units would assemble near Frankfurt, where McConneld, Barsohn, and the others would join them.

Over the next hours, reports filtered in. Units were arriving in Frankfurt as planned. McConneld was happy to learn the SEALs were there. The helicopters and air troops were on alert.

The first results of the reconnaissance flights also arrived, after preliminary examination by Agency and military Intelligence analysts. More detailed ones would be forwarded. Films and technical readouts indicated isolated facilities, farm-like, surrounded by rough and forested terrain. The Swiss location included a mansion on a remote estate.

McConneld contacted high-ranking Swiss Foreign Ministry authorities, to notify them of and clear with their government the impending "visit" by U.S. troops. They offered assistance, which McConneld accepted in the forms of guides, patrol boats, transport, and "subtle sequestration" of the immediate area. This meant surveillance of the roads by Swiss officers, but no roadblocks, till the operation was under way.

Barsohn and McConneld divided command. Barsohn would oversee the *Rothaargebirge* raid. He would have a subordinate, in tactical command. Balkovsky decided to join Barsohn.

McConneld, with Marshall, David, and George along, would supervise the Swiss operation. He, too, would have an operational sub-commander.

The other raids would be commanded by members of the Services involved. Channing would coordinate from a mobile C3, created for the purpose, at Frankfurt Headquarters.

Contact with the Germans was limited. McConneld was hesitant, since he did not know how deeply the German Government, the military establishment, and the *Bundeswehr* had been infiltrated.

He also took a gamble not requesting the areas in question be cordoned off by German police or troops. Barsohn and he discussed the possibility and rejected it. They favored dispatching U.S. scouts, instead. The "bad guys" had demonstrated their "air transport," or quick-disappearance, capabilities. That was also his reason for not barging into the offices in Hamburg, where he saw Marshall with The Colonel.

* * *

In her hardtop Rover, parked on the path to the *Sihlsee*, Sam was watching the entry road to the estate. It was the late morning of 13 November. She left Zürich around 5 A.M.

On the way she stocked provisions. She was ready for five days of spartan eating and caffeine. She had been on stakeout for several hours when she saw the same jeep as before, go and come multiple times.

Near noon it was on its third return trip, when it was accompanied by trucks and two other jeeps. Things were quiet again for the afternoon.

* * *

Preparations continued through 13 November. Better photographic analyses and renditions of the target areas arrived from surveillance flights. Maps had also arrived, pinpointing physical features, distances, and possible landing zones. In the Swiss case, McConneld obtained grounds drawings and floorplans.

Barsohn, McConneld, and Marshall drew up tentative assault plans. Most, if not all, would have to be approached on foot. The troop-choppers would not come in until the follow-up troops and EOD were due. Even gunships would have to stand-off, unless absolutely necessary.

By late afternoon, McConneld, Barsohn, and Co. were prepared to leave for Frankfurt. All the units were there.

* * *

Things had been quiet for Sam since the convoy. Snow began to fall in the late morning. She hunkered down in her ski suit, drinking Cokes and coffee and studying the maps Klaus gave her. As the afternoon drew on, her mind wandered. Maybe she should've done what Liz suggested. Doubts crowded her thoughts. The snow continued to fall heavily.

She was awakened from her free association by a rap on the passenger window. She clutched the 9mm in her right-hand ski-jacket pocket. It was Klaus.

"Christ! You scared the shit out of me! I told you I could take care of myself!"

"*I owe your old man too much,*" Klaus replied. "*Besides, do you really think you could find that tunnel alone. In this?*"

"*I guess not,*" Sam conceded, grudgingly. She was disappointed, in one sense, since she had wanted to do this without any man's help.

"*I bet you forgot a shovel,*" Klaus said.

"Wrong! I have my handy-dandy trench-tool," Sam said, proudly.

"*Then, we're both well-equipped,*" Klaus replied, unfazed. "*We'd better scout out the entrance.*"

"*I was waiting till dark,*" Sam said.

"That's first-rate thinking . . ." Klaus said.

"You're the second guy to say that to me in as many days," Sam snapped. *"You men can be so condescending, and you're not even aware of it."*

Klaus replied, *"I'm not disagreeing. I only meant if whatever else you're doing in civilian life doesn't work out, you have a real future as a burglar."*

Sam smiled at his joke. *"I guess I'm jumpy, but you're right. We might have to go in sooner."*

"Maybe I was a bit patronizing," Klaus said. *"Evening is not far. What do you really expect to find here?"*

"If I'm lucky," Sam sighed, *"my father. If he's not here, maybe a lead to him."* She felt cool, in control, no tears.

The two studied the map of the estate and surroundings. It appeared the tunnel opening was down the shore a brief distance. Evening settled, with snow continuing to fall. By then it had covered the Rover.

In the darkness, Sam and Klaus searched for the opening. Sam carried the two 9mm pistols in her pockets. She had left the *Uzi* in the lower, rear section of the Rover. The map showed only the tunnel's general location. It seemed to be at least a kilometer to the house.

Down the shoreline not far from the road, Sam and Klaus found the mouth of a tunnel, recessed in a slope. It looked like the end of a sewer line, four or five feet in diameter with thick overgrowth, like a curtain, over part of it. It was cut through rock. There was a regular trickle of water, flowing from it.

Klaus compared its location with the map. *"It looks like we didn't have to dig, after all,"* he said to Sam.

He went to the Rover and brought back her pack with assorted tools and supplies. Klaus led.

"Oh, God!" Sam whispered. *"There are rats in here, aren't there?!"*

"You can still go back."

"I'll stay close," Sam said. *"They can't chomp us both."*

The floor was coarse and full of dips and bumps, with a gradual incline. Sam felt entombed.

Images from her dreams flashed in her mind. All she heard

were the echoes of the water, an occasional scurry up ahead, and their own footsteps.

After ten or fifteen minutes, the crouching was getting to her back. They squatted, where there was no water flow.

"This must be centuries old," he said, *"maybe older."*

They found a circular opening in the ceiling and the remnants of an iron ladder. Sam shone her light up the overhead shaft. It rose thirty feet or more and was covered. They had been in the tunnel over an hour, only quiet starkness and shaft ahead. And no rats!

Klaus guessed they had traveled a kilometer, when they took a rest. By his compass, the tunnel was in the correct direction.

More crouching, more time, more tunnel. Sam's back and shoulders were sore, and she felt a damp, penetrating cold. There were more overhead shafts like the first. The ladders were crude iron or wood, in various conditions of disrepair or decay.

Darkness at the end of the tunnel, Sam had thought. Sam and Klaus found a stone wall, with chunks of it broken out. The tunnel width shrank to a meter. There was a greater stream of water on the floor and the incline became sharper. Sam and Klaus shimmied on hands and toes.

Finally, they came into an underground chamber and shone their lanterns around it. The tunnel climaxed on the lip of a spring. On either side of the water were stone ledges, inclined as well, and bounded by coarse rock walls. There were no modern additions, or even torches.

The ceiling was high. The ledges converged further on into one path. There, rough-hewn steps ascended into more darkness.

Sam and Klaus each took out pistols and attached sound suppressors. They headed up the stairs, crouching, but not against physical restrictions.

The steps stopped abruptly, with a solid wall of rock in front. To the right was a sheer drop, to the left a very old-looking wooden door, with a bolt on the inside and a keyhole. The door gave way, grudgingly, as Klaus pushed it. Its very old hinges moaned a two-octave groan. Klaus closed it after them. This space smelled of ancient mold and mildew.

They were in another chamber, with dirt walls and floor. There was a single exit, through the roof, by way of another deteriorated iron ladder. Some rungs were attached on only one side. Over the hole there was a cover.

"I suggest we go back to your vehicle," Klaus whispered. "We need other things . . . the Uzi you didn't bring."

"Guilty," Sam confessed. "But let's at least see what's up there."

* * *

The interior of the briefing room seemed so familiar, Marshall thought. It was like Uncle Sam to stick with the same architecture. He was at a table in the front with McConneld & Co. and another senior officer, a brigadier general.

In the room were officers and NCOs, in battle dress, from the units chosen to carry out the raids: Rangers, Special Forces, SEALs, EOD personnel, and pilots.

The general introduced McConneld and the others and took roll. Then he turned the briefing over to McConneld and Barsohn.

McConneld explained the raids. From briefing boards, he and Barsohn completed details with photos and maps. Each assault team had allotted time to reach its objective, do its reconnoitering, and get in position for action.

"Each of you has a binder in front of you," Barsohn said. "Open it now." The operations would be coordinated by Frankfurt Ops-Cen. All teams were due to "jump off" at 0500, the next morning, 14 November.

The tactical commanders would have considerable flexibility in execution. All would make direct pre-assault and action reports to the operational command center in Frankfurt, overseen by Channing and the brigadier general.

The weather forecasts for each area showed the Bremen area was expected to be clear, while conditions deteriorated farther south. Ironically, the southern areas were expecting or were already getting snowfall.

"I want to re-emphasize," McConneld said, when Barsohn

finished. "These are dedicated fanatics. Expect the worst. The SADMs, and probably MADMs, may be armed. They have plenty of conventional ordnance. You must get in and secure these sites fast, with EOD right behind you. You airborne and air assault people'll follow up. Questions?"

Hands went up. Most were particular planning queries or requests for clarifications. Barsohn handled them.

"Rules of engagement?" the final questioner asked.

"Disable, if possible," McConneld answered. "But protect yourselves. It would be nice to capture canaries, but don't risk casualties." No more hands went up.

"One more thing," McConneld said. "Mr. Marshall here has volunteered to lead the reconnaissance squad on the Swiss raid that I'll be on. Tell your guys, he's the best. He had time in 'Nam."

"Don't let my baggy eyes fool you," Marshall said. "I've still got my edge. And I owe the bastards."

Barsohn read the names of five tactical commanders. "We'll see you after this," he said. "Dismissed."

One commander, a reactivated Navy SEAL officer, would be in command of the attack on the site near *Pfalzer Bergland*, west of the Rhine and north of *Kaiserslautern*. McConneld was particularly anxious to speak with him, Lt. Commander Robert Pemberton, USNR. McConneld saved him for last.

"Good to see you, Bob," McConneld said, finally. "Sorry about your father."

Pemberton returned the pleasure. "I understand you asked for me by name, sir."

"I owed it to you," McConneld replied, "besides being partially responsible for your father disappearing and for your other recent assignments."

"I had a hunch The Agency was involved," Pemberton replied.

"Especially after I told your sister to lay that story on you."

"You put her up to that, sir?"

"I had to," McConneld answered. "I couldn't afford having you blowing loose. But when you have a task, you're golden. You'll probably make admiral someday."

Barsohn explained the mission.

"I'm hoping we'll find a lead to your father," McConneld said, when Barsohn was finished.

McConneld recounted Liz McGonnville's report about Professor Pemberton. He omitted the part about him being a prisoner. He also did not tell Bob about Samantha's escape from D.C.

There would be time for all that, after the raids were complete. Bob Pemberton did not need to know those things then. He had a job to do first.

XXX

"Hold on! Almost there," Klaus whispered, as he hauled the rope through the opening in the floor. Sam was at the other end, suspended over the room they found after the rock stairs. As soon as she was within reach, Sam grabbed the side and dragged herself up.

"Are you all right?" Sam asked.

Klaus lay beside her, panting heavily and gulping air. *"Yes. Give me a minute."* His face was reddened.

This was another earthen-floor room, with a wooden door on the far wall, but no ceiling holes. The walls were irregular slate slabs. The swollen, antique lumber of the door resentfully gave way slightly.

Beyond, there was a hewn-rock hallway, with iron brackets on the walls that once held torches, but were empty. Sam could hear muted voices some distance away. *"A secret passage?!"* she whispered.

"I think we should go back," Klaus murmured, *"and get the Uzi. This'll keep. There is no reason to rush into these things."*

Sam unloaded her pack, leaving the contents in a corner of the room. They backtracked their trail, with Klaus lowering her by rope to the first chamber and himself hand-sliding the ladder. Except for the stretch between the spring and the broken stone wall, the descent was not too tough. The scent of cold, fresh air was alluring after the dampness and ancient mildew.

They emerged beside the lake. The snow was still falling, but heavier now. It was after 8:30 P.M.

The Rover was predictably blanketed in white, but Sam got in through the rear compartment. She removed the *Uzi* and its clips and gave them to Klaus. She pulled out sleeping bags, packed more food, and locked the vehicle. Klaus had Sam's pack and *Uzi* slung over his shoulder. Sam carried the sleeping bags.

Before they entered the tunnel, Klaus handed Sam a flask.

"Take a swig," he said to her. *"It'll keep you warm and courageous."*

Sam took a short swallow. As she was lowering it, Klaus quickly tipped it upward. The extra shot scorched her throat. He took one long drink, then put it in his pocket.

"I needed that!" he said.

"I'm not sure I did," Sam blurted. But emboldened by the brandy, she took the lead.

Back in the room, at the top of the stone staircase, Klaus helped Sam up the ladder first. She was clinging to the vertical supports, wrapping her arms around them in an incomplete hug, while juggling a flashlight. This time she had the pack.

When she was over the lip of the hole, she lowered the rope after tying it to the handle of the door.

"*I don't need that*," Klaus said, swatting at the rope. *"The ladder's a lot stronger than it looks."*

Three-fourths of the way, he misstepped. The rung where his foot landed snapped. His foot dominoed through more rungs. Off-balance, he clutched for the rope, but missed it. Arms flailing, he fell sideways and backward. *"Shit!"* he groaned from the darkness.

Sam ran the light over the floor. Klaus was on his left side, stretched full-length, moaning. She climbed down the rope.

"I told you not to come," Sam said. *"I could take care of myself."*

"Don't remind me," he replied, trying to sit up. *"I should've listened and used the damn rope! I think my leg's broken."*

"Can you move?"

"Down the tunnel? Probably not without a splint."

"I'll go back and see what I can scrounge," Sam said. She dragged him to one wall and leaned him against it.

Down the tunnel she went. She felt guilty about him, but shook off those thoughts. He was right: it was his fault.

When she was clear of the entrance, she crouched against the slope. As she was nearing the road, she heard voices. Sam peeked around a corner. Three men were at the Rover. Two of them had rifles slung over their shoulders, while the third had a weapon in his hands. She returned to Klaus and told him.

"*Pray they don't look in here,*" he said. "*I hope we can go back to it.*"

"*How's the leg?*"

"*My endorphins haven't worn off yet,*" he laughed. "*The brandy's helping. But every time I move, I hear from another part of my body.*"

"*Let's have a look,*" Sam said. "*The leg, I mean.*" Sam lifted his pants leg. He grimaced, as she did. "*Well, it looks like no compound fracture.*"

She unzipped the sleeping bags and packed them around him. "*If we're lucky, your shock might not be too bad.*"

"*Where're you going to sleep?*" Klaus asked, as Sam tucked the thermal layers around him.

"*I'll make out,*" Sam answered. "*The floor's not too hard. And my suit and gloves're warm.*"

"*You could come in here with me,*" Klaus said. "*I'm harmless.*"

"*No doubt,*" Sam smiled. "*But not on the first date. Besides, you need your rest. I'll find something to ad-lib a splint.*"

"*You're not going up there? Alone?*"

"*You have a better idea?*"

"*At least rest yourself. My leg's not going anywhere.*"

"*For you, there's always time, isn't there? Maybe you're right,*" Sam said.

Klaus closed his eyes, as if drifting off. Sam patted his face and awakened him. His forehead was clammy, his heart-rate fast, but his respiration regular, not shallow. His pupils were undilated and reacting to light.

"*How am I, Frau Doktor,*" Klaus asked.

"*Not too bad, though it could be touch-and-go. I'll take a little rest. If you feel yourself drifting off again, wake me up. And stay off the brandy.*"

Sam curled up on the dirt, a few feet from Klaus and closed her eyes.

* * *

"*How long'd I sleep?*" Sam asked, stretching.

"*A couple hours, maybe,*" Klaus said. "*I figured you needed it.*"

"How did you stay awake?"

"I didn't. I dozed off..."

"You should've awakened me," Sam protested.

"At least my leg didn't hurt," Klaus said. "I'm still here, aren't I? A few swigs of brandy helped."

"I'll see if I can find stuff for a splint. You still have your automatic? Keep warm. I shan't be long."

Klaus patted his right-side pocket. "I'll be OK. Hurry up, before I leave without you."

Sam started up the rope, with the *Uzi* slung like a bandoleer. She was surprised at how easy the climb was.

In the room, she shoved the door open to its limit and scanned the corridor. On the left was straight hallway, to the right a short stretch before a stone staircase hugged one wall. The corridor continued beside it. Sam climbed the steps, avoiding large cob- and spider-webs, durable and enduring artifacts of long-dead makers.

At the top was a breach in the wall, without door or frame. Through it was another dark corridor of hewn rock.

She swept her light behind her, then to her front. In her other hand, she held the *Uzi*. She fought the feeling of a cold, lurking presence, succeeding her into each turn of the maze and waiting to ambush her.

So far her hunt was fruitless. There was not even broken wood, only dirt, dust, and webs. She considered trying to break one of the doors, but she needed a saw. And if there had ever been torches in this century, no one had restocked the brackets in decades. *Maybe the new owner really hadn't found this*, she thought.

Further on, the walls were stone slabs, as panels, with slits between them. The rest were limned with mortar. There were peep-holes with iron rectangles over them.

Sam climbed another staircase. She was frustrated and about to backtrack to that first, pivotal turn, when she heard muffled voices.

They were up ahead, though with muted echoes. The specter, at her rear? They became slightly louder, recognizable as live, human voices, rather than broadcast or reproduced substitutes.

From an occasional higher-pitched intonation, Sam picked up German words. They were coming from the other side of a panel to her left.

She stepped slowly and used one of the listening devices Klaus had given her, until she could hear every word. The conversation was indeed in German. There were at least two, maybe three, participants.

"The old man get off all right?" a first said.

"His helicopter should be landing in Munich shortly, but he was still pissed," said a second. "He couldn't stop talking about incompetence."

"He'll be back," the first said. "But not before he's gone to ground for a while."

"God knows, he's got enough money hidden for five lifetimes," said the second. "Any more success with our guest?"

The first said, "Do you really want to learn anything from him?"

"Not really," said the second. "It's too late to be helpful. I want the pleasure of watching him suffer, before I kill him."

"Perhaps you want to work on him yourself?"

"Not for now. Keep him downstairs. Beat a little more shit out of him, for fun. And don't let him sleep."

"Sir, three of the guards found a Land Rover, parked near the See," a third voice piped in.

"On the property? Anybody with it?" asked the second.

"No," replied the new person. "They found tracks in the snow that ended at the See. Other ones led off into the woods away from here."

"Someone perhaps needed a swim!" said the second. They all laughed. "Tell them to keep an eye on it. But don't worry too hard. Probably hunters. When the snow lifts, we'll be moving everything out of here."

"Should we feed our guest?" asked the first.

"The condemned man's entitled to his bread and water," said the second. "But don't give Pemberton much else. I don't want him puking on my floor. Dismissed."

The mention of the name startled Sam. She shivered with a combination of relief and fear. Only she could save him! She would! Alone?! Panic, till the *Uzi* calmed her. Quiet, assured tenacity replaced her fear. She inspected the wall for any lever, or opener, into that room. *Was that a door closing?*

* * *

"That's a roger, Frankfurt," McConneld said through his headset. He was next to the pilot in the lead chopper. The tactical commander, an Army lieutenant-colonel, Marshall, the Israeli agents, and some troops were in the passenger-cargo section. They had been in the air almost two hours.

"Go ahead, Chuck." McConneld listened. "Rendezvous in fifteen minutes. Copy Harvey on status. Keep me advised. Out."

He checked his map of the *Sihlsee* region and enlarged reconnaissance photos. He confirmed the Landing Zone with the pilot and the tactical commander, where they would meet Swiss troops. The LZ was over two miles from the target. Swiss troops would also guide SEALs to motor boats on the *See*.

Theirs was a full flight of helicopters. Escorting them were Apache gunships. Those would remain in stand-off posture, unless needed. Behind was the airborne follow-up, in Hueys, UH-53s, and *Chinooks* once the first wave ascertained the weapons' status.

McConneld put on his night-vision goggles. "Coming up on LZ, sir," the pilot said to him. "There on the left."

There was a large pasture, acres in size. On one side was a line of vehicles, trucks mostly, neatly parked. *Swiss precision had struck again*, McConneld thought.

The pilot established clearance with the Swiss troops. Over the next ten to fifteen minutes the flight was tandem landing and unloading the assault troops, equipped with night-vision gear and dressed in snow-camouflage battle dress. Before leaving Frankfurt, they had changed from their standard greens-and-browns to white.

McConneld and the tactical CO met with the Swiss commander and his adjutant, at the lead vehicle of the column. McConneld mapped out the preliminaries, while the tactical CO briefed them on the operation.

The Swiss advised them of the terrain and conditions near the target. Marshall and the Israelis, also in snow-white battle-dress, joined them.

"The local power authority's granted your request," the Swiss commander said. "It will shut off electricity for the estate for half-an-hour. Exactly at 0500."

"Four-and-a-half hours from now, give-or-take. That should be right," the Tac.CO said. "If your people cover the east side of the lake and the roads, we'll be all set."

The Swiss commander radioed nearby Swiss units, already in position. "The sooner you retrieve those weapons and remove them from our soil, the better my superiors will like it," he said to McConneld.

The convoy set off southeast toward the estate. McConneld, the Tac.CO, and Marshall were in the point-vehicle with the Swiss officers. George and David were in the second. McConneld ordered the Tac.CO to apprise Frankfurt of their progress.

* * *

"Message, 'Chocolate One,' sir," a communications Spec4 said to Channing and the brigadier general.

Channing monitored the transmission. "McConneld's Tac.'s reporting Swiss rendezvous complete and on-the-way to target. ETA at debarkation point thirty minutes. Weather's thick. Lots of snow," he told the general.

The general said, "It might slow them down, but the bad guys won't expect them."

"Anything more from the others? 'Big Foot?'" Channing asked.

"Colonel Barsohn reported Arrival and Debarkation, scouts out. 'Swamp Creature,' 'Alsace One,' and 'Oktober First,' all report on schedule," the general said, "or close to it. Your man's was the last to take off."

* * *

Sam listened as closely as her electronics allowed. Another

door seemed to slam. She loosened a small metal slab on the wall of the tunnel with the tire iron from her pack. Cautiously, she peeked through the hole. It was dark inside, but she could see window shadows, reflected against an interior wall.

Her examination of the wall disclosed two vertical levers, one on either side of the panel, recessed in the stone-work and jammed from decades of disuse. Sam dislodged them. She replaced the peep hole cover and pulled down with all her weight on one lever. It stuck, functioning more like a curling bar, as Sam lifted herself off the ground. *What a time to forget the WD-40!* She snickered.

She hung from the cold iron, bobbing up and down, and hoping there was no one in the next room to hear her. When the bar jerked loose, unexpectedly, Sam fell in the dirt. *If the situation weren't so serious, this could have been a great sight-gag,* she thought, as she brushed herself off.

When she pushed the bar fully down, something, inside the wall panel, rose from the floor. The other lever was an equal adventure.

She dug in her boots and pushed and pushed, each time harder. The wall moved forward, sluggishly, like an elephantine revolving door. *What a time to be without a man,* she grunted, *when she needed dumb, brute force!*

At last she had a crevice into which she squeezed sideways. She clutched the *Uzi* tightly and scanned the room. She was alone, and still in the dark.

It was a huge room, high-ceilinged, with a chandelier, apparently a library or study. Bookcases covered the walls, except the one from which she emerged. That had a fireplace. The hearth was cold, but smelled of ash and lingering wood-smoke.

Sam closed the panel, after she found a way to reopen it. She had only till the snowstorm was over. *Would they kill her father, before she could help him escape?*

She looked out one side of the high windows. The snow was still falling. Her watch read 1:52 A.M.

How to proceed? Search inside the house? Go back to the left turn she bypassed? Wait for someone to come here? There were too many chances to get caught beyond this room. Wait for a possible hostage to show? Take chances?

"Hostage?" Sam caught herself. What was she thinking? Could she take a male one and win? Could she kill if she had to?

She had the *Uzi*. The *Uzi* was power, the power she needed. She'd win. Sooner or later, someone would come. Maybe the voice that spoke her father's name. She decided to wait.

But, first, she did a search. The furniture included a large oak desk, chairs, tables, and the ubiquitous bookcases. There was an automatic pistol in a desk drawer. She put it in her pocket.

There were also two large closets. One had coats, outerwear and harmless such. The other was a storeroom for small arms, ammunition, grenades, "LAWs." There were also wood pieces that could work as a splint.

Sam settled into the store-closet, with the door ajar. It was closer to the study door, than the other closet. *Good thing she slept*, she reflected. *This could be a longer than hoped-for eve...*

* * *

McConneld, the Tac.CO, Marshall, and the Israeli's were concealed in a patch of woods next to a road. It ran past the land entrance to the estate. There was a vehicle, though temporarily a snowpile, parked near the lake.

"Roger, Red-Dog Five," the Tac.CO said into his headset. "The patrol's linked up with SEALs," he said to McConneld. "Down the lake, past that dock area."

"That closes the vise, doesn't it?" Marshall asked.

The Tac.CO answered, "Our guys have the place completely surrounded and all the escapes covered."

"Any hostiles encountered?" McConneld asked.

"Avoided and under surveillance," the Tac.CO replied.

"Copy to Frankfurt," McConneld said. Frankfurt acknowledged and reported the other teams' status. Two were on schedule. The others were experiencing unanticipated delays and difficulties. HQ still expected H-Hour for 0500.

"Look at this," Marshall said to McConneld. He pointed out something on one of the maps McConneld received from the

Swiss. "It's not far. Colonel?"

"If it gets us in faster and safer," the Tac.CO said, "let's go with it. The electric company pulls the plug in two-and-a-half hours. But Frankfurt's waiting for 'Swamp Creature' and 'Oktober First.'"

Marshall called David and George. They put on their headsets and tested them. Reception was fine.

*   *   *

Inside her adopted closet, Sam was bored. If there were an "after," after all this, she already eliminated one career choice from her list: private investigator. Stake-outs were not her thing. There would be no problem with ammunition, if her own clips ran out. There was plenty of it that fit the *Uzi* and one pistol. She only hoped she had the time to reload her magazines. She found a field cap, and, stuffing her hair up into it, put it on.

What a pity her father never taught her the care-and-self-destruction of hand grenades, she thought, after cradling one in her hand. She remembered John Wayne movies. Pull the pin. Release the lever. Throw?

Sam heard footsteps out in the hall. She turned out the closet light, and closed the door to a paper-thin sliver of vision. She picked up an LAW and watched at the crack.

The hall door opened and the room lights went on. Footsteps came closer. Sam gripped the green tube tightly, like a stubby baseball bat, ready for her one and only strike. The closet door opened.

Sam swung with all the force she could muster, aiming for the shadowed face that suddenly materialized there. The blow caught the man unprepared and sent him reeling backward. He fell to the carpet on his back. His nose and mouth were bleeding.

She sprung from the closet and struck him hard, again, on the head. He moved. Sam hit him again. He was still. His face, though bloodied, was otherwise pale. She did not recognize him, but was relieved she had not killed him.

Dragging him by the feet, she got him into the closet and tied him up with rope she found there. He was on his stomach, legs and hands bound, then tied together. She gagged him.

What had she done?! Instinctive! Victorious! Shaking with the adrenalin rush, Sam was drenched in sweat. One down, God-only-knew how many more to go! What if someone came looking for him? Her own Rubicon!

She locked the door to the hallway, turned off the room lights, and returned to her closet. The excitement and the adrenalin had exacted their tolls. Sitting on the floor, Sam dozed.

From somewhere outside she heard footsteps and a voice. She snapped upright. It was not a conversation, only one person, in German, talking to himself. This time she had to take whoever it was with the *Uzi*, not a smash on the head. *Could she really shoot someone?*

The door creaked open and slammed. One set of feet came in and passed by. They became slightly fainter. *"Verdammten Idioten!"* the person said. Something about *"useless subordinates,"* among other things.

Sam recognized the voice, the accent. They belonged to the second speaker she heard, who had mentioned her father by name!

Holding the *Uzi*, she cautiously nudged the closet door open. There was no break in the soliloquy. She peeked out.

The speaker was in front of the desk, across the room from her, his back to her and the hallway door. He was bald and dressed in street clothes.

She eased the closet door open and slipped out. Never losing sight of the new arrival, she slid over to the hall door and locked the deadbolt, while still holding the *Uzi* toward him. She popped a bottom bolt into the floor. When she was finished, she grasped her weapon tightly, tiptoeing toward him.

He must have heard the floor bolt. His head perked up, his jabbering stopped, and he looked over his shoulder, casually.

THE FACE! The photos, but older. The Dream, but no *SS* uniform. The room, before Liz rescued her. The Berlin sewer worker. He pivoted suddenly and fell back against the desk front. *"Oh, fuck!!"* he said in German. *"Israelis??!!"*

Sam was alert again, and gripped the *Uzi* tightly.

"How'd you get in here?!"

"*Don't move!*" she said, quietly, coolly. "*Hands up!*" She motioned with the muzzle.

He raised his hands slowly. "*You'll never get away!! My men'll kill you before you get a foot out of here!*"

"*Shut up!*" Sam said, as she moved warily, methodically, toward him. "*Get down! On your stomach! Now! Move!*"

"*All I do is shout,*" the man said. "*My men'll be in here.*"

"*You do and you'll be dead, before you hit the floor!*"

"*I know your face! You're no Israeli! That shit Pemberton's daughter,*" The Face said. "*I should have had you killed in Vienna!*"

"*You're Colonel Johannes Krattmay! Sans hair! Down! Now! You bastard!*"

Krattmay slowly knelt, arms raised, and seemed startled she knew his name.

"*On your stomach, shithead!*" Sam said, getting closer.

He lowered himself to the floor, his arms outstretched beside his face.

Sam made an arc and reached him from the side. "*Nothing sudden!*" She had taken out one of her pistols from a pocket. She hit him on the back of the head, rendering him unconscious, and patted him down. When she was satisfied he was unarmed, she pushed him on his back, stood back, and waited for him to awaken.

* * *

"Looks like someone's been here ahead of us," Marshall said to David and George. They crouched at the mouth of a tunnel beside the lake. "The snow's filled the tracks."

Marshall shone his light up into the tunnel, seeing only empty stone conduit. He was on the point and reported developments to McConneld.

"It reminds me of a sewer," George said, "in Tehran."

"I remember that one," David said.

"Everybody forgot about this one," Marshall said, as they ascended its incline. "Till a little while ago. These are fresh muddy footprints."

They found overhead shafts and climbed through the remnants of a stone wall. The width of the passage shrank. It ended at an underground chamber with a spring in the center and two concentric ledge-walks around it.

On a stone staircase, the three men had to climb, sideways and single file. In the room at the top of those steps they found a man, bundled in unzipped sleeping bags, asleep. Marshall recognized him. *"Klaus?!"* he said, patting the sleeper on the cheeks.

"What the devil . . . ?!" Klaus said, awakening. He squinted into the beam of George's light. *"Marshall?! John Marshall?!"*

"You know this guy?" George said.

"As it happens, I do," Marshall said. "Tom Pemberton helped him escape from East Germany. I haven't seen him in years."

"Is there anyone you don't know?" George asked.

"What're you doing here?" Klaus asked.

"Sounds like Swiss-German," David said. "Can you manage it?"

Marshall quipped, "After Hebrew, anything's a breeze. Western language, that is."

"You speak Hebrew?" George said. "Control never told us that."

"I had to," Marshall said, "when I was on post in Tel Aviv." Then to Klaus, Marshall continued, in the Swiss-German dialect. *"I could ask you the same thing. I see a rope over there. And another set of footprints. What happened? You got a partner up there? Is Samantha Pemberton with you?!"*

Klaus told him about his leg and Samantha.

"I'm going up," Marshall said. "One of you guys should help my man, while the other brings reinforcements and medics."

"Your turn, partner," David said to George, who headed back the way they had come.

* * *

In Frankfurt ComCen, Channing and the general received final, pre-assault reports. It was 0403. All but one team were in position, with reconnaissance complete or nearly so.

"That transmission was from 'Oktober First'," Channing

said. "They reported ready. That means everyone but 'Swamp Creature', is in position and Green. Well, General?"

"Give them till H-Hour," the general said. "If not ready then, we'll order the other four to go. Cross our fingers those don't warn Swamp Creature's target."

*   *   *

Sam stepped back from Krattmay's still-prone body. Slinging the *Uzi*, she took out her two 9mm pistols. They each had sound-suppressors. As his eyes opened, she stepped further back.

"What the . . . ?!" he said, trying to sit up. *"Oh, shit! I thought it was all a dream!"*

"I might be your worst nightmare," Sam replied. *"Up, slowly. Nothing sudden. "*

He rubbed the back of his neck. *"I owe you one, lady!"*

"Right. One father, intact," Sam answered. *"You'll get him for me."*

"You think we're going to waltz out of here, and I'll lead you to him?"

"A variation on that."

"I hate to be the bearer of bad tidings," Krattmay said. *"But he's not here. The Baron took him, when he left."*

"Nice try, putz-breath," Sam said, raising the pistol in her left hand. *"He's here. The sooner you retrieve him, the better off you'll be. The longer I wait, the more itchy my fingers get. I may scratch them by blowing your head off. The only reason you're not tied and gagged is you're getting my father brought here."*

"Dream on, lady," Krattmay said, stepping toward her.

Sam tensed the weapons suddenly, as though about to fire.

"You won't shoot me," Krattmay said, backing away, toward the desk. *"You have no stomach for it. You shoot me, you're flushed. You'll have to admit you're no better. Just another murderer."*

"A little bit of us . . . " Sam murmured. *"Call a flunky and get my father brought up here! NOW!!"*

Sam squeezed off a shot from the pistol in her left hand. The slug tore the corner of the leather chair, behind him.

"*Why you!...*" Krattmay made as though he would lunge at her, when she snapped the pistol back at him.

"*I've got fourteen more where that came from,*" Sam said. "*One way or another, you're getting my father for me.*"

"*You'll never get away from here,*" Krattmay said, slowly backing around the desk. "*I'll kill you both, in the end.*"

"*I may surprise you,*" Sam said. "*Now, make the call, struntz!*"

Krattmay reached for the receiver on the phone console.

"*On speaker!*" Sam said. "*Remember, I understand every word you say. The wrong one, and you won't say another.*"

He spoke into the console's speaker. He told someone named "*Schmidt,*" to bring the elder Pemberton to his study. "*Are you the reason my man didn't come back?*"

"*I never saw him. Nobody here but me...and my...Uzi,*" Sam sang, to the tune of *Me and My Shadow*.

A few minutes passed, but no one had come. Sam's frustration grew. "*You'd better call that stooge of yours,*" she said.

A knock on the hall door. Sam paralleled Krattmay to it. She slipped into the storage closet, its door slightly ajar.

"*Herr Oberst?*" came a voice Sam recognized as the first one she heard in the earlier conversation.

"*Nothing stupid!*" Sam whispered. Out of the Colonel's gaze, she switched the pistols in her hands.

Krattmay released the floor bolt on the right-hand door and opened it. In came a man, with Sam's unconscious father propped against him.

After he passed the closet door, Sam motioned to Krattmay, with her left-hand pistol. She watched fleetingly, as the man put her father in a chair, before the desk. She ducked behind the door as he turned.

"*Schmidt! Storage closet!*" Krattmay yelled.

When Sam heard this, she kicked the door out of her way. The other man hurried toward her. She aimed her right-hand pistol and fired at the floor ahead of him.

He stopped abruptly, but his body's momentum propelled him. He fell onto the carpet on his face.

"*Hold it, Colonel!!*" Sam said to Krattmay. "*Get over here, and tie him!*" She threw him some rope from the closet.

Schmidt had not recovered from his fall. Krattmay began to help him up.

Sam ordered, *"On his stomach! Tie him!"*

Krattmay did as he was told. *"Sorry, Schmidt,"* he said.

Sam stepped back to the door and relocked it. She tossed rags to Krattmay to gag him, while pointing both pistols at them.

"You'll pay for this!" Krattmay snarled.

"*I already have,*" Sam responded. *"You're just not to be trusted, are you, Colonel?"*

"My compliments on your marksmanship," Krattmay sneered. *"I thought you were aiming at him."*

Her father had not stirred. His face was bruised and bloody, his eyes blackened, nose and cheekbones swollen. His hands were tied behind his back, with his arms over the chair-back. He smelled of human waste.

"You swine!" Sam spat at Krattmay. She put one pistol in her pocket, came out with a small knife, and cut the rope on her father's wrists. Immediately, he slumped forward. Sam replaced the knife and held the second pistol again. She tried talking to him, but he did not respond.

"Pa!" Sam persisted. "It's I. Milli. I'm here! Everything's OK! We're getting away!" No reaction from her father.

"Sam?" a muffled voice unexpectedly spoke from behind the fireplace. Krattmay also seemed surprised by the new entry and was stepping slowly toward the desk.

Sam back-pedaled, carefully, and listened at the fireplace. "Marshall?! How the hell?!"

Suddenly, Krattmay reached into the desk's top drawer.

"Looking for something?" Sam asked, as casually as she could. *"It's resting comfortably in my pocket, Colonel. So, move back where you were."*

Through the wall, Sam explained the mechanism to Marshall. His eyes and nose were soon peeking through the peephole. The fireplace turned, its left side pulling from the wall. Through the mobile doorway stepped Marshall.

"Who're you, a marshmallow man?" Sam asked, laughing.

"My men told me you were dead," Krattmay said, in English. "In the lake that night. If you want a job done . . ."

"Sorry to disappoint you, Colonel," Marshall replied. "Christ!" he said, after he saw Sam's father. "Both of them?! Who's that?" He jerked his head in Schmidt's direction.

"Another flunky," Sam replied. "I had a little trouble."

"Goddammit, Sam! I told you to stay put!" Marshall said. He hurried to Sam's father.

"Typical man! Not even, 'Hi, honey, how was your day'?"

"From the looks of it, busy," Marshall said. "You don't know how to listen to *anyone*, do you?"

"I've been listening to everyone else all my life, Mr. Marshall," Sam huffed.

"Just shut up and keep him covered."

"Believe it or not," Sam said, "I'd figured that out by myself, and was doing fine before you showed. Ask Struntzy Putz-breath over there. I found his automatic in the desk. He tried for it and thought he could make a big play. But you still haven't answered me."

"I'll explain it all soon," Marshall said. "But we've got to get Tom out. He's got internal injuries."

"*Hey, you! Colonel! I told you to get away from there!*" Sam said. "*Back where you were.*"

Krattmay was standing behind his desk. She glanced at her father again.

"Watch him," Marshall said. "He's the king of diversions." Marshall looked over his shoulder. The Colonel was aiming a small-caliber pistol at them. "Sam! Look out!"

He shoved Sam out of the way. Her left-hand pistol flew from her hand. She bounced behind a chair.

Krattmay fired. Marshall felt a sharp pain across the top of his left shoulder before he landed. He pulled Sam's father down with him.

The Colonel got off other shots before Sam returned fire with a pistol from behind a pillar. He was crouching near the passage's entrance, left open from Marshall's arrival.

Sam's first shots missed. Krattmay popped up and fired again. Before his next burst, she played a hunch. Her next shot caught him in the hand. His pistol went flying and landed away from him.

He scampered for it, but Sam laid shots across his path. He recoiled toward the hole in the wall, disappearing behind the bulk of the desk.

"You're done, Colonel," Sam said. *"Give it up."* She stood, able to see to the wall. He had vanished. She recovered her other pistol and reloaded the one she had been using.

"Is it bad?" Sam said, stooping over Marshall. Her father, lying beside him, was stirring. "Pa! I'm here. You're safe!"

"Mil!" He groaned a subdued, though excited, response. He squinted, grimacing from the pain. Sam sat them both up against the chair and embraced her father.

"It only grazed me," Marshall said. "But it's one *mean* burn!"

She took Marshall's helmet off, unbuttoned his battle jacket, and examined his shoulder. It was bleeding, but the wound was on the surface.

From the clothes closet, Sam took coats. She tore pieces from one lining as makeshift bandages. Balling up another, she put it under her father's head. Sam covered Marshall with a third.

"McConneld and half the American Army're going to be here any minute," Marshall said. "Where's he going? Do you have any clue where that shaft leads? . . . David, are you monitoring?" he said into a headset he had taken from his pocket.

Marshall listened. "Krattmay might be headed your way and is armed . . . Right . . . Tell George. I need a medic. Out."

Marshall looked for Sam. She was gone. He got up slowly and helped Tom Pemberton to a closet, locking him inside. His holster was empty. He stumbled to the fireplace, picking up Krattmay's gun on the way.

* * *

Sam pocketed her other pistol and had the *Uzi* over her shoulder. In the passage she examined the dirt floor with her light. There were no tracks to the left, an unexplored area. Tracks led to the right.

Some were her own or Marshall's. Krattmay had to be running, but the dirt was too dark to reveal any bloodstains. She thought she heard something up ahead but was not sure. *Were there any hiding places she remembered?* She swept the beam ahead of her. No Colonel materialized. Before this, the specter she sensed was her own fear. Now, it had a human face.

* * *

After reentering the passage, Marshall turned to his left. He doubted the Colonel would head into oncoming traffic. His flashlight, given him in Frankfurt, was dim. *Billions for defense, but not a penny for new batteries*, he thought.

He could not tell if there were fresh tracks in that part of the corridor. After a minute, Marshall decided his hunch was wrong. He turned back for the more traveled way. When he reached the panel into the library, it was still open. He peeked in. Nothing had changed. As he turned, something struck him on the back of the head, and he blacked out.

* * *

Not far from the tunnel entrance, George met McConneld and the Tac.CO. He gave them his report. "Great Trojan horse possibilities," he said. "Marshall figures they don't know this way."

The Tac.CO's communications officer came over to them. "Patrols report sounds like weapons fire inside the house, sir. Sporadic, then multiple. Things're stirring outside as a result."

"Marshall, you think?" McConneld asked George.

"Could be," George replied. "I say, go in."

"What's your opinion, Colonel?" McConneld asked the Tac.CO.

"It's your call, sir," he replied. "But it's thirty-six minutes ahead of scheduled H-Hour. And Frankfurt HQ should be consulted."

"OK, Colonel," McConneld said. "SOP's satisfied. Give me man-to-man."

The Tac.CO said, "If he were my friend, no question."

"Give the order, Colonel," McConneld said. "All units move in. Target communications. Advise Frankfurt of the emergency on my authority. And send a detachment with George."

* * *

Sam reached the wooden door, where she first entered the passages. It was closed. She flashed the light down the corridor she had not taken. The dirt there showed no signs of being disturbed.

She pulled open the wooden door. The room was empty. She called through the floor hole to Klaus. David told her he was asleep, with medics on the way.

Back in the passageway, Sam hustled toward the library. *He must have escaped,* she thought. But, just in case, she would be cautious.

* * *

"The lead group reports sentries taken out," the Tac.CO told McConneld. They were advancing with C3 and EOD personnel through the woods, between the lake and the access road. The snow, still falling, slowed them down.

"No sign of the weapons, sir," the communications officer said. "But there are trucks. SEALs have the dock area under control. No firefights, as yet."

"Anything from George?" McConneld asked the Tac.CO.

"We lost contact with them," the communications officer replied. "Probably too far underground for the equipment."

"Copy to all teams," the Tac.CO said to the communications officer. "Look especially for any underground storage or sheds."

* * *

Sam covered the distance to the library quickly. It was no more than ten minutes since she started the pursuit. Wherever Krattmay went, he was not in that passageway.

The library panel was barely open when she reached it. She grabbed a glimpse inside, through the crack. Marshall was face-down on the floor near the desk. Across the room, Krattmay was bending over Schmidt, untying him with only one hand. It was tight, but she slipped back through the crevice, with two pistols in her hands.

Krattmay must have heard. When he saw her, he stood, holding his own in his left hand, pointed at Marshall. His right hand was wrapped in white cloth and was close to his chest.

"Checkmate, Miss Pemberton," he said, sounding cocky. "What we have is a Mexican stand-off. Even if you kill me, you stupid bitch, your friend is toast. And your side can't stop us. Things're too far along for that."

Sam decided it was time for the performance of her life. She faked the best expression of defeat she could, as she slowly lowered her pistols. Krattmay seemed to be let down, a tiny bit.

As quickly, she raised them and squeezed off shots from both. She aimed for the knees and apparently hit one of them. Krattmay's right leg gave way, and he collapsed. A shot discharged from his weapon. He looked up from the floor, and pointed his pistol at her.

In the next second, she heard the metal click of an empty gun. Springing at him, she kicked the gun from Krattmay's hand. Krattmay's right hand, bandaged as it was, was clutching his knee. He writhed.

"Sam?" a weakened Marshall called. "What hit me?" He got up slowly, on his knees and elbows.

"He must've bushwhacked you," she answered. She raised the pistol in her right hand again, pointed it at Krattmay, and aimed.

"Christ, Sam!" Marshall cried out. "What're you doing?!"

"Settling a score," Sam replied. "This bastard killed my mother!"

Krattmay looked up at her. His face was pale, his arrogance gone. "My, God! You're not here for your father at all!."

"Finding him was luck," Sam said. "I *was* looking for him. But I never expected to find him here. I only knew I'd find you here, you slimy bastard!!"

"When did I kill your mother?!" He sounded pathetic, pleading, like a child answering a parent.

"In an airliner that you blew up," Sam said, calmly.

"You can't kill him in cold blood!" Marshall said, out of breath. "Wounding him in a gun battle's one thing. But this is murder! You'll be no better than he is!"

"What'll it matter?!" Sam answered. "The scum deserves it! Besides, only you'll know the difference. No jury in the world would convict me!"

"They wouldn't. That's what frightens me. But that's not justice, Sam. Only revenge."

"So be it," Sam said. "A minute ago he was ready to kill you. I saved your life, you ungrateful jerk! And you'd deny me my rightful justice?!!"

"*You*'ll know! You won't be able to live with yourself! Don't do it! Please!"

"Sorry, John," Sam said. "I've got to do what I've got to do."

With the gun aimed at Krattmay, she squeezed off shot-after-sound-suppressed-shot from the pistol in her right hand, until it was empty.

"That pays back many debts," she said, lowering the 9mm. Krattmay was motionless, his body spread-eagled on the rug.

"I can't believe you could kill anyone, Sam!" Marshall said. "You're not the woman I thought I knew. You'll have to kill me, too, if you want to keep this a secret!"

"What're you going to turn me in for?"

"Murder, of course."

"But I haven't murdered anyone," Sam said. She was smiling. "I haven't even killed anyone."

"But I just watched you empty a 9mm clip into him."

"Take a look, Smarty."

Getting up slowly, he walked to Krattmay's motionless body. "He's breathing!" Marshall exclaimed. "You couldn't have missed him! What the hell's going on?!!"

"I used rubber bullets," Sam replied. "If you look closely, you'll see the slugs. He must've passed out. He does have two real wounds, but I couldn't let him kill you. Pa always taught me to shoot, to disable."

"Stop rambling, you wiseacre," Marshall smirked. "You made him evacuate, too."

"Pa! My God?!! Where is he?!" Sam asked, feeling her first true panic of the night.

Marshall pointed to the closet. The two retrieved the elder Pemberton and headed into the secret passage.

"What time've you got?" Marshall asked. Sam was between them, propping them both up, to varying degrees.

"5:01," she answered.

"McConneld and the boys should be here soon," Marshall said.

They heard noise and saw more lights up ahead. David, some U.S. soldiers, and George reached them. Four soldiers accepted delivery of her two burdens. Sam told David what to expect and where to find it.

She followed the soldiers as they carried her father and Marshall to the room with the hole in the floor. She felt an incredible sense of relief, though she half regretted having pulled the triggers. She had her father back, alive, and she had exorcised her own ghosts of guilt.

"A little bit of us," she murmured, as she walked. *Ends and means? New guilt?*

* * *

"They've found four madames and two SADMs in the stables," the Tac.CO told McConneld.

They were at the tree line, observing the operation, with the communications officer and a security team of riflemen.

"And the SADMs had detonation packs with them," he continued. "None was armed. They were getting ready to ship them out."

McConneld said, "Any casualties on our side?"

"No KIAs, thank God," the Tac.CO answered. "Eight or twelve wounded. Hammer Three reports the house's secure. They've linked up with your guy, George. We'll set up a CP inside."

* * *

In a ground-floor banquet room, Marshall was being treated

by two medics. Sam was sitting nearby. Other medical personnel were tending to her father, who was on a stretcher. McConneld, after talking with the Tac.CO, came over to them.

"Things look wrapped up," McConneld said. "Weapons are intact, plus some conventional stuff from NATO depots. Nowhere near all of it, of course, but a start."

"Anybody talking?" Marshall asked. "The Colonel?"

"A few small-fry we took outside, but most shagged it when things got crazy," McConneld said. "He's not talking. I think he's in shock, after what Ms. Pemberton did to him. I'd have paid to see it."

"No, you wouldn't," Marshall said.

"Which reminds me," McConneld said, looking at Sam. "I thought I told you to stay home!"

"Do all you guys have the same scriptwriter?" Sam shot back.

McConneld waved her off. "But I'm sure glad you didn't listen this time. Your father mightn't have made it if you had. But if anything like this happens again, Bob will sign the papers, to stop you."

"Bob! Good God! We both owe him explanations!" Sam said.

"I took care of that end. You'll see him soon," McConneld said. "He commanded the 'Alsace One' operation. According to the last report, he was fine, and his people had the situation in hand. Your father's being evac'd to Frankfurt, ASAP. You're going with him, aren't you?" Sam nodded.

"Ms. McGonnville's got a lot of explaining, when I finally see her," McConneld said. "I smell insubordination."

"Easy on her," Sam said. "She's a good agent. Besides, if you're too hard, you'll lose her. I told her we'd give her a job, if you canned her."

"Did she ever set you up, too?" McConneld asked Marshall.

"Welcome to the club, pal," Marshall said.

"There's only one small matter remaining," McConneld said to Sam, lowering his voice. "You must never disclose, make public, or hint at the existence of these occurrences or their details. They never happened. Understand?"

"I'll think about it," Sam answered. "I wish it were true."

The Tac.CO joined McConneld. "Frankfurt says all the ops

are complete. Ten SADMs recovered. With what we found, that makes sixteen altogether." He glanced at his watch. "In the bag, sewn up by 0900. Can't ask for better precision than that."

"Berlin makes nineteen," McConneld said. "Still one out there, somewhere."

"What time did you say it was, Colonel?" Marshall asked.

"0900," the Tac.CO said. "Got a plane to catch, sir?"

Marshall said, "McConneld and I have a date with a ship."

"What the devil're you babbling about?" McConneld asked. "Ship?"

"Get hold of the Germans," Marshall said. "And the *Wilhelmshaven* Port Authority. Call Harvey Barsohn and Balkovsky. They'll want to be there. Colonel, we'll need your guys one last time. You want your twentieth bomb?"

To the medics treating him, he continued, "Bandage it up. Tight. With something for pain. This is one curtain-call I don't want to miss. Sam, I'll see you back in Frankfurt."

* * *

Zürich-Frankfurt-Bremen, with stopover in Frankfurt, and short diversion to *Marburg*. That had been Marshall, et al.'s flight itinerary en route to *Wilhelmshaven*. He was reflecting on the slapdash trip as he watched his helicopter land in a field west of the last city. The pain shot the medic gave him, at the estate, was still working. He also had pills for when it wore off.

They refueled in Frankfurt and changed battle-dress. The stop in *Marburg* was for scooping up Barsohn and Balkovsky. In *Bremen*, the SEALs assigned to them picked up scuba equipment from NATO stores.

A British detachment from the BAOR drove them to the outskirts of the harbor area. A quick call to the German Interior Ministry, from Frankfurt, set them up with the harbor patrol and the portmaster's office in *Wilhelmshaven*. Coastal patrol boats would keep a certain vessel from leaving.

At the portmaster's, Marshall received the pier number of the S.S. *Trujillo,* a freighter with dual Liberian and Panamanian registry. He borrowed workmen's clothes and a seaman's jacket.

"How do you know the name?" McConneld and Barsohn asked him.

Marshall turned to them. "Ever heard of Section 16 of the Securities and Exchange Act?" he asked. "Or Rule 10-b-5?"

Both men shrugged.

"To paraphrase Will Rogers, 'I can see we're gonna get out late tonight, folks. It's the explaining the jokes that takes the time'," Marshall said. "How 'bout, if I said, insider trading?"

They nodded.

The ship was docked at a pier at the south end of the harbor, near warehouses. The ship's gangway was manned by one seaman. Others periodically came and went.

McConneld and Barsohn's raiding force consisted of twenty-five SEALs and twenty Special Forces and Ranger troops. Not far from the berth, but still out-of-sight, five SEALs were dropped off at an empty wharf. They were to set its propellers and rudder for disablement if the ship tried to escape.

The rest of the team, including Barsohn, Marshall, and the others, infiltrated the warehouse area in pairs. Marshall led them to the rear of a smaller, apparently abandoned warehouse, closest to the pier. Barsohn sent a handful of troops in to check it. It was empty, though with signs of recent occupation.

McConneld said, as they watched the vessel from the warehouse, "Cut the secrecy shit and tell us what all this is about!"

"Your twentieth bomb's on that ship," Marshall said.

"You've already told us as much," McConneld said.

Marshall interrupted, "What I want now is a 9mm and a ten-minute head-start. If I'm not back then, storm the damn thing."

"Are you nuts?" McConneld asked. "How're you getting on there?"

Marshall shrugged. "I'm making it up along the way." He took a pill before he left by a side door.

The gangway was aft, beyond sight of the bridge. Only the one seaman was in view.

Marshall stumbled his way across the loading and dock areas, to the gangway. He had his hand in his jacket pocket, holding the pistol. Tripping up the walk, he was met by the seaman, who tried to turn him back and send him ashore. Marshall spun around, slugging him with the pistol. Dragging the body through a doorway, he stuffed it in the first closet he found. His shoulder throbbed.

He started down one corridor, the pistol back in his jacket, and listened at each door. There were no sounds from the first ones.

Down a staircase, he heard a conversation from another stateroom. The voices were familiar: Jaime Rodriguez' and the physicist's.

The conversation stopped. Footsteps were coming. He ducked inside the doorframe of a room down the hall. Rodriguez entered a stateroom. He did not emerge.

With his pistol out again, Marshall went in. A gargling noise stopped. *"That you, Doctor?"* Rodriguez asked in Spanish. *"Emilio?"* Rodriguez' voice was coming from Marshall's right. He appeared, in his underwear, with an electric razor whirring.

"You?! What?!..."

Marshall already had his pistol pointed toward his right as the Cuban came into view. "Don't bother asking," Marshall interrupted him. "I want the weapon now." He moved to his left, to cover both the door and Rodriguez.

"What if I said I don't know what you're talking about?"

"You know," Marshall said, softly, but angrily, "the Colonel almost killed me 'cause he thought I was in it with you. Now, it's payback time."

"What're you going to do with it?"

"My government would pay a good reward for its return. Or I could sell it to the highest bidder."

"It's not yours to sell," Rodriguez said.

"Yet," Marshall interjected.

"How did you know where to find me?"

"Good detective work," Marshall answered.

"You come here alone," Rodriguez said, finishing his shave, "and think I'll hand it to you? And not just hand it over, but let you walk away with it? Man, you're certifiable!"

"You like your life more than that, pal," Marshall said, pulling the hammer back on the pistol.

"Kill me, and you don't have shit."

"Repeat after me. I like my life," Marshall said.

"No way, man."

"You're not indispensable. Searching this scow's no problem," Marshall replied. "The captain's probably corruptible a second time."

"You're wrong there," Rodriguez said. "He's one of us. I'll tell you, since you won't live to tell anyone. We got ships under dual registry, Panamanian and Liberian, running American stuff into Cuba all the time."

Marshall said, "Then the guy I conked to get on this bucket had it coming. Now, we can do this easy or hard." He lowered the pistol, so that the muzzle was pointing at the Cuban's groin. "Let's see how your *machismo* survives as a soprano."

"All right! All right!" Rodriguez said. "I'll take you to it. It's in Hold 2." He hurriedly got dressed from clothes on the bed. "I believe you *would*'ve shot my balls off." He was putting on boots.

"What's this 'would have,' Gracie? I still might."

Suddenly, Rodriguez leaped at Marshall, grabbing his pistol hand. They struggled to the floor and smashed into furniture. Marshall's shoulder erupted in pain as he landed against the wall.

Rodriguez saw him grimace and slammed him into it again. He wrestled the gun from Marshall's hand and scrambled to his feet.

"Get up, asshole!" he said, stepping back to the center of the room. "Maybe I'll blow *your* nuts off, here and now!"

"*Jaime? Que pasa?*" came a voice from the hallway.

"*Emilio, come in, amigo,*" Rodriguez called.

Emilio appeared, gun in hand. "*Heard you banging in here! What the fuck?!*"

"*This scumbag wanted our new toy,*" Rodriguez scoffed. "Cover him, while I get something to tie him up with. We'll dump him at sea."

"Afraid I can't let you," Emilio said, in English. He turned his gun on Rodriguez. "Drop it, old buddy. Kick it over to him."

"What the fuck're you doing?!" Rodriguez exclaimed. He put the gun on the floor. "Are you out of your fucking mind?!"

Marshall held the pistol on Rodriguez. "Good to see you again, old chum." He smiled at Emilio.

"Are you OK, man?" Emilio asked Marshall. Marshall told him about the wound.

"You fucking sellout!" Rodriguez said to Emilio. "Selling your soul to the fucking CIA!"

"I didn't," Emilio replied. "He doesn't work for them. Or any American intelligence group."

"That's right. I'm a freelance interloper," Marshall added. "Emilio and I are just good, old friends, from New York days."

"You sold out to *somebody*," Rodriguez said. He spat on the floor. "*Puta!*"

"Let me give you some advice," Marshall said. "I hope you've got bank accounts squirreled away, pal. 'Cause when Fidel finds out how you fucked up, *he*'ll have your *machismo*s chopped off. And he's going to find out. Now's the time to think of a change of profession or employer."

"And be whores like you?" Rodriguez replied.

"You know what all you guys forgot?" Marshall asked. "Revolutions aren't just about kicking out the bad guys. They're conditions of the soul and the mind. That's why I rile when I hear '94' and 'revolution' in the same breath. Coup-by-ballot-box by reactionaries is no 'revolution.' Fidel's problem is he's forgot that, too. Now, he's as repressive and murderous as Batista was. He thinks it's OK, since he's doing it for The Cause."

"You finished with the bullshit?"

"No, I've got one more thing," Marshall said, "so you understand where I'm coming from. I wouldn't let Corporate America or The Mob take over Cuba again, either. Why don't we let the Cuban people run their own lives? Now, where's the boomer?" he asked Emilio.

"Cargo Hold 2," Emilio replied.

"At least you told me the truth," Marshall said to Rodriguez. "All I want's the package. You fade off for all I care."

Marshall heard a voice over a bullhorn. It was the German Federal Police, instructing the ship's master to prepare to be boarded. Harvey Barsohn's voice was next.

"I always did have a taste for Russian undressing,"

Rodriguez said, "especially the New York variety."

Marshall watched as Rodriguez climbed through the porthole and disappeared. Marshall followed Emilio from the cabin.

XXXI

At the Frankfurt Post Hospital, late on the same afternoon, as the raid on the Colonel's estate, Sam was in her father's room. He was under sedation after hours of surgery. He had been awake briefly, though not long enough to acknowledge her. His nose was splinted, his head, torso, and chest bandaged.

He opened his eyes once more. "Hi, Mil," he whispered.

"I love you, Pa," Sam said. She held his hand and kissed it. "You're going to be fine. God, it's good to have you back! Bob and the Twins will be so excited, too!"

"I'm sorry I left you," he said. "But I've been after The Colonel a long time."

"I guess I have been, too," Sam said. "Only I didn't know it."

"Couldn't... tell you about it," he said, "wanted to protect you. But I won't leave you again."

"Of course you will," Sam said, smiling. "But it's all right. I'm OK now, too." She kissed his forehead.

"For once, I'm glad you didn't listen. You're not my little mademoiselle any more." His words trailed off, as he fell asleep.

"Love you, Pa," Sam said, kissing him on the forehead again.

Liz and Regina came in, having flown there from Berlin. Each gave Sam a hug. They went out to the corridor to talk.

"The doctor told me he'll be recovering for months," Sam said. "At least he didn't lose anything important, especially at his age."

"I'm looking forward to finally meeting him," Liz said. "What I told you, when we first met, about admiring his work, was true. I'm psyched!"

"Sorry to hear about your step-father," Sam said to Regina. "Mr. Channing told me. Any idea where he might've gone?"

"No," Regina said, looking down. "They could not trace him from Munich."

Sam embraced and patted her softly on the back. She sensed

Regina wanted to cry, but wouldn't or couldn't. Regina's attempts at invulnerability only made her the more vulnerable. Sam reflected how, after their first meeting, she would never have foreseen getting this close to Regina.

"My life's changed completely," Regina said. "I don't recognize it. I am not sure what to do, or where to go... who I am."

"You could come back to school with us," Sam said, as they separated. "Or, I should say, with me, since Liz the Ringer won't be there anymore. What a threesome we might've been."

"What's this 'might've' stuff?" Liz asked. "You aren't getting rid of me that easily. Besides, did you forget? You offered me a job?"

"I figure Mr. McConneld will keep you," Sam said. "What're a few disregarded orders among professionals? But the offer stays open."

To Regina, she said, "You'll always have me for a friend, as long as you don't have any designs on my father."

Regina smiled. "I make no promises. But thanks."

"Me, too," Liz added. "I'm sorry for what I had to do to you earlier. And that stuff about shooting, I didn't really mean that. At least not now."

"Bail out, while you're ahead," Sam mumbled to Liz.

"Has your brother been here yet?" Liz asked, taking the cue.

Sam replied, "He said he'd get here ASAP."

"In a strange way I am even more thankful to you," Regina added, "for ridding me of the first guy my step-father had working with me. You know, I have also learned something about myself through all this. Perhaps there are a few changes I should make... But perhaps it's too late."

Sam noticed Mr. McConneld coming from the far end of the hall. Mr. Channing, George, David, the Army officer who had been in the sewer with Channing, and one other man, were with him. Mr. McConneld asked about her father. Sam repeated what she told Liz.

"They brought John in three hours ago," McConneld said. "He's downstairs, whenever you like. Bill Washbourne will be disappointed. I think he has a thing for you. Oh! I saw Bob at debriefing."

"Where's Colonel Krattmay, that struntz?" Sam asked.

"The Swiss authorities have him for now," McConneld said. "He's facing certain extradition to Germany. But I don't know after that. They can't do a public trial and keep the thing under wraps. We'll have to wait and see."

"I'm about to ask you the same question I did when we first met," Sam said to McConneld.

"Now I can tell you. Your father was spying on von Markenheim's Cartel for decades for me, after he 'retired,' too. His relationship with The Baron goes further back. Your two families have been acquainted since even before, with your grandfather. He knew von Markenheim and his father, and so on."

McConneld described how this mission came about, how her father did not tell him the particulars of The Cartel's plan. The Professor intended to deliver The Cartel, but was taken prisoner before he could. McConneld concluded, "He wanted to get Krattmay, personally, for your mother's death."

Sam said, "A lot of that was going around in our family."

"What's next for you?" McConneld asked.

"I'll get Pop back on his feet."

"I said 'for you.'"

"I'll probably finish school, maybe at Georgetown, maybe not," Sam said. "I'll see how my own stock's doing. And there's John, too."

"By the way, the Chancellor's arranged a reward for you, at my suggestion. It's a tidy sum. It should cover your bills for a long time. After all, he only owes his government and his life to you," McConneld said. "I wish you well. This isn't the last time you'll see me, I'm sure."

Sam turned to leave. Liz started with her.

"Hold it!" McConneld said. "Ms. McGonnville! Front and center. Red hair and all! Now that you've *finally* reported."

"Uh-oh," Liz murmured, as she stopped in mid-step.

"I can't charge you with insubordination," McConneld said, "since I never ordered you to keep Ms. Pemberton in Washington, or to report on her movements. But if..."

"Before you go on," Sam interrupted, "I remind you that I've offered Ms. McGonnville a *very* lucrative position with our family. I hope she takes it."

"But, if you ever play freelance gunslinger again," McConneld continued, "you will be reassigned permanent desk duty, sorting faxes till pension. Clear?!! Dismissed!"

Sam and Liz started briskly down the hall. Regina followed them in more of a glide. They disappeared around a corner.

"Well," Balkovsky said. "You've got your devices back. I've got my President. At least, he still is for now. It's time to turn out the lights."

"Not so fast, big boy," McConneld said. "Our spouses'll have to wait a while longer. There's mopping-up to do. That idiot Kinnean was right about one thing. It's going to take time to root them out, a long while to de-Nazify both sides of the Atlantic. The New Fascism won't be stopped overnight. Between Tom Pemberton's information, the major's files, Tripleleaf's operations, and The Cartel's, we're going to be busy. Not to mention tracking down The Baron. I can still count on your source, can't I?"

"Of course," Balkovsky answered. "At least with regards to some. This situation has taught me to trust again."

"Harvey? Chuck? Messrs. Arad and Cohn?" McConneld asked.

"What about The Baron?" Channing asked.

"As far as the Germans go," McConneld said. "He's still a sacred cow, even if he's dropped out of sight, at least until Tom Pemberton's well enough to talk."

"I still find it hard to believe," Barsohn said, "they actually thought they could pull it off and get away with it. Take over Germany. Economically dominate Europe, East and West."

"Consider," Channing said, "they surgically nuke or bomb key political and military centers, hiding behind terror groups they recruited and could blame later. They walk into the void, like good 'patriots,' and that's it. Dr. Johnson was right. 'Patriotism *is* the last refuge of scoundrels."

"That and religion. What's so hard, Harvey?" McConneld said. "They were in The Big Lie Biz. Tell it loud enough, long enough, and create a specter or a threat."

"Or scapegoats," Balkovsky said, quickly.

"Get 'them-versus-us' going, and people believe it," McConneld concluded. "It worked once. It's working again, too."

"And not only here," Channing said. "Remember what happened with the original *Reichstag* fire. The Nazis set it before their bluff elections in February 1933, 27 February, to be exact. Recall Pemberton's last message."

"Yeah," Barsohn said. "What'd that mean?"

"He was trying to tell us, '27 February *Reichstag*.' It came to me after Marshall's calls. The Nazis blamed this mentally handicapped Dutch Communist—tried, and executed him. They used the incident as an excuse to blame the Communists and pretext Hitler's demand for total powers."

"The Red Menace," McConneld interjected.

"By then, there were enough Nazis in the *Reichstag,* and the center went along," Channing said. "They voted Hitler all the power he wanted. After the war, it was discovered *Goering* himself was in the building, along with others, torching it."

Barsohn said, "The Germans have ordered all Tripleleaf's businesses and assets frozen. That's something."

"But he was a tip of the iceberg," Channing said. "Something tells me we'll never ferret out The Cartel's holdings."

"Let's get lunch before we head to the Embassy," McConneld said. "Ferreting out fascists always gives me a big appetite."

"Give me a raincheck," Balkovsky said. "I'm seeing my son and another friend. I'll see you back there."

"Your son?" McConneld asked.

"Long story," Balkovsky said. "I'll explain later."

On the way from the hospital floor, McConneld reflected on events. *Did every generation have to fight its version of Nazism? Or Fascism? Or to exorcise personal demons? . . . Would there ever be a generation not so "blessed?"*

*   *   *

At the nurses' station on the second floor, Sam asked for Marshall's room. A nurse led her, Liz, and Regina to Room 245.

Sam went in first, then Liz and Regina. Marshall was dressed in hospital gown, sitting up, reading a newspaper.

"John!" Sam said, scurrying to the bed. They kissed. "I'd like you to meet two friends. This is Liz McGonnville."

"Oh, shit!" Marshall said, suddenly.

"It's you!" Regina exclaimed.

"You know each other?" Sam asked.

"I was afraid this'd happen," Marshall said. "But I hoped you'd forgotten me."

"Forgot you! Yes, I know this weasel!" Regina said, coming over to the bed. "But his name wasn't John. What is it really?" Sam told her.

"When I met him in Nice," Regina said. "It was *Louis-Napoleon Chalmont*. And he was supposedly a French aristocrat and businessman, on holiday. I actually fell for you, you snake! Then he stood me up at the train station. We were going off to elope! Whose house was that?"

"A friend's," Marshall answered. "That part was true."

Liz laughed, recalling Regina's many earlier references to Nice. "This is Mr. Special?! I love it!"

"I didn't mean to hurt you," Marshall said. "But I was on a job. You happened into it, and I had to get you back out. If I hadn't, you might never have played the violin again."

Sam said, "Poor Regina. How could you do that to her? You can be such a jerk!"

"OK," Marshall said. "Next time I'll let the bad guys take her out. And I ain't talking about socially."

"What kind of 'job'?" Sam asked.

"I'll explain it all soon," Marshall said. "On second thought, what business is it of yours?"

Liz grabbed Regina by the arm. "Come on, Regina . . . Sam, we'll see you downstairs."

"But I was only getting started!" Regina protested. "You're lucky you already *are* in hospital!" Liz was finally able to push through the doorway and drag Regina after her.

"Well, hello to you, too," Marshall continued. "How am I, you ask?"

"So I'm sorry," Sam said.

"The doctor says I'll be here a couple of weeks. You'd like her, a nice major, named Rosie Gallo."

Sam looked out the window at the sunset. "John," she said, without turning. "I've been thinking... Since the other day... and this morning."

"And what's your cogitation produced? About us? I'm sure that's what it's been about, right?"

"Not us, alone, but 'we' were certainly prominent," Sam said, sighing. "What you said about shooting? About Krattmay? I can't believe I did it, either," Sam said. "I can't believe I shot him. I shouldn't have. I was wrong."

"Watch my lips," Marshall replied. "You did the right thing. The only good liberal, or leftist, is a live one. I've seen enough martyrs. They only benefit the opportunists, never themselves."

"At least I didn't kill him," Sam said.

"That's right. Your rubber-bullet trick was insidious. But you inflicted a much more serious punishment on him. A guy like that's more afraid of living than dying. He's going to be scared shitless for a while. I've always been ambivalent about whether the only good Nazi's a dead one, or one locked up for life."

"On another plane," Sam said, "so much has happened in my life. I've been somebody's daughter, and somebody's sister, and somebody's victim for so long, that this is really the first time I've felt like somebody. Can you understand that?"

"Perhaps better than you think," he said, reaching his hand out to her.

Sam grasped it, and squeezed softly. "Now that I am 'someone,' I want to hold that feeling for a while, before I consider whether to be somebody's someone ever again."

"I understand," Marshall said. It was his turn to sigh. "I was wondering when you'd catch up with yourself. And get over the father-figure gig. But, if you expect me to..."

"Oh," Sam said. "I don't. Really. I want us to be friends. Maybe even lovers. But I need space."

"And time? Well, don't get the idea I'd be that easy. Just 'cause you're a knockout, both inside and out, don't think I'm that kind of guy. Many a woman's tried to get me to the altar and failed."

"Why, you self-centered jerk!" Sam said, crossing her arms. "Besides, how would you contribute to us? Financially, I mean. I heard you use the word 'job,' but I'm sure that kind comes and goes real fast. You'd be off on the next 'job.' You don't know it, but you're married to thrills. How *do* you support yourself? Not that I expect any man, besides my father, to have done that. And how many more of our past-lovers are going to show up?"

"I'll let that last one go without reply. If you want my rating, call Dunn and Bradstreet. I'll give you the quick tour. When I was in 'Nam, lo those many years ago, among other jobs I worked on was breaking up currency black-marketeering. I cracked some big ones. And I wangled finders' fees. One was worth $50,000 to me. A few others, even more. When I got back here, I invested it all and had some good picks. I got into the personal computer thing early and parachuted at the right moment.

"I'm not hurting, but I end up giving a lot of income away. No one to spend it on. Not really. Till now. I've got two trips to Israel to arrange. And you. But don't expect me to disappear from your life. You need time; I'll go along with that. But don't forget. Neither of us is getting any younger."

"I owe four people, too. Maybe *we*'ll go see them," Sam said, kissing him, hard, on the lips. "Or have November in Paris. Or April. Maybe we're not getting any younger, but we're also getting a little better. And badder, too," she added, before kissing him again.